Others Available by DK Holmberg

The Dark Ability

The Dark Ability
The Heartstone Blade
The Tower of Venass
Blood of the Watcher
The Shadowsteel Forge

The Cloud Warrior Saga

Chased by Fire
Bound by Fire
Changed by Fire
Fortress of Fire
Forged in Fire
Serpent of Fire
Servant of Fire
Born of Fire

The Lost Garden

Keeper of the Forest
The Desolate Bond
Keeper of Light

BLOOD OF THE WATCHER

THE DARK ABILITY
BOOK 4

ASH Publishing
dkholmberg.com

Blood of the Watcher

Copyright © 2016 by D.K. Holmberg
All Rights Reserved
Published by ASH Publishing

Cover art copyright © 2016 Rebecca Frank
Book design copyright © 2016 ASH Publishing

ISBN-13: 978-1532914317
ISBN-10: 1532914318

Disclaimer: The book is licensed for your personal enjoyment only. All rights reserved. This is a work of fiction. All characters and events portrayed in this book are fictional, and any resemblance to real people or incidents is purely coincidental. This book, or parts thereof, may not be reproduced in any form without permission.

ASH Publishing
dkholmberg.com

BLOOD OF THE WATCHER

THE DARK ABILITY
BOOK 4

CHAPTER 1

A SLIVER OF MOON PEEKED OUT from behind a thick bank of clouds. Gentle rain drizzled down, leaving the stones in this part of Lower Town slick beneath his boots. Rsiran shifted the sword still sheathed at his side, a flush of embarrassment coursing through him that he still carried it with him. He had no ability with the sword, and if it came to actually *using* a sword, he would be in more trouble than if he were to simply Slide away.

Jessa stood at his side, holding tightly to his hand, as if she were concerned that he might leave her behind. He suspected that she'd seen something on his face, maybe the tension as his jaw muscle twitched, or the fact that he continued to check his knives to make certain they were still there.

The darkness in Lower Town didn't bother him as it once did. There were shades present that had not been there before, and a certain clarity that he wasn't accustomed to seeing. Once he would have been thankful for such a change, now he only worried about why it had.

A single cat yowled down a distant alley. He didn't wait to see if it would repeat.

"I heard another," Jessa said.

"Doesn't matter," Rsiran answered.

"Of course it matters."

He shook his head. He hadn't managed to shake the foul mood he'd been in for the last few weeks. They had walked along the docks, Jessa guiding him and likely knowing that he normally found the waves crashing along the shore soothing. Not today. Now with each wave, he felt a surge of anxiety, as if the water simply served to remind him of how much danger he posed to his friends.

"Brusus wanted us to meet him here again tonight," Jessa said.

The Wretched Barth had once been a place of safety to them, a place where they could meet, and dice, and discuss plans, all with some semblance of comfort. That had been before Lianna had died, and before everything that Rsiran did drew them ever deeper into the plans of the Forgotten and Venass. Now the pub held nothing but memories of Brusus's attack, and when Thom had Compelled Haern to attack them.

"What was he thinking having us come here?" Rsiran asked.

Jessa pulled the door open—he could tell from the brief widening of her eyes that she hadn't been certain whether she could without having to pick the lock—and stepped into the tavern.

The soft sounds of a lute played near the far end of the tavern, though Rsiran saw no one there. A fire crackled in the hearth, giving a warmth to the place. The scent of roasted meat and hot ale filled the tavern.

"I thought the Barth was closed," Rsiran said, confusion replacing some of the worry he felt. After the attacks, the tavern had been shuttered. What would make anyone want to return here?

Brusus came from behind a door that led to the kitchen and saw them. He carried a mug of ale in one hand, and when he saw them, a wide smile spread across his face. "Ah, finally you've come!"

Rsiran glanced over at Jessa and she shrugged.

"Brusus?" he asked.

He tipped his head in a nod. "Thought some ale might cheer us all up."

"What are we doing here?" Rsiran asked.

Brusus's brow furrowed and he gave a puzzled smile. "What do we always do here?"

He sat at a table, pulled a packet of ivory dice from his pocket, and set it on the table next to his mug of ale. As he did, the door opened and Haern entered. His eyes took in the tavern with a quick sweep and then he grunted, flopping himself onto a stool.

"You're going to have to get your own ale," Brusus said to him.

Haern studied Brusus's face for a moment, and then he shrugged and made his way into the kitchen, returning a moment later with a full mug.

"You two going to just stand there or are you going to join us and dice? I admit, it might not be as spirited as when Firell joined us," he said, his face clouding for a moment, "but I think we can all admit that it's been too long since we took the time to sit together and simply relax."

"The Barth is closed," Rsiran said.

Brusus looked around and laughed softly. "Closed? Looks like we've got it open, doesn't it, Haern?"

Haern grunted. A coin flipped between the fingers of his left hand while his right hand traced over the scar that ran along the side of his face. "Open enough."

Jessa shrugged again and took a seat next to Haern.

He glanced at her, tipping his head to the side, and his eyes went distant for a moment as they often did when he attempted a Seeing. When they came back into focus, he nodded to her. "You're still well." It came out as a statement, rather than a question.

Jessa patted him on the shoulder and smiled. "Still well, Haern."

Rsiran shook off his confusion and took a seat. Brusus rolled the dice across the table and nodded toward the kitchen. "You might want to get yourself a mug of ale."

"Since neither of you two was accommodating, I'll get us each one," Jessa said.

She made her way to the kitchen, and Rsiran watched her go before turning his attention back to Brusus.

"What is this?" Rsiran asked. "I thought Karin closed the Barth after the attack and put it up for sale."

Brusus nodded. "She did. And it sold."

It took Rsiran a moment to make the connection. "You?"

"Of course me. Who else were you thinking?"

"You're not concerned about what happened here?" Rsiran asked.

Brusus waved a hand as he took another drink. "What's to worry about? The Forgotten got what they were after, and as far as they know, I'm dead."

"They weren't after you," Rsiran said.

"Maybe not. Either way, they think I'm gone."

"But the tavern—"

"Was bought by a certain Tolstan Imolat."

Rsiran looked from Brusus to Haern, frowning as he did. "Who is Tolstan Imolat?"

Haern started shaking his head. "Damn fool, that's who he is," he said. The coin that he flipped between his fingers continued to move, spinning atop his knuckles. When it came to rest, he slapped it onto the table and picked up the dice, shaking them in his hand.

"You?" Rsiran asked Brusus.

He shrugged. "Thought I needed to take on a different name, especially after what happened to me. Can't have the Forgotten hearing my real name bandied about. Kind of ruins the ruse."

"But it wasn't the exiled Elvraeth who attacked you," Rsiran reminded.

Brusus looked around the tavern, his eyes darting toward the door to the kitchen. It still felt strangely empty in the Wretched Barth without Lianna, as if the spirit of the place had changed when she had died. Then it had been a place of safety, where they hadn't needed to fear attack or poisoning, but after Lianna's death, Brusus had been poisoned and Rsiran and Jessa nearly killed.

"It wasn't only Venass, either," Brusus said.

Jessa pushed open the door to the kitchen, walking stiffly. For a moment, Rsiran worried that something had happened to her while she was there, but she came out carrying two large mugs of steaming ale. She smiled broadly as she weaved around the tables in the tavern, making her way to where they sat, and managed to set them down without spilling any.

"Looks like someone could use a job," Brusus said.

Jessa punched him on the shoulder. "You hire your own help if you're intent to run this place."

"You knew?" Rsiran asked.

She shrugged. "When he asked us to come here, I suspected. I'd heard that the Barth had sold, but I didn't recognize the name. A little digging, and it seems *no one* recognized the name. Figured his invitation to meet here was too much of a coincidence to be only that."

She dropped a hand to his shoulder and leaned into Rsiran's ear to whisper. "Besides, it's good to give him something else to worry about, you know? Everything else that's going on, he's starting to feel helpless."

Brusus tossed a handful of coin on the table. "You know, I can hear you."

Jessa twisted to look over at him. "Why else would I have said it?"

Brusus slapped Haern's hand, and the dice went spinning across the table. "Now you're only being mean. Besides, I thought you'd want to have someplace safe for us to meet."

Jessa took a seat and spun to face Brusus. "This isn't safe. They know that this has been our place. What happens when the Forgotten come after us again?" she asked, lowering her voice as she did, even though they were the only ones in the tavern. She turned to Haern. "What happens when Venass makes a play at us again? You know what they're after—"

"What we *think* they're after," Brusus countered. "There is a difference."

Jessa grabbed the dice and tossed them across the table. "Whatever. Now that Thom and the rest of Venass know what Rsiran can do, we're not really safe anywhere."

Haern clasped his hands together on the table and looked to Rsiran. "No. I suppose we're not."

Rsiran glanced toward Brusus, but he just sipped his ale and shrugged. "That's why we're here," Brusus started. "Have to figure out our next move."

Haern reached over and grabbed Rsiran's wrist. He was much older than Rsiran and didn't have the strength that years spent working at the forge afforded Rsiran, but there was strength in his grip. "As much as Brusus likes to think he's the center of our world, since we met you, *you* seem to be in the middle of everything that happens. We have years of knowing how to be careful—"

"Some of us fewer than others," Jessa said.

Haern ignored her and kept his focus on Rsiran. "One lesson you needed to learn was that there are times when you have to be hard, and others when you have to be compassionate. So far, I've seen only compassion from you even when it places us in more danger. Time for that to change."

"He's not soft, Haern," Jessa said.

Haern released Rsiran's wrist and picked up the dice. He flipped them between his fingers, twisting them slowly and then dumped them onto the table. They landed a pair of ones. "Never said that. Boy wouldn't have survived half of what he's been through if that were the case, but he's got a gentle heart, and that's going to get one of us killed."

Rsiran wondered if Jessa had shared with them that Josun had escaped. That Firell had freed him in exchange for his daughter. So far, it hadn't mattered. Josun hadn't come back for them. But he would. He'd already proven how far he would go, first killing Lianna, then capturing Rsiran, and most recently having taken Jessa prisoner.

It was the reason that Rsiran always kept himself on edge, always looking around. But how far *would* he go? He hadn't been willing to kill Josun. Anyone he *had* harmed, he'd done out of a need for self-protection. Haern might think that he needed to be harder, but what happened if he found he enjoyed it too much? What happened if his abilities turned him into something darker?

Jessa watched him as if Reading him. She shook her head slowly from side to side.

"Listen, are we going to dice or are we going to sit here and talk?" Brusus grumbled. "We've got this wonderful tavern all to ourselves. I thought you all would *want* to be here, but all I get from you is arguing. And I get enough of that from Haern." He took them all in with a glance, then quieted. "Let's have a quiet, enjoyable night, and then we can start figuring out what we need to do with both Venass and the Forgotten tomorrow. Seems like it's time for us to sort that out."

Haern looked at Rsiran for a moment more and then picked up the dice, rolling them in his hand and dumping them on the table one more time. "Tomorrow," he agreed as the dice settled, again coming up with ones.

Rsiran couldn't help but wonder if another day mattered. He might have held one of the Great Crystals and had sat next to the Great Watcher, but what did that matter when the Forgotten and Venass were after him? How many times would he be able to Slide away before one of them caught up to him? And then what would he do? *Would* he be hard enough to do what was needed?

This time, Haern watched him, his eyes slightly distant as he attempted a Seeing. He blinked and sent the dice sliding across the top of the table, all without taking his gaze off Rsiran.

CHAPTER 2

THE POUNDING ON THE DOOR to the smithy woke Rsiran. His head pounded in time, almost as if whoever was on the other side managed to reach inside his skull and assault him. He stood slowly, wobbling as he made his way to the door, wishing he hadn't had that third mug of ale last night. The second had helped him forget about the fear he had of who might be out there still after him. The third had simply been excess.

He glanced over at Jessa and found she was already up and gone, leaving little more than a nest of blankets curled up where her body had been. How late had he slept?

At the door, he hesitated. Other than Jessa, there were only a few people who knew of the smithy, but why would they have come early in the morning? And why would they beat at the door like this?

"Open the door, Rsiran. Jessa tells me you're still there."

Haern.

He slipped the locks, marveling at how Jessa managed to lock them again and wondering if he would ever really be able to seal up the smithy, and pulled open the door. Bright sunlight spilled in, and he had to shade his eyes. Haern wore a dark cloak covering up a shimmering shirt that practically pulled light away from it. Rsiran had seen it before, but that had been when they snuck into the Alchemist Guild house.

"Haern? What are you doing here?"

Haern shoved past him and glanced around the smithy. "Been a while since I came here, so I thought I would see if you—"

He spun, and a knife came streaking through the air toward Rsiran.

Rsiran *pushed* on it and caught it just before it would have pierced his leg. Not a killing throw, but one that would have hurt. And lorcith, so he suspected this to be some sort of test from Haern.

"Good. At least you keep your reflexes active. Have to be with what's coming." Haern grabbed the knife from Rsiran's hand and kicked the door to the smithy shut. "You going to stand there and gape at me, or you going to ask the question that's on your mind?"

"I repeat, what are you doing here?"

Haern started toward the forge and stopped at the long table that held Rsiran's recent forgings. It had been days since he'd worked at the forge, and the smithy didn't smell quite so strongly of lorcith, but the top of the table was littered with what he'd made. Now that they didn't sell his lorcith creations, he kept them all here, and they accumulated.

At the table, Haern took a pair of knives and flicked them toward Rsiran. It was an almost casual motion, and he smiled as he did it.

Rsiran *pushed* the knives, slowing them enough that he could catch them. "Haern?"

"This," Haern began, grabbing an iron plate that Rsiran had made, "is about your training," he finished, spinning the iron plate at Rsiran.

Iron didn't react the same as lorcith. He ducked, but wasn't fast enough. The plate caught him on the arm and sent him spinning.

In that time, Haern crossed the distance between them, a steel knife appearing in his hand. He slashed at Rsiran.

Rsiran Slid back two steps, emerging near the door.

Haern stood and smiled. "Good. Can't forget all your abilities, can you?"

He flicked a pair of knives that Rsiran hadn't seen. Neither was lorcith.

Rsiran emerged on the far side of the smithy, wanting to be farther away when he emerged. "Training?" he asked. His mind still hadn't cleared, but what was Haern doing?

"Told you that you'll need to be harder. That you'll need to learn how to use your abilities. Now you're going to learn." Another knife streaked toward Rsiran that he Slid away from. "You really need to think quicker when you're attacked. You use one of your abilities at a time, when you've got two."

Haern rolled, sending another knife at Rsiran and then leaping toward him.

Rsiran Slid to emerge behind him. If Haern wanted to play at an attack, then he suspected he would have to oblige him. He pulled a pair of knives from the table and sent them spinning toward Haern, blunt end forward. Rsiran didn't want to hurt Haern, but he wanted to prove that he was capable enough.

A short sword appeared in Haern's hand, and he swatted the knives from the air. Rsiran had never seen Haern with a sword, and was surprised to note the bright gleam to the steel. It was finely made, but not one of his.

"That might work, but you forget that I can See." He jumped toward Rsiran, the tip of his sword stabbing toward him.

Rsiran Slid two steps to the side. "I thought you couldn't See anything involving me."

Haern spun and darted toward him again. A tight smile spread across his face. Haern didn't seem winded, and actually seemed to be enjoying himself. "Can't See *you*, but when you send knives at me…"

Rsiran had another pair of knives ready and sent them flying toward Haern. The man spun, his steps quick, and slashed the knives out of the air, before spinning back toward Rsiran, and jumping with more agility than Rsiran would have expected. He landed in front of Rsiran, his sword nearly stabbing into his chest.

"You see, you hesitate," Haern said, jabbing at him with the tip of the sword. "What would have happened had I *wanted* to hurt you?"

Rsiran Slid a step back, but Haern had been ready. When he emerged, Haern's sword remained stabbed toward his chest. "I think that I could get away."

He eyed the sharp edge of the sword and noted how close it was to him. In spite of his ability to Slide, it was still dangerously close. He thought of when he'd been attacked by the Forgotten Sliders after they'd poisoned him. He hadn't been able to do much more than escape then. What would have happened to him—to Jessa—had they been even slightly more capable?

"There are times when your abilities fail," Haern said. "Times when you either can't—or don't want to—run. You need to know how to use your combination of abilities, because I assure you, there are others out there who have honed their gifts and will not hesitate to do what they need to do in order to survive."

Rsiran met Haern's eyes. "I've done what was needed to survive."

Haern laughed darkly and slipped his sword into an unseen sheath. "You mean those men you fought in Asador? Or Thom when he Compelled me?" Haern grunted. "Jessa thinks you'd do what is needed, but she also thinks you fear it'll turn you into something else." Rsiran hadn't known that Jessa had discovered his concern. But then, she knew him better than anyone. "Trust me when I tell you that I've lived with darkness, Rsiran. There are things that can break a man, but you have to be willing to be broken. From what I've seen, you keep yourself too grounded for that to happen."

"I don't think I'm grounded."

Haern swept his hand around him. "No? You don't think this place gives you some purpose? It might not be what you expected, but I've seen the way you look when you talk about your work. And Jessa. Even if you never stood in front of your forge again, I think that girl would be enough to keep you straight."

Rsiran turned away from Haern and stepped in front of the anvil. He lifted one of his hammers and slung it over his shoulder. There was a reassuring heft to the hammer, a familiarity that had come from all the years he'd spent pounding with it. "That's the problem, isn't it? I'd do anything to keep her safe."

"And you fear what that means," Haern said. "You think that just because you killed Shael, and were willing to kill others, that you might have to do it again. And I can't say you won't, not with what we're dealing with."

Rsiran swallowed. It was as if Haern Read him, but that wouldn't be possible, not from Haern. "I fear what I've become. And I fear what I'll be forced to become."

"As you should," Haern said softly. Rsiran turned to him and Haern shrugged. "You know where I studied. There's a darkness to what I did, and what I *had* to do, but even as I learned, I never questioned whether what I was doing was right. I never wondered whether what I learned was right, only that it was necessary. You're different. If you weren't, I wouldn't let Jessa stay with you." Haern slipped his sword into his sheath. "Did you feel a thrill when you killed Shael?"

Rsiran thought about the way the knife had torn through him. There had been no choice. Had he not, Jessa and he would have remained trapped. He remembered the sadness, and the fear, but there had been no thrill. "What do you mean by a thrill?"

"Some feel it when they kill. Not you?"

Rsiran shook his head.

"Good. Even if you did, doesn't mean you're some sort of killer. Oh, maybe it means that you *could* be, but I think there's a darkness within each of us, and we have to know when and how to control it. When you're threatened, that darkness comes forward. It's a natural survival instinct and you sometimes lose a little control. If it didn't manifest, either you'd be dead, or someone you cared about would be dead. For Jessa's sake, I think you *need* to have that part of you. But like I said, you need to control it."

Rsiran set the hammer back down on the anvil, wondering whether Haern was telling him what he thought he wanted to hear or whether it was the truth. "I don't know that I can keep her safe, Haern," he said softly. "With what I know is out there—the Forgotten and Venass…"

"And the alchemists," Haern reminded.

"And the alchemists," Rsiran agreed. He hadn't forgotten about them, but the alchemists seemed less of a threat than the Forgotten and the scholars of Venass, especially since he hadn't heard anything from them in the months since he had infiltrated the guild house. "All of that makes me a target, doesn't it? As long as Jessa stays with me, then *she's* a target too. I can't be the reason that something happens to her."

Haern returned to the table at the back of the room and picked up one of Rsiran's knives. He spun it in his hand, moving with a casual grace that did nothing to mask how deadly he would be with the knife.

"That's why I came to you today. You've got it right. You have a target on you. With what happened with Josun and what you've been forced to do, there's no one else who's in quite as much danger as you. I think it's about time we do something to make sure you get the training you need to ensure that if someone comes after you again, you won't be the reason others get hurt. It's time we make sure that, if anything, you're the reason we remain safe."

"I don't know…"

"What's your hesitation? Do you think that if you don't learn to control your abilities, you won't have to use them?"

"I know how to control them," Rsiran said.

"Right. You can travel from one place to the next, and you can *push* your knives at me. But is that control, or is that the most basic level of what's possible? Seems to me that there are layers of ability. I'm guessing you haven't done much more than scratch at the surface of yours."

Rsiran considered what Haern suggested. He had seen how deadly Haern could be. And the man moved with such a confident grace, how could learning such skills not be helpful? But, if he did, what other skills would he commit himself to learning? What would Haern force him to do in order to master his abilities?

"And if I do this?" Rsiran asked.

Haern frowned. "What're you getting at?"

Rsiran shook his head. "What's the price?"

Haern flipped one of the knives and spun it so quickly that it seemed to practically hum in the air. With a quick flick of his wrist, he sent the knife spiraling toward the opposite end of the smithy where it sank into the wall. "There's always a price, Rsiran. You don't think it's worth it to make certain you're not the reason we get hurt? That you're not the reason *she* gets hurt?"

Rsiran considered the many things that had happened of late as he watched Haern. He could learn much from this man, especially if he had studied in Venass and knew some of their secrets. Rsiran didn't know what else the scholars might want from him, but it clearly had something to do with his ability to Slide past the alloy. It was the same knowledge that the Forgotten wanted from him.

The scholars had claimed that a time would come when they would call Rsiran to them, when they would demand that he fulfill his promise to return so they could study him. Thom had already called him once before attacking them, but Rsiran had refused. What that meant for him remained to be seen, but he didn't think he would escape unharmed. And his friends would likely suffer from it as well.

But he owed the scholars of Venass a debt. That had been the deal when he'd gone for the antidote, one that, in the end, he had not truly needed for Brusus… but had needed for himself. If nothing else, Venass had *saved* him. But he found it difficult to imagine that had been the intent when they had given him the antidote. Given that Thom was likely behind the poison attack on Brusus in the first place, it was almost certain that Venass had only intended the antidote be given to him. And, as far as Venass knew, Brusus was dead.

He sighed, and frowned as Haern smiled at him. What price would he exact to help teach him what he needed to keep himself—and Jessa—safe?

Was there any price that was too high?

CHAPTER 3

The edge of the Aisl Forest carried none of the heavy fragrance of the sjihn trees that it did deeper in the woods. The trees along the edge were enormous and towered over the edge of the city as if ancient guardians observing the city itself. Only Krali Rock reached above the height of the trees from here; otherwise, the city sloped down toward the bay and the steady waves crashing along the shoreline.

Pale sunlight streamed through the upper branches, bouncing off the thick leaves, casting a wavering shadow that danced across the forest floor. Other than his own footsteps, Rsiran heard nothing else moving. Thankfully, the strange howls he had often heard when deep in the forest were silent on this occasion.

He waited for Haern, his heart racing, knowing that at any moment, the man might appear, and attack. Training, he called it, but Rsiran felt that, so far, it had been little more than testing of his ability, almost as if Haern wanted to take stock of what he could do. If he didn't know how implicitly Brusus trusted Haern—as did Jessa—he might have questioned what he'd been asked to do. As it was, he went along with Haern's requests but wondered how long he should.

They had spent an evening in the smithy, much like when Haern had first appeared. Somehow, Rsiran still didn't manage to get the best of Haern, in spite of his increasing attempts to at least catch him once with the edge of one of his knives. None had connected. Haern rolled each time, either the knife missing or with him managing to bat it out of the air, his ability to See giving him awareness of where Rsiran's attack would likely come from.

It had grown frustrating.

When Haern suggested they meet at the edge of the Aisl, Rsiran figured he might have some advantage. He had spent his boyhood in the forest and could Slide and appear anywhere while Haern would have to move in the open, but then, Rsiran wondered if he really had any advantage when it came to Haern.

There was one thing that Haern had told him that was true: he needed to master his abilities or he would end up failing Jessa, and he might end up used by those who were after him. For her, he would do what he needed to keep them safe. Even if it meant embracing the darkness of his abilities.

Rsiran Slid from tree to tree, not willing to stand in a single place for too long. He emerged long enough to glance around, knowing that Haern would be there soon, and not wanting to be caught unprepared again.

After a while, when Haern failed to appear, he began working his way deeper into the forest. At one point, he paused near the plain wooden hut where his father had been housed after Rsiran had brought him back from Asador. He still didn't know why the Forgotten wanted his father, and what they might have been after before Rsiran had brought him back to Elaeavn. Without returning to Asador, he might not learn the answer, though from what he'd discovered, the Forgotten had been targeting smiths. But why? And why had Josun been sending lorcith to Asador?

Questions without answers, much like why the lorcith supply in Elaeavn had dried up. There hadn't ever been that much lorcith in Ilphaesn, at least as far as the Elvraeth and the Miners Guild knew. Only Rsiran knew the secret of how much lorcith remained hidden in the mountain.

Grass around the hut had grown long. When he had come the last time, it had been trampled down by dozens of different feet, leaving a path that led up to the entrance of the hut. Rsiran didn't need the path, nor did he need to worry about the lock on the door.

Since Haern hadn't appeared, Rsiran Slid inside.

A place like this would have been too dark for him even a month ago, but since holding the crystal, his vision had changed, though he still didn't understand exactly how. Della claimed she had changed after holding the crystal, and she expected that he would as well, though she didn't know how that change would manifest.

Now, he was able to make out the simple sleep pallet along one wall in this barren space his father had briefly called home. The pair of chairs angled near the hearth, almost as if to leave an opportunity for conversation. The stale scent of burned logs, the residue of the char still hanging in the air, lingered. There was an old odor of sweat, and the stink of the man who had lived here for… What had it been? Weeks? A month? All that time, and Rsiran had only come to him once before needing him to find Thyr.

Rsiran should have taken the opportunity to ask questions, but instead, he had held onto his anger, never able to move past it. How much could he have learned had he only been willing to ask?

His father knew more about what it meant to be a smith than Rsiran had been able to discover on his own. It was more than what the man could teach him about working the forge. It was the teachings of a master smith, those invaluable lessons and insights that come from years of honing one's craft. Skills that Rsiran still hadn't mastered despite all the lessons the lorcith had provided. There were techniques that he might begin to discover if he took the time, but would never truly master, not like his father, and not without having a true master to work under.

Rsiran sighed and turned away from the hearth thinking of the journey he'd forced his father to take to Venass, during which he'd learned that his father had spent time in Thyr. He should have asked more questions during that journey, when he had his father in somewhat captured company, but he had not. What else had he missed out on the opportunity to learn? He had never known that his father had spent any time outside of the city, and now might never know why, or the reason he had returned.

Everything about the hut came as gradations of shadow, but as he glanced over near the pallet, a shimmer of color seemed to catch his eye.

Rsiran leaned over the pallet searching for any sense of lorcith, and found none. What had he seen then?

The pallet was little more than straw stuffing, with blankets lying over the top. At first, Rsiran wondered if he had seen nothing more than colors from one of the blankets, regardless of how valuable such linens might be. With what they'd discovered in the warehouse along the docks of Lower Town, there were things that Brusus had taken and used that were incredibly valuable, so Rsiran wouldn't have been entirely surprised to learn that he had taken something like that and left it here for his father.

But that wasn't what he had seen.

Along the wall, there was a long mark, as if carved. Rsiran leaned toward this mark and realized that it had been gouged into the wood. He reached toward it, running his fingers along the rough edge of the crack, suspecting that his father must have made it.

It was deeper than he would have expected, and any more light would likely have faded into the shadows, but in the darkness he could see the crack.

Not only the crack, but the way something had been stuffed into the crack.

Rsiran used one of his knives to pry at the wall. Lorcith was hard metal, particularly when forged by someone like himself who understood the way the metal called to him, but it could be brittle as well. He dug at the crack, wiggling the tip of his knife from side to side until the crack in the wood began to widen.

The wood separated enough for him to feel a long sliver of metal.

Not lorcith, or it would have tugged on his senses. And not heartstone, though he wouldn't have expected his father to have anything of heartstone here. This appeared to be a mixture of metals, but one of iron and grindl, a rare enough metal that could be formed into fairly beautiful patterns if made by the right smith. The mixture of iron and grindl was not one of the alchemists' sanctioned alloys, though nor was it forbidden, not like using lorcith in the way that Rsiran did. Streaks of green melded into the black of the iron, giving it the shimmering color that he had seen, but how had he managed to see it from the other side of the room?

Rsiran studied the piece of metal. It was a flat sheet, seemingly plain, but as he tipped it from side to side, he realized that there was a pattern to the streaks of grindl that ran through the iron, almost as if intentional. Why would his father have hidden this?

Or had he?

Thom had been here, and had known about Rsiran's ability. It was possible that Thom had left it, hoping that Rsiran or one of them would find it. For all he knew, he had been Compelled to find it, some strange plan of Thom's.

But why these metals?

Grindl might be rare, but it wasn't particularly expensive, not like lorcith. And iron was common. No, this wouldn't have been Thom. This seemed more likely to have come from his father.

Then what was it? Why would his father have placed something here? Unless he had known that he would be dragged away.

Rsiran didn't think that likely. If his father thought that he might be dragged away, and that something else was going to happen to him, he wouldn't have stored something here. He would have kept it on him.

Then what?

Maybe he had it wrong. Maybe this was nothing of his father's at all. He would have to ask Brusus.

Rsiran tucked the piece of metal into his pocket and scanned the rest of the hut. There was nothing else here that he could see. His father had been held here in the months following his capture, and Rsiran thought he should feel something, some emotional reaction. But he struggled to come up with any sort of sympathy for his father after what he'd put Rsiran through. In spite of that, he still wanted to find out why the scholars had taken him when they arrived at the Tower of Scholars. What did they intend for him?

He shook away those unanswered questions, realizing he'd spent enough time here. He needed to find Haern and continue the training that he intended. Rsiran Slid from the hut, emerging just outside the door.

As soon as he did, he sensed lorcith.

Without waiting, he Slid forward two steps. Something struck the door behind where he'd been standing. He spun to see a lorcith knife protruding from the door. Rsiran Slid again, this time a dozen steps to the right, *pulling* on the knife intended for him at the same time and sending it whistling back in the direction that he'd sensed it. It streaked into the trees and fell to the ground.

Damn Haern for testing him like this.

In the smithy, Haern stopped using lorcith blades, knowing that Rsiran could detect them easily enough, even with knives that he had not made. Haern had thought to test him in the Aisl, and probably knew that Rsiran wasn't ready for anything *not* made of lorcith.

Rsiran sensed no other lorcith, but doubted that Haern had departed. If it was Haern, then this was all a part of his training. If it was not… Rsiran didn't want to think of what might happen if it wasn't Haern. He had to find out who was hiding in the trees. If it *wasn't* Haern, he needed to know.

He didn't want to move until he knew what he might be dealing with. Any movement might give him away. Even Sliding could do that. Jessa told him what she saw when he Slid, the flash of colors that came with it, so he wanted to avoid giving himself away.

How would he be able to determine who might be out there, especially if they didn't carry lorcith—or heartstone—on them?

Maybe he couldn't, and maybe that was the point Haern wanted to make. Rsiran might have certain abilities that protected him and kept him safe, but unless his attackers carried lorcith, his ability was neutralized.

That didn't mean he was in danger, necessarily. Especially when traveling alone.

When Jessa Slid with him, he had to worry about something happening to her. He had to ensure they kept in contact so that if something did happen and they needed to escape, they could.

Alone, he could Slide quickly. Even the ripples formed by his Sliding should be minimal.

What he needed was a better way to see. A better vantage. That would be his best option, but there was nothing but trees all around him. He might be able to Slide onto a high branch, but he could just as easily fall attempting that. Sliding someplace like that was no different from Sliding to a narrow ledge.

But he could *pull* himself, couldn't he? He had another way to Slide, one that didn't require him to step into the Slide. There was a different type of control when he did that.

Looking up, he surveyed the trees and considered which one to start with. The sjihn trees here were all massive. The hut was situated deeper into the forest where more mature trees grew. They were not quite as tall as some that grew deeper in the forest, those that lived even beyond where Lianna was buried, but should be enough for him to get a better look at what might be moving around him. One thick branch seemed to stretch between trees, something like a walkway.

Rsiran focused on it, and rather than stepping into the Slide—a movement that might be visible to someone with Sight—he *pulled* himself toward it. The difference was subtle, but it changed the way that he traveled. With Sliding, there was the sense of movement, and of flashes of color, and even the bitter scent of lorcith. Sliding this way had no real sense of movement, none of the wind that whistled through his ears. Muted white light surrounded him and the air smelled almost fragrant.

When he emerged, he stood balanced on the branch and looking down at the forest floor below. From this vantage, he could see some of the city through the trees, but the buildings were little more than gradations of color. From outside, especially from the sea, the city had been designed to flow into to the rock. Above it all rose Krali Rock, towering over the city.

Rsiran turned his attention away from the city and looked to the forest below him. The hut occupied much of a small clearing. The grasses that he hadn't thought trampled appeared more compacted now than when he'd been down on the ground. Not only could he see his boot marks, but those of others, though he couldn't be sure how many others without getting much closer. Small scrub plants cropped up near the edge of the trees, but otherwise, nothing but the sjihn trees grew here.

He moved slowly along the branch, looking for any sign of whoever had thrown the knife, staring at the ground. Probably Haern, but a nagging worry made him wonder if he was wrong. Nothing moved that would explain what might be here.

Rsiran reached the trunk of the tree and leaned back against it. Somehow, he was missing something. He shouldn't remain here, not by himself, but what if it *was* only Haern? How would he explain that he'd Slid away at the first sign of an attack, especially after what Haern had been trying to demonstrate to him?

No, he needed to find him.

He looked deeper into the forest, and away from the clearing, toward another large tree with a similarly large branch. Focusing on it, he *pulled* himself in the Slide, again choosing this technique rather than stepping into the Slide. When he emerged this time, the darkness of the canopy hung overhead, filtering out more of the light and making it harder to see anything.

Rsiran studied the ground. Movement should be easier to find. He scanned from tree to tree, but saw nothing that indicated anything—or anyone—moving.

Maybe he'd been mistaken.

Had Haern climbed into the branches to hide? He wouldn't put it past him, but if Haern had climbed into the trees, Rsiran would be better equipped to chase after him. He didn't have to crawl along the rough sjihn bark, or try to scale the massive trunks.

With his attention turned to the trees, he almost missed the sudden flare of lorcith again.

Rsiran frowned. The sense was back near the hut.

He fixed his attention on the tree that he'd just come from, and *pulled* himself back to the branch.

When he emerged, he saw movement below him. The door to the hut hung open—likely forced open, from the way that it hung half-splintered on the frame. A solitary figure stalked around the edge of the hut.

At first, Rsiran thought that it was Haern and nearly Slid down to surprise him, but he hesitated. There was something different about the posture and the way the person flickered as he moved that made him hesitate.

Flicker.

Not Haern.

Rsiran's heart started pounding so loud that he feared someone who might be a Listener could hear. He slammed heartstone-infused barriers into place in his mind, suddenly concerned. And he understood why he hadn't detected lorcith before now: Whoever was down in the clearing below could Slide.

CHAPTER 4

Rsiran should return to the safety of the smithy, or at least to the outskirts of the forest and find Haern, but first, he wanted to find out who had come to the hut, and why.

Whoever it was must have detected him Sliding and known he was here. The attack as soon as he Slid outside the hut had told him that. But why kick down the door if whoever this was could Slide as well?

Another figure emerged from the hut. A tall woman with dark eyes and deep black hair slipped out from the door. She held a short sword in hand and walked in a casual way that reminded him of the Neelish sellsword who had nearly killed Brusus. Her lips were pressed into a thin line as she surveyed the clearing, pausing to turn to the remains of the door where the lorcith knife had pierced the wood.

She traced her fingers along the wood for a moment before craning her neck so that she could see behind her. Rsiran clung to the tree, ready to Slide if needed, as she surveyed the forest.

"What is it?" The other figure appeared from the side of the hut and pushed a hood back revealing a youthful face with short brown hair and a thin beard to match.

"Your knife," the woman said.

Their voices carried to him, but barely. Rsiran strained to hear, wanting to know if these were Forgotten or Venass or some new enemy. He wasn't sure that he was prepared to have one more group that might be after him.

"What about it? I threw it blunt end so it wouldn't kill, and he Slid before it hit him."

"Yes," the woman said, "then where is it?"

The man stalked past her and leaned into the door. He touched it much like the woman had, and his fingers traced a pattern across the wood. "Why would he linger long enough to take the knife?"

"Did you see him do that?" she asked.

The man flickered and appeared at the edge of the trees. There seemed to be a slight swirl of colors as he did, and then he emerged nearly directly below Rsiran. "Didn't see him, but only a fool would have taken the time to fetch a knife…"

"Unless he didn't know we were here."

The man grunted. "You certain that he didn't? Seemed to pause long enough, and you said he Slid as soon as the knife started toward him."

The woman tilted her head in agreement. "That's what I said."

"Then where did he go?"

Her eyes scanned the trees. "It doesn't work like that," she said.

The man Slid back to her, emerging near the hut. Rsiran noted how quickly he moved, blinking from one place to the next, almost as if sprinting. The Forgotten that he'd met had similar speed with Sliding, not to mention Josun's control. Was there a benefit to Sliding quickly? He hadn't found one, but that didn't mean that one didn't exist. Rsiran didn't have the same advantage as others with his ability; there was no one to ask about technique, and ways to use Sliding, not like those with different abilities had.

"Then tell me, Sarah, how does it work?"

The woman flipped her sword toward the man, but he simply Slid a step to the side. As he emerged, essentially flickering back into view, he swung his sword up and knocked hers down.

That was what Haern wanted Rsiran to learn.

"Know that it doesn't," she said.

The man laughed softly. "You lost him? After all the time we spent searching for him, and now you've lost him?"

She fixed the man with a hard-eyed expression. "He's not nearly as easy to detect as some."

"I thought you said he was loud?"

"At times. As are you."

"And what does it mean that he's loud?"

Sarah looked beyond the man and shook her head. "It means strength, Valn. This one… he is incredibly strong."

"Stronger than—"

As he asked, Rsiran slipped on the branch.

Sarah glanced at the trees and her eyes went wide.

He didn't dare wait any longer, and Slid.

Rsiran emerged briefly, standing on the edge of the dock, before Sliding again, this time to the alley along where his father's shop had been, and then once more, finally to his smithy. If Sarah was able to follow his Slides, he didn't want to take the chance that she might be able to track him back to the smithy. Chances were that she already knew where to find him, but if she didn't, then he wanted to be careful.

And here he'd been concerned that his Sliding could be influenced. That wasn't the only risk anymore, not if there was someone with the ability to track his Slides, as well as someone else who was able to Slide. They could possibly follow him anywhere.

Wasn't that the reason the Forgotten didn't Slide often? They feared their Sliding might be influenced. And, it seemed, for good reason.

A heavy pounding came on the door to his smithy.

Rsiran jumped. He had six knives on him. Enough for the most part, but what if Sarah and this man Valn had followed him? He was protected by the heartstone alloy in the walls of the smithy, but he might not be protected if they simply tried to kick in the door.

The smithy was supposed to be a place of safety, but what if it no longer was?

Sliding—though this time, *pulling* himself rather than stepping into it—he emerged on the roof of his smithy. From here, he could see the street, though part of it remained obscured by the overhang of the roof. The air smelled of the filth from this part of Lower Town, in so many ways the stench worse here than in the rest of Lower Town, the benefit being it masked the smell of lorcith that might emanate from the smithy. Inside, that stink could be ignored, and the lorcith that he forged often overpowered it, anyway. He looked down, worried about what he might find.

Haern stood outside the door to the smithy alone.

Rsiran Slid to him, grabbed him by the sleeve, and then Slid back into the smithy, *pulling* through the bars of heartstone alloy.

Haern jerked his arm away as they emerged inside. Rsiran twisted the knob on the lantern on his table, letting pale blue light spill across the smithy.

"What the—" Haern started. "Rsiran, where were you?"

He shook his head, touching his pocket to feel the small sheet of metal that he'd discovered in the hut, wondering why his father might have stuffed it into the wall.

"When you didn't come, I made my way deeper into the forest," Rsiran said.

"I told you to wait. That was part of the training."

Rsiran breathed out softly, trying to keep an image of Valn and Sarah fixed in his mind. He needed to know whether they were with the Forgotten or if they were with Venass. Until he knew, he wouldn't be comfortable. Valn and his Sliding ability seemed more likely to make him one of the Forgotten, but the woman Sarah looked nothing like someone of Elaeavn. She was short, compact, and appeared deadly.

"I went to the hut," Rsiran said. "I hadn't been there since…" He shook his head. Haern wouldn't understand why he'd felt the need to return to the hut, and truthfully, Rsiran didn't really know, either. He'd gone because he'd wanted to see the inside, because he'd been thinking about his father, and because he couldn't shake the idea that there was something about Thom that he needed to know, only… what he had found had been different.

"I know. Since Thom convinced you to go to Venass," Haern said. "There's nothing there. Brusus locked it after you left. Best we not use it, anyway, especially if Thom knows it exists."

Rsiran nodded. He should have been smarter than that and should have stayed away. "When I Slid out of the hut, I was attacked," he went on. "At first, I thought it was you, that maybe you were playing some sort of training game with me, and when I couldn't find you, I went to the trees. From there…"

"What?" Haern asked.

"There was activity near the hut. A Slider and a woman who I think can sense Sliding, much like Della. They were waiting for me."

"Are you sure they waited for you?"

"They knew I could Slide, Haern. They were expecting it. The woman said she could sense it, and that my Sliding was loud."

Haern breathed out a soft swear. "Same thing Brusus used to say about your thoughts. He tell you that?"

Rsiran had forgotten about Brusus telling him that, but then that had been before he started blocking his thoughts with lorcith and heartstone.

"What did they want?" Haern asked.

"I don't know. I didn't remain behind long enough to find out."

"You certain it was you they wanted, though?"

Rsiran thought about what he'd overheard from them. "Yes."

Haern started pacing along the length of the smithy. One of his knives flipped into his hands, and he twisted it as he walked. "Could you tell where they might be from?"

"That's what I was trying to do," he admitted, "but I… I slipped and she heard me. I had to Slide away before finding out who they might be with."

Haern paused and faced him. "Sliding likely means the Forgotten."

"It could mean Venass," Rsiran said. "They were able to direct my Sliding when we were there."

"Damn," Haern whispered. "And there's nothing I can See, at least nothing bright enough, to know what they might be after. We haven't heard much from either of them over the last few weeks, not since you escaped from the palace and Thom attacked. I kept thinking that they might come back to us, or that word of them might reach us, but there's been nothing."

"Not even in the palace?" Rsiran asked.

"Brusus's contacts haven't got much to share, and without anything to really bribe them with, we're not likely to learn much, anyway."

Rsiran glanced at the table covered with his lorcith forgings. Brusus had used the forgings as a way to get information, but had stopped when Rsiran had asked him to.

Hearn followed the direction of his gaze and shook his head. "Don't matter that much anyway, Rsiran. There's only so much you can learn from the palace. They're not likely to share with Brusus anything about your break-in, and the Forgotten… well, that's sort of an off-limits topic."

"I don't want to be in the middle of all of this," Rsiran said. "I don't want to be the reason anyone gets hurt."

Haern grunted. "The way I see it, there's not much that you're going to be able to do to avoid it. Some things drag you in, regardless of whether you want them to or not."

"You're the one who told me what's coming," Rsiran said.

Haern nodded. "That I did. And that don't change anything that is to come, now does it? You want to keep yourself safe, and you want to keep your friends safe, but what's going on is bigger than all of us. And they don't want no one interfering."

"So what can I do?" Rsiran asked.

Haern lifted a knife off the table and flipped it toward him. Rsiran caught it easily from the air. "Seems to me that you're already doing what you need. If you don't want to get caught in the middle, you have to learn to master your abilities, whatever they are." He tipped his head to Rsiran and touched a finger to his nose. "And there's more to what you can do than what they know. I think that's part of the reason you intrigue them so much."

"But, Haern, what can we really do if war comes like you say?"

Haern laughed and started to the door. "Pick a side. That's all any of us can do."

He pulled open the door and leaned out, pausing to turn to Rsiran. "We'll pick up our training again tomorrow. Let this settle down a bit before we go at it. The forest?"

Rsiran sighed, wishing what Haern suggested wasn't necessary but knowing that he was likely right. "Not the edge of the forest," he said.

Haern frowned. "Where then?"

"Deeper. Where Lianna was buried." At least there he didn't think they'd be discovered.

Haern nodded once, then pulled the door closed as he disappeared down the street.

Rsiran slipped the locks back into place around the door, knowing they did nothing to stop Jessa, but then he had no reason to obstruct her access. As he made his way to the forge, he wondered how he could do what Haern suggested. How could he pick a side if he didn't know what each side wanted? And how could he choose when each side had done nothing but try to use him?

CHAPTER 5

THE FORGE GLOWED A COOL ORANGE. Sweat dripped from his brow, and Rsiran set the hammer down atop the anvil. He went to the bucket of water where he'd left the knives he'd forged, and pulled them out. These were smaller than his usual knives, and laced with heartstone in a single strip that ran along the blade.

"You finally done?" Jessa called from their bed.

He took the knives and placed them on the table, arranging them in a line. It would take more effort to *pull* on them, but then he needed the practice. And this way, he had something that no one else could use. At least so far. If Venass and the Forgotten had their way, they would learn how to replicate his ability.

"Done for now," Rsiran said. He hadn't noticed when Jessa had returned, but then he had been focused on the forge, and the metal, letting it clear his head as it so often did.

Jessa stood and came to the table where she examined one of the knives he'd made, holding it up and turning it from side to side.

"Interesting texture on this one. It's almost as if you've put two knives together."

Rsiran could feel the way the metals sat on each other. Forging this had required folding the metals together rather than simply mixing the alloy, and he'd let the lorcith guide him with the forging. "Something like that," he agreed.

Jessa set the knife back down and took his hands. "Haern tells me that you've been practicing with him."

Rsiran grunted. "Not only him, it seems."

"What does that mean?"

He shook his head and told her about the others he'd seen near the hut.

"What do you think they were after?" she asked.

"Besides me?"

She punched him in the shoulder and leaned toward the pale red flower that she stuffed into her charm today. Standing this close to her, the bright fragrance coming off the flower drifted to him. It pushed back some of the bitterness in the air from the lorcith, as well as some of the strange sweetness that came from heartstone.

"Yes, besides you. Do you really think that the forest is the best place for them to grab you? They were looking for something."

Rsiran hadn't pieced that together, but maybe she was right. He reached for where he'd left his cloak draped over the table and pulled the small sheet of metal out and handed it to her.

"What is this?"

"What I found in the hut. This was buried in the wall, stuffed there, I think, by my father."

Jessa held it out and examined it much like she had with the knife. She turned her head slightly, as if trying to get a better view, and frowned. "There's something here, isn't there?"

"I don't know. I haven't had a chance to look at it much."

She passed it back over to him. "This is skillfully made, but it's different from your forgings." She looked up from the metal. "You think your father did this?"

Rsiran studied the piece of metal. It had been a while since he had seen anything made by his father, but the way the metal was folded together made it seem unlikely. The grindl mixed into the iron, but not in an alloy, and not like what was done with metals like steel. This was more like what he did with the heartstone, especially with the knives that he'd just made. There was a certain artistry to the metal, a pattern to the grindl within it, that didn't really suit the utilitarian designs he'd seen his father favor.

"I don't know," Rsiran said. "There was a reason he thought to hide it, though."

Jessa took it back from him and placed it near the blue heartstone light. The blue light could help augment what someone Sighted could see, while the orange light, like the lantern that had been in the Ilphaesn mine, made it more difficult for someone Sighted to see anything.

"You think these patterns mean anything?" she asked.

"Not that I can tell. I can barely see them."

"The way this green metal—"

"Grindl," Rsiran said.

"—seems to repeat," she went on. "Almost like there is an intentional pattern to it, but nothing that I can really make out or understand."

Rsiran could see the pattern, but if it were made with lorcith or with heartstone, he could *feel* the pattern. What he could see didn't really give him much of an idea about whether the pattern itself meant anything, or whether there was something more to this metal than simply demonstrating technique. But the fact that it had been hidden within the wall of the hut made him think that there *had* to be something important about it.

"So you think they were after this?" Jessa asked.

"I don't know that they knew it was there. *I* wouldn't have known it was there if not for the darkness."

"Someone Sighted would have seen it," Jessa said.

Rsiran wondered if that was true. If they were Sighted, the shadows in the room might have obscured the ability to see the crack where this had been stuffed, especially with a fire burning in the hearth as there had been the times that Rsiran had visited.

"How has your training gone?" Jessa asked.

"Haern thinks we'll need to choose sides," Rsiran said.

"Sides?"

"With what's coming. This… war," he said. He ran his hand above the knives he'd just made, feeling the way that lorcith and heartstone called to him, each with a different type of intensity. It was different from the way the alloy pulled on him.

"Which side, Rsiran?" Jessa asked. She pointed to the forge, and then to the lorcith items spread across the table. "Do you support the Elvraeth in the palace? Because that's who controls the city. Or do you mean to support the Forgotten, those the Elvraeth have decided were too dangerous for the city? The same Forgotten we've seen willing to poison us to learn what you know. The same Forgotten willing to torment you—*us*—simply so that they could attain more power?" Jessa touched the nearest knife and sent it spinning in place. "What about Venass? The scholars didn't seem too interested in your safety, either, did they? They were perfectly content to leave you trapped, and only after you managed to escape were they interested in helping. Even that came with a cost, now didn't it?" Jessa turned to him and crossed her arms over her chest. "So which side, Rsiran? Tell me what you think we should do?"

"I don't know," he said softly. Hearing her put it that way made it clear that there was no side that was the right one for them to choose. How could he work with any of them, especially if all of them seemed willing to harm whoever they had to in order to keep their control?

"We need to keep safe and stay out of whatever they plan," Jessa said. "That's how we'll get through this. Let the Forgotten do whatever they want to the Elvraeth, and let Venass continue to do… whatever it is they do. But we don't need to get mixed up in it. That only leads one place."

Rsiran nodded. That Jessa was right didn't mean that he knew how they would remain safe, or that they would somehow manage to stay separated from what the Forgotten or Venass had in mind, especially if they had already come looking for him.

"That's my concern," he said. "I don't think there's any way that we're going to stay out of this. What if the way out is to stay *in*?"

Jessa shook her head. "That means you intend to engage in whatever Venass and the Forgotten want. We already know the power the Elvraeth hide—and protect—in the palace. You've said it yourself that it needs to stay there, that the crystals are too powerful. What if Venass gets ahold of them? Or the Forgotten?" She grabbed the spinning knife and slapped her hand onto it. "How many of them do you think there are? How many compared to us? We're nothing, Rsiran. That's why they haven't been opposed to using us for what they want. When they're done using us, they won't have any problem simply throwing us away again."

Even though he agreed with Jessa, Rsiran couldn't shake the sense that Haern might be right. The Forgotten and Venass had proven that they would keep coming. They would be forced to make a choice at some point, but how could they? What they knew of the Forgotten was that they were willing to sacrifice anyone—and anything—to achieve whatever their goals might be. And Venass? He still didn't know what they were after, only that they wanted to understand how he could Slide past the heartstone alloy. That, and they wanted the crystals in the palace. Thom coming after them made that clear.

They needed to know more. In that, Jessa was wrong. If they waited, if they remained in the dark, they would always be forced to react. If they learned more, maybe they could stay in front of what came.

But that meant putting themselves in even more danger.

Rsiran watched Jessa. She touched her one hand to the charm hanging from the lorcith chain. Her eyes darted around the smithy, always searching. What might she see with her enhanced Sight that he could not? In the smithy, with the pressure of lorcith all around him, he doubted that she would see much more than he could sense. But elsewhere? It was why he was thankful for his enhanced Sight since holding the crystal.

Every so often, Jessa would sniff at the flower. He had yet to learn why she chose to place a flower in the charm. Maybe only because she wanted something other than the stink of Lower Town, or maybe there was more to it.

Before, he had thought to barricade himself in the smithy. That was the reason for the bars of heartstone alloy running along the smithy. It had taken Jessa and his friends to convince him to give up on that notion, that he couldn't remain hidden, because others would come for him, regardless. And now that he knew more about everything was that took place around them—how much greater it was than he imagined—he knew he *couldn't* keep them safe within the smithy, even if he wanted to.

But remaining ignorant of what awaited them wasn't helping them, either. Waiting did nothing but put them in more danger, and let others prepare.

What he needed was to understand what was at stake. It might be about the crystals at the heart of the palace, but there might be more as well. And what would happen when the attack came to Elaeavn? Would they be ready?

Rsiran found Jessa watching him. "I see what you're thinking."

He shook his head. "I'm only thinking that we need to know what they're after."

"We tried that once."

He nodded. The image of Shael lying dead because of his knife remained burned in his mind. Haern claimed that he had only done what was needed, but what if the Great Watcher intended for him to embrace the darkness and to use his ability in this way?

Rsiran couldn't do that to Jessa. He would not do that to her.

Then he needed a different plan. Only… he didn't know what that would be.

CHAPTER 6

"YOU HAVE TO FIND A WAY TO MOVE and attack at the same time."

Rsiran wiped the sweat dripping from his forehead and glanced up at Haern. Somehow, the older man seemed barely bothered by the sparring, his breathing easy, and no sign of sweat. He scarcely seemed to have exerted himself.

How could Rsiran be so exhausted? He spent hours hammering away at the forge without any need to slow, but practicing with the sword… that had been a different sort of exertion.

The heartstone blade touched the floor, the tip resting against the wood. Rsiran was surprised to note that where it touched, it left small charred traces behind.

He sighed. "Why do I need to learn to fight like this?" he asked Haern, motioning with the sword. The question was not a new one, and he expected the answer.

"What happens if there are no lorcith knives for you to *push* or *pull*? What happens if you can't Slide somewhere? Do you want to feel helpless like that?"

Rsiran shook his head. That was the last thing that he wanted. "But you're letting me use this," he said, holding up the heartstone-forged sword. "If I have this—"

"Haven't I shown you how that can be stopped?"

Rsiran nodded. The first time he'd tried *pushing* the sword at Haern, he had simply ducked and grabbed the sword out of the air. Rsiran *pulled* on it, but Haern had managed to resist, holding tightly to the sword. Rsiran still didn't know how Haern had managed that.

"You're using that sword because you need to learn how to attack creatively. With your abilities, you should be able to attack in ways that I can't, but you still haven't managed to even disarm me, let alone defeat me."

And Rsiran felt a growing frustration about that as well. Each time he tried—and failed—Haern smacked him with the flat of his sword. His arms and legs stung from each one, a painful reminder of all the times he had failed.

"I can Slide away if I am attacked, Haern."

"Yes. That worked so well for you with Shael. And the Forgotten."

"Shael had the Elvraeth chains."

Haern nodded. "You make my point."

"That's just it, Haern. Had I *not* been trapped by the chains, I'm not sure that I would have learned about how I could connect to the heartstone."

Haern's eyes narrowed. "You think that it was a good thing that Shael attacked you? That he trapped you on Firell's ship?"

"Not a good thing, no," Rsiran started. The time he'd spent trapped on Firell's ship had been torment, but mostly because he didn't know what had happened to Jessa, where Josun had dragged her. He would have done anything to find out. "But good came from it."

"And Venass?" Haern asked. "You were trapped there, I seem to remember you sharing. Do you think that some good came from your time there?"

Rsiran didn't think that anything good could come from a place like Venass. After they had trapped him, essentially buried him in lorcith until he managed to find a way free, the only thing that he had gotten from Venass had been an antidote that hadn't even been needed for Brusus. But hadn't he come to understand that they were a threat?

Haern shook his head and grunted. "Always so damn positive. If you think that there were lessons you were meant to take from that place, then you are a fool," he said. "From that line of thinking, then you'll probably think there was a good reason you ended up trapped by the Forgotten."

Of all the times he'd been trapped, for some reason, it was that time that had left him feeling the most helpless. He couldn't stop what they did to him, how they assaulted him. Not the physical attacks so much, but the way they had attacked his mind, attempting to steal knowledge from him, secrets that were his alone.

Because of that, he hated the Forgotten the most. That, and the fact that they had not only poisoned him, but Jessa as well. They had forced Firell to help find him, tormenting him by threatening harm to his daughter.

"Not good. But at least I know how far they'll go to get what they want."

Haern grunted again. "You could have learned that without getting abducted. Think about how long they have been in hiding, with no sign that they were organized as they are. Even Brusus hadn't learned about the extent of their organization."

"Or you," Rsiran said.

Haern often downplayed his connections, but he had been an assassin before coming to Elaeavn. Those skills would have given him a different sort of insight than someone like Brusus who had been born and raised in Elaeavn, even if his mother had been exiled.

"Yes. Or me," Haern said.

"You've never told me much about your time before Elaeavn, other than the fact that you were an assassin," Rsiran said.

Haern's face remained neutral, but there was a certain tension to his shoulders. His hand clenched around the hilt of the steel sword—one of Rsiran's that Haern had asked him to make—and he took a slow breath. "There aren't many who know of that time."

"Jessa knows."

"Jessa knows some."

"How did you end up in Venass?"

Haern's eyes seemed to take in everything in the smithy, before pausing on Rsiran. "You don't end up in Venass. They claim you if they think there's something you can do for them. Like your abilities."

"They wanted what you can See?"

Haern traced a finger along the scar on his face. "Seers have different levels of ability, you know that, Rsiran?"

He didn't, so he shook his head.

"Don't really know how it works, but it's like each person catches a different glimpse of what the Great Watcher knows. You take all of that, and you piece it together…"

Rsiran thought he understood. Venass could use the combined knowledge gained from Seers in some way. "When did you remove it?"

Haern tapped the scar. "You can never really get away if you continue to use what they give you. That's something I learned early on. But it's been hard. A man gets used to having certain gifts. Thing like enhancement to Seeing, that was useful in my line of work. Can't say I don't miss it."

Rsiran realized that was part of the reason Haern pushed him as he did. He wanted Rsiran to be better prepared for whatever he might face, including the possibility that his abilities would fail. "You're still gifted."

His eyes went distant. "That's the thing. I was never a strong Seer before I went to Venass, so when I took away what they gave me, the implant, I expected it to fade. Only… only I retained more than I expected. Sort of like I gained strength through use."

"Is the scar from when they implanted you with lorcith?" He didn't know if it had been lorcith or heartstone, but Venass seemed more likely to use lorcith.

"From when it came out. Jessa's father… He helped."

Haern fell silent and Rsiran decided not to push on that issue any further. "That's why you helped her? She told me that you rescued her."

Haern's face darkened. "That would be as good a way to put it as any," he answered.

"Where was she? I mean, she told me that slavers thought to sell her, but not where."

Haern shook a moment. "What would you do, Rsiran? You think you would go to Eban, find the slaver responsible for what happened to her, and get revenge for what they did?"

What they did? Jessa hadn't said anything about what they had done to her. "I didn't mean—"

"It doesn't matter, anyway."

"Why not?"

"Because I already took care of them," Haern said.

He said it with such force, and an edge of darkness, that Rsiran took an involuntary step back.

"Elaeavn is protected," Haern went on. "And that isn't necessarily something that should change. Most who live here do not know about the darkness that exists outside the city, and never learn how *hard* a place it can be. You've seen some of it—more than most who have lived here their entire lives—but you've been protected as well."

"I've seen what Venass did. I've seen what the Forgotten—"

Haern laughed. "The Forgotten. They only matter to the Elvraeth, and to Elaeavn. But what of other places? In Elaeavn, we think the Great Watcher has granted us abilities, and that makes us special, but there are other places and other abilities. The only thing special about Elaeavn is that we know so little about the rest of the world."

Haern raised his sword and held it out. "Now. We need to continue to practice. If you lose your connection to lorcith, you might need to know simple technique. I don't think to make you into a Neelish swordsman, but you can learn enough to get past someone who knows less than you. That might make the difference between getting caught and getting to safety."

"Haern—" Rsiran started.

Haern shook his head, cutting off additional questions. Then he leapt forward, swinging his sword in attack.

CHAPTER 7

The bandolist playing in the back of the Wretched Barth was a man Rsiran had seen before, and the mournful tune he played was familiar. There was a certain soothing quality to the fact that he could sit at a table in the Barth again, and hold a mug of ale. Perhaps in that, Brusus had been right to buy the tavern.

Jessa sat across from him, absently rolling dice in her hand, shaking them before letting them spill out across the table. Her ale sat untouched. Since returning to the smithy to see him practicing with Haern, she had been quiet, though Rsiran hadn't learned why. She had whispered something to Haern before he left, making him promise to meet them at the Barth later. And now they were here.

"What is it?" he asked.

She shook her head. "When Brusus gets here," she said.

Rsiran took a long drink and set his mug back on the table. His eyes darted around the Barth. There were others here tonight, the first time that he'd seen that since it had reopened. A couple sat along one wall, eating a plate of beef and bread, speaking quietly. Rsiran couldn't help but check for weapons, or anything that might put them in danger. Four men sat around a table near the bandolist. They diced and talked too loudly to be much of a threat. He saw nothing about them that made him uncomfortable. Unfortunately, he'd learned such an observation didn't mean they were harmless. He'd thought there was nothing to worry about from the waitress when Brusus had been poisoned, and he'd nearly lost a friend that night.

No other patrons sat in the Barth, though Rsiran figured that was probably for the best. Too many people would make him suspicious about why they had suddenly chosen the Barth. Even under Lianna's management, the Barth had never been all that busy. She had been busy enough, and her cooking had brought in more people than had come under Karin's management, but that had been part of the Barth's charm.

"When will he get here?" Rsiran asked. He shifted on his stool, trying to find a comfortable way to sit, but his body ached from working with Haern all afternoon. As fit as he felt, given his working the forge, it seemed his training introduced him to muscles he didn't even know he had. Somehow, even his buttocks throbbed.

"Don't know."

"Jessa?" he asked. There was tension in her voice. Had he not known her nearly as well as he did, he might not have heard it, but he was around Jessa pretty much every day, and he knew her as well as he could know anyone. He leaned toward her and rested his arms on the table, reaching for her hands.

She swallowed as he touched her. "Not yet." She pulled one hand away and touched the charm she wore, now with a bold yellow flower inside. The large petals fell from the charm, making them look as if they had been formed together. Rsiran wondered how she managed to stuff the flowers inside.

"What are you keeping from me?" he asked.

She looked over, and her eyes were drawn, but she only shook her head.

Rsiran waited. If Jessa didn't want to answer, then he wasn't going to push, but whatever she wasn't saying troubled her. He continued to drink his ale, while she occasionally picked up the dice and tossed them across the table. She never bothered to look at how they landed.

Rsiran didn't know how much time passed before the door to the Barth opened. They both glanced to look. Haern came in and wiped a trail of rain off his cloak, sending splatters of water to the ground. It hadn't been raining when they arrived at the Barth.

"Is he with you?" Jessa asked.

"Coming," Haern answered. He took a seat next to Rsiran. An amused smile came to his lips as he saw the way that Rsiran shifted on his stool. "You look like you're sore."

Rsiran rubbed his thighs and shook his head. "How is it that I hurt like I do?"

"You need practice. Muscles take a while to get accustomed to different movements. Maybe you're not as strong as you think."

The comment brought a smile from Jessa that faded quickly. "He's strong enough."

"Better hope so," Haern said.

Jessa shook her head.

Rsiran looked from Haern to Jessa. Neither was willing to meet his eyes. "What does that mean?"

"Wait for—"

"Yeah, Brusus," he said. He reached for Jessa before pulling his hand back. What wouldn't she tell him? Why keep something from him? Didn't they share in the risk together? What didn't she want to say to him?

He began to feel a growing irritation the longer he sat there. Had she learned something about the pair he'd seen in the forest? If so, why not tell him?

He drank his ale, finishing the mug in a long draught, and nodded when one of the servers came by to check if he wanted another. Jessa only watched him.

Rsiran lost track of the time before Brusus finally arrived. He swept into the Barth, his eyes surveying the tavern, flaring slightly darker green as he did, before he pulled off his cloak and hung it on a hook near the door. When he took a seat across from Haern, he pulled a stack of coin from his pocket and set it next to the dice.

When no one reached for it, he shrugged. "Thought we'd dice, but you all seem a bit somber tonight. Maybe it's the music?" he asked, turning toward the bandolist. He motioned to the man, and the song changed, getting a little louder, and bawdier. The song picked up in rhythm, and the singer's voice rang loudly through the tavern.

Brusus leaned forward, the amusement in his face gone. "Rsiran," he started.

Rsiran took a long drink of his ale and slammed it down with more force than he intended. "I've been waiting for you. Jessa won't tell me what's bothering her, and Haern remains silent. Seems like you still want to hold us all under your control." The words spilled out, more influenced by drink than anything. Rsiran flushed and sighed. "I'm sorry, Brusus. I don't mean—"

Brusus shook his head. "Doesn't matter. Jessa didn't want to say anything to you until I got here because I suspect she wanted to wait to know if I learned anything different than she had." Brusus glanced at Jessa, who nodded.

"Learned anything about what? Why wouldn't she tell me what she'd learned?"

"Because she's afraid of what you might do, I suspect," Brusus said.

"Do?"

Brusus looked over at Jessa and leaned forward, lowering his voice. "Even after everything you've been through, you've proven to be far more forgiving than most," Brusus went on. "Most of us don't really understand, and that's why Haern has been working with you, wanting to harden you a bit."

Rsiran looked around the table. Everyone here was his friend, but they all watched him as if afraid of how he might react.

What did they know?

"Forgiving of what?" he asked. He looked to Jessa, but she wasn't willing to meet his eyes. Instead, she picked the dice off the table and shook them again, rolling them in her hand. "You mean my father, don't you?" he asked.

That had been the point of contention between him and Jessa. She never understood why he had been so willing to forgive his father, even if Rsiran didn't really consider it forgiving. He couldn't find it in himself to hate his father, even after everything that he'd done.

Jessa looked up and met his eyes. She shook her head and set the dice down, not rolling them across the table this time. "Not your father."

"Then who?" he asked.

Brusus answered for her. "It's your sister, Rsiran."

"What about my sister?" The last time he'd seen Alyse, she had been making her way through Lower Town. Alyse had always been the most blessed of them, gifted by the Great Watcher with both Sight and Reading. Dual abilities were uncommon outside of the Elvraeth, enough to ensure that Alyse would marry well.

Or it had, until their father lost the smithy. Then she had suffered a fate similar to Rsiran. She had been forced to find work, something that Alyse was particularly ill prepared for.

"When you learned that she was in Lower Town," Jessa started, "Brusus asked me to keep an eye on her."

"Like you did with my father?"

"It's not like that, Rsiran," Brusus said.

He turned to Brusus. "No? It seems to me that when my father lost the smithy, you knew long before I did. How long ago did you learn about Alyse?"

"Only today. Jessa has been watching for her, helping if she can—"

"You've been *helping* my sister?" he asked her.

"Not so that she would notice," Jessa answered. "But I've been doing what I can."

"Why?"

"Because she's your sister," Jessa answered. She reached toward him, and he let her take his hands. "I know how you feel about her. You never wanted to see her hurt, even though they hurt you. And I know that you still care what happens to her."

Rsiran didn't know what to say. He hadn't seen his sister in months, and had even made a threat to his father that he would allow Alyse to be harmed, but Rsiran would never have really done anything to her. Regardless of what Alyse had done to him, she *was* his sister. It was the same reason he struggled with his father's disappearance. "And my mother?" he asked. He'd thought so little about her since he'd been sentenced to the mines. She had never stood up to his father and had never been willing to argue when his father drank too much, or said too much, or any of the dozens of other things that his father had done over the years. Like Alyse, she had never intervened on his behalf, almost as if she didn't care what happened to him.

"She remains in Lower Town," Jessa said. "She's safe, if dirtier than you remember."

"What happened?" he asked. "Where is Alyse?"

Jessa looked over to Brusus and let him answer. "When Jessa sent word that she'd gone missing, I began my search," Brusus said. "Lower Town can be dangerous, especially to someone who's not prepared for it. Like you, she lived her entire life above us, sitting closer to Upper Town than the docks."

"I've been safe enough," Rsiran said.

Brusus smiled sadly. "You've had help. You have people who care about you, and who want you to do well. Do you think that your sister has the same? You came to Lower Town because you wanted to. Your sister came here because she *had* to. There is a difference, and it is not insignificant."

"How do you know that she's gone?" he asked.

He presumed that she was still working for whomever she'd been working for when he'd run into her, hidden in some part of Lower Town where they would never find her. What if Jessa had simply overlooked her?

That didn't change the fact that, something had happened to her, Rsiran wanted to know. She was his sister, even if she never managed to get past the fact that he could Slide. There was a connection there. One that she might not understand, but one that if Rsiran were honest with himself, he still felt.

"Because the man she was working for hasn't seen her in the last week," Brusus said. "And the others working for him don't know where she might have gone."

"You don't know what that means," Rsiran said. "We should go talk to the man she's been working for together… find out what he knows—"

"There's no need to do that," Brusus said.

"But if he knows something about Alyse—"

"He doesn't. I've asked."

Rsiran pushed back from the table. "How do you know he's telling the truth? What if he's trying to keep something from you?"

"I can be persuasive," Brusus said simply.

Rsiran stared at Brusus, realizing that Brusus could have Compelled or simply Read the person Alyse worked for. Brusus would know, even if someone didn't want to talk. There weren't many with his ability to augment their minds with heartstone, or even lorcith, to keep from allowing a Reader access. Some man along Lower Town would certainly not be able to protect himself if Brusus wanted answers.

"What do you know?" Rsiran asked.

Brusus leaned forward and rested his hands on the table. "She hasn't been there in days. She's considered reliable, a good worker, and has never not shown up for her work. The fact that she didn't tells him that something either happened—not all that uncommon in Lower Town—or that she simply decided not to come to work for reasons known only to her."

"She needed the work," Rsiran said.

Brusus nodded. "That's the way it appeared."

Rsiran looked to Jessa. "What do you think happened? Was it Josun?"

But even as he asked, he wondered if maybe it might not be. What reason would Josun have to reappear in the city after Firell freed him? Rsiran doubted that Josun would risk coming after him so quickly, but what did he really know? And if it was Sarah and Valn…

Jessa might not want to answer, but she would. For him, he knew that she would.

Jessa sighed. "I don't know. I thought maybe she'd moved on, gone to another job," she started, looking over at Brusus. "From what I can tell, it wouldn't have been the first time she's changed jobs since moving to Lower Town, but the last time was for a much better position. The man she had worked for before this one… well, he wasn't very nice."

Rsiran didn't like the idea of someone hurting his sister. Even after what he'd been through, he didn't want her to suffer. It was bad enough that his father had lost the smithy, but for Alyse to suffer because of it—and possibly for something that he had done—that bothered him.

"But I can't find any evidence that she's moved on to another job. All the other businesses with openings in this part of the city haven't seen her."

"What if she took a job in Upper Town?" Rsiran asked.

He could imagine his sister trying to move up from Lower Town. It was a better fit for her, anyway, with better opportunities than she'd find in Lower Town, but then he didn't know what kind of work she had done. When he'd seen her before, she had been returning from the market, carrying a basket of fish toward some house near the docks. She had still had the same strength that he'd always seen in her, but some of the arrogance had been shaken. Losing their father had affected her and had forced her into a role she never had thought that she would have to play.

"I don't think that's likely," Haern said. His eyes had gone distant like they did when he used his ability. The green to them took on a faint film, and the scar along his cheek twitched. "I don't See much of her, but were she in Upper Town, I suspect the visions would be clearer. That they are not…"

Rsiran swallowed a lump in his throat. "Then what?"

"I think," Brusus began with a sigh, "that whoever is trying to reach you thinks to use her to get to you."

He couldn't shake the memory of Sarah and Valn, and the way they had appeared in the forest. They would have been able to find Alyse if they wanted to.

He would have to find them to get answers. Or find Alyse. Either way, he already knew he had to do something.

Jessa watched him, the corners of her eyes pulled in a frown, but she said nothing.

CHAPTER 8

Rsiran stood on a darkened street of Lower Town, listening to the sounds of waves crashing along the shore. Down here, he could practically feel the power of the ocean as it slammed against the rocks, much like he had when he'd been on Firell's ship. At least here, he didn't fear falling from the ship into the water. Always before, he'd been afraid that if he ended up someplace where he couldn't move, he wouldn't be able to Slide himself to safety, but now he knew how to Slide without stepping into it. It still didn't make him feel safer.

Gulls circled overhead, casting moon shadows across the ground. Rsiran ignored them, and ignored their harsh cawing as they hovered, occasionally diving, before flying off with whatever they caught. In some ways, he felt more like the fish, waiting for the gull to dive and snatch him away from everything he knew, much like what had happened to Alyse.

Jessa stood along the rock, dipping her boot into the water and tracing a pattern in the foam. She had been silent since they left the

Barth, knowing that he needed a chance to process what he'd learned.

And what did he know? If Alyse was gone, and abducted because of him, what could he do about it? Haern had suggested that he needed to pick a side, but how could he when he had no idea which side wanted him and which side wanted only to use him?

Worse, as easy as it was to believe that Alyse had been abducted because of him, there was the possibility that she hadn't. What if it wasn't tied to him at all, but to his father?

Rsiran thought that Venass had wanted his father because they wanted some leverage over him, but maybe there was more to it than that. What if his father was more valuable than he had realized?

That would give Venass a reason to abduct Alyse. His father would do anything for her.

Still, he didn't know, and that left a worried knot that grew with every passing moment.

"You're silent," Jessa said.

"So are you."

"I know what you're thinking, and I don't think I like it," she said. Jessa lifted her foot from the water, and a long strand of seaweed clung to it. She shook it off and left it lying across the rock. A gull nearby hopped to the rock and grabbed it, taking to the air and flying off.

"What exactly am I thinking?"

"You want to do something." She jumped from the rock and touched his arm. "I've seen you like this before, Rsiran. It was the same way that you looked when Brusus was hurt. The same as when you decided we needed to find the Forgotten. Damn, Rsiran, it's the same as when you decided to Slide into the palace." She looked over his shoulder, and he didn't have to follow the direction of her gaze to know that she looked at the Floating Palace. From here, it would stand out starkly from the rock, and appear as if it hovered, as if the Great Watcher held the palace in his hand, holding the Elvraeth above them.

"I..." He hesitated. Jessa was right. He not only wanted to do something, but he *needed* to do something. "If they're willing to take Alyse—"

"You worry what will happen if they come for one of us."

"They already have," he said. "Both the Forgotten and Venass."

"Josun wasn't with the Forgotten. From what Inna told you, they didn't sanction what he did."

"You're making excuses for them. They were plenty willing to attack me—"

"Evaelyn didn't seem too pleased about that, either."

Rsiran sighed. "What would happen if I hadn't been able to find you when Josun took you?"

Jessa squeezed his arm and smiled. "I always knew that you would," she said.

He remembered his terror all too well. Finding her hadn't been guaranteed. "And the next time?" he asked. "Now that Inna knows how I feel about you, what happens the next time? Or the time after that? We always have to be on watch."

"There's no way to avoid that. And it's no different from what we've done in Lower Town for as long as I've been here. You find a way, Rsiran. That's how it is. There are those with power, and then there's us." She shrugged. "With Brusus, we've always managed to stay safe, or safe enough." She kicked at the foam, sending it splashing. "And now we've got you. You're added safety."

There had to be a way to find real safety. There had to be a way for him to find a home where he didn't always feel like he was in danger of losing it. The smithy was safe enough now, but it wouldn't always be that way.

With what he'd seen in the forest, he knew it couldn't. Having his Slides influenced was bad enough, but he thought that heartstone could keep them protected. Having someone able to follow his Sliding, even with heartstone, meant that they would never have real peace. There would always be the concern that he'd have to watch behind him, fearful that someone would be tracking him. With the Forgotten, and the gifts that the Elvraeth possessed, he would never be able to learn enough to counter them, regardless of what Haern thought to teach him.

"They need to fear us," he said softly.

Jessa glanced over at him, and laughed. "Fear us? What are we but a few to their many? They have nothing to fear from us. No, Rsiran, I think we make all the preparations that we can, and settle in."

"Settle in for what? For this war that is coming? What does that get us, but chased? Constantly harassed by others where we don't even know what they intend. How many more of us will need to be in danger before we stop settling?" he asked.

Jessa cupped a hand around her charm and made her way across the rocks, jumping from rock to rock until she reached a small point that stretched away from the shore. Rsiran Slid to join her.

"What happens if we go after them?" she asked. "What then? I worried about you when we went for the Forgotten, but what you intend to do here is different. We can't stop them, Rsiran. We're not enough. Not strong enough, not many enough, not… just not enough. I didn't agree with how we hunkered down in the smithy before, but I do now. I understand the value in having a place like that to keep safe, where we don't have to worry about what might be coming after us."

"But it's not safe," he said. "If there's someone able to—"

He cut off, detecting the sudden appearance of lorcith. The sense of it came from down the street, nearer the rest of Lower Town and away from the docks. The suddenness of it made it almost certain that someone had Slid to them.

"What is it?" Jessa asked.

He focused on lorcith, shifting his attention to the knives that he carried. If needed, he could *push* them from him, but he didn't want to have to attack if he didn't need to, not until he knew if there was anything to be worried about. Maybe this was nothing but lorcith that had been there all along, and he'd not detected it before, but Rsiran didn't think that likely. Had there been lorcith before, he would have noticed.

Strangely enough, this was not one of his forgings.

Still, he could *pull* on the sense of lorcith, could draw on it if needed. Lorcith that he forged always answered him better, but all lorcith was attuned to him in some ways.

"Lorcith," he whispered. He dropped to the rock, pulling Jessa with him. He didn't want to Slide, not until he knew whether this was the person able to track his Sliding.

Jessa rolled on the rock to get a better view, and tilted her head toward him. "Where would lorcith have come from?"

Rsiran shrugged. "Same place it did when I was in the Aisl."

Jessa pieced what he said together quickly. "If it's them, can you Slide us to safety without them following?"

"I don't know." There seemed to be something that he'd done that she hadn't been able to track, but Rsiran wasn't sure what that was. When he'd Slid from the Aisl, he'd made a few different jumps, each time emerging only long enough to get his bearings and then take off again. It would be different were he to try the same with Jessa with him. Not slower, but he suspected that whatever ripples he formed would be louder, and easier for the other woman to follow.

"Then we sneak," Jessa whispered.

She slid off the rock, moving silently. Rsiran followed her, keeping low, suspecting that if whoever was after them was Sighted, they'd easily be able to see them, but Jessa slipped across the street and stopped in a pool of shadows left by a small tree. She held a hand up to silence him, not that Rsiran needed the warning here.

Rsiran knew that Jessa was incredibly skilled as a sneak, but he'd never had need for her to prove it before. Always before, he had been able to Slide them to safety. And he *could* Slide them now, but he didn't want to risk it.

He needed to know if it was the same two people that he'd seen in the Aisl earlier. If it was, the next step was learning *why* they had come for him, and then if they were responsible for what happened to Alyse. Maybe if he could get close enough, he could find out whose side they were on. Or, as he'd feared earlier, if he had a new enemy altogether. That would be valuable to know. And if they had taken Alyse, could he capture them and force them to tell him where they'd taken her?

Jessa pulled on his sleeve, urging him onward. She raised a finger to her lips, keeping him quiet. "What do you think you're doing?" she asked.

"I'm…" He stared down the street, trying and failing to get a clear view of who might be down there. The sense of lorcith remained, but didn't move any closer. At first, that reassured him, but what if they knew of his ability with lorcith? Josun did, which meant that the Forgotten could by now. They could use it to distract him, and lull him into a sense of safety, before coming after him. "I need to know who it is," he said, careful to pitch his voice low like Jessa did. "After what happened with Alyse, and what I saw in the forest…"

Jessa stared at him for a moment and then nodded. "Let *me* sneak down there," she whispered. "You're too noisy."

She crouched as she darted down the street, somehow finding a way to remain hidden in the shadows along the rocks. At this time of night, there were many places for her to fade into the shadows, and Jessa managed to find them all. Rsiran remembered how she had once described her Sight, and the way that it gave her the ability to see gradations of shadows in the dark. Did she search for the darkest shadow or was there some other trick that she used?

Jessa moved silently as well. Whereas Rsiran *was* too noisy, each step practically scraping across the stone, Jessa padded softly, the soles of her boots designed for her to sneak with as much silence as she did.

Nerves caused his heart to flutter as he watched Jessa fade to little more than a dark figure outlined in the night. As she walked, he focused on the lorcith she carried with her. The charm pulled on him easily now. Rsiran made a point of keeping his connection to it and allowed the lorcith to guide him. Were he to ignore the lorcith, and focus on the heartstone in her chain, he had another way to keep track of her.

Jessa stopped moving. He shouldn't have allowed her to go without him. What had he been thinking? She was a skilled sneak—at least Brusus and Haern certainly felt that she was—but if Sarah and Valn had returned, and had found him… then Jessa would be in real danger. He could hold onto her, connected with the lorcith, but what if they Slid her someplace so quickly that he lost his connection to the charm or the necklace?

Now that she had gone, there was nothing to do but wait, only Rsiran didn't care for waiting. It left him feeling helpless, a sensation that he'd gotten far too familiar with over the last few months.

Then the first sense of lorcith that he'd detected disappeared.

Rsiran held his breath, checking to make certain that Jessa hadn't disappeared, but she was still there.

Slowly, the sense of her made its way back toward him. When she was barely two-dozen steps from him, he sensed the return of lorcith, this time much closer.

Rsiran didn't dare wait.

He Slid to Jessa, grabbed her, and Slid away.

*****

The Slide pulled him quickly, the flash of colors and the hot, bitter scent of lorcith streaking past, almost the same as if he stood in front of the forge, and then they emerged. Rsiran's Slide had brought them to Ilphaesn, but the part of the mountain that had once been hidden from him. This was where he thought Josun had been mining, though he still didn't know what Josun had hoped to gain by providing lorcith to the Forgotten.

As he emerged, he listened to the sounds of the mountain around him, the call of lorcith. Something about it had changed, but he wasn't completely certain. Had he more time—and more willingness to search without Jessa—he thought he might be able to figure out what seemed different.

Jessa released his arm. "What was that? They had disappeared. And why did you bring me *here*?"

Rsiran hated that he had to bring her to this place, but this was the first place that came to mind when he thought of finding a safe place to Slide. He could have Slid them to the smithy, but he didn't want to risk them following them there, and at least here, they might follow, but there would be no way that they could Slide past the alloy that Josun had placed in the mouth of the cavern.

"They hadn't disappeared," he said. "Not entirely. When you made your way back down the street, they had reappeared."

"Are you sure?"

He pulled on the lorcith charm. "I could sense it when they left, and then when they returned. They must have known to follow you."

He looked at the walls of the mine. The walls seemed to have something like a faint glow to them. Rsiran suspected it was his newly enhanced Sight that allowed him to see the change, but he still didn't have nearly the skill Jessa did.

"Damn," Jessa whispered.

"Did you learn who they were?"

She shook her head. "Not well enough to know who might have chased you to Elaeavn."

"Not just me," he reminded.

"You don't know that they were the same ones that took Alyse. For all that we know, they're separate issues."

The likelihood that there would be two different attacks at the same time seemed unlikely, but then again, the idea that there were multiple groups trying to gain access to the Elvraeth and what they stored in the palace would once have seemed equally unlikely. Even the idea of one other group trying to reach the palace would have surprised him, but that had been before he knew what he did now. In that way, he *had* been protected living in Elaeavn.

"If they're separate, then I still need to find out what happened to Alyse," he said.

"Only Alyse and not these other two?"

They *had* to be connected, why else would Sarah and Valn appear in the city at the same time Alyse went missing?

And he needed to know if they were the Forgotten or Venass. Though both wanted to use him, knowing changed how he approached them.

He sighed, took another look at the mine, feeling the pull of the lorcith, before grabbing Jessa's hand. "Are you ready?"

"Where now?"

"The smithy. I think that it'll probably be safe to return from here to there. The alloy should shield us."

He hoped that it would, but what if it didn't? What if he couldn't be safe anymore? What if even Sliding had been taken from him as a way to keep Jessa and his friends safe?

CHAPTER 9

"Tell me again why you want to walk?" Brusus asked.

Rsiran shook his head at his friend as they made their way along the street. It was true that Rsiran rarely *walked* anywhere. Why walk when Sliding took him all that much faster? More than that, he had the need to practice, to improve his Sliding. Or, he had, until he began to fear the safety of Sliding.

"I told you what I saw."

"You don't know that they can track you. Didn't Della tell you that ability was rare?"

"I don't know much about that ability," Rsiran said. "Only what I had heard. Why risk it?"

Brusus sniffed. "Because you have me walking through *here*," he said, pointing at the alleyway in disgust. "This place… If we could have found you a smithy anywhere else, I think we would should have."

Rsiran glanced back down the street, toward the old smithy he'd taken over and made his own. He had to admit that it felt good in some ways to actually walk. "This location has its advantages. I mean, who in this neighborhood would bother reporting the noise to the constables? And why would the constables bother to believe them even if they did? Besides, this keeps me out of the eye of the Smith Guild." He wondered if the guild even knew of his smithy. They had to have kept records of all the smiths in the city. Would they continue to track the ones that had supposedly shut down?

"That *was* part of the appeal at first."

"Where else would we find a smithy like this?" Rsiran asked with a laugh.

"No place safe," Brusus answered. They turned onto a wider street and started down toward the docks. "You sure this is what you want to do?" he asked.

Rsiran had thought about it for the last few days. "I think this is what I need to do."

"And Jessa?"

"She isn't convinced."

Brusus watched him a moment, his face pulling into a broad smile. "Not convinced? You didn't tell her, did you?"

Rsiran didn't answer right away. What was there to say? That he *hadn't* told Jessa he intended to come down to this part of Lower Town, or that he wanted to know what might have happened to Alyse, or even that he intended to find his mother to see if she knew anything about what happened?

He'd tried using the lorcith Alyse wore, the chain that their father had forged for her, to find her, but had so far discovered nothing. Until he knew about Alyse, he wouldn't be settled. Only after he understood could he begin to move onto the next step that needed to happen, whatever that might be.

Only, he began to suspect that the next step involved finding out more about who targeted him in the city, and then he would need to find a way to deter them, however he could. A part of him feared what that might require. If he wanted his friends to be left alone, if they were to be allowed peace, then it might take a more aggressive stance than he'd taken so far. Jessa didn't understand that, but he'd seen the lengths that the Forgotten would go; he'd seen the way that Venass had sought to use him. He began to think he needed to do more than deter them; he needed to frighten them. Maybe that started with Sarah and Valn.

"Jessa doesn't agree with what I think needs to happen," Rsiran said.

Brusus tipped his head to the side and studied Rsiran for a moment. "You need to be careful, son. She's the type that doesn't react well to being excluded. And I've seen the two of you together. You have abilities. Damn, but the Great Watcher knows that you do. There are things that you can do that I can't even begin to fully understand. But that doesn't mean that you can close out those who care about you, especially when they share your bed."

He smiled and patted Rsiran on the arm then led them down a narrow street. They wound into a part of Elaeavn that Rsiran wasn't familiar with. That was one downside to his ability to Slide everywhere. He never learned the streets, not like Jessa or Brusus did. If he needed to travel somewhere, he could simply take himself there, missing all the parts of the city along the way. It shielded him in some ways.

The muted sounds of the waves crashing along the shore carried to him, and the smell of salt cut through the other stink of filth along the street. They encountered no one else. Rsiran wondered if that was because of the time of day, or whether that was due to something else. The two of them might not look terribly imposing, but Brusus walked with purpose. In this part of the city, anyone moving as quickly as he did likely had something unsavory in mind.

"Are you sure this is the right area?" Rsiran asked.

Brusus glanced over and watched him a moment before laughing. "Right area? You know this is no different from the area you call home? In many ways, this is *cleaner*."

They hadn't passed any of the stagnant pools of water like were found near the smithy, which kept the stench minimized. All parts of the city were designed to drain back out into Aylianne Bay, but over time, many parts of Lower Town had become obstructed, the drains failing. When they failed in Upper Town, the Elvraeth made certain to send the city engineers to repair the problem. Down here, there was not the same urgency when the drains failed.

The bright sunlight didn't manage to pierce the space between buildings as it did higher in the city. That was by intentional design. When the city had first been built, the Lower Town buildings were the first placed, and they were set in ways that obscured the city from the water, attempting to blend into the rock. Rsiran had seen the city from above, and from a distance, and there were times when the illusion was better than others.

A door opened, and a young faced peeked out, before closing quickly.

Rsiran glanced at Brusus, and he shrugged. "You're scary," Brusus said.

Rsiran smiled. Were that only true. Then he might be left alone. Then all of them might be left alone. It raised a question for him: how could he be truly frightening to those chasing him? What could he do that would make them hesitate before coming after them?

Not his abilities. There didn't seem to be anything about his abilities that scared them. Rather, his ability to Slide past heartstone and lorcith made him alluring. That was the reason they *wanted* him.

It would have to be something big enough—or he would have to become someone frightening enough—to keep the Forgotten and

Venass from coming after him. Maybe the secret involved his training with Haern.

There was another option, one that he hadn't put as much thought into, but as he watched Brusus, he recognized the threat the Elvraeth posed. If they could somehow convince the Elvraeth to recognize the risk from the Forgotten, or from Venass, they wouldn't be in as much danger.

Brusus stopped in front of a worn brick building. Like the rest around here, it flowed from one to the next, no real separation. Walls were shared between buildings here, and in some places the brick cracked and fell. He tapped on a rough wooden door with gaps around the frame, stepping back after he did.

"Be ready," Brusus warned.

Rsiran focused on the knives in his pockets. At least that ability still didn't seem limited. If it ever were limited, he would truly feel isolated.

The knives tilted forward, ready for him to *push* them through the fabric of his cloak.

The door opened a crack, and an older woman peered out. Her eyes were a darker green than most in this part of Lower Town, and her mouth wrinkled as she pressed her lips together. A faded gray scarf covered her head.

In spite of that, Rsiran recognized his mother.

"What do you want?" she snapped.

"Miss," Brusus began, stepping forward. "We have a few questions for you is all."

She glanced from Brusus to Rsiran, and he realized that she didn't recognize him. In the time since he'd left home, his physical appearance had changed. Primarily due to the manual labor he'd done in the mines, and more recently, his work at the forge, giving him strength that he hadn't had before, but he had also experienced much. No longer was he the same sheltered boy he'd once been, a boy who looked up at the Elvraeth palace and wondered why they were given the right and the ability to rule when he was given so little. Now he understood that they had taken that right, much like others wanted to take it from them.

"Questions?" she echoed. "What kind of questions do you have? Are you with the constables?" She eyed Brusus's fine jacket with the embroidery that ran along the sleeves with a splash of color not common in Lower Town, and then she looked to Rsiran, her eyes seeming to take in his cloak, the fabric much finer than would be found here. "Not constables," she said. Her eyes widened and she took a step back. "The palace?" she asked with a gasp.

Brusus frowned and glanced at Rsiran. "Not the palace. Please, we have a few questions is all."

She recovered quickly. "Then if not the palace and if not the constables, I have nothing to say." She slammed the door shut on them, and a heavy lock slipped closed.

"Well, that was interesting," Brusus said.

"She didn't recognize me."

Brusus clapped him on the shoulder. "Rsiran, if I hadn't been with you for the last few months, I'm not sure that I would recognize you."

"What does that mean?"

"Only that you've changed. Not just your appearance, though that has changed too. But the way that you carry yourself. You were plenty timid when we first met, afraid to upset your father and risk your 'ship. I think that's changed the most." A playful smile worked across his face. "Well, that and the fact that you've got yourself a woman. That changes a man plenty too."

Brusus pulled out his lock-pick set and unrolled it. He poked at the lock until it clicked and pushed on the door. It didn't budge.

"Didn't expect that down here," he muttered.

"What?"

"Feels like they placed bars into the ground. Not many with the know how or the skills to fashion something like that."

"My father would have," Rsiran said.

Brusus nodded. "Should've thought of that." He stepped back, rolling the lock-pick set back and slipping it back into his pocket. He crossed his arms over his chest as he surveyed the street. "Need to find another way in, but one that doesn't make *too* much noise. Constables don't patrol in this part too often, but they do send men from time to time."

"Let me Slide us through," Rsiran said.

"Thought you didn't want to do that. What if it draws those from the other night in the forest?"

Rsiran considered the door. He needed to learn what happened to Alyse. To do that, he might have to take a few risks. He could minimize them, and maybe a short Slide like this wouldn't be enough to trigger any sort of attention.

"It might," he said.

"Then we'll have to be ready." Brusus tapped his pocket.

Rsiran could sense the four knives Brusus kept in his pocket, plus the one that he kept tucked into his waistband. He grabbed Brusus's sleeve and focused on the other side of the door. He didn't know what was on the other side. There could be nothing, or she could have placed some kind of heavy barricade to block the door. Sliding into that could create some risk.

But if he *pulled* himself into the Slide… that might allow him the time to determine whether the Slide would pose a danger. Sliding in that way gave a different type of control, and he thought that he might be able to Slide away if something went wrong.

They moved slowly at first, a steady drawing sensation that brought them past the door. For the first time, Rsiran had a sense of control of the speed, as if he could move more quickly or more slowly were he to need to, and the colors that flashed past during the Slide were plain browns, those of the door itself.

When they emerged, he checked to ensure they were safe, before letting out a shaky breath.

"Damn," Brusus whispered.

A woman screamed. A long length of iron came swinging toward them. If Rsiran did nothing, Brusus would get hit in the head with it.

He sent the knives streaking from his pocket to block the iron. With the force of his *push*, he sent the bar arcing up and away, flipping from his mother's hands. The knives hung in the air a moment until he *pulled* them back to him.

She stared at him, her eyes wide.

"You…"

Rsiran nodded. "Me."

"How is it… How are you… He said you were dead!"

Rsiran glanced over at Brusus, but he'd crossed his arms over his chest and kept his face neutral.

"Who said I was dead?" Rsiran asked. "Father?"

That would be the final piece, wouldn't it? The last brutal part of his punishment for his father to claim to the rest of his family that he had died. That explained why Alyse had been so surprised to see him, but why hadn't she shared the truth with their mother?

"Not your father. He regretted what happened. Never said it, but when he drank…"

Rsiran didn't need her to finish. His barriers would have been down, and she would have been able to Read him. That was an advantage that Rsiran would not share.

"Who told you that I died?"

Who else would have cared what happened to him? Who else would have wanted to tell his mother that he had died? Other than his father and the fact that he was completely disinterested in what happened to him, Rsiran couldn't think of anyone who would have reason to tell her that he'd died.

"It doesn't matter," she said. She took a step toward him before catching herself and stepping back. "You… You look different."

"Being sent to the mines will do that," Rsiran said.

She stared at him for a moment. "I wish he had never done that, but Neran always thought that he could keep you from…" She caught herself and shook her head. "Perhaps that is in the past. What has happened, has happened. And now that Neran is gone, it doesn't matter, does it?" she said, mostly to herself.

Brusus looked over and caught Rsiran's wrist. "It seems that you are more welcomed than you expected. Do you need me to be here?" he asked.

Rsiran looked at his mother, at the deep wrinkles that had formed along her eyes, and the way that her face wore a mask of concern that she'd never had when he lived at home. What had happened to his family? So much had changed, not only for him, but for them as well. Seeing her, and seeing that she seemed almost relieved, left him with questions that he suddenly found he needed answers to.

His mother watched him, and there was a hint of… worry or hope or… something written on her face. As much as he needed answers, it seemed that she did as well.

"I think that I'll be fine."

Brusus turned to the door.

"Brusus?" Brusus paused and turned. "Can you find Jessa and tell her where I am?"

Brusus smiled. "Probably wise that I do. Better be ready to answer a few questions."

"I am," Rsiran's mother said.

Brusus tipped his head to her. "That's good, but you're not the person I meant."

With that, Brusus pulled open the door and stepped back into the streets of Lower Town, leaving Rsiran standing with his mother, alone for the first time in ages.

CHAPTER 10

When Brusus left, Rsiran debated what to ask first. His mother saved him by motioning him into the small home. Rsiran followed, noting the utilitarian furniture, a far cry from the plush chairs and the warm decorations found around their home when he'd been growing up. Here, nothing adorned the walls other than a few lanterns to provide light, thick oil burning within them.

The smells were familiar, though. He caught the scent of bread rising and the fragrant aroma of roasting meat as she stopped at a small table and touched the back of a chair, motioning for him to sit.

Rsiran settled onto the chair and rested his hands on the table. "What happened, Mother?" Rsiran asked.

She took a seat, balancing on the edge of the chair and clasping her hands in her lap. Her fingers played with the fabric of her dress, and she shook her head softly. "What happened, he asks," she whispered. "So much. So much. How can you begin to understand everything that we've been through?" she asked him, barely meeting his eyes.

"Everything *you've* been through?" he said. "You think nothing of what I've been through, only the hardships that you've endured?"

Her gaze drifted to the door, where Brusus had disappeared. "You travel in the company of the Elvraeth now. I think you have endured much less than we have, Rsiran."

Rsiran smiled inwardly. Brusus would have been either amused or annoyed that his mother identified him as one of the Elvraeth. Born to one of the Elvraeth, Brusus had been exiled as surely as his mother. "He is not one of the Elvraeth."

"No? I thought…" She shook her head. "It doesn't matter what I thought. Much as it doesn't matter what happened to us in the time you've been away. We have suffered, that is all that you must know."

Rsiran thought of how he'd been tortured, the friend he'd lost, the way he'd been abducted. "That's not all that I must know," he said. "What happened?"

"When you left—"

"Left? I was sent away, Mother. Don't make it seem like it was my choice."

"You could have listened to him," she said.

Rsiran sat back in the chair and shook his head as he studied his mother. "Listened to what? He wanted to change who I was. He wanted me to refuse the abilities that I have been given. How could I listen to him?"

"Neran only wanted what was best for you, Rsiran. He knew what would happen if you were to use them, and how others might use you. You don't understand… You can't understand. And now he's gone."

"I'm sorry about that," Rsiran said.

"You couldn't know," she answered, clenching her hands more tightly in her lap. "After… after you left, he fell into the ale even more. Neran always had a problem, always thought that drinking could help him ignore…" She shook her head. "It doesn't matter now."

"He lost the smithy," Rsiran said.

She nodded.

"I saw it," Rsiran admitted.

"You know your father. Maybe not as well as you should have, but you should know that losing the smithy—especially after losing you—was the worst thing that could have happened to him. More than anything else, it changed him."

"Why did he leave you?"

"He… He was ashamed, I think. And afraid that if he stayed, they would hurt the rest of us."

Rsiran frowned. "Who would?"

His mother reached toward him, before pulling her hands back. "It doesn't matter."

"It does matter. To me, it matters."

"Why? Because you're still so angry with him for what happened? What does that change, Rsiran?"

Would it change anything for him to know?

It was possible, he realized. He still didn't know why his father had been taken to Asador, or why Venass had claimed him. Rsiran still didn't really know why his father had been to Thyr before, or even how. He had thought he'd spent his entire life in the city, but if that wasn't true what other secrets could his father be hiding?

"Do you know where he is?" he asked.

"Gone," she whispered.

"Do you know who took him?"

"Rsiran," she said, a pleading note entering her voice. "You only put yourself in danger by asking. Why do you think I've come here, to a place where *they* won't even search for me? Why do you think I had Alyse find work, and put her out from my home, separating her as much as I could? She needed to be safe."

"They? You mean the Elvraeth?"

"Please don't ask."

Rsiran wondered what secrets she was keeping. There was more to his father than he had realized. And here Rsiran had thought that he was the one that the Forgotten had come for, but maybe there was more to it.

"Why was he in Asador?"

She looked up, her eyes reddened. "What?"

Rsiran nodded. "When I found him, he was in Asador, locked away like nothing more than a prisoner."

"Neran lives?"

Rsiran sniffed. "You haven't answered. Why would he have been in Asador?"

"They wanted smiths with skill, master smiths they claimed could hear the call of the ore. Your father, he…"

Rsiran nodded. "He can hear lorcith," Rsiran finished. He *pulled* on the lorcith knives in his pocket and sent them hovering above the table. They *pulled* on his awareness, calling to him. Rsiran noted that there was no other lorcith in her home, not as there once had been. Lorcith had always been a part of the home, always a decorative metal. In that way, they were blessed nearly as much as the Elvraeth, at least he had always thought that to be the case.

"Great Watcher," she whispered. "When you did that before, I thought it some trick."

"No trick. *This* is what father fears. This connection to lorcith. It's this connection that's kept me alive when so many have tried to kill me. Tell me, how could this be dark?" he asked.

Her eyes fixed on the knives, as if unable to move away from them. "Stop that."

Rsiran sent the knives spinning. Since holding the crystal in the heart of the palace, his connection to both lorcith and heartstone had increased. Now he could easily spin and hold the lorcith in place, and could more easily detect heartstone around him.

"Stop!" She smacked at the knives with her hand and they dropped to the table.

Rsiran *pulled* them back to him, and slipped them into his pocket.

"You've been around Father too long if you fear that," Rsiran said.

"Not your father," she whispered. "You don't understand anything, do you?" she asked. "Perhaps Neran was right. All this time, I thought that he had been wrong sending you to the mines, that he had made you suffer needlessly. I tried telling him that you could learn, that you needed time to understand, but he saw what I could not."

Rsiran's back stiffened. "And what is that?"

"That… what you just demonstrated… is dangerous. That leads to darkness."

He sat frozen for a moment, unable to even answer. How could his mother believe that his ability with lorcith was dangerous? It had been Sliding that they feared, not his connection to lorcith. Only when he'd begun listening to lorcith had his father decided that it was time Rsiran be punished.

"Dangerous," Rsiran said. "This dangerous ability kept me alive when I was trapped in the Ilphaesn mines. This dangerous ability helped save me when one of the Elvraeth thought to use me. And it helped keep me safe as I began to realize how much danger exists outside of Elaeavn." He stood, knocking down the chair as he did. "Is there anything you wish me to tell Father if I see him again?"

"You know where he is?"

"I told you that I found him in Asador."

"Found. What does that mean?"

Rsiran stepped back, moving toward the door. It had been a mistake coming here. All that he had done was dredge up the same feelings of inadequacy that he'd had all those years spent living at home, feelings that he'd managed to move past with the help of his friends, and Jessa.

When his mother had first welcomed him into her new home, he had thought that she might have been happy to see him, but now he realized he'd been mistaken. She wasn't happy to see him at all. All she cared about was what happened with his father, and how that had affected her. Did she even know about Alyse? How would she handle that news?

"It means he was in Asador. He is not any longer."

"Where did they take him?" she asked. She stood and reached toward Rsiran. "What did they do to him?"

"He's in Thyr. I don't know what they did to him," Rsiran said.

"What? Why would they have taken him to Thyr? That leads to nothing but…"

"But what?"

She shook her head. "What does it matter? You don't care what happens to your father. You can leave, go back to wherever and whatever has become of you, and enjoy the finery of your new station. Leave me here in this part of the city," she said, her nose turned up as she did, "and don't worry about us."

Rsiran should have left, but he hesitated. "You think that I don't care, but when I learned he was the man I'd brought from Asador—"

"You brought him back from Asador?"

He nodded.

"Neran was here and he didn't come for us?"

"He wasn't allowed."

"By who?"

Rsiran crossed his arms over his chest. Brusus didn't deserve the blame for what happened with his father. What had happened with him was on Rsiran. "Because of me. There was something I needed in Thyr, and when I learned that Father had been in Thyr before, I took him with me."

She sucked in a soft breath. "So you know."

"Know that he hasn't spent his entire life in the city? Or that he feared me becoming what he already was?"

Rsiran felt certain that part of his father's concern with his ability with lorcith stemmed from his own ability, or possibly inability, to ignore the call of lorcith. Rather than ignoring it, Rsiran had embraced it.

She turned away from him. "Did he tell you?"

"Why don't you?" Rsiran said.

She leaned on the nearest chair as if for support, but didn't turn back to face him. "You are more like him than you realized, you know that, Rsiran? Only, he was much harsher to you than his own father ever was to him."

Rsiran never knew his grandparents. They had been gone, returned to the Great Watcher long before he ever had a chance to meet them, but his grandfather had the smithy before his father. And his father before him. The smithy should have eventually passed to Rsiran, and now it never would.

That would have bothered him more only months before. Now, he had grown accustomed to the fact that he would never know the smithy where he'd first swung a hammer, and would never work over the anvil of his forefathers, heat the same forge that his ancestors had heated. No, now he would only work at the hidden smithy, always fearing what would happen were the constables to discover his presence, and always fearing what his ability would compel him to create next.

"Harsher how?" Rsiran asked. He didn't want to know—whatever had happened no longer mattered—but a part of him needed to know. Had his father gone through something similar? If so, how could he have thought it fair to put Rsiran through the same? After what Rsiran had gone through, he could never do that to another, especially family.

"Do you think you were the first to hear the way the metal called to you? Do you think that you were the first to struggle with control?" She sniffed and wiped her arm across her face. Rsiran realized that she was crying. He couldn't find it in him to feel sorry for her.

"Was Father sent to the mines by his father, like he sent me?"

"No. And he recognized the mistake as soon as he sent you, but how could he call you back without sharing what you needed to learn on your own?"

"I learned how to nearly die," Rsiran said softly. "Was that the lesson he wanted me to learn?"

"He knew what it was like. When he was about your age, he was sent from Elaeavn much like he sent you, only he was sent farther from the city. His father wanted him isolated from the call of the ore, and thought that sending him away would weaken it. Neran should have done the same for you. It would have been less cruel."

It wouldn't have mattered where his father had sent him. With his ability to Slide, nothing weakened the call or limited him other than his willingness. And maybe, had his father sent him anywhere *but* Ilphaesn, the others who knew of Sliding, and how to control it, would have reached him sooner.

Could it be that his father had *protected* him?

Not intentionally, but nevertheless, maybe he needed to give up the anger and hurt that he'd been feeling since he was kicked out his home and focus on what he'd been given. Sometimes, it was easy for him to forget about all that he'd gained, the friends—family, really—and the understanding of his ability. That might be more valuable than anything else.

"Where was he sent?" Rsiran asked.

His mother turned to him. Tears streamed down her face, leaving her eyes streaked with red. "I thought you said he told you."

Rsiran stared at her and said nothing.

"Thyr. His father sent him to Thyr. Far enough from the city that he wouldn't feel the draw of it."

"Why Thyr?" Rsiran asked. His father had never answered that question for him, or told him why he'd left, but now that his mother had, Rsiran thought he understood.

"There were craftsmen in Thyr who worked with him, men who knew how to work with other metals and helped turn him into the smithy that he is—or was. That was where we…"

Rsiran could imagine what had happened. His father sent from the city and forced to ignore the drawing of lorcith, learning to work the forge until he no longer heard the draw of lorcith. Using iron or steel or any other metal, until using lorcith was a faded memory and his forging ability became second nature. Had Rsiran been forced to learn the same way, what would have changed for him? What would he have learned? Maybe the same skill as his father, or maybe less. Lorcith had turned him into the smith he was now, guiding him at first, helping him draw shapes from the metal that he wouldn't have known possible.

Something his mother had been about to say pulled on his attention. "What were you going to say about Thyr? That was where you what?"

She wiped her arm across her face, smearing the tears that had streamed there. "It no longer matters, does it? All of that is in the past."

"It matters," Rsiran whispered.

"Thyr," his mother said, "it is where we met."

CHAPTER 11

THE WORDS TOOK A MOMENT TO SINK IN. If his parents had met outside of Elaeavn, there could really only be one reason for it, but the reason made no sense, not given what he knew of his parents. They had always followed the Elvraeth rule and had served as expected, living quietly within Elaeavn, or had until Rsiran had been sent to the mines.

"If you met in Thyr, that means that you're one of the Forgotten," he said.

Her entire body stiffened. "You think that I could have been exiled?" she asked.

Even the term she chose matched what the Forgotten used. Exiled, not Forgotten.

But that meant that *he* had ties to the Forgotten. Had Evaelyn known? Was that part of the reason they had wanted him?

No. They wouldn't have poisoned him, trying to force answers from him if that were the case. Unless Inna didn't know. Evaelyn had been upset at how she'd used the slithca syrup on him.

He needed to find Della. She might know more.

Rsiran turned his attention back to his mother. "What did you do?"

She pulled her chair back and took a seat. "I did nothing but have the misfortune to be born outside of the city," she began. "Your father returned me. Such a thing is allowed, but there is monitoring, and a price to pay."

"What kind of price?"

"The kind your father paid," his mother said.

Rsiran frowned. "What does that mean?"

"It means that he had permission to return with me to Elaeavn, but there would come a day when he would be asked to do more. You, like your father, are descendants of the ancient smith blood. There is power in that." She pointed toward the pockets of his cloak where he'd tucked the knives. "Even *they* know that."

"The Forgotten. Father was called to help them," Rsiran said. "That was the price? That was why he was in Asador?"

"He was called because the metal began to flow freely again. Whatever restriction had been on it was eased. As a smith—one of the true smiths—your father was summoned."

From what Rsiran had seen, he hadn't been the only one summoned. Many of the smithies within Elaeavn had been shuttered. He had thought it due to the lack of lorcith, but his mother was right: the flow of lorcith had increased since the restrictions had eased. For the Forgotten, he knew Josun was their supplier, accessing Ilphaesn from the other side of the mountain. For the rest of Elaeavn, he was quite sure the mine he'd worked in was their only source.

But someone had been controlling the output generated from Ilphaesn, hadn't they? Why relax that control?

Everything began to make some sense, though questions remained.

He wished Brusus hadn't gone. He was connected well enough to understand the strange politics and knew what questions needed to be asked.

"That was why he was in Asador," Rsiran said.

She nodded.

Rsiran made a slow circle around the inside of her home, pacing as he often did when in the smithy, trying to piece together what he knew. He had answers to why his father had been in Asador, if not the reason they had wanted lorcith forged. He might even understand why Venass wanted his father if they thought to either learn what the Forgotten wanted from the smiths or thought to prevent them from claiming it.

That left Alyse.

"Why did you come here, Rsiran?" his mother asked. "You knew about your father, but not enough to have come to me. Why now, when you clearly have known how to find me for some time."

He blinked, pushing away the questions. He would begin to work through them another time, but not on his own. Jessa could help, would have to help, and Brusus.

"I haven't known that you were here," he said. "Only that you were in Lower Town."

She nodded. "Why today?"

"Did Alyse ever tell you that she saw me?"

The corners of her eyes tightened when he mentioned his sister's name. Could she know where she was? If she was afraid of the Forgotten, could she have somehow found a way to sneak her from the city to keep her safe?

But how would she have managed that?

Here, in this part of Lower Town, she had no leverage, no capacity to reach help. Maybe once they would have had a way, but no longer.

"She did not."

Rsiran sniffed. For whatever reason, his sister had kept his existence from his mother. Maybe he should do the same.

"It's Alyse, isn't it?" she asked. "That's why you came today. What happened to her?"

"I don't know. She's not been seen in a week."

"Seen?"

"One of my… friends," he said, "has been watching out for her, monitoring her location. And now we don't know where she is." Rsiran took a step toward his mother. "You wanted to know why I came here today. Well, it's because I'm trying to find out what happened to Alyse."

He had thought her disappearance might have to do with him, but now he wasn't certain, especially if his father had been working for the Forgotten. If they were trying to find him, wouldn't it be possible that they would appear in Elaeavn and grab Alyse, thinking to draw his father back to work?

She dropped her head to the table, resting her forehead on her hands. "Not Alyse as well," she whispered. "Haven't we been through enough already?"

"You were afraid this might happen," Rsiran realized.

"You can go. You don't have to pretend concern for your sister."

He snorted. "I came here, didn't I? Is that not demonstrating some level of concern? I might not show it the same as you and father, but then, I didn't realize that sending your son off to the mines was father's way of showing concern for me."

She turned her head toward him. "There was always a threat that something would happen to you or your sister if your father didn't answer the summons."

A summons sounded too much like what he expected to receive from Venass to be chance. So far, he'd received no summons from Venass since Thom attacked, but that didn't mean that one would not come. Maybe that was what the two people he'd seen in the forest were sent to do, or those from the street when he had been with Jessa. Had they come to draw him back to Venass?

"What can you tell me?" Rsiran asked.

His mother shook her head. "There is nothing to tell, only that if she is gone, there is no way for me to find her. I had thought her protected from all of this, that by coming to this part of the city, we could disappear, but even that wasn't enough."

"The Forgotten. Tell me what you know."

She took a deep breath and her back straightened. "If I tell you anything, I only put you both in danger. You're better where you are, Rsiran. Stay with your friend in Upper Town with your fancy clothes and whatever you have decided to do with yourself. Find happiness."

He laughed bitterly. "You don't understand, do you? I'm already mixed up with the Forgotten. They know about me, and about what I can do. And I've already escaped them once. Trust me when I tell you that it is unlikely Alyse will be able to escape from them."

His mother didn't need for him to tell her how Alyse might get drugged and forced to share secrets about herself and her family, even secrets she didn't realize that she possessed. Without the ability to protect her mind, Readers like Inna or any of the other Forgotten, would be able to torment her. And for what? Information on what happened to their father? Alyse wouldn't know that.

"Then you already know why I can't say anything," she said. "And they will not harm her."

Something about the way that she said it troubled him. "How can you be so certain that they won't harm her?"

She stared down at her hands. Rsiran wanted to shake answers out of her, but that wouldn't get him any closer to knowing why Alyse had been taken or where she was now. "Who are you protecting?" he asked. "What do you know?"

"You should go, Rsiran. You should not have come here."

He waited for something more, but it didn't come. He stopped at the door and looked back at her over his shoulder. "Who was exiled?" he asked.

She blinked.

"Of your parents. Who was exiled?"

She swallowed. "Both."

Both. That hadn't been the answer he expected, but then, he hadn't known what he should have expected. Not that his grandparents were Forgotten. Not that he shared something more with Brusus than he realized.

He waited, hoping she might offer more but she didn't. She turned her back to him, and Rsiran knew that he wouldn't get anything more from her.

He stood for a moment, debating what else he could say. His grandparents were Forgotten? Didn't that change things for him?

He thought of Haern's warning that they would all have to pick a side. If he *had* to choose, shouldn't he side with his family? Knowing his mother was born to exiles, and knowing his father had followed his orders to serve the Forgotten, it would seem they'd chosen their side long ago.

But could he choose to side with the very people who'd been tracking him down? Attacking his friends? In that way, they were no different from Venass.

Or were they?

He cast one more glance to his mother before turning away. When he reached the door and pulled it open, he saw Jessa standing in the shadows just outside, waiting for him. A deep blue flower was tucked into her charm today, and she glared at him, punching him as soon as he stepped from the home.

"I'm sorry," he said softly.

"You run here, after everything they did to you, and don't bother to tell me?" Her voice was higher than normal, and she punched him again to emphasize her irritation. "Is that the kind of relationship that we have now?"

As he closed the door behind him, he saw his mother watching him. "I'm sorry," he said again.

"You don't have to be alone, Rsiran," Jessa said. "Haven't I shown you that?"

"I could always use a little more explanation." He reached for her hand, and she let him take it, though punched him a third time as they started down the street.

"I'm not sure that you deserve that," she grumbled.

"You found me fine."

"Well, Brusus told me you were here, and so—"

"You knew where she was, too, didn't you?"

Jessa bit her lower lip.

"It's okay. I don't think I was ready to see her before today."

"And now?" she asked. She tipped her head toward the flower in the charm and took a deep breath. It was times like this, when walking through these parts of Lower Town, that Rsiran wished he had something similar. At least then he wouldn't have to smell the stink.

"Now I know that we have more in common than I realized."

Jessa frowned. "What does that mean?"

"Only that my mother's parents were exiled." He smiled at her. "Makes me a child of the Forgotten as well."

"Oh, Great Watcher," she said, stiffening next to him.

"What?"

"Do you think they want to claim you because there is some sort of connection?" she asked. "They knew about my parents, and you saw how they treated me."

"Not a connection," Rsiran said. "But it helps me decide something that Haern told me I'd have to."

"And what is that?"

"He told me that we would have to pick a side."

Jessa pulled away from him and looked over. "And you want to side with the Forgotten?"

"I…" He didn't know. That was the problem. But knowing what he did about his family, and Jessa's, even Brusus's, he wasn't sure that he knew the answer anymore. "I don't know," he said finally.

"And your sister?"

He wasn't sure how Jessa would respond to what he would tell her next. She didn't think that his family deserved his attention, not after what they had done to him, but then Alyse didn't deserve to be abducted because of something their father had committed to. And it was Rsiran's fault that their father was no longer in Asador. Had he left him there, the Forgotten wouldn't have had any reason to come for Alyse. But he had had taken him from the city, drawn attention to himself, and in doing so, put Alyse in danger.

How could he not try to help her?

CHAPTER 12

THE SMITHY FELT AS MUCH LIKE HOME as anyplace ever had. He stood inside the door, now with the bars of heartstone slammed into the ground and over the doorframe, and surveyed the smithy, wondering if it ever could be home. There had been a time, especially after he first met Brusus and the others, when he had thought that it would be. But what if that could never be?

"What do you think you're going to do?" Jessa asked.

He leaned against the door. It felt strange walking to his smithy rather than Sliding, but the risk of being tracked while Sliding was still top of mind. Now even more so. Until he knew whether they were actually in danger, or whether the two he had seen in the forest were people he needed to worry about, he would walk.

But walking left him missing the experience of Sliding. He missed the movement, the speed, and—if he were honest—even the smells that came with the Slide. The bitter scent of lorcith had become calming, a familiar scent that reminded him of the forge, but also of the freedom he'd gained learning how to control his Sliding.

"I don't know yet," he said.

"But you intend to find her? How do you think we're going to do that?"

It was a question he didn't have the answer for yet. He could find the Forgotten again, but what would he do then? Go and demand his sister? That would give them leverage over him as well, not that they needed any more leverage than they already had. But there was another reason to find the Forgotten, one that he could tell from the way Jessa watched him that she feared. A reason that had to do with all of them, something that unified them in some ways.

But that would come later.

First, he needed a better understanding of why his father had been in Asador in the first place. Short of returning to Venass and demanding access to his father, he wasn't sure that he could figure out what his father had been up to there.

He remembered that piece of metal that he'd found in the hut. Would that somehow provide him with answers?

He hurried across the smithy to the table where he'd left the small piece of metal. Grindl and iron, a strange combination, and one that he couldn't believe the Forgotten would have been interested in.

He tried once again to examine the patterns in the metal. Even with his new Sight, he couldn't see them well enough to understand if they meant anything. Jessa could see them, but she didn't understand metal as he did. He thought if only he had her Sight, he could understand, but then he realized there might be another way.

Rsiran took a small piece of lorcith from the bin that Shael had brought him. At least that had been a gift that had served him well, regardless of the fact that Shael had not intended it that way. Shael had wanted him to forge something for him, though Rsiran still didn't know what that had been, other than proof of his ability to create the alloy.

As he waited for the forge to heat up, he held the metal out to Jessa. "He hid his. There has to be a reason that he thought this important enough to hide."

"What if he didn't hide it?"

"You think Brusus put it there when he had the hut built?"

"Not Brusus, but you know that your father wasn't the only one in that hut."

"Thom?"

She shrugged. "Can we be certain that it wasn't Thom?"

Rsiran looked at the metal and couldn't think of any reason that Thom would have hidden it in the wall. "This has to be my father," he said.

"But you said you don't know what it is. Why are you getting the forge ready?"

Rsiran ran his hands along the surface of the grindl. The pattern created ridges that his fingers traced. "I can't see what it is, and I can't feel it, but if I use lorcith, I might be able to feel what this is for, and understand why he took the time to hide it in the wall."

She stared at the flat sheet of metal for a moment and then shrugged. "If you think so," she said. She took a seat on the bed near the hearth, leaving Rsiran at the forge.

He started by taking the small lump of lorcith and heating it, getting the coals glowing to a bright orange, and then red. As he waited, he considered the sheet of metal in his hand and realized that it would be a mistake to use lorcith. Lorcith took much greater heat than either iron or grindl. Were he to use it, he would end up destroying what his father had left.

When the lorcith was ready, he listened to it a moment, gathering what shape it would take, before beginning the process of forging it. A long-bladed knife emerged. Different from the kind he usually forged, this knife was meant for throwing or *pushing*. It was intended to be carried for defense. The knife would be for Jessa.

As he finished, he studied the sheet of iron and grindl again, convinced that lorcith wasn't the answer.

Some of the soft metals would work. Gold, if he had it, would be particularly effective. But it was too expensive to use on something like this, and it wouldn't give him any more connection than he already had with the sheet of metal. The same went for silver.

What he needed was something soft enough, but that wouldn't destroy what his father had made, at least until he knew what it was for.

The only thing that might work was heartstone.

Rsiran didn't know how well it would work. Heartstone was softer and required a lower temperature to work effectively, but it also was unpredictable. What would happen when he heated it and added it to the grindl?

He didn't know. But if he wanted to understand what his father had left behind, he would try.

The box containing the remaining heartstone was nearly empty. He had acquired some that they'd found in the warehouse, but Rsiran hadn't been able to come up with any more than what they had already discovered, even after reaching out for it with his ability.

After finding the Forgotten Palace, he knew there were places that possessed much more heartstone, enough that it wasn't nearly as rare as what he had thought, and in pure form. Likely that was because the Forgotten didn't have anyone able to create the alloy. That might have been why they wanted the smiths, and part of the reason they had wanted him. From what he'd seen with Josun, the Forgotten *wanted* the alloy, but they had no way of obtaining it.

He did not need a large section of heartstone. And unlike lorcith where he had to work the entire piece, leaving the rest unworkable once it had been heated, heartstone was different, allowing him to pry off only what he needed. For this, he didn't need much more than a small piece of the soft, gray metal.

At the forge, it took heat quickly. Rsiran set it into an iron pot, letting the heartstone turn to a softly glowing liquid. A faint, deep bluish color burned within the heartstone, much darker and hotter than it should be. Lifting the pot of heartstone away from the coals, he surrounded the iron and grindl sheet with long bars of iron, creating a box form. Then he poured the liquid heartstone onto it.

He cleaned his work while waiting for the heartstone to cool. As he cleared the remaining heartstone from the iron pot, a flash of green and blue flame burst from the form holding the heartstone.

"Damn!" he swore, dropping the iron pot and running over to the form. The heartstone glowed a bluish green, and flames flickered across its the surface. He slapped the table in frustration.

"What is it?" Jessa asked.

She peered into the form, nose turned up at the stink from the burning metal, as she studied what he'd made.

"The grindl. I don't know the different temperatures required to heat heartstone and grindl."

"But you've worked with them before."

He nodded. He was an idiot, and had he any true training as a smith, he wouldn't have made the same mistake. "I've worked with them before, but not together. They must have a similar heating point." He shook his head. The only thing that he could think had happened was that the heartstone had fused with the grindl. "Now I think I've ruined the plate." He slapped the table again in frustration.

It hadn't been the only plan he had to find some way of learning what his father might have been doing for the Forgotten, but it had seemed the easiest, and even that had proven not nearly as easy as he'd hoped.

Anything else would be riskier.

"Wait until it cools," Jessa said.

"Won't matter."

She laughed softly. "You don't know that. Wait until it cools and then see what you can learn. Don't let yourself get too upset just yet."

Rsiran nodded, but didn't have much hope that it would work. And if it didn't work, for him to find why the Forgotten had used his father meant that he—likely *they*—would be taking another dangerous trip.

Part of him actually looked forward to it. If he could understand what happened to his grandparents, to Jessa's parents, even to Brusus's mother, maybe he would better understand what the Forgotten were after.

Jessa watched him, almost as if Reading his thoughts, and Rsiran turned his attention back to the form around the heartstone.

When the metal cooled, Rsiran pried the iron bars away, tapping at them with a hammer to separate them. It probably didn't matter how gentle he was with the bars. There wasn't anything that to destroy within, anyway. Pouring the heartstone onto the plate had probably already done that.

With the bars removed, he dropped them to the floor of the smithy and kicked them to the side. He'd have to clean the heartstone off them later.

The light gray heartstone atop the plate had hardened to a smooth sheen. Once heated, heartstone cooled much harder than it was in its raw form. Lorcith had strange qualities like that as well, making it so that it couldn't be reheated once it took a shape. Heartstone could be heated again, but it would never be as soft as it was when first shaped.

Rsiran turned the block of heartstone over in his hands. The metal surrounded the plate, leaving barely an edge free. Had he been more careful with the form—or even more prepared—he might have a better chance of getting the plate separated from the heartstone. Now it didn't really matter. The grindl would have fused with the heartstone. He might be able to pry the iron portion of the plate off, but even that wasn't guaranteed.

"Did it work?" Jessa asked.

"Not like I'd hoped. The grindl and the heartstone fused during the heating process."

"Like an alloy?"

He hadn't known that grindl would join with heartstone before. If nothing else, some good could come of his mistake. "Something like that."

"So now you can't separate them?"

She took the brick of heartstone from him and ran her fingers across the surface. Heartstone was slick, much like how it felt when he tried to *push* or *pull* on it. There was always the sense that it would slide free of your grip, and *pushing* on it was no different. Jessa held it tightly, as if afraid that she would drop it.

"Not that I can tell," he said.

"Can you, you know, *sense* it?"

He should have thought of that first, and not needed Jessa to suggest it to him. "Maybe…"

He took the brick of heartstone back from Jessa, gripping it carefully, and ran his hand over the surface. The heartstone pulled on him, but the way that it did had less intensity now. That must be the grindl, he realized.

Rsiran pushed away the sense of lorcith in the smithy, forcing it to the back of his mind so that he could focus on heartstone. With lorcith pressed away, he could feel the draw of heartstone, and he felt the steady sense tickling in his mind. Rsiran focused more intently, drawing the awareness of heartstone even closer.

Something like an image bloomed in his mind with flashes of color, both green and a deep blue. He could see it, as if it were right in front of him. The ridges that he'd detected had meaning, but what?

There was almost a familiarity to it, as if he'd seen it before, but he couldn't tell why. The intricacies of the metalwork amazed him. Whoever had made this was an incredibly skilled smith.

The contours that he detected reminded him in some ways of the Ilphaesn mines, almost as if this was intended to serve as some kind of…

"It's a map," he whispered.

"A map?"

He nodded. That had been what he'd sensed, the rough sense that he'd felt beneath his fingers. Now that he'd said it, he felt even more certain that it was some sort of map, but a map of what?

And why would his father have had it? There had to be something, some reason for his father to have this, but Rsiran couldn't think of one.

Unless Jessa was right. Could Thom or someone else with him have hidden the plate in the wall of the hut after he'd left?

If so, why? If they had intended for Rsiran to find it, there were better places to have hidden it.

That left his father. The fact that Alyse had been abducted made it even more likely that his father had left it, and that whoever he'd taken it from wanted it back.

Maybe that was the reason his father had been locked in the room where he'd found him.

When he'd gone to Asador, he'd found his father trapped in a building barricaded with alloy that made it difficult for him to Slide past.

He'd never really considered the reason that his father would have been held like that, but maybe this was it.

Could it be the reason Alyse had been abducted?

And now, without his father here to ask, he had no way of knowing why he'd left this behind, and no way of understanding why it might be important.

CHAPTER 13

Rsiran slid the page across the table. Brusus picked it up and leaned toward it, frowning as he studied it. Haern glanced at it, but shook his head as he had the first time Rsiran had shown him the drawing of the map that he saw within his mind.

"You say this was on a sheet of metal?" Brusus asked.

Rsiran nodded. Movement near the back of the Barth caught his attention and he turned. Ever since the attack, he didn't feel nearly as comfortable here as he once had, regardless of the fact that Brusus now owned it and claimed it safe. A lute and bandolist played together tonight, the combination almost haunting.

He picked at the carrots on his plate. He'd eaten everything else and mopped them through the remaining gravy. His ale sat relatively untouched in front of him. "It was what I found in the hut. That's what those other two were after, I think."

"Thought you said they were after you," Brusus said.

That had been what he'd assumed, but if they know of this map, and if they thought that he had it, could it be that they'd come after him for that, rather than his ability to Slide past the alloy?

"I don't really know," Rsiran said. "Did they want me or my father? They probably knew that taking Alyse would motivate him more than me."

Brusus touched the page, letting his fingers trail across the ink. Rsiran had done the best that he could reproducing what he saw in his mind, but he didn't have any real artistic skill. Copying the map was difficult. There was a sense of elevation in the map that he couldn't reproduce on the flat page.

"You ever see anything like this?" Brusus asked Haern.

Haern's scar twitched, and he rubbed his fingers over it. "Not like that. Venass don't use maps like that. Don't need to," he said. His fingers ran along the surface of the scar—a memento of his escape from the clutches of Venass.

"You've been other places besides Venass," Brusus suggested.

Haern shook his head. "Map like that, you've got to know what you're looking at to know why it's important."

"Are you sure it's a map?" Brusus asked.

Haern touched the page again. As he had when Rsiran had first shown it to him—when Haern had come to resume his training—he tipped his head to the side, and his eyes went distant. "It's a map," he said. "Can't See what it is. Rsiran blocks it."

Brusus sat back and waved over the waitress. She was an older woman, with gray hair pinned up. The green in her eyes had a softer hue, less intense, and almost muted compared to everyone other than Brusus. He whispered something to the woman and she nodded curtly, making her way back to the kitchen.

When he turned back to the table, he smiled sheepishly. "Have to keep the tavern running, you know?"

Jessa looked up from the dice she spun on the table. "Tell Rsiran he should let this go," she said to Brusus.

Brusus met her eyes and something passed between them. Silence settled over the table for long moments. The sound of the music and the voice from the few other patrons around the tavern filled the silence.

"She dies if he does," Haern said.

Jessa looked over. "Who dies?"

Haern nodded to Rsiran. "His sister. Can't See it well, but what I See tells me that if he does nothing, she dies."

"And if he goes looking for her? Who dies then?" Jessa asked.

Rsiran hadn't realized that Jessa felt so strongly about him trying to find his sister. He knew that she didn't feel that he owed his family anything, but more than that, she hadn't shared. Did she fear losing him, that he'd return to his family if he tried to help? She should know him well enough by now to know that he had no interest in that.

But how could he leave his sister? Especially if she would die if he did nothing?

"Can't See that, either," Haern said.

Jessa slapped the dice and swept them into her hand. She shook them forcefully and spilled them across the table, letting them go skittering across, stopping when they clinked against Rsiran's mug. "You can't See much of anything, now can you? There's not much good to your visions if they don't help us, Haern."

Haern frowned, the long scar on his face twitching again. "Never said there was much good to what I See. Sometimes, all they offer is fear. But I'm not telling you what might happen. I'm telling *him*."

Jessa pushed on Haern's arm. "And what about me? I thought you cared what happened to me."

When Jessa finally relaxed, Haern put his arm around her shoulder and pulled her against him. "You know that I care. I know what you been through, girl. And I know what happened, how it eats at you. You can't want the same for him, not if you have a hope for more."

Jessa lowered her head and didn't meet Haern's eyes. Rsiran reached for her, but she pushed him away as well. "How can we even think about more when all we have in front of us is darkness? Everything we do leads us deeper in, doesn't it? First with Josun, then with Venass, and now what will this bring?"

Jessa had never shared her concern with him before, not like this, and not with such sadness. Rsiran had many of the same concerns, but he had thought Jessa would support him with what he needed to do. If she didn't, he wasn't sure that he would be able to go alone.

"Don't know where this will end," Haern said. "I've been trying to See that since we first met Josun Elvraeth. But those visions are closed to me. Too dark, or... something. I can focus only on what I *can* See. That's all I can do. And she dies if he does nothing."

"Can you See where she is?"

Haern shook his head. "Not that clear. I think your connection to her blurs her. When I focus on her, try to See her, I get flashes of color, and then darkness. When I add you," he said, nodding to Rsiran, "the flashes continue. Without you, she's gone. With you, she's got a chance. Don't even know what that is, though."

Jessa laughed bitterly. "Flashes of color. That's what you want Rsiran to base his decision on? What if those flashes of color are wrong? What if he tries something and she dies anyway?" Her voice caught. "What if he tries something and *he* dies?"

No one spoke for moments. Brusus finally broke the silence. "What do you intend to do? I can see from your face that you have a plan."

Rsiran caught Jessa's eyes and tried to hold her attention, but she shook her head and looked away. "I can't do nothing," he said. Even before Haern had shared his vision, he knew that he couldn't simply do nothing, not if his sister was in danger, and not if there was something that he could do that would help.

"What you plan means going after the Forgotten," Brusus said.

He'd thought about that, but there was no guarantee that the Forgotten were responsible for abducting Alyse. The more he thought about it, the less the Forgotten made sense. His mother wasn't Elvraeth, and the Forgotten—those he'd found in the Forgotten Palace—had all been Elvraeth once. So while his family might have been exiled, they were not Elvraeth, and not like the Forgotten they'd faced before. In that, he was more like Jessa with her parents, and less like Brusus.

The Forgotten had wanted to use his father, though. That much was undeniable. Rsiran might not know why, but he needed to understand if he wanted to help his sister. Which meant he needed to reach his father. Either he needed to get word to him, or he needed to find someone who could.

And he thought he had a way of finding someone who could.

"Not the Forgotten," Rsiran said. "They may have been responsible for taking Alyse, but there are too many places for them to hide her. I need to know what they want from my father."

"You can't intend to try and pull him from Venass," Brusus said.

The thought had crossed his mind, but he didn't think that would be possible, not without help, and knowing more than he did about Venass. He'd been working with Haern, but he still had far to go before he was even as skilled as Haern. And if a single man without the ability to Slide could deter him, what would happen if he tried going to a place where there might be several, dozens even?

"Not that."

"What then?" Haern asked.

Rsiran scanned the tavern, then directed his answer to Haern and lowered his voice. "You know about my connection to lorcith and heartstone," he started.

Haern's mouth tightened. Rsiran worried what Haern might say about his plans even more than Brusus or Jessa.

"I can use that connection to find the metal. It's easiest when I've sensed the metal before. Well, really it's easiest if I've forged the metal before, but if I've sensed it, there's a certain signature that I can follow."

"Aw, damn, Rsiran," Brusus said. He glanced at Jessa whose face had turned into a neutral mask. Rsiran noted the tension in her shoulders and the set of her jaw and knew that she was angry. "You think you can find your father, don't you?"

He nodded. "I need someone who knows Venass—"

"Haern knows Venass," Jessa said.

"Who knows it today. And Thom knows Venass. They must trust him, or at least control him enough for them to have sent him after us. If I can find him"—he caught Jessa' eye—"if *we* can find him, use Thom to either reach my father, or get word to him. Either way, I think that's the first step to learning what happened to Alyse. Maybe finding out who's after me in the city."

"First of all, why do you think he'll do your bidding? And secondly, do you not remember what happened the last time you encountered him?" Brusus looked at Haern as he asked. "If he's that skilled with Compelling, you put yourself in danger. What if he's able to Compel you? Or Jessa, since I assume that she's going along with you."

"I'm going to have to find a way to convince him to help," he answered, but didn't yet know how. "And I don't think he can Compel me."

"You place a lot of trust in your ability to prevent a skilled manipulator from reaching your mind. Trust me when I tell you that it can be more difficult than you realize."

Rsiran solidified the barriers in his mind, adding the connection to lorcith and then adding a hint of heartstone. He'd always thought that he did it by imagining the connection to the metals. Lately, he wondered if maybe he *pulled* on something in the metals themselves, almost as if whatever arcane properties they possessed that allowed him to reach them, to *push* on them, also allowed him to draw on their strength as he protected his mind.

"Try to Compel me," Rsiran said.

Brusus smiled and shook his head. "You know that I can't Compel—"

Rsiran snorted. "You Push, but I think it's all part of the same ability. How long has it been since you've been able to Read me?"

Rsiran used lorcith constantly to hold his mental barriers in place. It was the easiest for him to connect with, and almost as secure as heartstone. There had been a time when Brusus had claimed his thoughts were too loud, and he realized he was at risk when his barriers were down. Since then, he'd taken to maintaining a constant barrier, strengthening the connection with heartstone, trying to silence his thoughts, at least to prevent other skilled Readers from accessing them. Had he not, some of the things that he knew, that they'd learned, would be dangerous for them.

"It's been a while," Brusus admitted. He shifted his attention to Haern and then Jessa. "Not that I try often, but Rsiran was challenging. When we first met him—"

"You don't have to explain," Rsiran said. He remembered how Brusus had tried Reading him, and how he had used the barriers that he'd learned to form in his mind because of Alyse. That had mostly blocked Brusus. When he'd met Josun, he realized that he was able to crawl beyond those barriers, as if they were no obstacle to him whatsoever. "But try Compelling me," he said.

Brusus shrugged and rested his arms on the table. His eyes flared a deep green. Like when he used his abilities, he could no longer focus on Pushing out the image of pale green eyes as he hid his natural strength. Pressure built in Rsiran's head, and he felt the attempt and used a combination of lorcith and heartstone to push back. Brusus grunted and let out a frustrated breath.

"Fine. I can't."

Rsiran nodded. "When we were in the Forgotten Palace, Evaelyn tried and failed. Della said that she's incredibly skilled. Thom might have honed his ability to Compel, and might even have learned something in Venass that makes him even more dangerous, but I can keep him from affecting me."

Brusus nodded slowly. "You can't go by yourself."

"No."

"I should be safe as well," Brusus said. "With a shared ability, it's unlikely that he'll be able to Compel me, either."

"He's not leaving me here," Jessa said.

"If you come," Brusus said, "you run the risk of being used against us."

When Rsiran and Jessa first met Evaelyn Elvraeth, she had used Jessa that way. That was when Rsiran realized he needed to be more careful with what he shared, even with Jessa. She might not *want* to betray him, but if she was Compelled, there might be nothing she could do to stop it.

"There might be a way," Haern said.

They all turned to him.

"When I was in Venass," he started, touching the scar on his face, "when I still had my… implant… I was protected from men and women like Thom. Whatever Venass did to me kept me from being used."

"What do you suggest, Haern?" Brusus asked. "You want us to place something inside Jessa to keep her safe? I know she trusts Rsiran, but I think that might be straining it a bit, don't you think?"

Haern actually smiled. "You could always ask Della," he said.

"You're serious?" Jessa asked, shooting Haern a dark look.

"Not serious, at least not about that," Haern said. "But you don't need implants for some of the things that are done in Venass."

Rsiran remembered the piercings that the scholar had. Lorcith bars that went through his lip, his eyebrow, his stomach, and probably places that he hadn't seen. "I'm not going to do that to Jessa."

"Not a piercing," Haern said. "Though contact is important. Don't know why, but that's what I was always told."

"You think Rsiran can make something that might keep her safe?" Brusus asked.

"I already have," he said, pointing to her charm. Between that and the heartstone alloy necklace, she wore his forgings. Then there was the long-bladed knife that he'd forged from the lorcith he'd heated when trying to decipher the map. She had that strapped to her thigh. Another layer of protection, and one that he approved of. "It didn't keep her safe when we were in the Forgotten Palace."

"There is a certain shape that's needed for it to work," Haern said. He ran his finger along the scar on his cheek. "Not sure that I fully understand, but it's keyed to each person differently. You have a connection to lorcith, Rsiran. You should be able to figure out the shape, don't you think?"

He thought that it was possible, but that meant he'd have to somehow get the lorcith to understand what he intended, and then create the shape. If it worked, Jessa *might* be protected from someone Compelling her. If it didn't… well, then she'd be controlled, and possibly a danger to them.

As he looked over to her, he realized that she wouldn't let him leave her behind. That left only one answer: Rsiran would have to get it right.

CHAPTER 14

THE FORGED GLOWED AGAIN, this time heating the entire smithy, pushing back the growing chill that threatened to work through the cracks in the building. It reminded Rsiran of when he'd first taken over the smithy, and all the repairs that had been required before the smithy itself had been functional. They had repaired holes in the ceiling, and cracked and crumbling brick, but all from the inside of the smithy. They couldn't have the outside looking too well kept. There was value and secrecy in the dilapidated structure.

He had not lit the hearth, so Jessa curled in a chair, wrapping her arms around her legs close to the forge itself. She had spent countless hours with him as he worked in the time since they first met, and had more than a passing familiarity with the rhythmic hammering of metal on metal. Rsiran suspected that she would be able to replicate some of his workflow simply from watching, though she had never once made an effort to pick up a hammer. She usually had other tasks elsewhere, for which her skills were more valued, leaving him for stretches of time to work alone.

He stood in front of the large bin of lorcith. Every time he looked into the bin, he thought of Shael, and the way that he'd sneaked the ore into the smithy. At the time, Rsiran feared that he was committing himself to whatever Shael had wanted of him. Now he was thankful for the ore, and the fact that he would not have to return to Ilphaesn any time soon.

Strangely, there was a part of him that missed the mine, that longed for the familiar scents and sounds found within the mine itself. He had nearly died several times over while working there, but no longer did he feel the same fear about its emptiness. Now he could use the lorcith to guide him, much like he did with the heartstone in the map that he now possessed. His strengthened Sight helped take away the sheer overwhelming blackness that often greeted him in the mine. Would it be so bad if he had to return? There was much he could learn there; he still hadn't explored the mines Josun used, or determined why the supply coming from Ilphaesn had been constrained. Nor had he spent the time to figure out where Josun had gone.

He pushed those thoughts away from his mind and focused on the sense of lorcith, holding an image in his mind of what he wanted to accomplish. Haern suggested that lorcith could be used, something that could help protect Jessa from influence, from whatever Compelling that Thom might attempt. Had he only known *what* to make, Rsiran might be better equipped to forge it.

One lump called to him more than the others.

Rsiran had experienced that often enough that he had counted on the lorcith itself guiding him somewhat. When he first began working with lorcith, he had selected the ore at random, and it had called to him, demanding he create specific forgings. The longer that he worked with it, the more he recognized the connection, so that now when he wanted to create a specific shape, he knew to search for lorcith that was willing to work with him and take on that shape. Doing anything different would have required forcing it into shapes that it wouldn't want to take. That was the way other smiths worked.

He pulled the lump of lorcith from the bin. It was of average size, but it sang to him, drawing him to the forge. Rsiran held onto the desire that he had, the need to create something that would protect Jessa, as he brought it to the coals and began to heat it.

When it glowed with red-hot heat, he moved it to the anvil. This was the part that he was least certain of. If this worked, the lorcith would guide him, and he would simply follow the forging. If it didn't… there would be wasted lorcith.

Rsiran began hammering. At first, he worked with an irregular pattern. He tried keeping in mind what he wanted of the lorcith and the fact that he needed something that would protect Jessa. If he failed in this, he wouldn't feel comfortable with her coming with him to find Thom.

The longer he worked, the more he fell into a pattern. The desire he held in mind began to fade as he was seduced by the song of the lorcith. It took over, much like it used to do when he was first learning to work with it.

Rsiran lost track of how long he worked. He hammered, the steady, rhythmic pull on the metal, periodically bringing it back to the coals to heat it again. His mind was blank, nothing but the call of the lorcith.

Time passed, and he had no way of knowing whether it was minutes or hours.

Then he stopped.

The forging was complete.

He set the hammer down and wiped sweat from his brow, hot from the work he'd been doing. The smithy itself was cool. Rsiran looked at the table where he'd set the completed project and was somewhat surprised by what he found.

Two small circular bands that looped around themselves and then back, the ends not touching, rested on the table. The metal was twisted, spiraling around in a symmetric pattern. One free end curved inward.

"Is it done?" Jessa asked.

She stirred from the chair where she sat, watching him. He held the forgings out to her, uncertain whether these bracelets would work. Never before had he gone to the lorcith with nothing but a desire in mind. He'd always wanted something in particular; he could envision its shape. Usually it was knives, or the sword, but this time, it had been a request to the metal to shape something to achieve a specific goal.

"I think so," he said.

Jessa took the bracelets with a frown. "They look like the chains you put on Josun," she said. "Only as usual, yours are fancier."

"Those were heartstone and lorcith," Rsiran said.

"You don't think these will prevent my Sight?"

"I don't know how these will work. I've never done this before."

"Done what?"

"Trusted the metal to show me what I needed to do."

Her frown faded and the hint of a smile tugged at her lips. "The way you talk about it… it's always so interesting to me. Almost as if it's alive, that it talks to you."

Rsiran listened for a moment. The lorcith in the bracelets *did* talk to him, and he could hear from it the entire history of the metal, from the point where it came out of Ilphaesn, all the way back to when it had been nothing more than a part of the mountain. "It is alive," he said. "Not the same as us, but lorcith is alive more than any other metal. I can hear it, and I think I can talk to it." He shrugged, letting go of the connection and the song of the lorcith from the bracelets. "I know it sounds strange, but…" He shrugged again.

Jessa slipped one of the bracelets onto her wrist. The metal pulled on her palm before getting past her hand. She twisted it in place, tracing her fingers along the metal. "I don't think they'd fit anyone else," she said as she slid the second one over her other hand. "My hands aren't the biggest. Had you made them any other size—"

Rsiran chuckled. "They were made for you. I told the lorcith what I needed, and *why*. That's the important part. There has to be a reason."

She tugged on each bracelet until she seemed satisfied with how they settled on her arms. "How do the other smiths use it? They don't listen like you do."

"They ignore the call," he said. "They force it in ways that they want. It's why my father was so particular about lorcith when I was in my apprenticeship. In his mind, you have to ignore the call of lorcith, and you have to focus on what you want it to become. I think that weakens the forgings in some way."

He'd never really made the connection before, but now that he had, that seemed truer than he realized. The forgings that he'd made, the ones where he listened to what the lorcith wanted him to forge, seemed the strongest. His connection to the lorcith made it stronger. Forcing it as his father did seemed to make the metal more brittle. His forgings were never as brittle as what he'd known lorcith to be when he was growing up.

"Will these work?" she asked.

"There's only one way to know."

"Brusus will be busy," Jessa said. "And I get the sense that you don't really want to wait to find out if these are going to work."

He smiled. She knew him too well. "I've got another idea."

Rsiran took her hand and squeezed.

"Are you really sure it's safe to Slide?"

"We haven't seen them for a while. And we're starting from the smithy. I think that helps."

Just to be safe, he grabbed the heartstone sword and slipped it into a loop on his belt. Heartstone had to protect him, didn't it? That was why he hadn't been influenced before, other than by Della. And at some point, he'd have to make a more formal sheath, mostly to protect him. He was as likely to kick the blade and slice himself as he was to need it.

Focusing on where he wanted to go, he Slid them to Della's home.

A small flame crackled in the hearth. Rsiran didn't know what time of night it was, but wasn't entirely surprised to see that she was up. Della often seemed to know when they would need her.

"About time you came. I was getting worried that I was wrong."

She stood behind a long counter and tapped one of her jars, spooning powder out before tipping it into a mug. She took a kettle and poured steaming water into it and then stirred it.

"You knew we were coming?" Rsiran asked.

"Knew? There are things that I See, but knowing is something different. You make Seeing anything difficult, Rsiran Lareth." She made her way around the counter and took a seat in front of the hearth. "Much like you make staying awake to wait for you difficult. I'm not as young as I once was, you know. What was easy for me years ago is no longer quite the same. Now sit, let us test what you have made."

Rsiran glanced over at Jessa and she shrugged. Della had often managed to know things that she shouldn't. "Did Brusus tell you what we were going to do?" he asked as he took a seat.

"Not Brusus. Haven't seen him nearly as much since he decided to take over the tavern. Can't say that I blame him. It's important to him."

"There are other taverns," Jessa said. "Ones where the Forgotten don't know how to find us."

"You think that's true? That the Forgotten don't know where you are, and that Venass won't be able to find you if you don't want them to?" She sniffed and took a sip of her tea. "You're smarter than that, Jessa. You know that they can and will find you if that's what they want to do."

"I still don't know why he risks himself like that. Having the tavern puts him—and us—in danger," Jessa said.

Della smiled. "Memories. That's the reason that Brusus risks it. There are memories in the Barth, and he's afraid of losing them. Some might call that sentiment, but to Brusus, it's just a part of him." She scooted to the end of the chair and reached for Jessa's wrist. "These are what you made?" she asked, reaching for Jessa's other wrist and looking up at Rsiran.

He nodded. "We don't know if they will work. That's why we came here."

"You think I can Compel with enough strength to test this?"

Rsiran didn't know enough to say with any certainty. In addition to being a Healer, Della was a strong Reader, but that didn't mean that she also could Compel with the same strength, not like they'd seen from Evaelyn or Thom. "I thought you might," he said.

A sad smile came to her face as she took a long drink of her tea. "Perhaps once I would have claimed skill with that particular talent, but it's one that I haven't practiced over the years. After what happened with Evaelyn… I could not bring myself to attempt it. Now it's something I only use to keep myself safe."

Rsiran should have expected something like that. As a Healer, Della should have had countless others coming to her for help. And maybe she did, but only when they weren't here. But from what he'd seen, she never Healed anyone else. She remained hidden, tucked away in this part of Lower Town, avoiding Healing others.

"Why don't you help anyone else?" Rsiran asked.

Jessa squeezed his arm to silence him.

Della sighed. "It's okay, dear," she said the Jessa. "There was a time when I helped all who came to me. It is… difficult to take on that much risk."

"The rest of us take on risk," Rsiran said.

Della nodded. "I know that you do, and I can only think that the Great Watcher intends for you to assume such danger, but the last time I did, someone I cared about dearly was lost."

"You couldn't Heal them?"

She shook her head once. "There are some things you don't Heal."

Rsiran frowned. "What kinds of things? You've managed to Heal pretty much everything that's come through here."

She sat up. "Not everything is a physical injury, and not everything is poisoning," she said. "There are times when even those you wish to remain can no long do so."

"You mean exile," he said.

Della nodded. "Exile. Forgotten. Either way, banished from the city or risk death."

"Who was it?" Rsiran asked.

Della sipped at her tea and stared at the flames crackling in the hearth. "A friend. Someone with a good heart, but who risked himself when he did not have to."

She took another sip of tea, and Rsiran wondered if Della had lost someone as Brusus had, a lover, or someone else. Knowing Della as he did, it was hard to imagine either. She had always valued her friends and had kept them close, fighting for Brusus when needed. What would it have taken for her not to fight when someone she cared about was exiled?

"Let me see these," she said, setting her mug on the floor. She reached again for Jessa's wrists and took the bracelets into her own as she seemed to study them. "Contact with the skin. Good. Venass would think you need it to pierce the skin to be effective, but this should be effective." She trailed her thumbs along the metal twisted around Jessa's wrists. "The symmetry to these is impressive," she said with a soft breath. "I haven't seen metalwork like this in… in a long time." She looked up at Rsiran and shook her head. "You have learned much since we first met. Then it was all about knives and weapons."

"That was what I needed to make," he said.

She tapped a finger on her lips. "Perhaps. But this? These are exquisite. Even without knowing that you crafted them with intent, they would be considered valuable. You may have made them *too* valuable. If someone else sees them, they might find a reason to separate them from Jessa's wrists."

"Do they work?" Rsiran asked.

Della leaned back in her chair and took a few steady breaths. As she did, her eyes flared a deep green, darker than he'd ever seen before. Jessa gasped, and Rsiran feared that Della was harming her. Jessa shook her head when he squeezed her hand.

"Just cold," she whispered.

Della sat for long moments. The bitter scent of lorcith filled the air for a moment, and the bracelets took on a soft glow. Then Della blinked, the color in her eyes fading, and shook her head.

"She is obscured from me. I can't say that they will work for all, but they work. She should be safe." She leaned forward and rested her hands on her knees. "If the others learn of this, if they learn of what you are able to create… You are dangerous, Rsiran Lareth."

"Dangerous?" he asked.

"You can do things that they cannot. I do not have to warn you to be careful, but I will, anyway. If they didn't want to learn from you before, they will if they ever learn of those. Please. Be careful."

He nodded. "I will."

But as he said it, his mind raced. Was *this* the reason that the smiths had been taken from Elaeavn? Did the Forgotten think master smiths could forge items like this?

Della glanced over. "How do you intend to find this man you seek?"

"He's from Venass," Rsiran said. "Heartstone is implanted in him."

Della nodded. "Then find him. And find answers to your questions, Rsiran."

CHAPTER 15

As he so often did when he needed to search for something, Rsiran stood atop Krali Rock and focused on everything around him. Krali stretched high above the city, high enough that he had the sense that he could see anything within the city from where he stood, as if he were apart from it, looking down much like the Great Watcher, observing much like he had when he'd held the crystal in the heart of the palace.

Jessa remained down below in the city, waiting for him. She promised to find Brusus, but from here, he thought that he could find Brusus without her assistance. Like all of his friends, Brusus carried lorcith-made knives with him that Rsiran could find. There were dozens of his knives still in the city, many in the palace itself from when Brusus had used the knives to barter for information, but there were other forgings of his as well, such as those within the Barth, or in Della's home.

Lorcith wasn't the reason that he came here, even though lorcith was everywhere all around him. From here, he could feel the pull of

Ilphaesn, and even recognize that something about the mountain had changed. When he had more time, he needed to stop there. It had been too long since he'd been to the main part of Ilphaesn, and he felt a sense of possession about the mountain, and the lorcith within. Who else cared what happened to the ore as he did?

Ilphaesn wasn't the only place where lorcith in that quantity could be found. There were other locations, but Rsiran didn't know how much of it he could find. Enough that he was drawn to it when he left the Forgotten Palace. How many others knew about those places?

Not Josun, or he wouldn't have gone to Ilphaesn to secretly mine lorcith. More questions— questions that must wait.

Rsiran was here for a different purpose. He might be able to sense Thom's heartstone implant from inside the city, but there was strength to standing on Krali, and perspective that he valued.

The wind caught his cloak, making it flutter. Once, he would have feared falling from this height, but now he understood his ability better than before. He could Slide while falling, and could even Slide without stepping. He'd been afraid that he would end up trapped when he Slid, but if he didn't have to take a step to Slide, that wasn't even something to fear.

Heartstone. That was the reason that he'd come here.

Rsiran closed his eyes and pushed away the sense of lorcith all around him. As he did, he pulled the awareness of heartstone to him. Not the alloy, but pure heartstone.

Awareness of it came gradually. There was the heartstone within the smithy, and it drew him. There was a small amount of heartstone— pure heartstone and not the alloy—in the palace. He had the distant awareness of heartstone in another location within the city, and suspected that came from the alchemists. They might not work with the alloy any longer—though he wasn't convinced that they couldn't—but that wasn't what he searched for.

He sensed no heartstone within the city with the same alloy signature that he'd detected within Thom. Rsiran hadn't expected to find him in the city. Thom would have come for him sooner had he been here. Unable to sense him, he was relieved to confirm that he wasn't here.

Beyond the borders of the city, there was the sense of other heartstone. Heartstone had been plentiful within the Forgotten Palace, and he detected it now, far enough away that he would have to strain to reach it. The heartstone pulled on him, demanding his attention. At least Rsiran knew that he *could* find the Forgotten again when he wanted to.

Was Alyse there?

He doubted that she was. That would be too easy. Even if she were there, would he be able to Slide to her and then Slide away? Evaelyn now knew that he was able to reach her, when she'd thought herself safe inside the Forgotten Palace. He doubted that she would make the same mistake again. Sliding to the palace would place him in danger. Still, he considered it. If he could reach the palace and could find out where they had taken Alyse, his search would be over. He'd have no need of Thom, or even his father.

His attention shifted to Lower Town, to his smithy where Jessa waited for him. He could tell her what he intended, bring her with him… but that risked her almost as much as if they went to Thyr. And before they went to Thyr, didn't he need to determine whether he even *should*?

Taking one of his lorcith knives, he *pushed* it into the stone, sinking it deeply in case he should need an anchor to return. Then he focused on the sense of lorcith, casting it away before shifting his attention to heartstone. Without thinking about it too much, he Slid to the Forgotten Palace, transporting himself into the heartstone room.

He emerged surrounded by the pull of heartstone. It was everywhere, filling the room. This had been where he'd first met Evaelyn and where he feared finding her again. He readied his knives, preparing to *push* them, but the room was empty.

Rsiran looked around, glancing at the shelves lined with books, the plush carpet splayed onto the floor, even the paintings along the wall. All of it had the look of wealth.

He'd been to the Forgotten Palace before and had barely escaped. Now that he'd returned, he wondered what he had been thinking. He should not have come here, not without Jessa or Brusus or Haern. Worse, no one even knew that he'd come. What would happen were he captured?

Rsiran almost traveled back to Elaeavn, but hesitated. Now that he *was* here, what more could he learn? Would he find evidence of Valn or Sarah? Or his sister… he had been around her enough that he thought he could detect the lorcith chain that their father had forged for her, if only he could get close enough. Unless too much lorcith surrounded it, much like how Josun had hidden Jessa within the mine.

Sliding carried him outside the heartstone room and into the main halls of the Forgotten Palace. With each Slide, he ensured his mental barriers were in place, not wanting to risk someone Reading or Compelling him. He should have made bracelets for himself, but thought the barriers he could erect kept him safe. Still, he wondered if that were strong enough. When he Slid, there was a moment when he lost the barrier, and had to reassert it.

The hall was empty. Rsiran Slid, moving to the end of the hall, wishing that he'd brought someone with him who could Read, some way to keep himself safe.

He paused, looking around. The next hall was darker than the last. Nothing moved.

He focused on lorcith and detected large quantities of it distantly. But nothing nearby.

Another Slide, this one to the stairs. He went up, pausing to focus on lorcith, searching for signs of his sister, but found none.

If she still had her necklace—and why would the Forgotten have reason to remove it from her?—he would find her.

Rsiran made his way back down through the palace, relieved that it remained empty. Until he reached the lowest level of the palace. Voices drifted to him, and he froze, jamming the barriers that he created into place, holding them tightly, this time afraid to Slide.

"Where is she?" This came from a male voice, and harsh.

"Not yet returned, but she was to be right behind me. We have asked for a meet, but they have refused."

"They can't refuse for too long. One of us will find him."

Was it Valn? Rsiran couldn't be certain. He'd heard him only that one time, not enough to recognize the man's voice.

"What of the others?"

"We'll have most of the sm—"

"Why are you standing here?" This was a third voice, and one Rsiran recognized: Inna.

"Easy. We were waiting on you."

"Waiting. Get back to the mines. Check their progress."

"They refuse. They claim they can't hear it."

"They're smiths," Inna said. "They hear it. They choose not to help."

"We had one who was willing, but he's gone."

"Then convince them they need to help. Give them no choice, much like you have with the others."

"How?"

"Get creative. We need to prove how far we'll go. If they won't work for their own safety, maybe they will for another's."

Rsiran Slid forward a step, trying to better hear.

When he emerged, the voices had gone silent.

He waited, fearful that Inna and the other two might have heard him. Expecting one of them to appear at any moment, he finally began to relax when no one came.

Then he saw a faint sparkle of light.

Rsiran Slid back a few steps, afraid to remain where he was. Inna hadn't said anything more. Did they know that he was here? Had they discovered him somehow? He didn't know how they would, but he didn't want to risk it, either.

But her comment… that hadn't seemed the kind of statement she'd make if they'd already taken his sister. It sounded more like they planned to do something similar.

Did that mean it had been Venass?

A figure appeared in front of him.

Rsiran tensed, readying his knives.

Inna. She smiled darkly when she saw him, unsheathing a sword.

Rsiran didn't hesitated, and anchored to the knife atop Krali, and Slid away.

CHAPTER 16

Rsiran trembled atop Krali Rock, the wind pulling at him once more, a sudden change from the stifling sense within the Forgotten Palace, almost as if the wind blowing off the sea wanted to tear away the fear he felt after being in the palace.

He'd seen Inna. Worse, she had seen him. Would she send others after him now?

But it didn't sound like they had come for Alyse. Not yet.

That left him with needing to reach Venass. After foolishly Sliding to the Forgotten Palace—something he might keep from Jessa for now—he needed to find Thom.

Rsiran steadied his breathing, letting the sense of the wind help him relax. He focused on lorcith, then pushed it away, seeking instead the heartstone. Sources of heartstone pulled on him, some nearly as plentiful as within the Forgotten Palace. From the time that he'd held the crystal and seemed to float above the world with nothing but darkness below him, he had suspected that there would be other sources of heartstone, but detecting it made it more real.

A realization came to him, one that helped him forget about the Forgotten Palace: he might never run out of heartstone if he could mine it. Heartstone wasn't always as useful to him as lorcith, but when combined with lorcith, it created a way for him to avoid the Forgotten Sliders, and possibly even those of Venass. Rsiran could envision using enough heartstone and lorcith to create a place where he would be safe from both, not having to worry about his Slides being influenced, and not needing to worry about them attacking.

Thoughts of safety were premature. First he had to find a way to reach Thom, then his father, and then find his sister. Only after he did that would he consider the possibility that he might be able to find safety for himself. His friends. And maybe even his family.

From where he stood, he detected other sources of heartstone, but each was so small that it was difficult to know where exactly to find them. Rsiran began to fear that he wouldn't be able to find Thom, that his connection to heartstone wasn't strong enough. What options would he have then? He could return to the Forgotten Palace, but if he did that, he wouldn't take Jessa. Risking her for something that would be nearly certain danger wasn't something he was willing to do. He wasn't even certain that he would be able to take her with him to wherever he found Thom, especially if he found him somewhere that Haern or Brusus considered too dangerous. Better to take Haern.

And he could craft similar bracelets for Haern, protect him from Thom's influence, keep him from being used against them. Haern was skilled with knives and had the experience to be able to withstand an attack from Thom if he could prevent him from being Compelled. But Haern wasn't Jessa. There was a certain comfort that came from knowing that she would be the one watching over him, protecting him from whatever attack might come. And her Sight was valuable.

He had to focus. Standing here, he'd allowed himself to get distracted by thoughts of what he needed to do once he found Thom, but first he had to find Thom.

Knowing that he'd sensed Thom's heartstone before gave him a degree of confidence. He should be able to find him.

Reaching out, Rsiran ignored the larger collections of heartstone, pushing away what he sensed of the palace and the unmined heartstone. As he did, he felt a steady pulsing, a faint, dark draw, but one that he recognized.

Thom.

It was distant, but not so distant that he didn't know where he'd gone.

Rsiran should not have been surprised to learn that he'd returned to Thyr. Possibly even to Venass.

Finding him there would be dangerous. Within Venass were others with the ability to *pull* him to them, to influence his Sliding. He hoped that the heartstone he carried would protect him, but he'd never had the chance to test it as well as he would have liked.

Could he really take Jessa to Thyr?

She wouldn't let him leave her; he knew that with certainty. Which meant that he would take her. And she would want to help him, even if it meant trying to help his sister. He knew that she didn't agree with what he felt he needed to do, that she didn't agree with him that he should even help, but she wouldn't let him leave her behind.

Rsiran focused on the smithy. It was time to return, to make preparations for reaching Thom, and for leaving.

Then he Slid.

As soon as he did, he recognized that something was wrong.

He felt the *pull* of his Slide, as if another force tried pressing on him, drawing him from his intended target. Normally, Sliding to the smithy would be easy, something that he could manage without fear.

He should have been more careful. He'd seen the couple trailing him through Elaeavn, and knew that the woman Sarah at least had the ability to follow Sliding. It didn't take much to guess that she could influence it as well.

Yet, when Della influenced his Sliding, there was never the sense of a battle, not like he felt now.

This was a distinct awareness of what opposed him. Not the person, but the fact that there was someone wanting to *pull* him away from where he intended.

Rsiran reached for the sense of lorcith, searching for an anchor. He should have done that before. Knowing that Sarah was after him should have kept him more on edge.

The colors oozed past him. Lorcith burned in his nostrils as if he'd left it on the coals too long. He *pushed* back, terror filling him, trying to remain on Krali Rock.

An anchor. He needed an anchor that he could use. There were dozens around Elaeavn, but where could he go that would protect him? He needed to reach someplace where he didn't have to fear exposing others, especially if she followed him.

Not the smithy. He might be protected by the bars of alloy, but he didn't want to risk them finding the smithy. Not Della or the Barth or so many other places. All of the places that he considered, he had to ignore, fearing their exposure.

Where could he go?

As much as he fought, straining in the place between Slides, spending more time here than he ever had before, he felt himself drawn steadily forward. Eventually, without an anchor, he would be *pulled* away.

Then he found a piece of lorcith he'd forged, left unintentionally but not in a place that would expose him or anyone with him.

Anchoring to it, he *pulled* himself to the lorcith, and emerged near the docks. The remains of a broken knife rested between rocks. Rsiran left it, thinking that he might need it again, and then Slid, this time anchoring as he did, emerging in the warehouse, then the smithy. Hopefully, the additional stops kept him safe, but he wasn't sure. Maybe he no longer *could* be sure when it came to Sliding.

Jessa looked up as he emerged, and then ran to the door, sinking the bars of alloy into the ground and up over the frame.

"What happened?"

He trembled. After being discovered in the Forgotten Palace, and now this... Had Inna followed him? "I was nearly *pulled* out of my Slide."

"Like when Della does it?"

"This was different. Rougher."

She leaned against the door. "Do you really think it's safe for us to go then? Until you know, do you really think that we can rely on you Sliding us safely?"

"If I have an anchor, I'm safe." Inna wouldn't have followed him, would she? Not to Elaeavn. He was safe within the city. Outside the city, he didn't have the same number of anchors as he did within Elaeavn. "Besides, I still think when I have heartstone with me, I am protected."

Why had he left the sword behind? Why had he gone to the Forgotten Palace? What had he been thinking?

If he'd had it with him, he might have been able to avoid battling with whoever attempted to *pull* him from his Slide. He needed to take it with him when they went after Thom, but what if it didn't work? What if it didn't prevent someone from drawing him along out of his Slide?

"Did you find him?" she asked.

He nodded. "I think so, but you're not going to like it."

Jessa tipped her head, waiting.

"I think he's in Thyr."

She pushed away from the door. "You're right. I don't like it. I know that you've made these for me," she said, lifting one of her wrists. "But what if they don't work? What if when we're that close to Venass, they can overpower whatever you made? I know that you can protect your mind, and that Brusus can with his ability to Compel as well, but we're putting an awful lot of faith in these, especially when we're talking about being that close to Venass."

"I have to go, Jessa," he said.

"I know." She took his hands in hers and looked of at him. "Della was right. When she was talking about needing to do these things because of the memories, I understood. My parents," she went on, letting out a sigh that shook her body, "made me a part of what they did. It was dangerous, and it was the reason my father was jailed. And my mother… I don't even know what happened to her. After they took me, after they sold me, I lost her. Had it not been for Haern…" Jessa sighed.

Rsiran didn't need her to elaborate. Had it not been for Haern, she would have been sold into slavery, and forced into… what? Rsiran didn't know what would have been required of her, only that Jessa feared it. Any time she spoke of it, she tensed.

"You don't have to go," he said.

"No, that's not it. What I'm saying is that I understand," she said. "My parents, had they *not* involved me in what they did, I would never have been placed into a position where I had to fear like I did. For a long time after Haern rescued me, I was angry with them. For so long, I hated the fact that they had never lived in Elaeavn, that it took Haern to return me to where I *should* have lived all along, where I should have been able to grow up. But if I had a chance to talk to them today, even after what I went through, I'd take it in a heartbeat." She pulled him to her and hugged him tightly. "So I understand what you need to do. Even though they never treated you kindly, I understand the desire to know more. And I understand that you might not always like them, but you don't want something bad to happen to them."

Rsiran swallowed the lump that had formed in his throat. The possibility that he might not have Jessa's support had been the hardest part for him. Knowing that she would be there with him, and better, that she wouldn't be angry for what he wanted to do, took a weight off his shoulders that he hadn't realized had been there.

"I know this might not be safe, but I have to do it."

"I know."

"I'm afraid for you if you come with me."

She rose up on her toes and kissed his cheek. "And I'm afraid if you go without me. What if something happens to you while you're gone? I wouldn't know." She wrapped her arms around him and took a deep breath. "Trust me, it's better that we're together. If we weren't, and something happened, and I didn't know…"

He held her tight against him, understanding exactly what she meant. It had been the same thing that he had been afraid of when Josun took her. For him, at least he had the ability to Slide, to search, but Jessa would only be able to wait, to hope and pray that he found a way to get free.

"When do we go?" she asked.

A heavy knocking on the door answered her question.

"I guess now," Rsiran said.

CHAPTER 17

Standing on the rock overlooking the stretch of plains leading up to Thyr, Rsiran paused, debating whether he should continue forward. Night had fallen, and the thin sliver of a moon didn't give much light—more than before, now that he had a hint of Sight—but he could still make out the pale white tower gleaming in the distance. His heart fluttered as he considered it, debating whether he should Slide any closer.

"I'm still not certain this is a good idea," Brusus said. He crouched on the rock, his long, wool cloak catching the breeze that whispered past this high up on the rock, and cupped a hand over his brow, almost as if shielding his eyes from the light of the moon. Brusus was Sighted, but could the moonlight really make *that* much of a difference?

"It probably isn't," Rsiran agreed. "That's why I brought you."

Jessa elbowed him in the stomach and touched the pale blue daisy tucked into her lorcith-shaped charm. Rsiran still wondered if the flower sufficiently diluted the bitter odor of the lorcith. Having grown up around lorcith, the only time he noticed it was during a Slide, when for some reason, he always detected the scent of it burning in the air.

"Didn't you say the last time you came too close, they *pulled* you to them?" Brusus glanced from Jessa to Rsiran.

Rsiran touched the heartstone alloy sword, his cloak keeping it covered. He'd taken to wearing it since escaping from the palace a second time. There was reassurance to having a sword, even if he barely knew how to use one. But he hoped that with the heartstone alloy blade, he wouldn't have to worry about his Slides being *pulled* by someone like Sarah, or Della. As far as he knew, he was the only person able to Slide beyond the heartstone alloy, and probably the only person able to Slide *with* the alloy.

"I don't think they will find it that easy this time," he said.

Jessa looked at him with a troubled expression. He noted the deep crease in her brow, and she chewed on her lower lip as she often did when she worried.

"They'll only find another way to draw you in, Rsiran. You promised them, and Haern said—"

"Haern said they're dangerous," Rsiran said. "Well, I'm dangerous too." He glanced at Jessa and she shook her head.

"You're not dangerous. You're barely able to—"

He Slid to her in a heartbeat and cut her off with a kiss.

"Bah," Brusus said. "Even here? C'mon, we're on a job."

Jessa pulled him closer for a minute before giving him a shove away. "See? Not dangerous at all. You couldn't even stop me from hitting—"

Rsiran detected the sudden flash of lorcith and grabbed Jessa, pulling her back a dozen steps, Sliding faster than he once would have thought possible. He emerged long enough to grab Brusus, and *pulled* him into the Slide as well, drawing them behind a teetering tower of rock behind them.

Had they been followed? The fact that it was lorcith, and that he'd noted the same thing the other times made him afraid that neither the heartstone sword nor the way that he Slid kept them safe.

Brusus had a pair of knives already in hand as they stopped, and Jessa ducked down, peering around the bottom of the rock. The bracelets that he'd made for her bumped softly against the rock. With their Sight, she and Brusus would be best equipped to see what he might have detected.

"Lorcith," he said softly. He focused on the sense of it, trying to find where he'd sensed it. The faint presence of the ore had changed. Had it disappeared?

He couldn't have them attacked this close to Thyr. If they were followed, and someone prevented them from reaching Thom, he wouldn't be able to get answers about Alyse.

That meant confronting whoever might be out there.

He had claimed that he was dangerous, and he intended to prove it. Haern had worked with him enough that he felt more confident in his ability to keep himself safe if attacked, at least against someone not nearly as skilled as Haern. If he encountered another assassin who shared Haern's skill, then he would need to rely on Brusus and Jessa to help.

Rsiran stepped around the rock, five small knives already *pushed* out in front of him and now hovering in the air. If the lorcith had disappeared, that meant someone was Sliding. Maybe Valn and Sarah, even though he hoped they hadn't followed him from the city. Could the lorcith have been masked? This close to Thyr, with the Tower of Scholars in the background, he could think of only one reason it could be masked.

"Rsiran?" Jessa hissed.

"Wait for me," he said, stepping forward. The long cloak he wore to cover the sheathed heartstone sword caught the wind and flapped behind him. With each step, he *pushed* the knives before him, holding them floating in the air in an arc around him. He strained for the sense of lorcith, but didn't pick up anything more.

Experience had taught him that didn't mean there wasn't anything more there. Especially here, in the shadows of Thyr. Moments passed, and he detected nothing else. No sense of lorcith that flashed before fading. Nothing.

What of heartstone?

Drawing the knives back to him, he caught them in his palm and held them ready.

Detecting the alloy took a different sort of attention. He had to ignore the call of lorcith in order to hear heartstone, and when he did, it left him with no sense of the metal. Pushing away lorcith had become easier over time, and now he did it in a heartbeat.

The sword called to him, demanding he unsheathe it. The time he'd spent with Haern had made him passable with the sword, but he would need even more time to give him real competence. There was an almost angry sort of energy from the sword, as if it were something alive rather than forged from metal at his forge. Rsiran ignored it, pushing the sense of the sword away from him.

Then he sensed the alloy in Jessa's necklace and noted that she approached, ignoring the dangers of whatever he had sensed. "What do you sense?" she asked.

There was no other alloy nearby.

Reaching beyond him, he strained to reach a distant sense of the alloy and felt a moment of relief that there was something within Thyr made of the heartstone. It didn't move, and he worried that it wasn't what he had detected from Krali Rock. The heartstone—and Thom—was the reason they had come.

"I don't know," Rsiran said. "Probably nothing."

Brusus scraped along the rocks as he came out from hiding. His brow creased into a deep frown, and he stood on the ledge of rock overlooking the Thyrass River rushing with a white froth far below. "I've learned that when you're involved, it is always something," Brusus said.

"I sensed lorcith, then I didn't."

Brusus glanced over at him, drawing one of the small knives he kept with him from a hidden sheath beneath his cloak. He held it out to the bright moonlight, letting it spill across the blade. "Like you did in the forest? You think you were followed?"

Jessa watched him, biting at her lower lip as she did.

"It's possible," he admitted.

Brusus nodded. "Possible. You told me about the time in the forest, and Jessa told me about the time near the docks. You really think they would have followed you here?"

Rsiran shook his head, uncertain. The Forgotten Sliders had been afraid to venture too far from their hiding place. That had been one thing that he'd counted on, knowing that they would be protected in some ways from them by his willingness to Slide. And carrying the sword, he'd not noticed any influence on his Slide, but that didn't mean that the others weren't out there, attempting to follow. And Sliding three people would create enough ripples, noise of a sort, that someone like Sarah would be able to follow it.

"We should get to Thyr and get this over with," Rsiran said. "Find Thom, get to my father, and then…" Then he still had to figure out where to find Alyse. Only they couldn't do that without risk. Was he ready to expose Jessa to that risk?

"It's okay if we wait," Jessa said. "If we've already been detected, this might not be the right time."

Rsiran stared toward the city, one hand going to the hilt of the heartstone sword. It had a certain reassuring weight to it, and he pressed his palm into the simple leather wrappings he'd placed around the hilt. "You heard what Haern said. If we do nothing, she'll die. I can't wait, not knowing that I would be responsible for that."

"You won't be responsible, Rsiran," Brusus said. "Whoever did this to her, they are the ones responsible. And if it has something to do with your father, then *he* is the one who is ultimately responsible. Don't take blame when you have none."

"You know, after Jessa and I escaped from the palace, I thought the Forgotten would come after me first," he said. "And then we were attacked by Thom. Both want me afraid of them. And I am."

"You don't have to be ashamed for fearing. Damn, Rsiran, you've gone through more than any of us would ever want for you, and you've handled it better than I would have ever dreamed. And now? Now you intend to go into Thyr, after a man who attacked you. That's not fear anymore, that's bravery."

Rsiran sighed and turned away, focusing his attention on the distant city. From where they stood, Thyr in some ways looked no different from Elaeavn, just another city sprawling across the flat ground. The massive pale Tower of Scholars looked to be a part of the city, but he knew that they were separate. Other than the Tower, he had not been to Thyr, and couldn't risk Sliding them directly into the city. That was why he had stopped on the rocks overlooking the river, unwilling to take them any farther.

"He studied in the Tower," Rsiran said. After barely surviving Thom, and learning of the metal implanted in him, he knew that to be true. "Like Haern. I'm not sure going after him is bravery, or if it's stupidity."

"You've brought help. And we're as protected as you can make us," Jessa said.

Brusus smiled. "You've never told me what part of Thom had a piercing of lorcith. How you can find him."

"Not lorcith," Rsiran said, but tapped his head. Like Haern, Thom had a vicious scar along his face from what the scholars had done.

Brusus turned, frowning. "Then how do you sense him?"

Rsiran still didn't understand why Thom would have heartstone implanted beneath his skin, and what ability he hoped to gain. There was a part of Rsiran that was curious. Would he be able to gain similar abilities using the knowledge found within Venass? If he went to the scholars, could he learn to become a Reader? To Compel like Thom? Even if he could, what price would he pay for those abilities?

"Heartstone," he said. "He has a heartstone implant."

Brusus let out a sharp breath. "Did you talk to Della about that?"

"Why would it matter?"

"Because it's heartstone. The damn metal is strange, Rsiran. There's a reason you don't find it very often. I thought it gone completely until we found the samples in the warehouse." He cupped his hands together and squeezed. "You think lorcith has strange qualities, well heartstone has just as many."

"I know."

Brusus took a step back and looked over at him, a hard gleam in his eyes. "Yes. You do. You've seen what lengths others will go to hide it."

Rsiran nodded. He'd seen the way the Forgotten had hidden the heartstone in the Forgotten Palace, and the way that Evaelyn had protected herself with heartstone, practically walling herself into the palace with the metal so that none could Slide past. It was a metal that offered qualities different from, and sometimes more powerful than lorcith.

That was the reason the Forgotten wanted to find out how Rsiran managed to Slide past their barriers. More than that, and still not known to those who pursued him, was the fact that Rsiran could Slide *with* heartstone. He was just learning the breadth of what he could do with heartstone, and hoped it would help him now.

He needed to Slide, free of any fear of being influenced. With heartstone, Rsiran didn't *think* he could be influenced the same way, but then, he wasn't entirely certain, either.

It made coming this far north a risk. It made Sliding anywhere a risk. But he had no choice if he was going to find Alyse.

Brusus sighed. "Tell me again what you intend after you find Thom?"

"Find my father. And figure out why he was hiding the map in the hut and where it might lead."

"Let's play this out. What if he's not willing to share what the map is for? You said your mother told you that he worked with the Forgotten willingly. What if he protects them?"

"He'll do what he can to protect Alyse," Rsiran said. That was what he counted on. His father might want to protect the Forgotten that he worked with, but he would do anything to help his own daughter. He'd shown that over and again. Rsiran struggled with believing what his mother said about how he'd wanted to keep Rsiran safe as well. How would sending him to the mines keep him safe? How would letting him nearly die keep him safe? If he knew something about his abilities, why hide it from him?

"Are you ready to do what is needed?" Brusus asked. "If Thom comes at you, will you be ready?"

He nodded slowly. "I've been working with Haern."

"I know that you have, but there's a difference between learning how to defend yourself and actually doing what might be needed when the time comes. Had Haern been so unwilling to come even close to this place? He should be here instead of Jessa." Brusus tipped his head and shrugged. "No offense, Jessa, but he's the more capable one when it comes to stuff like this."

"I know he is," Jessa said.

"From here on out," Brusus began, watching as Jessa hugged her arms around her body and dipped her head toward the small flower tucked into her lorcith charm, "everything is dangerous in a way that we haven't experienced before." He pointed to Rsiran. "Even for me. You start with Thom, and you show Venass that we're willing to go on the offensive. We need to be ready. All of us need to be ready. You, Rsiran. You've a kind heart, and I'll be honest and tell you that's something that worries me. When it comes down to it, can you find the darkness you need?"

Rsiran watched Jessa. Brusus asked much the same as Haern. Could he? Would he really be able to attack—and kill—if it came to it? But he'd already shown what he would do for her when he killed Shael, so he knew that for her, he would do whatever was needed. "This is what we need to do, Brusus."

Brusus grunted. "Didn't say it wasn't the right move, only that it was dangerous."

There was a time when Brusus would have told him the next steps to take, but that was before Rsiran had shown them that the growing battles were about more than simply the Forgotten and the Elvraeth in Elaeavn. Even with that, there were questions they didn't have answers for. *How* could Venass use lorcith to recreate his ability? And if they could do that with lorcith, what else could they replicate? Or would it be like Della feared, that if they learned of how he could work with lorcith, and could use that connection to create items that would defend against Elvraeth abilities, would they seek to use that as well?

Now that he'd been to the heart of the palace…and maybe not even the palace—Rsiran wasn't completely convinced that he had still been in the palace when he'd Slid to the circle of crystals—he understood that there was something more to what Venass and the Forgotten wanted.

"Hopefully Haern helped me to be dangerous too," Rsiran said, trying to sound more confident than he felt.

Brusus clapped him on his shoulder and smiled. "You *could* be dangerous, Rsiran, but you've got to know when compassion gets you killed. You showed that with Josun—"

"And your father," Jessa added.

"Maybe him as well," Brusus agreed. "With what's coming, if what we *think* is really coming, I think you're going to have to harden your heart."

Rsiran looked to Thyr, detecting the call of the heartstone within the city that he suspected came from Thom. After what the man had done to Haern, and almost had done to Jessa, he didn't think he would have any trouble hardening his heart.

But Brusus was right. He'd been captured too many times, mostly because he *had* hesitated. What would have happened had he been willing to finish Josun when he first captured him? What would have happened had he been willing to take a harder stance when they found the Forgotten? Or Evaelyn? Even in Venass?

There was no guarantee that it would have worked, or that he would have survived, but so far, that was all that he had done. Survival was no longer his only goal.

He glanced at Jessa watching him with narrowed eyes, and knew she was doing that thing she did… somehow reading him. She knew him so well, how he thought, when he was troubled, or when he simply needed someone to listen to.

More than anything, he would do what it took to keep her safe.

He readied three knives, *pulling* on the lorcith in them. "Ready?" he asked, looking to Brusus and Jessa.

She took his hand, and Brusus hesitated, his pale green eyes flaring brighter for the briefest moment. Did Brusus think to Read him? With the lorcith-infused barriers that Rsiran kept in his mind, Brusus would have difficulty. Even more so when Rsiran strengthened them with the heartstone. That was what he counted on when it came to Thom. It was the only thing that would keep him safe. He didn't have the lorcith bracelets like Jessa did to keep him safe, and didn't have the natural ability to Compel that kept Brusus safe.

But what he wanted was no secret. The fact that he wanted to keep his friends safe was no secret. That he wanted to protect Jessa was no kind of secret.

Then Brusus grabbed his arm. "Careful," he said softly.

Rsiran focused on the distant edge of Thyr and, using the modified way that he'd learned to Slide, *pulled* them to the city.

CHAPTER 18

THEY EMERGED AT THE EDGE OF THE CITY. Thyr was one of the great cities, and a place where traders from all over came to convene. It was an open city, but still a massive wall that was a mixture of stone and iron enclosed it. He had made a point of emerging in the shadows of a clump of trees, and was glad that he had. Guards patrolled along the top of the wall, though Rsiran's Sight was still too weak to count more than a pair of guards. Each of the guards wore a short sword, and both carried crossbows held ready as they patrolled.

He shivered. Much like Asador, Thyr felt foreign to him. There were parts of Elaeavn where he felt equally out of place, such as the times he wandered through Upper Town, or when he had risked entering the Floating Palace, or even the Alchemist Guild.

Jessa squeezed his hand, as if she understood what he was thinking. Even though he could Slide, and even though his ability allowed him to travel wherever he could imagine, there was a part of him that did not feel at home anywhere, not anymore.

He glanced at Jessa, "Are you ready?" he asked.

"As much as I can be. You able to return us if needed?" she whispered.

There was the distant sense of Venass that pulled on him, though Rsiran didn't really know what it was that he detected. Was it the lorcith they used, or was there something else entirely? Not the alloy, though he suspected they were familiar with that as well. Whatever drew him was something else.

"You don't want to Slide us all the way to wherever Thom is?" Brusus asked Rsiran, motioning for them to start toward the massive gates allowing access to the city.

"I thought about it," Rsiran said, "but what happens if we emerge to find him with others? What happens if they're all armed like them?" he asked, motioning to the guards atop the wall. Closer up, he caught the way the moonlight traced silver streaks along their armor. Their chests and necks were covered, keeping them as safe as possible. His knives wouldn't do much good, at least, not short of killing, and that was something Rsiran wasn't ready to do. And there was a limit to what he might be able to do if surrounded by assassins. Haern had shown him that his ability to Slide and push knives could be countered by someone with incredible skill. "Besides, Sliding all the way to him is unreliable."

"I thought you had control of your gift?" Brusus said. He nodded to a guard stationed at the entrance to the city, keeping his head bowed and his eyes focused on the ground.

Rsiran copied the movement, and Jessa did the same. They would stand out here, not only for the green of their eyes—well, not Brusus Pushing with a subtle influence that masked the color of his eyes—but also for their height. Rsiran had noted the same when he'd been through Asador. The people he'd seen had all been shorter than he was, some significantly so.

"I've got control, but with heartstone…" He shrugged.

How to explain to Brusus what it was about the metal that made it so unique? There was less control with heartstone than with lorcith, and he didn't really know why that should be. It had a slippery quality to it, especially in the pure form. In an alloy—or what he called an alloy, since it never truly mixed with the lorcith—the heartstone gave him a bit more control, but nothing like the exquisite sense he had with lorcith.

That sense was even stronger than it had been, as were most of his abilities since he'd held the crystal. Even his sense of heartstone was improved, so it was possible that the control that he sought and feared he didn't have was actually much better than he believed, but he hadn't the time to truly test it in any meaningful way yet.

"Say no more," Brusus said with a wave of his hand.

Within the city itself, there was a cacophony of sound, even at this time of night. Occasional shouts split the night, some screams, and every so often, he heard the barking of dogs. No cats. Not like in Elaeavn. Music drifted toward him, though muted, and with unfamiliar instruments.

Smells assaulted him as well, that of sweat, and filth, and, surprisingly, blood. His boots rang off the hard stone, but side streets were nothing more than hard-packed earth. Piles of refuse littered these alleys, much worse than he'd ever seen in Elaeavn, even in Lower Town.

This was the place his father had been sent to avoid the call of lorcith. That meant there were smiths here, men his father had learned from. Could Rsiran find a master smith to learn from outside of Elaeavn? There was only so much that he could learn listening to lorcith.

A painful shout shook him from his thoughts, and he looked over to his friends.

"This is a mistake," he said. "This is worse than Asador."

Brusus laughed softly, shaking his head as he did. "You'll get used to it. Many of the 'Great' cities are more like the worst parts of Lower Town."

"Smells worse than Lower Town," Jessa said.

"Even near the docks?" Brusus asked, turning up his nose.

"You get used to the docks," Jessa said. "At least there's safety there. No fear that someone will grab you and…"

She didn't finish, but Rsiran didn't need her to and neither did Brusus. Had she ever been to Thyr or Asador before returning to Elaeavn? She'd nearly been sold into slavery in Eban. Was it a place like what he saw here? Looking at it, *smelling* it, made it possible that Thyr could be such a place.

The city made him wonder if maybe Haern had been right that he should have left Jessa behind. It would have certainly been safer. Her only protections were her Sight, and her ability as a sneak. Neither would be of much use when a knife or crossbow bolt came whistling toward her. He didn't want to be the reason that anything happened to her.

She elbowed him, almost as if Reading him.

"Which way?" Brusus asked.

They stopped in a square, and Rsiran pushed away the sense of lorcith as he reached for heartstone. If he didn't have to do that, he wouldn't be left so vulnerable, but he knew of no other way to reach for heartstone. When he did, he didn't have any of the awareness of the knives he carried, or of the charm he made Jessa, or even the blades that Brusus stored on his person. It was the reason he'd taken to carrying the sword, and the reason that he was thankful that he'd made Jessa the necklace for the charm out of heartstone.

Now that he'd pushed away the sense of lorcith, he sensed the heartstone within the city. When he'd been atop the rock overlooking the Thyrass River, and looking toward the city, the heartstone that he sensed had been like nothing more than a vague light in his mind. This close, he now noticed it as a burning, a calling to him, but even that was muted.

That was how he knew he had come to the right place.

He started forward, following the pull of the heartstone. Jessa came alongside him—her necklace told him that she did—and placed a hand on his arm to guide him. Rsiran left his eyes closed, letting him be drawn toward the heartstone.

He didn't worry that Brusus would follow. There was no sound from Brusus, but then he was nearly as skilled a sneak as Jessa. Perhaps more so, he decided. Brusus had been the one to train her.

"Rsiran," Jessa said gently, stopping him with a slight tug on his arm.

He opened his eyes and realized that he'd stopped in front of a building. The heartstone was beyond here, but he would have to go around. Rsiran tapped on the wall and shook his head. He should have paid attention to where he was going.

As he looked around, others on the street watched him. A group of men stood outside what he suspected was a tavern from the way the bawdy music spilled out. One man leaned forward, resting his hands on his knees, and vomited.

He could have done without his newly sensitive Sight showing him that.

"We close?" Brusus asked.

"Other side of the building. And we still have a ways to go."

Brusus reached into the pockets of his cloak at the same time four of the men started down the street toward them. "That's what I figured. We're going to have to make a decision here, it seems."

"What decision?"

"Either you Slide us, or we fight."

The men stopped about ten paces away. The nearest man had a thick mustache and dark, narrow eyes. He tapped the sword he carried at his side, offering Jessa a leering glance. The others stood on either side of him, slowly inching their way forward, as if they intended to surround them.

"What's your plan?" Brusus whispered.

Jessa gripped his arm. Holding on like that, he could Slide her to safety, but he'd have to grab Brusus. He could Slide quickly, reach his friend, and pull them away from the city. Then they could wait, and Slide back when the streets were safe.

But would they really be safe? He didn't know much about Thyr other than Haern's warning, but this wasn't a place like Elaeavn. Men carried swords openly and seemed to have no reluctance to attack.

A flash of metal caught his eye. One of the men had a crossbow and aimed it at Jessa.

Rsiran could Slide, but that meant that he risked the man firing. They were far enough away from Elaeavn that reaching Della from this distance posed a real risk.

"Easy, friends," Brusus said. His words were charged, and Rsiran recognized the way that he Pushed. In some ways, it was like Compelling, though Brusus claimed he didn't use his ability in that away. Compelling was a deeper piercing into a man's mind, and dangerous. "We mean you no trouble."

The nearest man pulled on the sword at his waist. "No trouble? Got enough from your kind these days, don't we? And that one," he said, nodding to Jessa, "she'll fetch plenty of coin." A dark smile crossed his face. "Leave her and you won't have much trouble."

Brusus pulled his hands from his pockets and held a pair of knives outward. He spun them in a quick flourish, nothing like what Haern would have managed, and then stepped into a defensive posture. "Don't think I can do that. Maybe you would prefer to return to your tavern, have another mug of ale. I'd even be willing to buy, if it would let this end peacefully."

"This ends peaceful enough if you leave her here."

Rsiran readied to *push* the knives hidden under his cloak. He didn't have to hurt the men that much. He could strike them on the arms, or the legs, enough to drop them so that they could move past and down the street. And then he would be able to go after Thom and the heartstone that he knew was in the city.

Brusus flicked a single finger to Rsiran, a warning to keep from *pushing* with his knives.

"Can't do that. You see, these two are pretty fond of each other, you know. Something like that is plenty hard to find, if you ask me. Don't want to lose it once you found it."

Even with these words, Brusus Pushed.

One of the men took a step back and lowered his hand from his sword. The man with the crossbow started to lower his hand, but then jerked it back into place, as if he recognized what Brusus was doing.

Could they know how to avoid Pushing? This close to Venass, he had to assume that they might. The scholars used lorcith, and the Great Watcher knew what else to replicate the abilities of those from Elaeavn, but even that might not be necessary, would it? The Neelish sellsword had managed to resist Brusus's attempt to Push him when they were attacked, so some trick must be known.

"You think your little tricks will work here?" the nearest man said. "If they worked, it wouldn't do us any good to take your woman, now would it? Don't know what tricks she has, but I can tell you that there are plenty of folks who would be pleased to find out." His dark smile spread. "Now, one hundred gold is a pretty hard price to pass up." He nodded to his friend, who raised his crossbow. "So as I said, step aside."

"Then I'm sorry," Brusus said. He nodded to Rsiran.

Rsiran had been willing to wait on Brusus, willing to avoid needing to harm these men, but he also was willing to do what was needed to keep Jessa safe. If they intended to attack them and take her, he would stop them.

With something almost like a flicker of pressure, he *pushed* the knives hidden beneath his cloak toward the three men. Each knife went a different direction, targeting each of the men.

The man with the crossbow was hit first, and dropped the crossbow. Brusus was there in a heartbeat, holding the tip of one of his knives against the man's throat.

The other knife struck the man with the sword in the shoulder, and he grunted, before dropping his sword. Rsiran unsheathed the heartstone blade and held it out from him. He had been training with the sword, but wouldn't be able to do much to defend them if it came to it. He was better with the knives. At least those he could control.

The third knife missed, and the man who had been backing away switched directions and reached for Jessa, wrenching her toward him, and away from Rsiran. He held his knife against her throat with a shaky hand and kept Jessa between Rsiran and him so that another knife wouldn't be a simple attack.

The nearest man smiled, unmindful of the knife protruding from his shoulder. "Seems we've got a bit of a standoff, don't we? And we've got your girl." He nodded toward the other man who started backing away, pulling Jessa with him.

Rsiran glanced over at Brusus, who appeared uncertain, his eyes slightly widened. As the man backed down the street with Jessa, his eyes narrowed. "If you think my friend is going to let you leave with her, you've made a bigger mistake than you realize."

The words came to Rsiran even as he was already *pulling* on the knife still embedded in the man's shoulder and Sliding to emerge behind him. With a flicker of power against the knife, Rsiran sent it spiraling into the man's back. The man staggered and fell, the knife falling harmlessly away from her throat.

Jessa looked at Rsiran, and he could tell that her neck was unharmed. He Slid again, coming to stand in front of the man with the sword. "You were given a chance to leave," Rsiran said, anger surging through him.

The man dropped his gaze to his fallen friend. "You don't even know what you've done, do you?"

Rsiran shook, feeling the anger in him burning more brightly than it ever had before. "Do you? We would have left you alone."

"Your kind never leaves us alone," the man said.

"Rsiran..." Brusus started.

Rsiran waved a hand toward him to silence him. "You think we would have harmed you had you not attacked? Do you think we even cared enough to come after you? But you do that," he said, waving a hand toward where Jessa backed against the building, "when you simply see one of our kind. How many others have you done that to?"

Was this the kind of man who had taken Jessa back in Eban? What did he think to do to others from Elaeavn? What would happen if there were Forgotten, or their children, those like Jessa, whose crime was only in living?

Before thinking about it any more, he sent the knife spinning toward the man. It caught him in the chest, and he dropped to his knees. He coughed once, blood bubbling to his lips, and fell forward.

What had he done?

Rsiran took a step back, unable to take his eyes off the man lying on the ground, dead because of the knife sticking out of his chest. The knife Rsiran had put there.

Brusus released the other man and gave him a kick that sent him running down the street. "Damn, Rsiran. I guess your time with Haern helped."

He swallowed and shook his head. How could he have killed a man? They had the situation in hand, and he hadn't *needed* to harm him anymore, but there was a deep part of him that had *wanted* to. In spite of the revulsion, a darkness within him thrilled at what he'd done. Just like Haern had warned him about.

Jessa took his hand and pulled on his arm until he turned to her. "You know what he would have done had he taken me," she said softly.

Was she hiding her own revulsion at what he'd done? Did Jessa look at him in a different way now that he'd killed this man?

Not only this one, but the other, the one lying on the street, with Rsiran's knife in his back. That one, at least, he could justify. Had he done nothing, the man would have pulled Jessa away from him. Tried to sell her to slavers. And the Great Watcher only knew what else he intended.

"We should move," Brusus said, pushing on them. "That one will go for friends. I'd suggest we not be here when they return."

Rsiran nodded numbly, pushing away the sense of lorcith. It receded from him slowly, as if the lorcith wanted him to remember what he'd done. When it was gone, he sensed the sword he held, Jessa's necklace, and… nothing else.

The heartstone was gone.

Rsiran blinked. "It's gone," he said.

"Gone? He can't simply Slide, Rsiran," Brusus said.

He didn't know if Thom could or couldn't, but there were others in Venass who could. And they had so much as admitted that they detected it when Rsiran Slid.

"He's gone," Rsiran repeated.

He'd killed twice, and for what? They hadn't even had the chance to find Thom and ask him about Venass. Worse, it was likely that Thom knew they were after him.

CHAPTER 19

"We need to keep moving," Brusus said.

Rsiran swallowed, looking at the dead men. Had Brusus known what he'd need to do? Was that why he'd pressed him so hard outside the city? He didn't know that he would have felt as compelled to fight so hard and prove himself had Brusus not mentioned something so recently.

Unable to think for a minute, Rsiran pulled on his knives, grabbing them from the air. He looked at them in his hands, the blood glinting off the lorcith blades. Had he not needed them, he would have left them there, but instead, he wiped off the blood and returned them to his pockets.

And now he had killed. Partly because he had needed to, but partly because—if he were honest with himself—he had *wanted* to.

"I've been to places like this, with men like that," Brusus went on, motioning to the fallen men, "and if we linger here too long, word is going to spread. We can handle a little rumor, but if it gets out that there's someone here with your particular abilities"—he tapped Rsiran on the shoulder—"we won't need to worry about keeping ourselves safe anymore. Venass will think that we're after them."

Rsiran shook away the growing concern he felt about what he'd done. That would be for another time. Like so much else, he needed to push it back and away, ignore it until he had time to spend thinking about it, time that he didn't have now. Right now, he needed to focus on Thom and determine if he was still within the city, or if he'd gone somewhere else.

Even within the city, Venass drew his attention. He looked over at the Tower, remembering the helpless fear that had burned through him when they'd been there last. That time, Rsiran hadn't known if Jessa was safe, or if he would be the reason that something happened to her. Had he not managed to Slide through the lorcith walls... He couldn't let himself think like that. He *had* managed to get past the walls. And he *had* managed to get to Jessa. They were safe.

"We can go where I sensed him the last time," Rsiran suggested.

Brusus's eyes narrowed as he started down the darkened street. Darkened to Rsiran, at least. To Brusus and Jessa, there would be different layers to the shadows. "Time to move," he suggested.

Rsiran heard the sound of boots across stone before he saw anything, and then saw the shifting shadows. He focused on where he had sensed Thom, pulling it into his mind. Carefully, he drew them forward in a Slide, knowing that if they emerged somewhere other than open space, he risked something happening to all of them.

A man's shout rang out as they disappeared from the street. He heard a whistling sound, and then they emerged.

Rsiran readied all the knives he carried with him, preparing to *push* them if needed as his eyes adjusted.

"Empty," Brusus said.

Rsiran relaxed his hold on his knives and looked around, trying to get a sense of where they might have emerged. The room was lit by soft blue light. Elvraeth light. The glow would enhance the eyesight of someone Sighted, enough where Rsiran even found that it benefited him.

He had expected it to be a home, or a tavern, or something like that, but they appeared to be inside a room of an inn. A simple bed rested along one wall, and a trunk lay open at the foot of the bed. Brusus hurried to the trunk, but Rsiran doubted that anything would be there.

Thom had expected them, and was gone.

"Was he here?" Jessa asked.

Brusus pulled a few things from within the trunk. He set them on the floor next to it. Most of what he withdrew were simple items: a length of rope, a dark shimmery shirt that reminded him of the one that Haern wore, a single knife—not lorcith made, he noted, and a small coin sack.

"He left quickly. He *was* here, but he's gone now," Brusus said.

Rsiran let out a frustrated breath.

"You'll find him again," Jessa said.

"Probably," he agreed, "but I was hoping to have this over with. Find Thom. Then my father. And then Alyse. That's what I need to do. And the longer she's gone, the more likely it is that they'll do something to hurt her. She might not have always been kind, but she's still my sister."

"We'll find her," Jessa said.

Rsiran wasn't as certain, but he would continue to search. If they didn't find Thom here, how else would he find her? Where would he look? Not the Forgotten Palace. He didn't think she was there, but he might have to go back, this time with help.

"Let me look around a bit more," Brusus said.

"There's nothing here," Jessa said.

"Probably not, but maybe there's something Rsiran can use to figure out where he might have gone."

"You don't think he would have returned to the Tower?" Jessa asked.

Brusus shrugged. "Still going to look."

He peeked under the bed and started reaching for something when he tensed.

Brusus scrambled back and waved them toward the wall, raising a finger to his lips. "Away from the door."

"What is it?" Jessa asked. She spoke so softly that it sounded like little more than a breath of air.

"Boots on the floor. They're coming this way," Brusus said.

Jessa pulled Rsiran with her, and they leaned against the wall on the far side of the door. Brusus stood on the opposite side, his knives out and ready. Rsiran *pushed* on a pair of knives, leaving them hovering in the air. Even Jessa pulled the long-bladed knife that he'd forged and held it like a short sword. To her, it served as something like one.

Voices drifted through the wall. Rsiran leaned his head against the wood and listened.

"You sure it was them?"

He recognized the harsh tone of Thom's voice. If he'd returned, why couldn't he detect the heartstone from him? He pushed away the lorcith and the alloy in Jessa's necklace, and listened for the pure heartstone again. No, it still wasn't there.

But that *was* Thom on the other side of the door. He was certain of the voice.

Had Thom learned some way to disguise his presence? If so, how had he known that he would need to?

"You warned us how he can control metal," another voice said. "Didn't say how. You know that Luke and Tolst are dead?"

"Then you should have gone after him, not the girl."

"The girl is worth more. They all are."

"Idiot. You were to delay him. I told you what I was willing to pay."

"You're not as consistent as them."

Jessa tensed, the knuckles of the hand clutching the knife going white. Rsiran rested a hand on her shoulder and pulled her back toward him. He didn't want her to spring forward in her anger, not if Thom was on the other side with someone else. There was no telling how many others there might be.

"Idiot," Thom said again. "Whatever happened is on you, not me."

"I came for you, didn't I?"

Thom snorted. "You didn't need to come *for* me. I could tell when he came near."

Rsiran's heart skipped a beat. How would Thom know that he was near? He'd made certain to shield his thoughts since leaving Elaeavn, using lorcith to fortify it. When they reached Thyr, he'd added heartstone to the protections as well.

If that didn't work, then he would be in danger of Thom Compelling him.

Rsiran had thought that he would be safe, that he could keep his mind shielded, but what if the heartstone implanted within Thom allowed him to sneak past even those barriers? Would he manage to get past the bracelets that he'd made for Jessa?

Would even Brusus be safe?

They should leave. He should grab Brusus and get them away.

But then he would lose the possibility of finding Alyse.

The voices fell silent and Rsiran waited.

The door swung open, and Thom leapt inside, sword swinging.

Brusus had been ready and used his knives to block the sword. He forced Thom back, swinging as he went, slashing with a free knife.

Another man barreled in behind Thom. He fell on Jessa.

Rsiran froze.

He needed to help both Brusus and Jessa. And he thought that he could, but doing so wouldn't be clean.

After kicking the door closed, he flicked one knife at the man who had wrestled Jessa to the ground. The man grunted and stopped moving.

At the same time, he sent two other knives that slipped past Thom. Rsiran *pulled* on them, reversing their direction. Had he not spent so much time practicing with Haern, he wasn't entirely certain he would have been able to do it.

Thom's head jerked back, and he raised his hands.

Brusus slashed at Thom. Blood stained his shirt, and Brusus held onto his side. They would need to return and get help from Della. Brusus shook his head, as if Reading him, but Rsiran didn't think that he had. With his barriers in place, he knew at least that Brusus couldn't Read him.

"Clever," Thom said. "Didn't think you'd be able to find me here." He seemed more at ease than a man with a pair of knives at his gut and another pair hovering near his throat should be. "Didn't think you'd risk coming here, though." He tipped his head to Brusus. "And good to see you, Brusus. It's been too long…"

"Not long enough," Brusus said. "You're going by the name Thom now?"

Thom shrugged. "I go by many names, Thom is only the most recent." Thom glanced at the man on the ground and Jessa kneeling next to him. She held her long-bladed knife toward Thom. He smiled as he saw it. "I think you're safe here, Jessa. Not my choice to try and sell you." His eyes narrowed, and Rsiran suspected that he tried to Compel her.

Jessa shook her head. "It won't work on me," she said.

"No. I see that it will not," Thom said with a frown.

"I need to know where my father is," Rsiran said.

Thom swung his gaze around to look at Rsiran. "Your father? Didn't think you two were on such terms that you'd risk yourself to come after him. Besides, when Venass summons, you'll get to see him soon enough. Maybe this time you'll answer. You won't find the rest of Venass as accommodating as I am."

Rsiran glanced over at Brusus, hoping his wounds weren't too serious, then turned back to Thom. "I think you violated the terms of the summons when you attacked us."

Thom tipped his head to the side, the smile never changing. "Did I? Venass rarely promises safe passage, and if they do, there are other stipulations." Shaking his head, he went on, "You made a bargain in exchange for an antidote." His gaze flicked over to Brusus. "And one that appears to have worked. But you have failed to fulfill your side of the bargain."

Rsiran bit back his retort. Sharing that Brusus hadn't needed Venass's antidote would only reveal Della, and he wasn't willing to do that. At the same time, he hated that Thom was right. Venass hadn't promised him safe passage, only the antidote. They hadn't endangered him, either, but that was more likely because he had something that they wanted.

"Where is he?" Rsiran asked.

Thom shook his head. "You think your threats are going to work on me? You don't understand the Tower, Rsiran, but you will. They've already begun to claim you. Once they do, there is no coming back."

"Haern came back," Rsiran said.

Thom's smile faltered a moment. "That one. He never really belonged, did he? He always thought that he was above the mission, that he could somehow avoid the calling."

Rsiran pointed to the scar on Thom's face. "You could too. Remove that—"

Thom laughed, a dark and horrible sound. "Remove? When it's given me so much?"

"How did you know we were here?" Brusus asked.

Thom glanced at Brusus and then nodded to Rsiran. "That one doesn't guard his thoughts nearly as well as he thinks. There are times," he went on, "when he simply screams. Surely you've heard it, Brusus? Maybe you've chosen not to share? You always did have your own agenda, even when you were working with others."

"Don't," Brusus said, his voice flat. "You will not divide this group as you have so many others."

Thom smiled again. "No? Look at him, Brusus. See how he considers what I said, and whether there is any truth in it."

"Rsiran knows all that I know, *Thom*."

"Truly? Does he know the way that you search for your mother, as if she still cares to find you? Does he know how it drives you?" Thom sniffed. "You're so weak, Brusus. Always so predictable."

"And if you think you can use my friends against me, then you're wrong."

Thom stood across from Brusus, the edge of a smile pulling at his lips. For long moments, neither of them spoke. "What now, Brusus? You intend to take me back to Elaeavn, and think that there's anything that they can do to me there that I fear?"

Brusus started to answer, but Rsiran had had enough. He grabbed Thom and looked over to Jessa. "Stay safe. I'll be right back."

Her eyes widened and she nodded once.

Rsiran Slid.

They emerged outside Thyr, standing on the rocks overlooking the city. Rsiran immediately *pushed* a pair of knives toward Thom, holding them against his neck, keeping him from moving.

He stumbled back a step. The confidence that he'd shown faded a moment. "Do you really expect me to believe that you intend to harm me?"

"I don't care what you believe," Rsiran said. He Slid forward a step, anchoring to his knives as he did. He wasn't sure whether there was anyone here who could disrupt his Slides, but he wasn't going to risk it. "You aren't going to harm Brusus, and you can't Compel Jessa. And me?" he said, Sliding forward another step. "I'm willing to do whatever I need to keep my friends safe."

"Throwing me from these rocks isn't going to get you the answers that you want," Thom said. "What good am I to you if I'm lying in the river dead?"

"Who said I wanted to throw you into the river?" Rsiran asked.

Thom frowned. "Why did you bring me here?"

"A demonstration. I know Venass thinks they can control me. Just like the Forgotten think they can control me. If you're unwilling to tell me where to find my father, then I will follow through with my alternative plan."

"Which is?"

Rsiran nodded to the west. He could sense the pull of the heartstone from here, almost as if he could see it if he closed his eyes. "I'm sure there are those among the Forgotten who would be interested in learning what you've done to yourself."

Thom smiled slightly. "Do you think that I fear the Forgotten?"

Rsiran was gambling here, but it was the only answer that really made sense given what he'd gone through. It was the reason Venass hadn't attacked the Forgotten yet. Something prevented it, if only Rsiran could learn what it was. "I think that you fear something about them, and that's the reason you went to Venass in the first place. Maybe even the Forgotten didn't want you, or maybe there's another reason, but you *do* fear them. Why else would you go through what you did?"

Thom's dark smile returned. "You know so little, Rsiran. You think that you can Slide here, and that you can pull me with you, as if I feared what you could do to me. Always so shortsighted. There are powers you don't understand, powers that exceed even your abilities."

"Did you take her?"

Thom tilted his head. "Her? If you're not faster, you'll lose your Jessa. But if you would trade, and this is really about your father…"

"Where is he?" Rsiran demanded.

"Ah, you think I can share. Not yet. You have something to find first. But perhaps you should ask where your friends have gone," Thom said.

Rsiran paused, listening for lorcith. Jessa and Brusus were where he left them, weren't they?

"I won't ask again," Rsiran said. "If you don't tell me, then I might see how you would like meeting with a woman named Inna." The corners of Thom's eyes twitched. "You recognize that name, don't you? I've experienced her first hand, so trust me when I tell you that if she comes after you, there will be little that you can do."

Thom snorted. "Still don't get it, do you Rsiran? This is bigger than me. Venass is bigger than me. You might Slide me away and leave me trapped with the Forgotten, but how can you be certain that isn't their plan? How can you know that all of this isn't their plan? Ask Haern. He'll tell you what they can See."

Rsiran shivered at the idea, remembering what Haern had said about his ability to See with his implant.

Thom shook his head. "See? As I said, you know so little. That you returned at all tells me that you are not ready. And probably will never be ready."

"Ready for what?"

Thom tipped his head to the side, as if listening. His mouth pinched into a thin line and he shook his head. "Better not linger, Rsiran, not if you want to help them."

Rsiran focused on the lorcith, pulling on the connection to Jessa's charm. It was still within the city, still where it should be based on where they had been the last time. The knives Brusus carried were there as well, neither moved.

Thom watched him, his eyes unreadable.

Thom would not tell him what he needed to know, and he didn't want to risk leaving Jessa and Brusus alone for any longer than needed.

Flipping one of the knives to the flat end, he sent it spinning toward Thom. It struck him between his eyes and he fell, letting out a soft gasp as he did.

Rsiran hesitated before returning.

He now could sense the heartstone within Thom, just beneath the surface of his skin, covering the bone of his cheek. Had he wanted, he thought he could remove it, but he'd need the help of a Healer to make certain that it worked.

But why hadn't he sensed it before?

Questions he didn't have time to ask.

And if he had more time, he would have bound Thom so he couldn't move. He would have to hope that he remained out long enough for Rsiran to get to Brusus and Jessa and return to him.

Without waiting any longer, he closed his eyes, focused on the inn where they'd discovered Thom, and Slid.

CHAPTER 20

RSIRAN EMERGED TO CHAOS. Brusus stood in the hall outside the room, both knives spinning as he darted forward, attacking as best he could. Jessa crouched inside the room, her long knife held out like a sword, but Brusus blocked her from getting too far into the hall. For that, Rsiran was grateful.

Jessa let out a relieved sigh when he returned. "Rsiran. What happened to Thom?"

"I left him."

"Where?"

Brusus grunted as she asked and stepped into the doorway. "Glad you're back, Rsiran. I could use a little help."

Rsiran *pulled* on the knives in his pockets and drew them out. "On the rocks outside of the city," he said. "I hope he's there when we return."

Jessa's brow creased in a worried frown, but she nodded.

Rsiran Slid forward, moving past Brusus.

Five men were in the narrow hall. Three held unsheathed swords. Two had crossbows.

He went after the men with crossbows first, sending two knives streaking toward them. The nearest man fell as one of Rsiran's knives pierced his chest. The other man managed to avoid the knife, stepping out of the way so it hit the wall. Rsiran *pulled*, Sliding as he did, and sent the knife crashing into the back of the man's head. He fell in a heap.

That left the three men with swords.

Brusus parried with one, moving quickly with his knives, dancing with nearly the deadly grace of Haern. But his shirt was already stained with blood from more than one injury, and Rsiran realized he was moving more slowly with each passing moment.

How badly was he hurt?

He shook away the question.

Rsiran could see the other two swordsmen moving into position on the other side, attempting to pin Brusus against the wall. Sliding, he emerged behind them. The nearest man spun, flashing his sword toward him. Rsiran sent two knives spinning toward it to block. The man slapped the nearest out of the air and raised his sword to attack.

Rsiran sent another knife out, but the man easily dodged it as well. He had a few remaining, but they weren't working, not here in the hall.

That left the heartstone sword.

Rsiran had never held it with a real intent to use it. All that he'd done was spar with Haern. This man moved with a deadly sort of speed, comfortable with his sword.

He unsheathed his sword, and the blade glowed with a dark blue light.

The man stepped back for a moment, then darted forward to attack.

Rsiran didn't have time to think, only to react. He caught the slender steel blade with the edge of the heartstone blade and deflected it.

Drawing on his connection to the heartstone, he *pushed* the sword, sending his attacker's sword toward the wooden floor.

The man pulled it back, slipping beneath the attack, and swung his sword back up.

Rsiran somehow caught the blade again.

The man twisted, and Rsiran dropped his sword.

With a dark laugh, the man spun toward Rsiran who stood unarmed.

With his sword lying on the ground and a pocketful of useless knives, he realized Hearn was right, and he would fail because he hadn't practiced enough. It would not be because he wasn't hard enough, or that he hadn't been willing to do what was needed to protect himself. He'd proven that he would. But it would be because he wasn't skilled enough.

With one final effort, he *pulled* on the sword using his slippery connection to the alloy, and felt it slowly move toward him, easing off the ground. Rsiran jerked on the connection, and it struck the man's leg.

Dropping to one knee, the man stabbed forward with his sword.

Rsiran Slid back a step, barely missing the attack.

He sent out one of his knives, and it embedded in his attacker's shoulder. Rsiran *pulled* on the knife, jerking it free, then flipped it around and slammed the hilt against the man's forehead.

Finally, the man crumpled to the ground and didn't move.

Rsiran picked up the heartstone sword and wiped the blood off the blade. The dark blue glow persisted. Rsiran had never seen it glow like that before, and wondered why it suddenly would.

Brusus finished off the two men he faced, stopping two in the time it took Rsiran to handle the one. His gaze swept over the fallen men in the hall and he nodded. "Haern was smart to work with you."

"I should have listened better," Rsiran said.

Brusus snorted. "Probably. Haern is often right." He leaned around the open door and then swung it wide.

Jessa crouched, holding her knife out from her. When she saw Rsiran standing there, she jumped to her feet and ran to him, throwing her arms around him. "Stupid. You should have let Brusus handle this," she said.

"Brusus isn't sure that he could have handled this on his own," Brusus said. "And he's plenty glad that Rsiran decided to help. Now," he went on, leaning to grab the knives that Rsiran had used during his attack and cleaning blood from the blades, "we really need to get moving."

"Thom knew that they were coming," Rsiran said.

"He told you that?"

"Not in so many words, but I think he was trying to buy time. I don't think he expected me to drag him to the rocks above Thyr."

"Did you bind him?"

"Didn't have anything to use. I hit him with a knife, though."

"Is he dead?"

"Not dead. Out. He won't be a problem for us now."

Brusus tossed the knives that he'd collected to Rsiran. "As long as he lives, he'll always be a problem for us. He's nearly as bad as Josun that way." Brusus turned to Rsiran. "I think it's time we get back to Elaeavn. We can stop and grab Thom, and see what he might know."

Rsiran shook his head. He wouldn't be able to carry all of them back to Elaeavn, not without risking them in the Slide. "Can't do that."

"We can't stay here," Brusus said. "Too many men, especially for a place like… Damn," he finished in a whisper.

"What?" Jessa asked.

"Why would Thom need so many men here?" Brusus asked. "Look

at this. It's nothing more than an inn. He has some of his belongings here, and a place to stay, but he wasn't even here when we appeared."

"He knew we were coming," Rsiran said. "He sensed us."

"Did he? Seems to me, if he was able to Read that you were here, he would have been able to Compel you as well." Brusus shook his head. "No, I think there was another reason all these men were here."

Brusus stepped around them and made his way down the hall. Rsiran looked at Jessa, who only shrugged.

They followed Brusus, waiting as he stopped at the end of the hall. The hall ended at a staircase that led both down and up.

"Which way?" Brusus asked.

Rsiran shook his head. "Does it matter? Thom isn't here to tell us what he might have been hiding here."

"Which is why we need to search," Brusus said. "That's why we're here, isn't it? You wanted to see if there might be some way you could reach your father and find out what happened to your sister. Well, now we have Thom out of the way, so you have the chance to find out what he might have been hiding here."

"I came for my father, not for what Thom might be hiding."

"We'll take what we can find, Rsiran. Then we grab Thom and find your father."

Rsiran closed his eyes and focused, listening for lorcith. If Thom *hadn't* used his ability to detect him, then there would have to be some other way that he masked his presence. Only, Rsiran hadn't noticed him even when he had returned.

But then, he'd been focused on lorcith, hadn't he?

With his attention on lorcith, he lost the connection to heartstone. It was possible that Thom had been there the entire time. Somehow, he needed to sense both lorcith and heartstone at the same time. Trying to split his focus like that put him in danger, and he risked missing things—sometimes important things.

But he didn't detect anything.

"I don't know," Rsiran answered.

"Down," Jessa suggested. When they turned to her, she shrugged. "Which way would you go if you wanted to hide something. Besides, look at the floor down there, Brusus. It's hard-packed dirt, not wood. Down is below ground."

"Damn," Brusus said. "Didn't even pay any attention to that."

"Yeah, well you're Sight isn't as good as mine."

Brusus laughed. "Keep telling yourself that."

"Just as you keep telling yourself that you can sneak as well as I can."

Brusus shot her a glare and then started down the stairs. He moved more silently than Rsiran could manage and reached the bottom of the stairs where he paused. "Careful here," he warned.

"What do you see?" Jessa asked.

"Nothing. That's what worries me."

Rsiran reached the bottom of the stairs and paused, too, listening again. For a moment, he thought he sensed a flash of lorcith, but then it was gone. Nothing more than a flicker, it might have been imagined rather than real.

Jessa grabbed his elbow. "I'll keep you safe here. You might have gotten some Sight, but you're still a babe in the dark."

He bit back the laugh, and followed as she led him through the hall. Brusus stopped every few feet and tipped his head. With his Elvraeth blood, he might have been Listening.

When they stopped, Rsiran took the opportunity to focus for lorcith. He didn't get another sense of it, not as he had when he reached the bottom of the stairs. The darkness reminded him of the Ilphaesn mines, only in the mines, he had the sense of lorcith all around him.

Here, there was nothing but blackness. At least he could tell where Brusus and Jessa were from the connection to the lorcith they carried. Had it not been for that connection, Rsiran might have Slid away.

"The hall narrows," Brusus whispered.

"Narrows?" Rsiran asked. "It's pretty narrow already."

"Yeah, and then it stops." Brusus pulled up and slapped his hand against something solid. "Damn. This goes nowhere."

"Then why is it here?" Jessa asked. "Doesn't make any sense for the hall to be here, to lead us into the dark."

"Unless it's some sort of trap," Rsiran said. Thom studied in Venass. Could they have placed something here thinking to draw Rsiran to it? "You said it, Brusus. There were too many men here if it's just an inn where Thom resides when in Thyr. What if they thought to draw us to him and then trap us here?"

"Can you Slide?" Brusus asked.

Rsiran attempted a short Slide, moving back two steps. Nothing restricted him, and he emerged where he intended.

"Yes."

"Then not a trap," Brusus said. "If it were a trap, they would find some way to prevent you from Sliding. They're not worried about the rest of us."

"Then why would they have so many men?" Rsiran asked.

Brusus slapped his hand on something again. Rsiran suspected it was the wall, but couldn't see anything clearly enough to know.

"They're protecting something here," Brusus said. Jessa squeezed Rsiran's arm, though he didn't think that they would have been holding his father here. The scholars had him, so there would be no reason for him to be out in the city. "Have to be," Brusus went on. "Only, how are we going to find what it is?"

CHAPTER 21

Rsiran stood before the wall, running his hands across its surface, feeling for anything that might indicate a door. The hall led somewhere, so there *had* to be a door, only he found nothing.

Jessa stood near him, staring at the wall. He sensed her from the charm and the knives she carried. She breathed softly, and every so often would walk up to the wall and tap on it again, before stepping away.

"There's nothing here," she said softly. "We should go. We can go up the other stairs and see if we find anything. But staying here only puts us at risk."

"Why risk?" Rsiran asked.

"There were too many men up there," she said. "And we made too much noise in the attack. How long before someone else comes?"

"Then we handle it," Brusus said.

Jessa sniffed. "You might be able and willing to handle it, but what if we don't want to fight again? Haern may have trained Rsiran, but he didn't help me, and if there are too many—"

"I'm not going to put you in danger," Brusus said. "We're going to find out if this leads anywhere, and then we'll go."

"The longer we remain, the more likely Thom will wake up and escape before we get back there," Jessa said.

"Rsiran said he was out."

"He is," Rsiran said. "But not bound."

Brusus grunted. "Can't go anywhere up there, anyway. He'd have to walk, which gives us the advantage. Let's find out what's here, and then we can go."

Could they have hidden Alyse here? That might be the reason for so many men, especially if they worried about Rsiran coming for her. But where would she be?

He turned to the wall and ran his hand along it once more, not really expecting to find anything. As far as he could tell, it was a solid wall. "Maybe this was something they were digging out," he suggested.

"Still doesn't explain why there were so many men," Brusus said. "Think about what you know of Venass. They would hide something like this. We need to figure out what they would have used."

Not lorcith. He had sensed nothing of lorcith to tell him that it might be here, but what of heartstone? Thom had proven that Venass were skilled with heartstone and that they would use it in ways that Rsiran might not have thought of.

He pushed away the sense of lorcith, that of the charm hanging from Jessa's necklace, the bracelets she now wore, and the knives all around him. Then he pushed away the sense of the alloy, that of the sword and the chain holding Jessa's charm. He was left with nothing, an emptiness.

He listened for heartstone.

Pure heartstone was different from both the alloy and lorcith. It called to him in a subtler way. There was a quiet intensity about it, a draw, and a demand for his attention.

It was here.

There was not much, barely more than a fingernail's worth, but Rsiran was certain that was what he detected.

And it was on the other side of the wall.

He considered where Jessa stood. If he told her what he needed to do, she would grab on and Slide with him. This he would do alone.

It would be risky. Sliding to unknown locations often was, but he'd done it once today when he'd appeared in Thom's room. Now he would risk himself a second time, but only himself. He would not put Jessa or Brusus in danger for this.

And he couldn't step into the Slide, not without knowing what was on the other side. *Pulling* himself would be much safer for him, and might even allow him the chance to escape if something went wrong with the Slide.

"I'll be right back," he whispered.

Then he anchored to the heartstone on the other side of the wall and *pulled* himself to it.

Rsiran rarely used heartstone to anchor. Lorcith was stout and gave him strength and a reassuring sense when he Slid. This Slide was difficult, but no more so than *pulling* himself through alloy.

When he emerged, he sensed the small lump of heartstone, but couldn't see it. Everything around him was dark. For a moment, he panicked, fearing that he might have trapped himself somewhere, but he could move freely.

He needed light, something to give him a way to see.

The heartstone sword. It had glowed before, would it still be glowing?

He unsheathed it. The blade glowed with the same dark blue light that it had before. The light pushed back some of the darkness, enough for Rsiran to see around him. He was in a small room, barely more than a dozen paces across, and all stone. Other than the sense of heartstone, he detected no lorcith. Nothing else moved in the room.

Rsiran turned, preparing to leave, when the light from the sword reflected off something in an alcove along the wall. He leaned toward it and touched the reflection.

Metal, and cool to the touch.

He frowned, pulling the metal to him, and nearly dropped it. It was a square sheet of metal—probably steel mixed with streaks of silver leaving it with an undulating pattern.

Without touching it, and without making a mold as he had with the sheet of metal he'd found in the hut, he wondered if this would be another map.

If it was, it meant his father had been here.

Rsiran pocketed the piece of metal and Slid back to the other side of the wall, returning to Jessa.

As soon as he emerged, she punched him. "You can't go off like that!" she hissed.

"There was something on the other side of the wall," he told her.

"What did you find?" Brusus asked.

"A map. My father was here, I think."

"Another map?" Brusus asked. "Like the first?"

Rsiran nodded, not certain whether they could see it in the darkness. "Like the other, but different. This is steel and silver, I think."

"Anything else?"

Rsiran shook his head. "Nothing other than a small piece of heartstone."

"Show us," Brusus said.

Rsiran grabbed them and *pulled* them through the wall, Sliding with more confidence now that he knew what was on the other side of the wall.

Brusus grunted as they emerged. "How did you see anything in here, Rsiran? Thought you barely had any Sight."

"I don't," he said. He pulled his sword from under his cloak and held it out. The blue light again pushed back some of the shadows in the small room, making it easier to see everything around them.

"Rsiran?" Jessa said.

"Yeah?"

"Why do you have your sword out?"

"You don't see it?" he asked. He twisted the sword, letting the blue light play off her cheeks, catching the charm she wore. Brusus appeared as little more than a shadow.

"See what? All I see is you holding a sword out toward the two of us."

Brusus stepped back. "Damn, Rsiran. Put that thing away! We're in a tight enough space as it is."

He slipped the sword back into the loop on his belt. "You wanted to know how I saw anything in this darkness. You don't see the light coming off the sword?" He kept his cloak pulled back so that the light of the sword still managed to spread around him. The longer he was here, the more his eyes adjusted to it, and the easier it became for him to see.

Brusus frowned and shook his head.

Jessa touched him on the shoulder. "I don't see anything, Rsiran. Are you sure that's what you're seeing?"

He looked down at the sword, wondering if he was imagining the dark blue glow from the blade. It *was* there, and it let him see the concern on Jessa's face, and the way that Brusus paced from side to side, though he didn't really need the sword to see that. He had a sense of that from the knives Brusus carried, and how they moved with his steps.

"Look," he said, pulling the sheet of metal from his pocket and handing it to Jessa. "This is what I found."

She took it and held it up to her face. "I don't know how you managed to see this in here. I can barely make it out. All I can see are slivers of shadows," Jessa said.

Rsiran took it back and pocketed it. He would have to make another mold like he'd done with the first one so that he could understand what the map was designed to show. "If it was here, that means that my father was," Rsiran said.

"Or they want you to think that he was," Brusus countered. "Think about it. Why would your father leave another map for you? This is the man who wanted nothing from you for years, and now he's suddenly leaving things for you to find?"

Rsiran had to agree that it didn't make sense. "Then why is this here?" He didn't have an answer, only more questions, and he was no closer to finding his sister.

Rsiran went and picked up the small piece of heartstone that he had sensed originally. Had he not known where to find it, he could have stepped on it. Other than someone like himself able to sense heartstone, he doubted that anyone else would have been able to find it.

But if it wasn't left for him to find, then who? As far as he knew, he had a unique ability to detect heartstone.

"We should go," Brusus said. "If we wait too long…"

He didn't need to finish. Thom waited outside the city and Rsiran was determined to get answers from him, anything that might help him reach his father, find out what he was involved in, so that he could find his sister.

And then… Then it would be time for Rsiran to find a way to keep his friends protected.

Taking Jessa's hand, and grabbing Brusus's arm, he Slid.

They emerged outside the city, standing on the rock overlooking Thyr, with the Tower of Venass in the background.

Rsiran readied a pair of knives, half-expecting Thom to leap at them.

"Where did you leave him?" Brusus asked.

Rsiran thought that Thom would have been here, but there was nothing. Not even a drop of blood that would make it seem like anyone had been here.

Nothing. How was that possible? He was sure he'd knocked him out enough such that he'd be here when Rsiran returned.

He focused on heartstone, pushing away all the sense of lorcith and the alloy as quickly as he could, and listened for heartstone. There was nothing.

Since Thom seemed to have some way to avoid Rsiran's ability to sense him, Rsiran hadn't expected to find anything to explain where Thom might have gone. Likely as not, he'd disappeared into Venass. Rsiran wasn't willing to chase him there.

And now there was no way to find what happened to his father, or to learn what happened to Alyse.

Because he hadn't taken the time to bind Thom, she might be gone for good.

Rsiran was surprised at how much that thought hurt.

CHAPTER 22

After searching the area for Thom, they Slid from Thyr, returning to Elaeavn and his smithy. Brusus had expected to find something that would reveal where Thom had gone, but Rsiran didn't. The fact that Thom was disappeared should not have surprised him at all.

Could Venass have been monitoring somehow?

Rsiran knew so little about what they were capable of doing, only that they trained deadly assassins. If they were able to control lorcith and direct his Sliding in spite of his best abilities to protect himself, why couldn't they monitor one of their own and rescue him?

And now that he'd lost Thom and was unable to detect the heartstone implant any longer, he had nothing. Whatever Thom did to shield himself was effective.

As always when he returned to the smithy since placing the bars of alloy all around it, there was a steady drawing sensation, as if Sliding through the narrow slats of the alloy that he'd arranged around the smithy threatened to pull him apart. Each time returning got easier for him. In that way, Sliding with the alloy, and through the alloy, was much like with lorcith: the more he practiced, the stronger he became.

Brusus glanced around as they emerged and shook his head, a hint of a smile on his mouth. "Still not used to that."

"Do it enough times, and it's not so bad," Jessa said.

"Easy enough for you to say. You *want* to be around him." Jessa shot Brusus a glare and he smiled, spreading his hands apart in a shrug. "You know I'm kidding." He watched Rsiran, concern wrinkling his brow as he fixed him with a nod. "You going to be okay? I know you wanted to find out what Thom might have known, but chances are good that he didn't know anything."

Rsiran nodded. But if that was true, he couldn't shake the sense that he'd missed an opportunity. Whatever had been held in that room had been meant for someone with the ability to sense heartstone. Like him.

But Brusus had been right when he said that his father wouldn't have left him messages. The man had spent the last few years trying to change Rsiran. For him to suddenly count on him to find something hidden… It made no sense.

There had to be another explanation, but Rsiran had none.

"How you doing with the rest?" Brusus asked.

"The rest of what?"

Brusus motioned toward the sword. "Needing to use that. The fighting. The killing." He took a deep breath and sighed. "Something like that can change a man. Trust me. I've been there. You don't have to hold it in if you need to talk."

Rsiran shook his head. "I'll be fine."

"Yeah, well I know that you will. And I think Haern was right in teaching you. You're skilled, and you have potential, but there are others out there with more skill, and more experience. With everything that we have going on, you're going to need to keep practicing."

Rsiran nodded. "I get the feeling that Haern enjoys that a little too much."

Brusus smiled. "Probably he does. It was the same when he started teaching me, you know?"

"Haern taught you?"

"As much as he could. Figured the more we got involved with, I should know how to use knives and a sword. In Elaeavn, you don't really get the chance to use a sword very often, but the knives have come in handy. He's never taught me some of the other skills he acquired, though."

"I think he wants to forget them as much as he can," Jessa said.

Brusus shrugged. "Some things are useful, even when you want to forget." He paused then clapped Rsiran on the shoulder and leaned into him to whisper in his ear. "I know you don't like what you did, but you had to do it."

"I know."

"You did only what was needed to keep us safe. I need to find Haern. He was worried about us going to Thyr."

"He probably thought we'd get pulled to Venass again," Jessa said.

Brusus nodded. "I think that was a part of it."

As Brusus started to the door, he tipped his head to Jessa. She released Rsiran's hand and made her way over to Brusus where they leaned together and spoke quietly for a moment. In the smithy, surrounded by lorcith and the alloy, their voices carried. Rsiran didn't think that they really intended for him to hear.

"Make sure he knows that we'll still help him," Brusus said to her.

"Are you sure that's the safest thing to do?" Jessa asked.

"We promised him that we'd help. And if Venass has her—"

"You don't know that they do," Jessa said.

"No, but there was an awful lot of protection there for some reason. And Thom seemed to be expecting… well, if not us, then someone. Just don't let him go off after the Forgotten again without help."

Jessa said something more, but Rsiran couldn't hear it. Brusus turned from her and walked from the smithy. Jessa closed the door and locked it tightly. The locks were all that kept them safe within the smithy. The bars of lorcith would block someone from Sliding, but a skilled lock picker could still manage to sneak past the door. It was the reason he'd set another couple of bars through the door that could be set into the floor and up around the doorframe. That way, the *only* way into the smithy was by Sliding.

"You want to talk about it?" she asked. "I saw your face after… after the first attack."

Rsiran turned away. His hand went to his pocket where he'd tucked the second map. "What's there to say? I saw you in danger, and I reacted. Haern was right. I needed to learn how to protect us."

Jessa motioned toward the hearth at the far end of the smithy and started setting a few logs in place, getting the fire crackling softly. Their bed was shoved into the corner near the hearth and she knelt on it, patting a spot to motion for him to sit.

When he did, he curled his arms around his knees. Jessa leaned on his shoulder. "There's something more than what you're telling me. I can see it in the way your eyes tightened."

"Brusus and Haern want to make sure that I won't hesitate if it's needed. How can I argue with that?" he asked. "Especially now, after what happened today?"

She sniffed and smacked him softly on the shoulder. "Brusus doesn't always know what he's talking about. If you go in, knives flying all over the place, what does that make you *but* a killer?"

"He's right, though. What happens if I hesitate? Too often, we've been in danger because I hesitated. What happens when that puts you in danger—"

"I think we've already seen me in danger. And you didn't hesitate this time. Damn, Rsiran, but you jumped out into the hallway, Sliding with your knives flying as if you were excited to be there."

There had been a part of him that *had* been excited to be there, the same part that had enjoyed the challenge, the test of his abilities. If he could Slide, and throw his knives, could he keep them safe?

So far, the answer was that he couldn't. As much as he thought his abilities gave him some advantage, the skill of others mitigated it.

"You can't be so willing to go into danger," Jessa said. "You took Thom away, and you don't know what he might have been able to do. What if he'd managed to Compel you? What if he'd attacked?" She shook her head. "And then you jump into the hall as if you had trained your entire life to fight, but you haven't. You've only been working with Haern a short while…"

Rsiran pulled her against him, only now understanding what bothered her. He might be afraid to lose her, but she was afraid to lose him too. He had focused so much on making certain that Jessa, and Brusus, and even Haern were safe, not caring as much if he was in danger. Since leaving his home, abandoning his apprenticeship, he had placed himself in danger enough times that he no longer feared it as he once had. Danger like that had taught him to listen to lorcith, had taught him to hear the call of the alloy and learn that he could control it, and had taught him that he could Slide past the alloy, even without a lorcith anchor.

But fear for Jessa changed that. It made him… almost reckless in a way. Haern thought he might hesitate, but that wasn't what he did at all. When Jessa was in danger, he attacked with abandon. He didn't want anything to happen to her and refused to be the reason that she was placed in harm's way.

And when he had attacked, when he'd let himself go, he had enjoyed the fighting. He couldn't hide that fact from himself. When he had saved Jessa from Josun, hadn't he enjoyed harming him? And even with Shael, had he sent the knife at him with more force than needed?

Was he losing control?

Another troubling thought crept in, one that harkened back to claims his father made about him, and about his abilities. What if there was something to it?

What if they changed him in some way?

Holding the crystal had changed him. He could no longer question that, especially with the improvement in his Sight. But now he saw dark blue light glowing from his sword when there should not—and maybe, could not—be there.

Had he changed?

Did Sliding and using lorcith change him in ways that he still hadn't understood?

When he first discovered his ability to Slide, he had thought that it was a curse. His father had convinced him that it was a curse. But he'd begun to believe—at least, to let himself believe—that it was not, and that Sliding could help and did not make him the thief and criminal his father feared.

What if he'd been wrong?

Rsiran thought about others he'd learned could Slide. Josun. Inna. The others within the Forgotten camp. Even those within Venass who had somehow coopted the ability to Slide, even if they never possessed it in the first place.

What if there was something about Sliding that twisted a person, that brought them to darkness?

Rsiran would never really have considered it likely, but that was before. He'd felt far too eager attacking, almost as if some sort of bloodlust had overcome him.

Jessa pushed away from him and rested her hands on his shoulders as she looked at him. With her Sight, she saw things that he couldn't even imagine. "Something else is bothering you, isn't it?"

He swallowed. "Not entirely," he admitted. Jessa wouldn't want to hear about this concern, he was certain. She believed that his Sliding had saved them, and had helped them, but she couldn't know what he felt.

"Then what?"

Rsiran hesitated. He *wanted* to share with her, but he couldn't. That would only open old arguments, ones that he didn't want to have again.

But if he couldn't tell Jessa, who could he tell? They had been through everything together. She was the reason he hesitated, the reason that Brusus and Haern thought that he had a soft heart. Without her, what would have happened to him? Would he have become a monster sooner?

"When I first learned to Slide," he started, thinking back to the time when he'd awoken atop Krali Rock with the wind blowing against his face. He'd been terrified, but also exhilarated at the same time. How long had he looked up at the tall rock peak, wishing he could reach the summit? Atop Krali, he could look over all of Elaeavn and see the city as a different place, and for the first time, he felt he was meant to be something. The terror had forced him to climb down the side of Krali slowly, always afraid that he would fall. And when he'd told his father what happened… "My father called it a dark ability, and said that it would turn me into a thief, or worse."

"You've told me this before," Jessa said. "Besides, what's so wrong with being a thief?" She smiled as she said it, but there was an edge to the question as well.

Rsiran shook his head. "When it first happened, I didn't know you, or Brusus, or Haern. All I knew was my apprenticeship." He looked over at the forge, his eyes lingering on the anvil and the tools arranged neatly on the bench alongside it. "That was all that I wanted to be. That was my future. I would take over his smithy, and then…"

He couldn't finish. That future was gone, taken from him. Most days, he knew that he was better off without having taken over his father's smithy. He would never have learned what he had about lorcith had he listened to his father. He would never have learned how to control heartstone had he listened to him. But then, he might have been safe. He might have had a home.

Only, it would have been one without Jessa.

And he would never have known about his parents, would he? How his mother was the child of Forgotten parents, allowed to return to the city because of his father. Or how his father had committed his service to the Forgotten.

Would he have been drawn in, regardless?

She watched him, waiting for him to be ready to go on.

"When he called it a dark ability, I didn't know what to think. I felt cursed by the Great Watcher, gifted with something that I couldn't use."

"But it's not a curse. We can't keep going over this, Rsiran. The things you do, the way that you've helped us…" She shook her head. "There's nothing dark about it. It's… It's beautiful." She glanced toward the door, and her eyes narrowed as they often did when she was thinking. She tipped her head down to sniff at the flower she had within the charm. "When I was younger, I wanted nothing more than to return to Elaeavn. I remember my parents telling me that we couldn't return, and I never really understood. They said it was better outside the city. That we were able to see things that those within Elaeavn never experienced." She smiled at the memory.

"And then they were taken from me, and I was nearly... nearly sold into prostitution." She swallowed. "Haern... Haern saved me. There was darkness in him that night, too, but without it, I wouldn't be here. And now I understand that what you can do, the way that distances don't matter, that's a gift from the Great Watcher that is greater than any other. You can see the other places in the world, and you can return home. Wherever that is."

Jessa patted him on the chest and stood on her toes to kiss his cheek. "You have a gift. You may have darkness, but we all do. It's a part of what we've experienced, not because of some gift the Great Watcher gave us. These gifts are simply that. *We* choose how to use them. When we fail, it is because of us, not because of something the ability does to us."

Jessa fell silent. Rsiran watched her, waiting for her to say something more, but she didn't. Instead, she rested her head on his chest and breathed slowly.

"You're right," he started. "Of course you are. Back then, back when I first learned of my ability and what I could do, I was different than I am now. I believed what my father told me. Only when I learned what Josun said of Sliding did I think that maybe he'd been wrong, that maybe he'd only listened to the same superstitions about Sliding that the Elvraeth put out there."

"That *is* what happened, Rsiran."

He shook his head and turned toward the fire glowing in the hearth. He didn't feel the warmth from it, not as he should. After the way he'd killed, the way that he willingly attacked, and the surge of satisfaction that he'd felt when he had, he wondered if he really should feel warmth. Maybe he didn't deserve to know warmth, or comfort, or a home.

"That's what I thought, but then I learned my father had spent time outside of Elaeavn, and had been to places like Thyr. If he's been to

Thyr, what are the chances that he knew others who could Slide? I'd never heard of my ability before waking up atop Krali. It's not so common that a simple smith should know about it."

Jessa's brow creased and she watched him. "I hadn't, either," she admitted.

And neither had Brusus, or Haern, and they had been away from the city. Only Della knew anything about his ability, but Della was turning out to be someone much more than she ever let on.

"What if my father wasn't afraid of my ability because of some superstition placed out there by the Elvraeth? What if he'd known others who could Slide and had seen what had happened to them?"

Jessa shook her head. "You mean the Forgotten."

Rsiran shrugged. "I don't know how deeply drawn into the Forgotten he had been, but what if it's possible?"

"Don't you think Della would have said something if that were true? If you trust anyone, trust her and what she knows."

Rsiran breathed out softly. Della had told him more about Sliding than he'd learned from any other, and had been the one to make a point of showing him how his Sliding could be influenced and detected. But she kept enough secrets that he wasn't entirely certain that he *could* trust her. He wanted to trust, and he knew that he probably needed to, especially given all that she knew about what had happened to him, but what if she kept something back from him, something like the crystals hidden within the palace?

Had they known about them sooner, they might have understood what the Forgotten wanted. They might have understood why Venass was so eager to replicate the abilities the Great Watcher had given them.

"Maybe she would," he said softly. He couldn't share those concerns with Jessa. She viewed Della differently than he did, and trusted her more than Rsiran now did. "Or maybe there is something about my ability when combined with what I can do with lorcith that makes it darker. Maybe that's what my father feared."

If only his father hadn't been claimed by Venass. He needed to find him. If not for the answers to those questions, then to find his sister.

But would he allow more darkness into his heart if he went searching for Alyse? Would he fight as hard as he had for Jessa if Alyse were in danger?

Jessa pulled him toward her and hugged him for a long moment. "You can't think like that, Rsiran. There's nothing that the Great Watcher would give us that we shouldn't use. I think of all the good that you've done with your ability, and I know that there is nothing to Sliding and what you can do with lorcith that makes it wrong."

Rsiran squeezed his arms around his legs. If it wasn't his ability, or the lorcith, then what if the problem—and the darkness—came from him?

CHAPTER 23

Rsiran stood over the anvil, holding an iron pot of molten heartstone. The air smelled of the sweet metal, and he breathed it in. He'd feared his Sliding ability was turning him dark, but what of his ability with lorcith? What if that was as dark as Sliding?

He couldn't think like that, not when that ability had saved him nearly as much—or more—than his ability to Slide.

The form that he'd created to hold the metal sheet that he'd found in the small room in Thyr was more secure than the last one that he'd used. Rsiran had taken the time to create a tighter seal, not wanting to waste any of the heartstone, and suspecting that the silver would meld to the heartstone when they touched, fusing much like the grindl had. With the last map, the iron had been the harder of the two metals, with this, it would be the steel.

Jessa had disappeared while he worked, leaving him alone in the smithy. Rsiran kept track of her charm, noting where she was within the city. Working with heartstone to liquefy it didn't require the same focus as attempting a true forging. With this, he simply had to heat it to the right temperature, and then he could pour it over the map.

Rsiran didn't know what to expect. Awareness of the last map still burned in his mind, but he had the heartstone brick that he'd made to create it as well. He could use that to visualize the map again if needed, but it did no good if he couldn't tell *what* the map was to be used for.

What if this one was the same?

But it was all that he had to go on. If this didn't bring him any closer to figuring out what had happened to his sister, the next step was one that Brusus and Jessa didn't want him to take, but it was the only one that he could think of: find a way to draw out Sarah and Valn. If he found them, he could force them to show him where his sister had gone.

Rsiran held the iron pot over the top of the form and hesitated. Heartstone was different from lorcith in many ways, not the least of which being the fact that it didn't seem to care that he'd melted it to use simply for a form. It hadn't mattered which piece of heartstone he used—and he'd gone with the smallest that would give him the information that he wanted—not like it would with lorcith. With lorcith, he would have needed to listen to the metal and find the one piece most willing to work with him.

Pouring the heartstone carefully, he made certain that it covered the entirety of the steel and silver plate. Unlike with the grindl, he hadn't been able to feel any pattern with his fingers. He could *see* the pattern, but if this didn't work, he risked destroying the plate.

With the heartstone layered over the plate, he stepped back and brought the iron pot to the coals to keep heating it so that he could clean the remaining heartstone from it. As he did, there was a flash of yellow light from the form, and the four sides framing it fell away, hitting the floor of the smithy with a clatter.

The heartstone exploded outward, and Rsiran was thrown back. Hot metal flew toward him.

He ducked, but as he did, he *pushed* against the heartstone. Had he not had a connection to it, and probably if he had not held the crystal, he wouldn't have been able to do it. As it was, he barely managed to keep it from hitting him.

Taking a few steadying breaths, he released his connection to the heartstone where it fell harmlessly to the ground around the anvil.

Rsiran dusted himself off, cursing aloud, as he reached for a blob of heartstone with the tongs. He needn't have bothered. The heartstone had already cooled, but the explosion left it running toward the edge of the anvil, covering the plate entirely.

Rsiran lifted it, forced to pry it free from the surface of the anvil.

As he stood there, the door to the smithy opened and Jessa slipped inside. Once in the door, she flipped the bars in place that locked the door more securely. She watched him, an amused smile on her face. "What are you doing with that?"

"Trying to keep it from exploding," he answered.

"It… *exploded*?"

He motioned with his leg to the frames of the form lying on the floor. "After I poured the heartstone over it. I should have paid closer attention."

"Did you know that it would do that?"

Rsiran turned the twisted lump of heartstone pinched between the ends of the tongs from one side to the other. "Heartstone doesn't react to steel. And I've never had silver to test it with."

"But it did something similar with the grindl."

Rsiran nodded.

"Should it have done that?"

"I don't know."

"Do you think that Venass…"

Rsiran didn't know. With all the protection around the building, it almost seemed as if they didn't want him reaching the metal. But what if that was the point? What if Venass had tried to draw him to it?

"Who would know?" she asked.

"Not a smith. They rarely mix metals. That was the purview of the Alchemist Guild."

Jessa's smile faded. "Oh, no. Not the alchemists."

"I'm not going to go to them for help with this," he said.

She stared at him as if she didn't believe what he said. One hand reached for her charm, and her fingers played with the violet flower she'd found today. "Did you figure anything out from it?"

Rsiran touched the heartstone with his free hand and noted that it had cooled. He set it back on the anvil and picked it up with his hands, turning it. The metal might have exploded from the form, but what remained had taken on a distinct shape.

"That's strange," he said.

Jessa leaned over his shoulder and studied the heartstone. "What is? The crazy lump of metal you're holding or that you nearly got blown up by a small sheet of metal?"

Rsiran smiled. After the chaos within Thyr, it felt good to smile again. He tried not to think of what might have happened had he *not* had the ability with heartstone. "Both? But not that," he went on. "There's a pattern to the way the metal expanded."

"Expanded?"

He held the heartstone out and shook it. "That's what happened here. When the metal got hot, it expanded. Usually it does that, but there's more control to it. This," he went on, "this was an uncontrolled expansion. I've never seen it with heartstone."

When he worked with heartstone before, there hadn't been any unusual properties to the metal. It always reacted the same. The only time it hadn't had been when he attempted to combine it with lorcith.

"What's the pattern?" Jessa asked.

Rsiran studied the heartstone, pushing away the sense of lorcith, ignoring the louder draw that it placed on him. He focused on the shape of the heartstone, straining for the connection.

When it came to him, he frowned. There was no map, not like with the other plate.

"This isn't what we needed," he said.

"No? Then what is it?"

Rsiran couldn't tell what shape the heartstone had taken, only that there was a pattern, and the pattern was one he didn't recognize.

If he had better Sight, he might be able to see what shape the heartstone had taken, but then had he better Sight, he wouldn't have needed to create the form and combine the metals in the first place.

He set it down and surveyed the various forgings on the table. There was the other brick of heartstone, the shape of the map still drawing him. Nothing else of heartstone called to him in the same way, not even the sword that he'd made.

The table contained dozens of other creations of his. The oldest were knives of different sizes, but the newer creations had taken on a different complexity as he began to master lorcith. Now when he worked with it, he often had something in mind, an intent of what he wanted to make, and selected the metal based on whether it would be able to help him form the shape.

"Did you find anything," he asked Jessa.

She shook her head. "Found Brusus, but not Haern. He hasn't seen him since we returned."

Rsiran wondered if that should worry him. With everything that they'd been through, any time they couldn't find one of their friends made him nervous. It shouldn't; if they were attacked, Haern was the most skilled of any of them, and would be the ablest to deflect an attack. Unless it came from someone like Thom. He'd shown that he could control Haern.

He would need to make something like the bracelets for Haern.

Rsiran turned to the bin of lorcith and focused on what he wanted, much as he had when trying to make the bracelets for Jessa. He placed the image of Haern in his mind and focused on the concept of protecting him, of preventing someone from Reading and Compelling him.

None of the lorcith responded.

Rsiran tried again, listening, knowing that at least one of the dozens of lumps of lorcith in the bin would have to respond, but none of them did. All ignored his request.

Either the lorcith didn't want to help Haern, or Rsiran wasn't convincing enough in his desire to help Haern.

He sighed, and leaned on the table.

"What is it?" Jessa asked.

"I wanted to help Haern. I wanted to find something like I made for you."

She held up her wrists, studying the bracelets. "I wasn't sure about them at first. They dig into my arms, you know? But when Thom came at us, they went so cold that they burned. It was as if they absorbed whatever he tried to do to me." She smiled. "Glad you made them for me. After what happened with Evaelyn, I don't want to risk anything like that happening again. I don't want to risk anything happening to *you*."

"That's why I thought I could try to forge something similar for Haern, but none of the lorcith responds."

"Maybe none of these pieces are meant to help him."

He nodded, a part of him wondering if it was something about him, or whether the metal didn't want to help Haern.

Since meeting Haern, Rsiran had conflicted feelings about him. Haern made no attempt to hide the fact that he wanted to ensure Jessa's safety, going so far as to essentially attack Rsiran under the guise of trying to help her. That had helped Rsiran learn about his connection to the lorcith, but a part of him remained uncertain about how much he could truly trust Haern.

Maybe the lorcith responded to that.

Rsiran pushed the thought away. Maybe all he needed was to find a different piece of lorcith that *would* be more responsive. But that meant going to the mines.

And he needed to return to the mines, anyway. It had been too long since he'd last been there, and too long since he felt the breath of the mines blowing against him, something that he once would have found difficult to believe that he'd miss. Besides, he still hadn't learned why the supply of lorcith had been controlled and limited by the Elvraeth.

"Anyway," Jessa said, tugging on his hands and drawing his attention back to her, "Brusus said that Upper Town seems agitated."

"Agitated?"

She shrugged. "Don't know what it means, only that's how he described it. You know Brusus, though. He can be dramatic at times."

Brusus was usually pretty well connected to the goings on throughout the city. Some of that was through the bribes that he made, and some came from other connections that he had. Brusus kept most of that to himself.

"Are you still trying to convince yourself that you're some kind of horrible person?" Jessa asked.

Rsiran inhaled deeply. When he worked at the forge, regardless of what metal he chose, there wasn't the opportunity to allow himself to feel bad. Standing in front of the heat pushed away all thoughts, good and bad, leaving him with nothing more than a blank mind. And peace.

"Not right now," he said.

Jessa studied him for a moment. "Does that mean that you're going to find a way to feel bad about yourself later?"

Would he have to kill again? Would he feel the same surge of excitement when he did, a thrill that he should not have, if he did?

Those were questions he had no answers for, and wouldn't until it came to actually confronting whatever he would be faced with, and whether or not it meant that his friends—what he considered his family now—were in danger.

And if they were in danger, could he really feel bad about what he might be asked to do?

When answers didn't come, Jessa smiled at him. "Come on, Rsiran. We've got a different issue to work through."

"What issue is that?"

She focused on the table where many of his forgings rested. She touched a few of the more recent creations, shaking her head as she did. "Such skill," she whispered. "You didn't have this same skill when you first started."

"That's the issue?"

"No, but another reminder." She sighed and looked up at him. "Where do you think he went?"

She meant Thom. "I don't know if he can Slide, but Venass would have helped. The scholars know something about Sliding," he said. At least, they knew something about the way to influence Sliding, even if they couldn't Slide themselves. The way that he'd been drawn to Venass had proven they understood Sliding, as did how they had been *pushed* away from the Tower as they left. "I just don't know how they would have known where to find him."

"What did Thom say about knowing that we were coming?"

"Only that he knew *I* was coming. He said that I was loud."

Rsiran still wasn't sure whether that meant that he'd actually heard him, and that the barriers that he used and depended on to keep him safe weren't effective, or whether there was another way he knew.

Could it be the fact that he'd Slid them all to Thyr?

Della mentioned the ripples that she noticed when he Slid, and how they were more prominent with each person that he brought with him. Carrying three through a Slide would have been enough for Della to hear, and maybe enough for someone less skilled, someone like Sarah.

And he *had* detected the sense of lorcith before they reached Thyr, however briefly. What if Valn and Sarah were with Venass and had been the ones to warn Thom?

"The ripples that Della mentioned, right?" Jessa asked.

He nodded.

"And those ripples are bigger when you're carrying others, aren't they?"

"That's probably what it was," he said. He hoped that it wasn't something else, that Thom had managed to penetrate the barriers that he used to protect himself, but would he really have known?

He should have thought about it before now, but maybe there was a reason that he hadn't. Maybe *that* was the reason he'd been so eager to attack. "We need to go to Della," he said.

"Why?"

"We've been saying all along that Thom probably knew we were coming." Jessa nodded. "And if he did, what if he Compelled me?"

"I thought you could protect your mind so that he couldn't?"

Rsiran had thought the same, but then Thom had managed to mask the presence of heartstone from him. If he could do that, and if the implant somehow made him that much stronger at Compelling, it was possible that Rsiran *had* been affected.

"I thought so, too, but after what happened," he said, looking over to where the heartstone had exploded, "I need to be certain."

CHAPTER 24

After grabbing three small knives—he no longer liked going without something that he could *push* if needed—Rsiran Slid them to Della's home. Each time that he visited Della, he had the memory of the first time he had come, when he had needed her Healing services more than anything. That had been before he had been willing to embrace his ability, and before he had known about the extent of his connection to lorcith.

As usual, a cozy hearth glowed with a warm light. The smell of the mint tea that Della preferred permeated the air, mingling with the scents of the herbs and ointments that she mixed for her healing. A single lantern glowed near the back corner, giving even more light.

Della stood behind the counter where she worked with a thick ceramic bowl, pressing a long pestle into it with a steady motion. She barely looked up as they emerged.

"I'm sorry to intrude," he said to her.

She sniffed, set the pestle down, and dusted her hands across her dress. Usually, she was dressed in vibrant colors, and today was no different, with stripes of orange and red spiraling around her dress. Her gray hair was tied back and twisted into a tight bun. "I've told you before, Rsiran, that you have no need to be sorry. Besides, I can always tell when you're making your way here."

She pulled a jar off the shelf behind her and propped open the lid, taking out a pinch and sprinkling it into the bowl on the counter. Then she picked up her pestle and began grinding again, moving with a steady determination.

"That's why we're here," Jessa said.

Della looked up and arched a brow. "Not many places you don't go together, now are there?"

Jessa smiled. "I thought you told me to keep him in my Sight."

"That is what I said now, isn't it?"

Rsiran hadn't heard that before, but shouldn't be surprised that Della was giving Jessa instructions on watching him. Probably Brusus had some as well.

"So you're worried about what I detect?"

"Not what you detect," Rsiran said. He stepped over to the counter and looked into the bowl. She worked a thick greenish paste and pulled another jar off a different shelf and placed three pinches into the bowl. "But what others can detect when I Slide."

"Not much to worry about in the city. There aren't too many with my particular talent." She looked up from the bowl and fixed Rsiran with a steady stare.

"There's another in Elaeavn who can detect Sliding," Rsiran said. Why hadn't he told Della about that sooner? Would she know Sarah?

Della paused and studied him. "Another? There hasn't been another outside the…" She shook her head. "Doesn't matter. Who have you seen in Elaeavn?"

"A woman named Sarah. She was with another, a man named Valn, when I saw them. They were following me."

Della nodded slowly. "That's why you've been training with Haern?"

"You knew about that?"

Della sniffed. "Not much that I don't know about when it comes to you." She tapped the side of her head. "Remember what I told you about my connections, those that formed after I held the Great Crystal?" He nodded. "Those connections let me See, much like Haern, only mine is different."

"Do you know of her?"

Della set the pestle down and stared at him for a moment. "I don't know who else might follow the ripples of your Sliding, Rsiran. If there are others, you are already in more danger than we realized."

"I know."

Della sniffed. "And still you Slide here, carrying another with you, knowing how the ripples form."

"Did you feel them?"

Della grabbed a spoon and started stirring the paste in the bowl, pulling it out and sliding it into another jar. She worked carefully, almost as if avoiding touching the paste. When she was finished, she carried the spoon and the pestle over to the fire where she set them in the flames. The spoon began burning, sending blue and green sparks sputtering into her room. The pestle simple charred, the same sparks shooting off it until the paste was burned free.

She glanced at Rsiran, as if waiting for him to ask what she was making. He was curious, but Della was a master Healer, and there were more herbs and medicines in her home than he could even begin to name.

"You think you've found some way to hide yourself? Is that why you risk coming?"

He tapped the sword he still wore beneath his cloak. There was less need to carry the sword in Elaeavn, and more risk—if he were caught with a sword, the punishment was severe—but he liked the idea that his Sliding couldn't be deterred when he carried it with him.

"You think heartstone keeps you safe?" she asked.

He thought that it had, but had never tested his theory. "They can't Slide past it."

"Yes, but *you* can. What if it matters little about the metal and more about the individual doing the Sliding?" Della asked.

"It's more than the heartstone," Rsiran said. "Since…" When had it been that he started Sliding without stepping into the Slide? Could it really have been Venass? He didn't remember doing it before then, and when he'd been there, it had taken all of his focus to maintain the connection to the distant lorcith that he detected. "Since Venass," he went on, "I've found a different way to Slide."

Della turned to him, and crossed her arms over her chest. "Different?"

He nodded. Maybe he should have been Sliding that way ever since he realized there was someone after him, but sometimes speed mattered. Rsiran had gotten stronger at Sliding—practicing daily and always bringing Jessa with him had increased his strength—and with strength came a certain speed. Could he gain the same speed *pulling* himself?

"This is less like walking than a drawing sort of Slide." He shrugged. "I don't think I can explain it any better than that."

"And you don't think this method can be influenced?"

"I don't know. I thought the heartstone helped prevent me from having my Slides influenced. I'm hopeful that this other technique keeps me from having my Slides detected."

Together, he might have a way to move safely, and not worry about what would happen when he Slid.

Della sighed. "You risk much not knowing how this actually works, Rsiran. Do you know with certainty that this technique is effective, or do you simply hope that it is?"

"I… Can we test it?" Rsiran suggested.

Della frowned, taking a moment to screw a lid onto the jar of green paste, before nodding. "I can try." She glanced up, a wry smile teasing at her lips. "It's been a few years since anyone thought to test me."

He forced a smile and nodded to Jessa.

"She can stay here. We have a few things to talk about, anyway. Why don't you travel someplace far enough where I can try to influence you?"

He considered where to go, before deciding on the place where everything had really started for him, and the place that he had meant to visit, anyway.

CHAPTER 25

Rsiran emerged from the Slide atop Ilphaesn. The air carried the bitter scent of lorcith and wind gusted around the massive rock in the strange way that it did here. He hesitated, listening to the call of the lorcith and the way that the mountain itself almost seemed to speak to him. Something had changed since the last time he'd been here.

It took a moment for him to understand what it was that he sensed: Massive amounts of lorcith had shifted within the mountain.

Why would the lorcith have changed?

He gazed toward the city in the distance. From atop Ilphaesn, especially at night, Elaeavn almost appeared to glow. There was a peaceful sort of light about the city, a brightness to it that he didn't appreciate when standing in the streets. From here, it was hard to tell the separation that existed between Lower Town and Upper Town. The palace looked a part of the city, rather than carrying the illusion that it floated from the wall of rock itself. Everything appeared simple, peaceful.

The first time he'd stood here, he'd been dragged from the city, forced to come to Ilphaesn and serve so that his father could prove a point, to force him away from his connection to lorcith, to try and prevent him from listening to the call of lorcith, as *his* father had forced him away from lorcith.

Only, by sending him to Ilphaesn, he had forced a tighter connection to lorcith than what Rsiran would ever have learned otherwise. Had his father really wanted to prevent him from listening to lorcith, he would have sent him away from the city as he had been. At least there, the temptation would not have been present.

Rsiran turned his focus back to the change within the mountain. Before thinking too much about what he did, he Slid into the caves within the mountain, emerging within the main part where he had camped for the weeks that he'd spent here. Normally, there was a soft draw of the orange light within the mines, but either that had been extinguished, or it was gone altogether.

When Rsiran had last visited, he had no Sight, nothing to help him find his way through the mines but the sense of lorcith in the walls. With that, he could create a map, and it formed within his mind as he stood there. The mines were more extensive than he'd last seen, as if the miners had taken a more aggressive approach. Not only more extensive, but more lorcith had been removed than ever before.

And here he had thought to come to the mines to discover why all the lorcith that he knew existed within the mountain remained hidden, and how the supply was constricted. Instead, he found that lorcith had been mined in massive quantities.

How long had it been since he'd been to Ilphaesn—really been here, and long enough to take a sense of the mines? A month?

Before sneaking into the palace again, he knew.

It couldn't be a coincidence that lorcith had been pulled from Ilphaesn around the same time that he'd Slid into the palace for the second time. That hadn't gone unnoticed, and the Elvraeth would not be pleased with the fact that he had managed to make it past their barriers, but he had not expected their mining patterns to change.

Unless it wasn't the Elvraeth.

The Forgotten had managed to gain access to lorcith as well. When he'd left the Forgotten Palace, he had suspected that their access was a mine other than Ilphaesn, but what if wasn't?

Or, what if the hidden mines, the ones that he'd heard someone working in during his time trapped here, had finally connected? Josun still lived, saved by Firell's compassion, so he didn't doubt that Josun had shared with the Forgotten the secret of the mines that he accessed.

Rsiran took a step forward, realizing as he did that the change in his Sight made the mines different as well. Since holding the crystal, his Sight had improved, but within the mines, it was more than simply improved. There were the gradations of shadows that Jessa had described when they had last come, but even more than that.

Much like with the heartstone sword, and how it glowed with a soft blue light—visible even here, he realized—light and color blazed off the wall, as if burning through the stone. It took a moment for him to realize that what he saw was lorcith.

And it matched the image within his head. Lorcith, all around him, and burning brightly. Would it be like the heartstone, that only he could see? Or had something changed here?

The longer he stared, the more intense the light coming from the lorcith became, eventually becoming practically blinding, it was so bright.

What had happened when he held the crystal?

He remembered staring down, as if from the top of a massive mountain, seeing flashes of white far below. At that time, he recognized that the white light he'd seen had come from lorcith, and now here within the mountain, he saw lorcith much like he had when holding the crystal.

Did that mean the other part of the vision was accurate as well?

He'd had the sense of a blue light, one that made him think of heartstone. Could he find that the same way? Would he *see* it the same way?

Noise from down the cave caught his attention.

Rsiran nearly Slid away, but decided against it. Now that he was here, he wanted to know what was happening within Ilphaesn. The Elvraeth may claim the lorcith as theirs, but he felt a certain possessiveness about it as well, as if the lorcith here were meant for him. Even knowing that was not the case didn't change how he felt. Given the abilities that he possessed, and the way that he could use lorcith, he couldn't help but feel that connection.

He started down the mine shaft, Sliding a few steps as he went, willing to risk small Slides without pulling himself along. The lorcith all around him, and the heartstone sword he carried with him, would protect him here.

After a dozen Slides, he stopped and listened for the sound. It was a different experience for him in the mine than when he'd been here before. There was always a certain terror to standing in the pure dark, not able to see anything around him. When he'd learned to use his connection to the lorcith to form a map, that had alleviated some of that discomfort, but part of it remained. Now, it seemed nearly as bright as daylight.

He paused, thinking of the map that had been made of iron and grindl. Could it be a map of the mines?

Trying to form an almost superimposed mental image of the two, he decided that it wasn't.

Rsiran sighed. That would have been too easy. And unlikely. Why would his father—or whoever had placed it within the hut—have had a map of the Ilphaesn mines?

The soft wind that blew through the mine touched his cheeks and pulled softly on his cloak. No sound drifted with it, nothing that would tell him that he wasn't alone.

Rsiran wondered if there were miners sleeping in the massive cavern as he once had. Without the light, he should have thought to check. What if the miners were down here with him? What if that was the sound that he'd heard?

Once he would have been afraid of that, but now he could take himself to safety. Now he had the knives with him that he could use to remain safe.

He made another few Slides. The slope of the mineshaft angled gradually downward. Rsiran passed places that he'd mined when his father had sentenced him here, places that had never looked as they did now with the bright light glowing from the walls. Even with as much lorcith as had been mined from Ilphaesn, massive amounts still remained.

He stopped in a wider cavern and glanced around. It was here that the foreman had collected the lorcith that was mined and recorded the haul for the day. Men would buy their freedom here.

A table and a chair had been here, as well as a lantern and scale to record the lorcith mined. Now this was nothing more than an empty room.

Not empty, Rsiran realized. The bright white light that he saw all around him concentrated in a corner of the room, burning brightly along the wall. With a Slide, he reached the wall. The light that he saw came from dozens of lumps of lorcith. One in particular was massive, almost as large as he was. His time in Venass had shown him that there were collections of lorcith as large as that, but he'd never seen lump lorcith that size in person.

He ran his hand along the top of the lorcith and felt the tingling energy of the metal. It called to him, the steady song that he'd long ago decided to listen to. One voice was louder than the others, and he was surprised to note that it was a smaller piece of lorcith that leaned against the wall. Rsiran pocketed it.

Most of this lorcith would have been enough to buy miner's freedom. Rsiran started to count, but realized there were simply too many for him to keep track of. He let the lorcith tell him how many there were.

Nearly one hundred, and each larger than any that had been found during his time in the mines. Enough to free *all* of the miners who had been sentenced to Ilphaesn.

More than ever before, he wanted to know what was happening here.

When he'd been in the mine before, he had known that there was lorcith all around. Most men went days without finding anything, and when they did, they came up with only small nuggets, never anything of much value. Rsiran had drawn several larger lumps out of the mountain while here, but had done so without knowing how much danger that placed him in.

He remembered overhearing men speaking about the limited supply of lorcith, but never really knowing why. But he thought he did now. Someone had Compelled the miners *not* to find lorcith.

And now the entire mountain had changed. He felt the energy within the mine differently. There was no sense from the lorcith whether the change was good or bad, only that it was different. But Rsiran worried. Why would so much lorcith be needed?

He'd seen lorcith used in dangerous ways before. Not only the way that he could control it, and *push* his knives, but also the way the scholars used lorcith, nearly sealing him inside of Venass, or to modify themselves, piercing flesh with bars of the metal. The scholar he'd met had used it to gain control over lorcith.

Even the things that he had made possessed power. There were the bracelets that he'd made for Jessa that prevented Reading and Compelling. The knives had a certain power to them, something like a life that he had given them, powered by his ability to *push* on them.

What else could he make?

Della had called him dangerous. With this much lorcith, not only might he be dangerous, but whoever intended to use it would be as well, especially if they had the ability to listen to the call of the metal.

Rsiran shivered.

He stopped next to the massive lump of lorcith. In some ways, it was already shaped something like a man, and twice as wide. Its song was not as strong as some—surprising, given its size—but there was a depth to it that he heard. As he rested his hand on the metal, he could imagine shapes it would take, possibilities of ways to manipulate it, if only he could find some way to heat it. This lump would let itself become many things…

Rsiran pulled his hand away.

Lorcith rarely had multiple shapes that it would take. The metal was often willing to let him shape it, to turn it into something different, but never had he known the lorcith to have many shapes it was willing to take.

He knew suddenly that he could not leave this here.

Taking it would reveal that he'd been here to whoever had pulled this lorcith free, but Rsiran didn't want to leave it here, especially with its willingness to take on multiple shapes, as the metal here was. He needed to take it with him.

But how?

It was too large to carry. Even smaller lumps of lorcith were heavy, and this was simply massive.

Could he Slide it?

Something like that would ripple, he suspected, enough that anyone able to detect Sliding would know that he traveled, but they wouldn't necessarily know anything more than when he Slid with Jessa and Brusus. Here was his chance to test the type of Slide, and confirm that no one could influence or detect it when he *pulled*, rather than stepped.

He hoped that proved to be true.

Where would he take it?

The first thought was to his smithy, but for some reason, that didn't feel right.

There was another place, but he didn't think he'd be able to keep it any more protected there than it was here. Yet, the more he thought about it, the more *right* it felt.

Rsiran wrapped his arms around the lorcith. He couldn't lift it, but had not really expected to be able to. If he could Slide without moving, he wouldn't need to.

Closing his eyes, he formed the image in his mind of where he intended to emerge. He'd been there enough that he wouldn't need an anchor—a good thing, especially since he did not have one—and held tightly to the lorcith.

Then he drew himself forward, albeit more slowly given the mass and weight of his traveling companion. Holding onto lorcith of this size, the movement was more like trying to Slide through the alloy, but not exactly the same. Going through the alloy was more of an oozing, a steady forceful push until he popped free. In some ways, he worried that there was a danger trying to Slide through the alloy. Not so much for him, but for those who traveled with him. He'd been torn from Jessa once, though that had been in the palace, and he suspected that there was more to what happened than what he knew.

This was a steady drawing sensation. He felt the effort of the Slide, but not the weight of the lorcith that he brought with him. Whatever he held onto came with him, as if a part of him.

Would he be able to bring something even larger if he wanted? It was hard to believe that he could bring anything larger than this lorcith, but if he could...

He emerged.

The air was damp and earthy, the scent of the Aisl Forest filling his nostrils, a sharp change from the mines of Ilphaesn. He stood deep in the forest, near a clearing where Lianna had been buried. This was a place that he had known well in his childhood, and returned to often when Sliding. It was a place like this that he had first hidden lorcith when escaping from the mine. It was far enough away from the hut on the edge of the forest that he didn't think it would be discovered.

Trees stretched high overhead, the enormous sjihn trees that were only found this deep in the Aisl Forest. The Aisl had once been home to his people, but they had long ago moved to the shores, with Ilphaesn towering in the background. There had always been a part of Rsiran that wondered what it would have been like to live in the Aisl. The trees gave him a sense of peace, and a sense of safety that he didn't have, even in his smithy. It was why he had chosen to come here with his Slide.

The massive lump of lorcith rested on the ground, as if it had always been there.

Rsiran pushed on it but it didn't move, and he found the metal surprisingly warm. How many men must it have taken to simply drag it up the mineshaft? If he couldn't even move it, he imagined there must have been a half dozen, possibly even more.

Here it would be safe. And then what?

Rsiran didn't know what he intended for the lorcith, only that he couldn't have left it in the mines. It was too large to work in his forge.

He remembered the massive lorcith doors in Venass. They must have been crafted in forges much larger than any that were found in Elaeavn.

He stared at the lorcith, content that it would be safe for now, and realized that it was time that he return to Della. Jessa would be angry that he'd been gone as long as he had.

With one lingering glance at the lorcith, he worried who mined in Ilphaesn, and why lorcith was suddenly allowed to be removed when it had been restricted for as long as he'd been alive.

CHAPTER 26

Rsiran returned to Della's home, drawing himself in the Slide. This time, now that he was not carrying the weight of the lorcith with him, it took him quickly, with a familiar sense of movement. He tried to take a moment to watch the Slide, but he emerged before he had the chance.

Not for the first time, Rsiran wondered what existed in that space between places. Always it had felt as if there was something else there. Before, he had seen nothing but colors, but with the gradual improvement in his Sight, he came to see shades and shapes that hadn't been there before. The only time that he'd come close to knowing had been when he had resisted the influence on his Sliding.

When he emerged, Jessa assaulted him. "Where have you been?"

He grabbed her fists before she had the chance to hit him again, lowering them and pulling her into a soft hug. She stiffened before relaxing. Della sat by her hearth, rocking comfortably in her chair, a mug of steaming mint tea in her hand.

How long had he been gone?

"Were you able to influence my Sliding?" he asked Della.

She glanced over, an amused smile quirking the corner of her mouth, and her gaze flicked to Jessa. "I think you might want to answer her question first, don't you?"

"Ilphaesn," he said. "I thought I should go someplace far enough away that if she could influence my Sliding, I would know."

"Why were you gone so long?" Jessa asked.

He shook his head. "I'll have to show you."

"Show?"

Della stood, her smile fading into a frown. "What did you find?"

"Could you influence my Slide?"

She tipped her head to the side, studying him for a moment. Then she shook her head. "I could feel the ripple when you traveled from my home, and subtle shifts when you were away, but then nothing more."

Had he stepped into the Slide when he left? He couldn't remember. But while in Ilphaesn, he thought that he could Slide without her noticing, but she had.

But then she had detected nothing. With as much as he carried, how could that be?

"You didn't detect anything?" he asked. He sat down and took the mug of tea Della pulled off a tray and offered to him. It smelled different from the usual mint that she gave him, more potent in some ways. "Not even when I returned here?"

She took a sip. "There were no ripples. It was as if you didn't travel. This is heartstone?"

He glanced at Jessa, feeling a growing excitement. If he could *pull* himself rather than stepping into a Slide, would he be able to mask his presence? Then he wouldn't need to carry the heartstone sword with him, fearing that the Forgotten or that Venass might *pull* him toward them.

"Not heartstone. You sensed me Sliding while carrying heartstone. Could you influence that?"

Della pursed her lips. "No."

Rsiran smiled. Could he have found a way to move safely? To Slide without worrying about the others affecting him?

That would be a way to safety. Then he wouldn't have to fear Sliding, to fear how he traveled, or worry about what might happen, and where he would emerge.

Jessa stood behind the counter and tapped her hand on it. Rsiran recognized her agitation. He should have returned sooner, but he got caught up in what he discovered in the mines.

"I'm sorry that I didn't come back sooner. When I went to Ilphaesn, I sensed something different with the lorcith. I wanted to look, to see if I could understand."

She smacked him on the chest. "You can't *see* anything in the mines, Rsiran! You might be able to detect the metal there, but when it comes to actually seeing what's going on, you're—"

"Not anymore," he said.

"You said your Sight had improved, but the mines are black. Even to me there is nothing but shades of color. You want me to believe that your Sight has gotten so good that you can now see in the dark?"

Della watched him, her hands clasped together over her lap. Rsiran hadn't shared with her the changes to his Sight, but she had told him that when she had once held the crystal, her ability had changed. What had she said? That she was able to see those that she was meant to help Heal?

"It's like the sword," he started.

"There was nothing about the sword," Jessa said. "Neither Brusus nor I saw anything!"

"But *I* did."

Della stood. "What about the sword?"

"When we were in Thyr, we ended up in a small room. It was dark. Too dark to see clearly. But the sword," he said, pulling his cloak away from the blade, "glowed, giving me enough light to see." He pulled it from the leather loop on his belt and held it out. He could almost make out the faint shimmering along the blade, but it was faded, muted almost. He wondered if the room was too bright. "And then in Ilphaesn—"

"This is your Sight?" Della asked.

"I thought it was," he started, but Jessa shook her head. "But if it's not Sight, then it's something about the metal for me that is different. Not only heartstone, but the lorcith in the walls of the mine was different."

"What do you mean that it was different?" Jessa asked.

Della leaned forward.

Rsiran slipped the sword back into the loop on his belt, thinking of how to explain. "When I held the crystal, I had what I thought was nothing more than a vision. It was like I was standing atop Krali, but even higher, as if looking down on the entire land below me. While I was there, I saw dots of light. Some where brighter than others." He closed his eyes, and he could *see* those lights, almost like a map.

"Where did you see them?" Della asked. She had stood and looked at him from across the counter. Her eyes were drawn, and the wrinkled lines on her face were deeper than usual.

"The white light that I saw was lorcith," he went on. "At least, I think it was. There was one brighter than the others that I think is Ilphaesn." The others he had thought were forgings, but from such a height as he'd been looking from—if he had in fact really been that high above the ground—he wouldn't have been able to see individual forgings, would he? That meant they were other collections of lorcith, unshaped, and possibly not yet mined.

Why hadn't he thought of that before?

"You can still see them, can't you?" Della asked.

He nodded. "The vision is there." It was the same as the map of the mineshafts within Ilphaesn. Were he to close his eyes, he could recreate them if needed, much like he could with the map formed out of heartstone.

Jessa pushed on him and he looked over to her. "That doesn't explain what happened in the mine. What are you talking about that you can suddenly see in the mine?"

"That's just it," Rsiran answered. "I don't know. When I was there, it was as if the lorcith all around me glowed. The light was bright enough that I could see. Even without the sense of the metal pressing on me, I think I would have been able to see."

Jessa glanced from Rsiran over to Della. "What happened to him? What did that crystal do to him?"

Was she more worried than she let on? Jessa wouldn't tell him if she *was* concerned, mostly because she thought to protect him, much like he thought to protect her.

Della sighed and shook her head. "The Great Crystals are a way to power," she said. "You knew that when you went there."

"I didn't want to hold it," he said.

"No? But you were meant to, otherwise you wouldn't have been able to reach it. That is how the Great Crystals work." She made her way around the counter and pulled a jar off the shelf. She pulled out five smooth stones and set them on the counter, arranging them in a circle. "Had you not seen the crystals, I would never share this with you. Even among the Elvraeth, the crystals are closely guarded. Only those with the potential to lead are given the chance to view them, and even then, it is not guaranteed that they will be given the opportunity to hold them."

Rsiran frowned. "I thought any of the Elvraeth could reach the crystals."

"Only if they are Seen to have potential. In that way, the Elvraeth serve as another layer of defense for the crystals. As you have learned, they have much power, and in that way, they could be abused."

"But if not everyone can reach them—" Jessa started.

"Yes, not everyone can reach them, and of those who do, not everyone can hold them. But there are some who fear that others could hold the crystals as well, and be given much the same power. From what I've seen, that is true."

Rsiran stared at the stones arranged on the counter. He could imagine them much like the crystals, the soft blue light emanating from them, with one of the crystals glowing slightly brighter than the others. That light had called to him, had drawn him to reach for it.

What would have happened had he not?

"You mean Rsiran, don't you?" Jessa asked.

Della sighed. "Rsiran making his way to the crystals only proved that concern for their safety is valid. I did not think that the Forgotten Elvraeth, or even the so-called scholars of Venass would have a way to reach the crystals, but Rsiran managed to make it past ancient barriers long felt secure. The fact that he did makes them vulnerable."

"But they're not vulnerable," Rsiran said. "Only because of my connection to heartstone was I able to reach them."

"Yes, and how long until others realize that is the key? The Forgotten now know of your ability. Worse, Evaelyn now knows. They will use that knowledge."

"Do you think there are others with the ability to Slide past the alloy?" Jessa asked.

Della's face remained neutral. "Others of the Forgotten?" she asked, and shook her head. "That is unlikely. While they may have never lost traveling, not as we have chosen to in Elaeavn, they would need a different set of skills to bypass the alloy. Their contempt for Rsiran tells me that it will be some time before they understand that they're looking in the wrong place."

"Then what?" Jessa asked.

The Forgotten weren't the only ones interested in learning about the crystal. Thom's attack had proven that. And Thom had thought that they had managed to find the crystal, or suspected that Rsiran would have been able to bring one away from the palace.

The interest Venass showed in the crystals wasn't what worried him, nor did he worry about their ability with lorcith. Even if they could Slide, there was no guarantee that they would be able to make it beyond the alloy-crafted barrier.

There *was* something about Venass that worried him, especially as it related to his ability.

"My father," he said. Jessa turned to him, and Della nodded. "That's what you mean, isn't it?"

"The Forgotten may not understand how the ancient bloodline of the smiths is important, but I will tell you that Venass are well aware. In that, they truly are scholars. Now that they have seen what Rsiran is capable of doing, they will think to find access to the crystals on their own."

"You think that's why they wanted my father?" he asked.

Della nodded. "Perhaps even your sister."

"But he doesn't know how to access heartstone. And Alyse…" Alyse had never set foot in the smithy. She would have no more ability to use lorcith and heartstone than Jessa.

"Are you certain? Where do you think your ability comes from, if not from the ancient smith lines? Long ago, our people understood that power and did not take it for granted, but the Elvraeth have forgotten."

Rsiran looked to Jessa, wondering what it was that Venass might be able to get from his father. Maybe nothing. If that was the case, then it wouldn't matter, and the crystals would remain safe, but wasn't it possible that they would use his father to learn how Rsiran managed to Slide past the alloy? Could it really be possible that his father could teach them?

"What ability of the smith bloodline?" Jessa asked. "Does that have anything to do with Thom and whether he Compelled you?"

"That's the real reason we came here," Rsiran said. "When we saw Thom, he mentioned that he could hear me. That I was loud. Brusus once said the same thing."

And he had thought the barriers that he could create protected him.

Della reached across the counter and touched his arm. A cold chill worked up his arm and spread through his chest, before ending in his head. For a moment, the chill lingered before it faded. Della released his arm and stepped back.

"You were not Compelled just now," she said with palpable relief.

Della might have been relieved, but Rsiran was not. If she had been unable to Compel him, it meant the darkness of the attack had come from him. It meant those men had died at his own hands, not those controlled by another. It meant the thrill that had come from the attack, and from hurting others had been his alone.

And maybe, it meant that his father was right.

Della studied him a moment, her lips tightening into a frown. "You do not seem relieved."

Rsiran turned away rather than answering. Jessa grabbed at his arm, but he pulled away from her as well. If his ability truly did change him, if there was something about it that made him darker, then he didn't want to cause her any harm.

Unless it was already too late. He'd brought her into everything that he'd done, subjected her to the risk that he'd chosen, only to see that so much had happened to her because of it. She would never have been abducted by Josun were it not for him. She would never have been trapped in a cell with the Forgotten were it not for him. And now? What fate would she suffer because of what he could do?

"He begins to wonder if his father wasn't right about his ability," Jessa said.

Della snorted. "Your father believed the myths that the Elvraeth placed out there, Rsiran."

"It's more than that. My father lived outside of Elaeavn. That's where he met my mother. He would have known others who could Slide. The Forgotten—"

"There is nothing about what you do that is any different from what the Elvraeth once did themselves," Della said.

"There is everything about my ability that's different," he said. "Did the Elvraeth have the ability to control metal? Did they have the ability to kill with a thought?"

Della leaned forward. "You remember what I told you about Evaelyn and why she was banished?" Rsiran nodded. "Then you will know that the Elvraeth certainly did know about how to kill with a thought. With the right Compelling, a person can be made to do many things. And trust me when I tell you that is a far darker art than anything that you could do."

Rsiran turned back to them and looked to Della. "What if…" He paused, uncertain how to phrase his question. "What if it's something about the combination of my abilities?"

Della tottered toward him, resting a hand on the counter as she went. "The Great Watcher alone knows why you were given the gifts that you were, but I know that you have no darkness within you. Anger, certainly. After all that you've been through, it is only natural to have anger. But darkness? That implies that there is a part of you that revels in killing."

Rsiran thought about how he'd felt after sending his knife through the man in Thyr. Hadn't that part of him felt a slight thrill as it happened? What did that make him?

As he looked at Jessa and saw the concern written on her face, he knew that he would do anything to keep her safe, even if it was of his own doing. Maybe, especially if it was his own doing.

CHAPTER 27

THE BLUISH LIGHT FROM THE BRACELETS burned against the darkness of the night. Rsiran twisted them, feeling the way the end of the metal pressed against the sensitive inside of his arm, and wondered if he would ever feel confident that he could rely on them.

The lump of metal claimed from Ilphaesn had responded when he attempted to forge a similar set of bracelets to what he'd made for Jessa, seeking assurance that he would not be Compelled. The bracelets that formed for him were different from the ones he'd made for Jessa, not only in the shape that they'd taken—a flatter, twisting shape that rotated in a tight circle—but in the fact that he'd needed to add heartstone to the lorcith. For some reason, the shaping had practically demanded it.

Heartstone layered along the top of the bracelets, running in a thin line throughout their entirety. It was this heartstone that glowed for him, but the lorcith had called to him, lorcith that he'd taken from Ilphaesn when he'd returned to clear out the rest of the lorcith that he discovered there. Now, much of it filled his smithy, but a few of the larger lumps he'd taken to the Aisl.

Now he would need to test them. That was why he'd sneaked here, leaving his barriers lowered. Without them around his mind, he felt naked, exposed somehow, but if this worked, and he didn't have to remember to maintain the protections that he had long ago learned to erect in his mind, then he might be able to divert some of that focus to other tasks. And he might not need to fear what would happen if they were lowered, or that he "shouted" as Thom suggested.

He stopped at the door to listen. To sense. Darkness and shadows stretched all around him, less than they once had in this part of Lower Town, especially at night. He sensed lorcith, but it was either on him, or within the warehouse, carried by Brusus.

Would Brusus detect him coming?

Focusing on the inside of the warehouse, toward the clearing he knew was within, he *pulled* himself forward.

Lights flashed around him, and he emerged to darkness.

Not pure darkness, though. The bracelets created a soft light, much like the Elvraeth lantern and the blue glow that came from it. The shadows around him receded, leaving him with shifting layers of gray.

The crates towered over his head, the same as the last time he'd been here. After what had happened with Josun, Brusus had mostly abandoned his plans for the items stored in the warehouse, but when Rsiran detected him here, mostly from the knife that he carried, he decided to test the bracelets.

Jessa waited for him in the Barth. And Haern… Rsiran still hadn't seen Haern since returning from Thyr.

That should bother him, especially since Haern knew what they were going through, and that they had risked themselves traveling to Thyr. But Haern could often be strange, and was known to often be silent for days at a time. Jessa didn't seem concerned. More than anything, that reassured him. Were there something for him to worry about, especially when it came to Haern, Jessa would know.

The sense of lorcith came distantly within the warehouse. Rsiran focused on it, noting that it was toward one end of the warehouse. As he thought about it, he realized that he detected lorcith where he would not expect to. Not unless…

He readied a pair of knives and *pulled* himself to the hidden part of the warehouse where he'd detected Josun's attempts at combining heartstone.

As he emerged, Brusus swung a pair of knives toward him.

Rsiran *pushed* on the knives, and kept them from hitting him.

Brusus let out a relieved sigh. "Damn, Rsiran. You shouldn't come sneaking up on me like that. You're liable to get yourself killed."

Rsiran grabbed the knives and handed them over to Brusus. "If you wanted to kill me, you'd use something other than lorcith-forged knives, especially knives that *I* made."

Brusus pocketed the knives and shrugged. "Yours are the most finely made knives I own. Can't say I want to use a different knife. Besides, if you come jumping out at me like that, you're the only one who would be able to control them, so I don't have to worry that I'll hurt you." He tapped the side of his head. "That's a benefit, if you ask… Why are you wearing the bracelets you made Jessa?"

Rsiran held out his hands. The soft blue light glowing from the bracelets persisted, brighter since they were in such a dark space, between the stacks of crates. "I wanted a physical form of protection so I didn't have to constantly hold mental barriers in place."

"Listen, Rsiran, you know Thom only said that to get to you. He was trying to evoke a response." He glanced back down to the bracelets and shook his head. "And seeing how you find a need to wear them, it worked."

"It's not Thom." Brusus frowned at him. "Well, it's not *entirely* Thom. When I Slide, I lose the connection to lorcith and heartstone," he explained. That had been the fear when Thom mentioned that Rsiran had been loud. Each time he emerged from a Slide, he reached for the connection to lorcith to strengthen the barriers, but if Thom or someone like him managed to Compel him in that moment, there was no telling what he would do. He wouldn't always have Della nearby to answer whether he'd been Compelled, and he didn't want to put his friends in danger with something that he did. Or might do, when forced. "This way, I don't have to worry about losing the connection."

Brusus's frown deepened. "Are you sure they work? I mean, you're putting a lot of faith in them. It's one thing if Jessa was Compelled. She has Sight, but you? If they don't protect you as you hope, someone could Compel you to throw your knives or Slide us somewhere, or the Great Watcher only knows what else. Damn, Rsiran, it might be better if you just maintain that barrier."

"I'll keep the barrier in place," he said, "but I don't want to need to rely on it." Had he something like these bracelets when the Forgotten had captured him, he wouldn't have needed to worry about them getting past his barriers, even when dosed with the slithca syrup. "Do they work?" he asked Brusus.

Brusus pulled his eyes away from the bracelets and fixed his gaze on Rsiran. Pale green eyes darkened, revealing the full extent of his ability, visible even in the darkness. How much of that was because of the glow coming from Rsiran's bracelets and how much was because of Rsiran's improved Sight?

The bracelets went cool and then, with a surge of blue light, went cold.

Brusus staggered back and grabbed his head.

"What happened?" Rsiran asked.

Brusus leaned forward, resting his hands on his thighs. "Damn," he breathed. "Was that a punishment for something?" he asked. "Not sure I care for it." He took a few breaths and then shook himself, standing and rubbing at his temples. "You want to torment me, you can just go dancing around with Jessa like you do. But that?" he asked, pointing to the bracelets, "that's something else."

Rsiran twisted them. Jessa said they went cold when Thom attempted to Read or Compel her, but his had done something more than simply going cold. There had been a flash of light, as if the bracelets defended him in some way.

Della was right. What he created *was* dangerous. Not only if the bracelets let him know when someone tried to sneak past his barriers, but because they assaulted the person who tried.

"I'm sorry, Brusus. I didn't know…"

Brusus shook his head. "That'll keep me from trying to Read you. But it's not exactly subtle, is it? Something like that, if it leads to… whatever just happened to me… makes it pretty clear that you have something powerful with you."

"But you couldn't Compel me?"

"Compel? Damn, Rsiran, I couldn't *Read* you. Whatever those things are, they keep me completely blocked from your mind."

Jessa's hadn't reacted the same way. If they had, then Della would have told them. And Thom would have reacted more than he did. That meant the heartstone in them changed the intent. He added heartstone because the lorcith seemed to imply that he should, that they would be more effective for *him*, but now he wondered if that had been the only reason.

Had he known that the heartstone would change the way the bracelets worked?

He didn't think that he had. Heartstone didn't have an intent behind it, not like lorcith. He had only followed the direction and guidance of lorcith itself, not something within him. Hadn't he?

Brusus continued to rub his head, and Rsiran scanned the area, trying to push those thoughts out of his mind. The more he thought about it, the more he began to wonder if there *might* be something within him that generated darkness. If so, then he would either have to stop working with lorcith and Sliding… or embrace the fact that he had changed.

"How did you get in here?" Rsiran asked.

When he'd tried reaching this part of the warehouse without Sliding, there hadn't been any opening. As far as Rsiran could tell, there still wasn't one.

Brusus motioned toward a crate three off the ground, staggering briefly as he started toward it. Rsiran Slid to him and put and arm around him for support, but Brusus shook him off. "I'm fine." His voice still sounded somewhat shaky, and he took a deeper breath than normal, but he managed to stand in front of the crate without any outward sign of weakness. "Look up there," he instructed.

Rsiran followed the direction of where Brusus pointed, and realized that the crate had a small opening. "You climbed through that?"

"Climbed doesn't really describe it all that well," Brusus said with a smile. "More like I *squeezed* through that. I tried prying it open more than it is, but I couldn't really get it to move. The wood of these crates is different from the wood used in other parts of the warehouse. Older. Haern tells me it's called ironwood, but I think he's making it up."

Rsiran scrambled up the side of the crates until he reached the opening. The edges were rough, and the wood cooler than he expected. "What's inside these?" he asked over his shoulder.

"Nothing in that one, at least not anymore. Dust, as if whatever had been inside degraded a long time ago. These others have been too hard to open."

Rsiran jumped back to the ground and listened for lorcith, straining to hear if there might be any in these crates, but not expecting to find any. When he didn't, he listened for heartstone, stretching out for the sense of the metal. He had discovered several crates with small amounts of heartstone, enough to keep him with supplies for his forgings, but that would run out much sooner than the lorcith.

Not surprisingly, there was none here, either.

Had heartstone been present, he suspected that he would have detected it sooner, unless this ironwood prevented him somehow.

"So you crawled—squeezed through this crate?" he asked Brusus.

"Don't say it like you're surprised," Brusus said. "I've basically torn wood away in strips to get inside some of these crates." He turned in place, scanning the wall of boxes all around them. "One of these days, we'll learn what's in each of these. Maybe there will be some we can move, or maybe it will be like that one with nothing but dust. Either way, the Elvraeth have left them here for too long. They belong to all of Elaeavn."

Rsiran smiled, wishing that he shared the same passion that Brusus felt about finding a way to get the contents of these crates dispersed throughout the city. For Brusus, there was probably more to his intent than simply wanting a sense of fairness. He would want to be paid for the effort, but Rsiran couldn't deny that he hated the fact that the Elvraeth left such wealth trapped here, abandoned.

When Brusus said nothing more, Rsiran asked, "Have you seen Haern since we returned?"

Brusus stared up at the wall of boxes. "Haern doesn't always want to be found, you know? He didn't like the fact that we were risking a trip to Thyr. I think he knew it was important, especially with what he claims he saw of your sister, but…" He pulled his eyes away and shrugged. "With Haern, it's not always easy to know what he's about.

The last thing he told me was that he was hoping to learn something about that map you drew. Hey," Brusus said, frowning. "Whatever came of that other slip of metal you found? The one from Thyr?"

Rsiran breathed out with a soft laugh. "Only that I nearly made the heartstone I used explode."

Brusus smiled. "So, not a map?"

Rsiran shook his head. "Not a map. Not sure what it—"

The sudden appearance of lorcith nearby cut him off.

Rsiran frowned and raised a finger to his lips to silence Brusus.

It wasn't the first time he'd suddenly experienced lorcith in this place. Josun had been here before, and had used it to try and force him to create the alloy. But Josun wouldn't return here, would he? After what he'd seen from Rsiran and how he'd been trapped in Ilphaesn for as long as he had, would he really risk returning here?

He didn't think that he would.

Rsiran leaned to Brusus and whispered, "Stay here. Keep your knives with you."

Brusus studied his face a moment and nodded.

At least he didn't argue. With Jessa, she would have demanded to go with him, or been upset when he returned. Brusus recognized that there were times that Rsiran needed to Slide alone.

He focused on a spot on the crates above, where he'd have a better vantage, and *pulled* himself to it.

When he emerged, he looked down at the rest of the warehouse. Maybe he should have brought Brusus with him. Without the same skill with Sight, there might not be anything that he could see. The dark blue light from the bracelets only let him see so far, and the weakness of his Sight didn't help.

But, as he surveyed the warehouse, he realized that it didn't matter.

A bright light bloomed below where he'd left Brusus.

At first, he thought it might be a lantern, but why would Brusus have lit a lantern? He wouldn't. With his Sight, he didn't need anything like that to see.

Then he realized it wasn't lantern light at all, but a softly glowing light from the lorcith that Brusus held.

Did his knives glow the same way?

He pulled one from his pocket and held it out from him. The knife glowed just like the others, and with a brighter light than the blue from the heartstone of the bracelets.

Rsiran smiled to himself. If lorcith would glow like this for him, he wouldn't ever have to be in the dark again.

He stuffed the knife back into his pocket. That would be something to understand another time. Now he had to focus on the lorcith that he sensed down on the floor below him.

Another light, one that wasn't Brusus's, moved on the ground below.

It came from the clearing of crates, the place where Brusus had first brought him when showing him what the Elvraeth possessed here in the warehouse, a way of demonstrating the wealth of the Elvraeth.

It was a place that Rsiran knew well.

Focusing on that place, he *pulled* himself forward.

When he emerged, he searched for the light that he'd seen, looking for the glow that came from whatever lorcith they carried with them. He found it barely a dozen paces from him.

"Where is he?" a deep voice whispered.

Rsiran tensed. Josun's voice wasn't that deep. This reminded him more of the man Valn. But how would he have known to find Rsiran here?

"I can only track him so far," a woman answered. "He has something that prevents me following. I only catch it in glimpses."

That would be Sarah, the woman who could follow his Sliding.

Had he been careless? Since learning that *pulling* himself rather than stepping into a Slide would keep him from detection, he had made certain to Slide in that manner only.

Hadn't he?

Rsiran wasn't sure. Sometimes, he Slid without thinking, so accustomed to simply stepping into the Slide, that he didn't pay enough attention. It was possible that when Brusus had nearly fallen that he'd Slid to him without *pulling* himself along.

Damn. If they had detected that, and come so quickly, then he really had to be more careful.

But he wanted to know who they were, and why they were tracking him. He suspected that they were either from the Forgotten—which he considered the most likely—or from Venass. And hadn't he noticed a flash of lorcith on the rocks outside of Thyr?

Maybe they had warned Thom.

Rsiran thought that he could incapacitate one of them, but both? And someone who could Slide as well as he could?

He doubted that he would be able to. Haern had shown him how ineffective he was at defending himself when it came down to it, especially against someone trained as well as they would have to be if they came from Venass.

Could he follow them? If he could, he might finally find out what happened to his sister.

"He's not here," Valn said.

The woman sniffed. "I would have detected had he left. He might travel quickly," she noted, but her tone made it sound as if she found that unlikely, "but everyone who travels leaves a signature."

"He knows we're here. It's possible he's chosen to avoid traveling."

The woman sighed. "You might be right. And we should get back.

Tonight is your turn to guard her."

"Guard her? She's not going anywhere."

"Still. You know what they want. And until we have *him*, we have to guard *her*."

With a flash, the sense of lorcith vanished.

Rsiran stood there, a trembling sense rolling through him.

He'd gone to Thyr in search of Thom so that he could find his father, in the hope that he could find his sister, thinking that whoever had come for her wanted his father. But that didn't seem to be the case at all. They wanted Rsiran.

But now he knew how to search. With the connection to lorcith, he thought he could find Valn, especially if he remained near the city.

There was no guarantee, but he would look. And he would get Alyse back.

CHAPTER 28

The night was cool and the distant cry of a cat echoed through the streets. Rsiran lost count of how many he heard. Enough that it didn't matter what kind of luck they indicated, even if he believed in such things.

He held onto the sense of lorcith that he had. It was close enough that he could *pull* himself to it, but that risked revealing himself sooner than what he wanted.

Jessa had asked him to wait. For her, and for now, he would.

But he wouldn't for much longer.

She pulled on his arm. "Come on," she urged.

"Why?"

"Haern wanted to talk to you."

Since leaving the warehouse with Brusus—Sliding back to the Barth—he had wandered the streets, focusing on the sense of lorcith until he found the distinct sense of where Valn hid. Once he latched onto it, he didn't have to fear losing the connection, even when it jumped—likely when he Slid. Now, Rsiran could follow him.

If only he had the Elvraeth chains. Then he'd have a way to hold Valn and keep him from Sliding, but he'd given them to Firell as protection against Josun.

"Where is he?" Rsiran asked.

"Back at the Barth. He arrived a little after you left."

Rsiran knew that he needed to speak to Haern, to understand what he might have discovered, but the sense of Valn was out there... He only had to Slide to him, and now that he had detected the lorcith Valn carried, he knew where to find him.

"What is it?"

Rsiran sighed. "I sense him," he said.

"Who? Thom? If you sense him, then we should get Brusus before you do anything—"

Rsiran shook his head. "Not Thom," he answered. He hadn't attempted to detect the heartstone within Thom since they'd returned to Elaeavn. There were other things that he'd been focused on, especially now that he knew Valn and Sarah had his sister.

He needed to follow the sense of lorcith with Valn and reach Alyse, but he didn't want to do it alone.

Would Haern help?

More than even Brusus, Haern would be able to help with someone who could Slide. Haern had already shown him how ineffective his attack would be, and that was with Rsiran's ability to *push* knives. Valn had nothing like that ability.

"When I was with Brusus in the warehouse," he started.

Jessa nodded. "You told me that they were there."

"But I haven't told you that I can sense him now. He has one of my knives."

Jessa frowned. "Why would he have one of your knives?"

Rsiran shrugged. "I don't know. Probably from something with Brusus—"

"That's not what I mean," she said. "You're thinking that they're with the Forgotten or with Venass?"

Rsiran nodded.

"But both now know about your ability with lorcith. They wouldn't carry it with them, would they?"

Rsiran hadn't considered that before, but now that Jessa said it, he realized that she was right. What if they carried one of his knives with them expecting him to come after them? If he did, he'd only be doing what they wanted then.

"Come on," Jessa said. "I can see that you're upset. Let's go to Haern and see what he found out. Then you can decide if you want to go running after this guy."

Rsiran smiled as he slipped his arm around Jessa, and then *pulled* them to the Barth.

They emerged in the alley outside the tavern. The street was empty, and the lantern light dim, barely providing anything more than light to pierce the shadows. The dark, cloudless sky overhead didn't help, either.

Rsiran took one of the knives from his pocket and held it out. The knife had a soft glow to it and pressed back the darkness.

"Thinking of attacking me?" Jessa asked.

He waved with the knife. "You still don't see it, do you?"

"I see the knife, if that's what you're asking."

"Not the knife," Rsiran said. "Well, the knife, but you don't see how it glows?"

"Nothing like what you're describing. Whatever happened when you," she lowered her voice to a whisper, "held the crystal, it changed something. I can see it in your eyes."

Rsiran tensed. He'd been afraid that he might have changed, and that change might put him or Jessa or Brusus, or even Haern, in danger. Not only his ability to see the glowing light of the lorcith, or the dark blue glow of heartstone, but there was the way he'd jumped into the fight in Thyr. Jessa and Della might not think that the changes were all for the bad, but he wondered.

And maybe it wasn't his ability that changed him. Maybe it was just the fact that he'd held one of the Great Crystals when he was not meant to. Hadn't Della said that only a few were chosen? Those few would have Elvraeth blood. Why would he think that he had the capacity to hold something meant for the Elvraeth?

Rsiran took Jessa's hand, thankful for the reassurance that she brought him. Without her, all of this would be much more difficult. Even with her it was difficult, but he couldn't imagine attempting any of it without her.

"You've got others who care too," Jessa said softly.

As she started toward the front of the Barth, Haern burst from the door and saw them. His eyes widened a moment, and he nodded to them.

"Come. We need to go," he said.

"What is it?" Jessa asked.

Rsiran readied to fight, *pulling* on the awareness of the knives he carried. He noted that Haern didn't carry any with him. That would be the reason that Rsiran hadn't been able to track Haern.

"Something I Saw."

Haern pulled them along the street, guiding them up, away from the docks.

"I could Slide us," Rsiran suggested.

"Don't need you doing that," Haern said. "Besides, you need to be better about walking, especially if these others can track you."

"Not when I Slide a different way."

Haern paused and glanced over his shoulder at him. "That's not what Brusus tells me. Says you were with him in the warehouse and they appeared. Wouldn't do that if they didn't know how to find you." He started back up the wide street leading away from the docks. "Seems to me that you might think you're safer than you are. Dangerous to think that way, Rsiran."

Rsiran glanced at Jessa and saw her concern. "If they can follow you…"

"Only when I'm careless," he told her. "With Brusus, after he tried Reading me, he nearly fell, and I reacted out of instinct, not using my new method."

"And if you're careless with Brusus, what makes you think you won't be careless where this one is concerned?" Haern asked, nodding toward Jessa. "When it comes to her, you don't always think clearly." He looked around long enough to catch Jessa's eyes. "Sorry, girl, but he doesn't."

"What did you See, Haern?" Jessa asked.

"Nothing different from what I used to See all the time."

"And what was that?" she asked.

"Darkness. Danger. Death."

He pulled them onto a side street as they approached the middle of the city, a place between the wealth of Upper Town and the poverty of Lower Town. It was a place often referred to as the mids, and had been Rsiran's home until his father exiled him to the mines.

Music drifted down the street, the kind of up-tempo tune that came from taverns that Rsiran had never dared enter when he'd apprenticed to his father. He hadn't dared, for fear that his father might find out and punish him, even though his father had never avoided the ale.

"Why here?" Rsiran asked.

He started to tense when they made another turn, switching to a street lined with storefronts. Bakers, seamstresses, candlemakers, and even smiths. It was the street where his father's smithy had been.

Rsiran slowed, but Haern barreled on, drawing Rsiran up the slope of the street.

Jessa pulled on his hand. "It'll be okay, Rsiran."

He shook his head. "I'm not going back there."

"How do you know that's where he's taking us?"

He could think of nowhere else that Haern would be leading them along this street. Were he taking them to Upper Town, there would be easier ways to reach it.

Seeing Haern stop in the middle of the street, Rsiran realized that he was right.

He tipped his head to Haern. "See?"

Jessa bit her lip. "I don't know why he'd come here. The smithy is empty, isn't it?"

The last time that Rsiran had been here, the smithy had been empty. He didn't expect that to have changed in the months since then. Other smiths might want access to the forge—his family smithy was one of the larger and best equipped—but it would take time for that to work through the guild, and the Smith Guild was nearly as difficult as the alchemists when it came to allowing movement like that.

"Let's see what he has to show us," Jessa suggested.

When they reached Haern, he still stood in the middle of the street. "You two think to take a little liaison before coming with me?"

"Shut it, Haern. We're with you, aren't we?" Jessa said.

"Only because you know better."

Jessa smiled. "Rsiran and I want to know what you think to show us here? Why did you bring us to this place?"

"*This* place? I know you recognize it, Jessa. You spent long enough watching it, at no small measure of danger to yourself, I would add."

In the middle of the street, with the dim lantern light on either side, Rsiran noted how her cheeks flushed. He'd known that Jessa had watched his father's smithy, but hadn't realized that she'd put herself in danger to do it.

"It was empty the last time I was here," Rsiran said.

"Yes. Empty. But why is it that I See movement around here?"

"See or *See*?" Jessa asked.

Haern only frowned. "I think you know the answer."

"I don't know. The Smith Guild wouldn't allow the transfer of the smithy until a specific amount of time has passed," Rsiran said. "There's an order to how that is done."

"Yes, unless they were under *other* orders to expedite it."

Rsiran wasn't as connected to the guild as his father had been. As an apprentice, and one not even a journeyman, there had been no reason for him to understand the workings of the guild. His father had made that clear on more than one occasion, usually to journeymen asking questions about the guild that his father thought unnecessary.

"Who would make such orders?" Jessa asked.

Rsiran glanced up the street. There were three other smiths nearby, each having operated at a similar level to his father. They were all skilled, and sold their forgings throughout the city. But he sensed no lorcith here, nothing like he would expect to have detected from active smithies.

"What about the others?" Rsiran asked.

Haern nodded. "You begin to understand."

"I don't know that I understand, only that I sense something is off."

"How?" Haern asked.

Rsiran looked up and down the street before answering. Talking about his ability with metal wasn't something that he usually did openly, much like Sliding wasn't something he did openly. But it was late, and the street was empty.

"There's no lorcith," he said. "With the smithies around here, there should be some, even if the supply is constrained."

But that wasn't true anymore. Ilphaesn no longer *was* constrained as it had been before. The massive amounts of lorcith stacked within the mountain were testament to that, but what were they for, if not for the smiths to use?

"The other smithies in this part of the city have been closed for the last month," Haern answered.

"Closed?" Rsiran repeated.

"Brusus tells me that they tried to remain open, but most relied on lorcith sales to the Elvraeth to remain open. When the lorcith stopped coming, and the sales stopped happening, most of the smiths weren't able to keep up. The guild now possesses each of these smithies."

"What happened to them?" Rsiran asked.

Haern shook his head. "I don't know."

"Don't know, or can't See?"

Haern sighed. "My ability isn't like that, Rsiran. I can't simply observe something like that without knowing more about it. Maybe it once was, back when I still served Venass, but not any longer. Now, I'm no different from anyone else with my ability."

"That's not true," Jessa said.

Haern sniffed. "You're right. Most with my ability are Elvraeth."

They fell silent for a moment. "I still don't know why you brought us here," Rsiran said. "What did you want me to see?"

"First this. I don't know what's happening here, but the disappearance of smiths is important somehow, especially after what happened with your father."

But he didn't understand why. His father might be able to work with lorcith, but he'd never been willing to listen to what the ore told him. Without that, anything that he'd make out of it was weaker than it could have been.

His father would never have been able to listen to lorcith to make bracelets like Rsiran had made. Even if he were willing to listen to the lorcith, he would have to have a well-enough stocked supply to be able to find a piece willing to work with him.

Would any other smith?

"You said first this," Jessa reminded Haern.

Haern nodded, shadows along his face making the deep frown appear darker, and the scar on his cheek, the one where his implant had been, starker.

"First this," he said again, gesturing around them. "It wasn't the only reason you needed to come here, but this was how I started to make the connection. When I realized what happened to these smiths, and pieced it together with what we know of lorcith, and what Rsiran has told us about Ilphaesn, I started to question other things that I've been hearing."

"What other things?" Jessa asked.

Haern shook his head. "It no longer matters."

"Then what does?" Frustration came out clearly in her voice, making her louder than she likely intended. Jessa was always careful with noise. It's what made her such an excellent sneak. "Come on, Haern, stop doing this to us. Why did you bring us here?"

He nodded to Rsiran. "Him. And what he found."

A chill ran along Rsiran's spine at the comment.

"I think I know what the map is for," Haern said.

Rsiran tensed, thinking of the dimensions within the map, contours that were *almost* familiar, though he couldn't piece together why they would be. That map had nothing to do with the other sheet of metal that he'd discovered, nothing that would tie them together with a unified purpose other than the fact that they both *seemed* similar.

"What then?" Jessa.

"I'm surprised he doesn't know. He's been there before. Hell, he's the one who took me there."

Rsiran felt his heart stop, putting together what Haern said, and beginning to understand why the map might be familiar. The levels and dimensions to it and a place where he had led Haern. A hidden place, and dangerous.

"The Alchemist Guild?" he whispered.

Haern nodded. "I think your map is a way through it."

As Haern said it, Rsiran sensed the sudden connection of lorcith, a flash from the knife that he'd sensed from Valn.

He grabbed Jessa and lunged for Haern, and then *pulled* them to Rsiran's smithy with a quick Slide.

CHAPTER 29

"I don't know how he found us," Rsiran said.

Haern sat near the hearth, moving a few small logs into place so that it took flames. He frowned as he worked, the irregular lump of heartstone from the explosion resting on the ground next to him. Every so often, he glanced down at it, and lifted it to inspect the heartstone as if something might change from the last time he'd checked it. Once in a while, his eyes wandered to the lorcith Rsiran had arranged around the smithy, before he turned back to the heartstone that had nearly killed Rsiran.

Rsiran wondered what Haern Saw. Was there something about the heartstone? Haern didn't have Jessa's Sight or Rsiran's ability with the metal itself, but he'd been drawn to it as soon as they emerged in the smithy.

"You said they can't detect you when you Slide with this new method," Jessa said.

"I don't think they can. Della couldn't."

"There are things Della cannot do," Haern said without looking over at them. "Don't tie your safety into what she can or cannot accomplish."

"I'm not tying our safety to it," Rsiran said, "only that she's proven capable of detecting and influencing me Sliding. If Della can't do it, then it isn't likely that it can be done."

Haern stood and dusted his hands off on his pants. "The others with your ability, you've seen them?"

Rsiran nodded. "I've seen Josun and a few others, why?"

"And you commented on how much stronger Josun Elvraeth was with Sliding than you."

The first time he'd seen Josun, he hadn't even realized that he had been Sliding. He had moved so quickly with every step he took, that it had been nearly impossible for him to know.

"Haern, I understand what you're implying," Rsiran said, "but this is *Della*."

"And she would be the first to tell you that she's not the strongest in everything that she does, wouldn't she? If we were talking about Healing, I might agree that there is no one like her. But we're not. And you don't know if these others can track your Sliding even when you do it this other way."

"But I heard what they said."

"Maybe they wanted you to hear that," Haern suggested. "Maybe they knew you were there."

Rsiran didn't think that likely, but it raised a different concern, one that he hadn't considered as fully as he should have. Della *wasn't* the strongest with all of her abilities, and he'd asked her to test Jessa's bracelets. What if they worked against someone like Della, but wouldn't work with someone stronger than her?

Maybe he needed to create another set for her, one with heartstone infused inside them. Heartstone had blocked Brusus, and he suspected that they would keep even Evaelyn from influencing his thoughts, or Compelling him.

"Even were that true, I didn't Slide there, Haern," he said.

"Then it's possible they have another way of finding you," Haern said.

Again, Rsiran wasn't in agreement with Haern's conjecture. Had they known another way of finding him, whether they could detect lorcith like he could, or even heartstone, they would have noticed him in the warehouse. But they hadn't. And they had thought he'd disappeared.

That meant that Valn had been at his father's smithy for a different reason.

He drew a handful of knives to him from the table and stuffed them into his pocket.

Jessa jerked her head toward him and her eyes went wide. "Rsiran—"

"I've got to see," he said. "You can't be safe with me, not if I need to move quickly."

"Don't do this," she begged.

Rsiran stopped in front of her and slipped his arms around her neck and hugged her. He couldn't—he *wouldn't*—leave without making certain that she would be okay with him going. "If she's there—"

"You don't know that she will be," Jessa said. "And they've managed to follow you all over Elaeavn. What happens if they capture you? We wouldn't know!"

"They're not going to capture me," he said.

"You didn't think Shael was going to capture you, either. Or the Forgotten."

"This is different," he said.

"How can you say that?" She clung to him, refusing to let him go, knowing that if she didn't, he wouldn't be able to Slide without taking her with him. "How can you know this will be different?"

Rsiran let out a steady breath. "Because I'm different. I don't Slide the same way that they do, and if you come, I'll be distracted." He glanced over to where Haern again leaned over the hearth, still studying the misshapen piece of heartstone. "Haern is right. When it comes to you, I don't always think straight. If I'm worried about you, I don't know that I'll be able to act as quickly as I need to."

"You did with Thom," she reminded.

"That was different. I was taking him away from you. I thought I was keeping you safer."

She shook her head and slapped him on the chest. "Didn't work out as you planned, did it?"

Rsiran forced a smile. "It usually doesn't."

Jessa sighed. "That's what I'm afraid of."

* * * * *

Rsiran emerged within the enclosed area outside his family smithy. It was a place he knew well, where he'd spent much of his days cleaning up scrap metal and arranging it so that his father would know that he'd been working. It was a place where he could get his bearings before Sliding into the smithy itself.

Little had changed since he'd last come here. At the same time, so much had changed.

The air smelled of metal. Iron and copper mostly, but there was a residual odor of lorcith, one that was not nearly as strong as what he sensed in *his* smithy. Under the metallic scent was the stink from stagnant water. Even with the dim light coming off the bracelets, he could make out a thin film that grew on the surface of the full bucket near the door.

His father never would have tolerated leaving this area so messy. Rsiran would never have tolerated it, either. A part of him had the urge to start cleaning, to organize the scraps, but that wasn't why he'd come.

A narrow window opened into the shop, and Rsiran peered through it.

Was there motion inside? He couldn't tell. There was nothing that gave him any sign that someone was in the smithy. For all he knew, Valn had simply emerged along the street by chance.

Rsiran wouldn't know anything without Sliding inside.

Before he did, he checked the door, but it was locked. It would have been too easy for it to be unlocked.

He considered where to emerge in the smithy. After all the time he'd spent here growing up, he knew this smithy nearly as well as he knew the one he currently occupied. His attachment to it was different, though. This was to have been his some day, but he'd abandoned hope of that ever happening the moment he Slid away from Ilphaesn and did not return. The smithy he had now suited him. Even if it would never officially be his.

Once he decided, he pulled the image into mind and Slid, emerging in his father's old office.

The last time that he'd been here, it had been empty except for a collection of papers that Rsiran still hadn't deciphered. Much like the rest of the smithy had been empty. It was the best place for him to emerge, knowing that if the office were empty, there would be no place for someone to attack him from behind.

He readied all the knives that he possessed, while at the same time fixing an image of the hidden mine within Ilphaesn in his mind. If he needed to Slide away, he would do so to somewhere they wouldn't be able to follow. The bars of alloy prevented anyone but him from reaching there.

Nothing moved.

Rsiran started to allow himself to relax, but was that a sound he heard?

He couldn't be certain.

He took a step forward, moving as quietly as he could. When he reached the door to the main part of the smithy, he hesitated. With the darkness—even with his enhanced Sight—he couldn't see anything. He needed light.

Or one of his knives.

Rsiran pulled a small knife from his pocket, careful that it didn't make noise jostling against any others. It glowed with a bright light that pushed away some of the nearer shadows, but not enough for him to completely see.

He *pushed* against the knife, sending it across the smithy before he *pulled* it back.

Rsiran wasn't sure what he expected to see. The smithy was empty, no different from when he'd been here before.

He sent the knife again, this time in a different direction, sweeping toward the forge. He didn't let the knife sail fully across the smithy, and *pulled* back when it reached the door. Still nothing.

Why had Valn been here?

There was nothing in the smithy to explain why he might have come.

And no sign of Alyse.

That was the worst part for him. All of this, everything that he'd been doing, for a sister who didn't care whether he lived. But Rsiran couldn't simply do nothing, not if she was trapped, and not if she needed help that only he could offer.

Rsiran stepped out of the office and into the smithy itself. As he did, the bracelets on his arms went cool, then cold.

Someone was trying to Read him.

Where?

He pulled three knives from his pockets and sent them around the room, leaving them in each of the corners. Not for anchors, though they would work in that capacity if needed, but for the bright white light that radiated from them. He didn't know if any others could see the white light—but since Jessa and Brusus could not, he didn't think others could—but the light somehow gave him enough to see, to clear the shadows out of the smithy.

Nothing moved.

The bracelets remained cold.

Someone tried to Read him, but they either weren't in the smithy, or they somehow hid from him.

He focused on lorcith, on the connection to the metal. When he'd detected Valn before, he'd carried one of Rsiran's knives with him. Only the knives that he'd brought into the smithy resonated for him.

But there was a distant sense of lorcith, one that he recognized, and different from all the others that existed throughout the city. With as much as he'd produced, there were many of his forgings scattered around the city, but that was *around* the city, this was *under* it.

Beneath him.

Like all buildings in Elaeavn, the smithy was built on the side of the rocky slope leading down to the bay. The palace stood above most—but not all; Krali Rock towered over everything, and there were a few buildings staggered around the base of Krali that rose higher than the palace—but like everything in the city, there was nothing but rock below the building.

Or so Rsiran had thought.

His father never revealed a lower level to the smithy, but what he sensed was unmistakable. It came from beneath him, and far enough that he could just barely get the sense of the lorcith.

Rsiran could Slide to it, use the knife he detected as an anchor, but what would he find?

Would he appear somewhere that Valn and anyone helping him would be? Or would it only be Valn?

Rsiran made his way around the smithy, looking for sign of something—anything—that would help him find a way below the smithy, but there was nothing.

Either he risked himself and Slid, or he didn't go down.

CHAPTER 30

Rsiran returned to his smithy. Jessa and Haern stood talking silently near the hearth. She looked up as soon as he emerged, relief washing over her face.

"What did you find?" she asked.

Rsiran held the knives that he'd used for light around the smithy, and shook his head. "Nothing in the smithy."

Jessa glanced at Haern. "I'm glad you came back to us—"

"I need to go back," he said. "But I need your help."

"What?"

"I didn't find anything in the smithy, but I sensed the knife—the same one I've sensed on Valn each time I've seen him—*beneath* the smithy."

Haern turned slowly. "Did you know there was a space beneath the smithy?"

Rsiran shook his head. "There should be nothing."

A troubled expression crossed Haern's face. "And you think to bring Jessa with you to find a way down?"

"I could Slide," Rsiran began, "but then I don't know where I would end up, or what I would find. If they know I've discovered it, any advantage of surprise we might have is lost."

"What if the only way down is by Sliding?" Jessa asked.

"There would be another way in," Haern suggested. "If there is something"—from his tone, it sounded as if he wasn't convinced—"then there would need to be a way in for those who couldn't Slide as Rsiran does."

That had been Rsiran's hope. Carrying someone else in a Slide was difficult enough. It got easier with practice, and he'd taken Jessa with him enough times that he did it without the same strain that he'd once experienced Sliding, but others who *didn't* have someone like Jessa would have to exert themselves significantly. It made it more likely that there was some other way below.

"I could use your help as well, Haern" Rsiran said.

Haern stared at the misshapen lump of heartstone on the ground and shook his head. "Not this way. I need to find Brusus and look into something first." He ran his finger along his scar, and his eyes went distant the way that they did when he attempted a Seeing. "I find him, then we'll come looking for you."

"You won't know how to find us," Rsiran said.

Haern frowned at him. "You think I can't follow you?"

"I don't want to wait," Rsiran started. "Not if they have—"

Haern looked up and nodded once. "Don't wait. What I can See tells me that you can't wait."

Haern made his way past Rsiran, pausing at the table to grab a pair of his knives, and then left the smithy, pulling the door tightly behind him.

Jessa locked the door, slipping the bars into place in the ground and over the frame. "What would he need to tell Brusus that was so urgent?"

"I don't know, but he told me not to wait." What had Haern Seen that would make him rush out? And what was it about the piece of heartstone that troubled him so much? Haern had stared at it from the moment he'd emerged in the smithy.

Rsiran lifted it from the ground and carried it to the table. As he did, he focused on the heartstone within it, connecting to the way the metal pulled on him. Was there something more to the heartstone than he realized? Was there something that Haern had detected that he had missed?

Rsiran found nothing that made any sense. He could tell the contours and the layers to the metal, but nothing more than that.

When he set it down, he turned to Jessa and she nodded.

Using his memory of the smithy, he Slid, *pulling* them forward, drawing them into the office of the smithy.

Something was different than it had been even moments before.

Rsiran raised a finger to his lips, warning Jessa to silence.

He pulled a pair of knives from his pocket and sent them skimming through the smithy. The light from them let him see, enough that he noted the way the stone near the back of the forge appeared different.

Had it been that way the last time he'd been here?

Nothing else appeared different. He *pulled* the knives back to him and kept them out, ready to *push* again if needed.

"What was that?" Jessa whispered.

"I needed to see if something was different," he said.

"With your knives? That glow I can't see?"

He held them out for her to take. The glow wasn't as pronounced as when he held them, but enough that it lit her face. "They give me light," he told her. "That's the change in my Sight." He had thought that when holding the crystal, he'd somehow been granted Sight, and he had, only it was different from the kind of Sight that Jessa possessed. His worked together with lorcith—and heartstone—to give him his ability.

"That's... weird," she said.

He shrugged. "It's what it is. Look near the forge. Tell me what you see."

Rsiran *pushed* one of the knives toward the forge as Jessa focused on it. She frowned, her brow furrowed deeply, and then shook her head. "I don't see anything," she said.

With the light coming off the knife, Rsiran could make out the way the stone pushed slightly away from the floor, but not directly under the forge, only behind it, in a place that would be otherwise difficult to reach.

"There's nothing here, Rsiran," she said.

That had been what he had noted. The sense of lorcith remained, but if anything, was even more distant than when he'd sensed it before.

Rsiran stopped at the forge and went to his knees and traced a finger around the stone. The difference was subtle, barely anything at all, but he'd grown up in the smithy and recognized when it felt different.

What he didn't understand was what reason the stone would be different.

"What do you see here?" he asked Jessa.

She came next to him and peered at the floor. Her fingers traced the edge of the stone slowly, and she let out a soft breath. "*You* saw this from back there?"

He nodded.

"Maybe not a babe anymore after all."

He chuckled softly. "I think it has more to do with the fact that I grew up here. My father was pretty particular about everything, so I learned to notice if there was anything out of place. *This* is different."

Rsiran couldn't explain it better than that, and wasn't sure that it mattered.

"You think this is an access to a level below?" Jessa asked.

"That's the problem. I don't know if there's anything to it."

"Well, there's a tracing here, and something else…"

She started crawling behind the forge. Rsiran had swept behind it, but had never placed his entire body behind it. He could imagine the reaction his father would have if he had. When he forgot to put out the coals, he got into enough trouble, nearly as much as when he thought to forge items on his own using lorcith. How would he have reacted to him searching for some hidden passage behind the forge?

Jessa started to back out. "It's nothing. A few strange marks is all. Nothing that would give us any way to get below."

Rsiran sighed and turned back to the office.

When he'd grown up, it was the one place that he'd been forbidden to visit. Within the office, his father kept orders and forgings that were special to him, but nothing else. It was where he would spend most of his time…

And if there *were* a secret access within the smithy, wouldn't it be within his office?

He hurried back there and looked around. When his father had cleared out the smithy, he had noted that something had changed, but Rsiran hadn't spent enough time in here, not as he had in the rest of the smithy, to know what it might have been.

"What is it?" Jessa asked.

"Can you tell if anything is moved?"

There was a bookshelf against one wall. When he'd caught glimpses inside the office, the shelves had contained the journeymen forgings, items that had been made to demonstrate skill before they moved onto another smithy. All were gone now.

The long table that was pushed up against the wall had once been stacked with papers, and was now empty. Once a chair had been in here, but that had been taken away as well, like so much else.

"Look at the floor there," Jessa said, motioning toward the bookshelf.

Rsiran let one of the knives float toward the floor, giving him enough light to see what Jessa saw without difficulty. On the ground where she indicated, faint lines scratched along the stone matching each end of the bookshelf.

He *pulled* the knife back to him and grabbed the sides of the bookshelf, expecting it to move slowly, but it eased away from the wall, scratching softly at the ground.

"Uh, Rsiran?" Jessa said.

She had moved out of the way and stood beside the table, but her eyes were directed toward the wall, behind the bookshelf.

He stepped around followed the direction of her gaze.

Set into the wall was a small curved metal panel coming up to his waist. Streaks of green ran through it.

"It looks like the metal I found in the forest," Rsiran said, crouching as he ran his hands along the panel. The darker metal was iron, and the green he suspected was grindl, just like what he'd found in the hut. He leaned back on his heels, studying the wall. On the other side of the wall was the fenced-in area outside the smithy.

How thick was the wall?

He could imagine this as nothing more than a repair made to the smithy, but the pattern of the iron and grindl made that less likely.

With certainty, he knew that whatever was behind this panel was connected to the map that he'd found, the one Haern thought was tied to the alchemists.

Jessa reached around him and traced her fingers around the edge of the panel. A curious expression pinched her mouth, and she pushed on a part of the panel that he couldn't see. Part of the metal popped out, leaving something like a handle.

"How did you know?" he asked.

"This isn't the first time I've found strange doors," she answered.

He waited for her to say something more, but she didn't. Instead, she grabbed the handle and pulled. It swung away with a puff of air that reminded him of the wind that blew through the mines. Darkness met them on the other side.

Rsiran sent a knife forward, using it something like a lantern, illuminating a cramped opening with darkness stretching down and away. Stairs were set into the stone that led beneath the smithy.

"Do you see that?" he asked.

"Yeah, but I still don't know how you see it." Jessa leaned back and took a deep breath. "What now?"

Rsiran wondered if he really wanted to risk Jessa going with him beneath the smithy, but there might be something she could see that he did not. Had it not been for her, he might not have found a way to open the panel. He might be able to Slide, but she had the experience sneaking into places like this, hidden places where trespassers weren't meant to go.

"Now I guess we have to see where it leads."

Jessa smiled and started into the space in the wall. He grabbed her arm and pulled, but she pulled back. "You think you should lead? I can see better than you. Besides, I'm quieter than you."

Rsiran let her go, and she moved down the stairs. He floated the knife alongside, watching as she descended, and then stopped.

"It levels out here," she said in a whisper.

"I'll be right there."

From inside the office, he closed the panel, sealing the wall shut again, and then pushed the shelf back into place. Then he focused on where he'd last seen Jessa, and started his Slide to her.

Just as he started his Slide, the front door to the smithy rattled, the sound like a key going into a lock.

Rsiran nearly lost his focus, but safely *pulled* himself down beneath the smithy.

The air was cool and slightly damp, and it took his eyes a moment to adjust to the glow from the knife. As they did, he found Jessa waiting for him down a narrow hall. Rock walls lined both sides of the hall, with a low-hanging ceiling overhead. He had been lucky he hadn't emerged with his head stuck in rock.

"What happened?" Jessa asked.

"We should hurry," he said. "There was someone coming into the smithy when I Slid."

"Thought it was empty."

"And I thought there was no passage beneath it. Doesn't change that we should hurry."

Jessa waved her hand. "Which way? This tunnel goes in both directions."

Rsiran listened for the sound of the lorcith that he recognized as coming from Valn. It was distant, but definitely coming from a specific direction. He pointed.

"That leads to Upper Town," Jessa said.

Rsiran hadn't made the connection, but now that she said something, he suspected that she was right. If he went the other way, the tunnel would lead down the slope, toward Lower Town. He couldn't say with certainty, but the sense of the knife came from the direction toward Upper Town.

Above them, he heard a faint scraping.

Jessa froze.

Rsiran *pulled* himself to her, and they hurried up the tunnel toward Upper Town.

As they made their way, he expected the ground to follow the slope found outside, trailing up the hillside as it made its way into Upper Town, but that wasn't case. The ground was flat and ran fairly straight.

Jessa led the way, moving quickly. Her feet were silent, much more so than his, and she occasionally glanced back his way and shook her head.

After they'd gone barely a dozen steps, a side tunnel opened up. Rsiran listened, and the sense of lorcith seemed to come from that direction. He pointed, and Jessa nodded.

They ducked into this tunnel. The walls were narrower here than in the other tunnel, and there was less a sense of wind moving, nothing like the Ilphaesn mines. Had he not had as much experience in the mines, this might have been a more terrifying experience, but no longer was he trapped in the dark. Now he had the strange light from the knives.

He took to floating one of his knives next to him, holding it hovering in the air as if some sort of lantern. When he first did it, he caught Jessa's puzzled look, but then she nodded.

"Wish I could see what you do when that thing is floating here with me." She spoke in a soft whisper, her voice barely carrying to him. At least it wouldn't reach far down the tunnel.

"And I wish I could see like you do without needing it," he told her, pitching his voice as low as she did.

They hadn't walked far before Rsiran saw a door.

This wasn't like the metal plate that had been behind the bookshelf. This was a wooden doorway, much like any other he would find throughout the city. A strange mark, something almost like a letter, was etched on the surface. Jessa traced her fingers along it.

"Where do you think this leads?" she asked.

"Don't know." The sense of lorcith came from behind the door, and no longer moved as it had. Rsiran wondered what they were beneath now. They hadn't gone that far, but far enough to have moved away from the smithy entirely. How could there be such an extensive network of tunnels down here?

And, more importantly, why?

He glanced back down the tunnel in the direction they'd come. Had they continued onward, they would have reached Upper Town, all without walking along the street above. This tunnel appeared old, the walls irregular in places that reminded him of the mines, but he detected no lorcith around him. In the mines, he sensed it all around, everywhere throughout the rock.

Jessa looked past him and pressed a finger to his lips. She leaned into his ear and whispered. "We need to be careful. Voices carry in places like this. Even whispers. We need to be quiet until we know what we're going to see."

He nodded. He had no doubt about what he'd heard before he Slid from the smithy. There was someone else coming this way, and given the fact that the smithy was otherwise empty, there shouldn't be anyone else in the tunnels.

The air in the tunnel changed.

Jessa reached for the door and tried the handle. It didn't open.

She dropped to her knees and pulled out her lock pick. Within moments, she had the door open, and swung it carefully, only enough to peer inside.

With the door open, she popped her head through.

Rsiran sent the knife floating back down the tunnel behind them. As he did, a shadow flickered.

He *pulled* on the knife, drawing it back to him quickly, and nudged Jessa through the door before whoever was in the tunnel with them could see them. It might already have been too late.

The space on the other side of the door looked like a large storeroom.

And they weren't alone.

CHAPTER 31

A LANTERN FLASHED ON, its bright orange light that would have weakened Jessa's Sight, but did nothing to impact Rsiran. He had a pair of knives ready and leaned against the door to keep whoever might be on the other side from coming in.

The woman he'd seen in the forest stood in the middle of the room, a dark cloak covering her shoulders, her dark eyes glittering at him. "Rsiran Lareth." She said his name with a strange familiarity.

Rsiran *pulled* another pair of knives from his pockets and held them ready. He hadn't seen Valn, but he sensed the lorcith knife he carried and suspected that he hid somewhere, if only Rsiran could find him.

"Far side of the room," Jessa whispered.

Rsiran flicked his gaze in that direction and noted a shadow there. It was the same place he sensed the knife.

"And you're Sarah," Rsiran said. He stepped forward, putting himself between Sarah and Jessa, making certain to keep a connection to

Jessa. If he had to Slide quickly, he would need to have contact with her.

Sarah glanced toward Valn before turning her attention back to Rsiran. "I am. How, may I ask, do you know?"

"You've been following me."

A smile pulled on the corners of her mouth. "Ah, so you were there. I started to question whether we were wrong about you, but he," she said, tipping her head toward the far corner, "was convinced that we were not."

"Valn?" Rsiran asked.

There was a flutter of color, and a swirling sense that Rsiran felt that faded quickly.

"Rsiran," Jessa whispered. "He just Slid."

"I know."

Valn appeared next to Sarah. The sense of the lorcith knife pulsed strongly from him, practically burning through the fabric of his pants.

"How did he find us?" Valn asked Sarah.

She studied Rsiran for a moment. "His father, I would guess."

"Only supposed to be guild members. That's how we keep—"

Sarah cut him off with a wave of her hand.

"Why have you been following me?" Rsiran asked.

Sarah hesitated. Darkness flickered across her eyes before fading. With the light from his knives, he saw the green of her eyes surge briefly brighter before fading, much like they did with Brusus when he Pushed.

Rsiran considered raising his mental barriers. Since forging the bracelets, he'd allowed himself to leave them lowered. With them down, he was more attuned to the lorcith, and felt a stronger connection to it. Maybe it was the reason he was able to suddenly see the light from the metal.

"We should go," Jessa said softly.

Rsiran could Slide them away, get them to safety, but he wanted answers. So far, Sarah and Valn didn't seem as if they were going to attack. "Tell me," Rsiran said. "Why are you after me?"

He didn't expect Sarah to answer. When he'd been abducted by Venass and then by the Forgotten, they had forced themselves on him. Venass had been willing to let him die if he failed to Slide from the cell, and the Forgotten had poisoned him, willing to do whatever it took to get the answers they wanted. Regardless of which side they worked for, they had shown the lengths they would go with him.

He would not let Sarah and Valn take him and Jessa without a fight. This time, he'd trained enough, and had some experience fighting, that he was willing to do what was needed to keep her safe.

"Because we need your help," Sarah answered.

Rsiran tensed. He didn't like the connotation of the kind of help they wanted. When he'd been asked to help before, they hadn't wanted his help so much as his ability. They had wanted to use him. "Who are you with?" Rsiran asked. "Venass? I refuse to answer the summons. I think I've shown Thom that I—"

"Not Venass," Sarah said, glancing over to Valn.

Rsiran let out a sigh. That meant the Forgotten. "Then if it's the other, I've already experienced how you ask for help. You can tell Evaelyn or Inna or whoever you're with that I have no interest in helping. Just leave me alone."

Sarah and Valn looked at each other. Sarah's eyes widened slightly. "See? He knows."

Valn considered Rsiran and shook his head. "He doesn't know. Look at him, Sarah. He asked if we came from Venass."

"Can you blame him? After what he's been through—"

"Tell me what you're talking about, or I leave. I think I've proven that you'll have difficulty following me."

He was already preparing where to Slide. They might be able to reach him if he was too slow, but he could take them to Ilphaesn and leave them in the mines, trapped like Josun had been. Rsiran wouldn't even feel any sympathy for them. It would be hard to find any sympathy after what he'd been through.

"Come with us," Sarah said.

Rsiran glanced at Jessa. "I'm not going anywhere until you tell me—"

"You want to see your sister, right?"

Alyse. "You have her?"

Neither of them answered.

Rsiran let out a sigh and looked to Jessa. He leaned toward her, making certain to keep his words as soft as possible. "You should go. Get word to the others. You don't need to be pulled into this with me."

She pounded on his chest softly. "You aren't leaving me *here*, you idiot."

"I could Slide you back and then return."

"Or you could Slide us both. We don't need to do this for her."

Jessa still didn't understand. "I do."

"Fine. If that's what you intend, you're not going without me. The two of us together have a better chance of keeping you safe than you do by yourself."

Sarah and Valn waited.

When Rsiran nodded, they turned and started across the room. Rsiran had expected them to go through the door, but they didn't. Then who was on the other side of the door? He had seen *someone* moving in the tunnels, if not Valn and Sarah, then who?

Unless they had been there to make certain that Rsiran didn't leave.

"How did you know that I'd come after you?" Rsiran asked.

Sarah paused and glanced over her shoulder. "We didn't."

"Then why were you waiting for me… If not me, who then?"

Sarah looked at Valn, then back to Rsiran. "It doesn't matter, not now that you've come."

They stepped into the darkness of another tunnel, though this one was wider than the last. Jessa held tightly to Rsiran's arm, clinging to him in case they needed to Slide quickly. With her behind him, at least he didn't run the same risk of surprise like he'd experienced with the Forgotten when they'd come behind him and smacked him on the head.

They passed other paths along the way, and Rsiran motioned to each.

Sarah turned a few times, enough that Rsiran began to lose track of where they were. If he wasn't able to Slide, he could be trapped down here. As it was, without knowing where they led him, there would be no way of getting back on foot.

He could leave anchors, though.

Rsiran considered dropping one of his knives, but decided to save it for later, for when he might have a greater need.

The tunnel began to widen, and as it did, a faint color came to the walls. Lorcith.

It glowed all around, slowly building with each step. Rsiran put the knife he carried away, no longer needing the light from it to guide him.

Jessa frowned. "What is it?"

He leaned into her. Sarah or Valn could be Listeners, but she needed to know what he detected. "Lorcith all around."

"Wouldn't you have known if there was this much lorcith within the city?"

He should have. That meant that wherever they were was either in some place where he couldn't detect the lorcith—unlikely as that might be—or it was in a place where there already was a significant amount of lorcith.

Either answer led to the same place: the palace.

Rsiran strained his awareness all around him, searching through the lorcith in the walls, seeking the connection to it. If they were in the palace, or more accurately *beneath* the palace, then there would also be the heartstone that he detected when here. As he focused on it, he realized that it was above him as well.

If they were with the Forgotten, had they managed to somehow burrow into the palace?

If that was the case, why did they need him?

Rsiran stopped and took Jessa's hand. "I'm not helping you break into the palace."

Sarah paused and looked back to him. "Break in? What are you talking about?"

Rsiran waved at the walls. "That's where we are. Beneath the palace. Don't pretend you don't know."

"Of course we know," Valn said with a grunt. "Can't reach where we're going without going through here. Not this way, at least."

Valn motioned for Sarah to follow and keep moving. Rsiran stood for a moment, debating whether he should follow, or whether he should Slide Jessa to safety. The longer he went, the less comfortable he felt.

But nothing he did by Sliding to safety would help him find what happened to Alyse.

That drove him in a way that surprised him.

They continued onward, making their way through the tunnels with the light from the lorcith all around. How was it that he'd broken into the palace now twice, but the third time, he was led inside?

And what would happen to him this time? The first time he'd gone to the palace, he'd been forced to nearly poison the council. The second time had been to discover what the Elvraeth protected, and to see if there was anything that he would need to do to keep it from Venass and the Forgotten. The third time… What would he be asked to do this time?

Jessa patted his hand in an attempt to reassure him. He was thankful for it. Without her, he didn't think that he'd be able to keep going.

Or maybe it was worse than that. Without her, would he go rushing in, unmindful of the risk to himself?

He sighed. Either way, she kept him safe.

How long, he wondered, would he be able to keep her safe?

CHAPTER 32

Sarah stopped at an intersection in the tunnel. Rsiran realized that wasn't quite right. The wall changed, no longer stone, and no longer glowing with the same white light. There was a subtle shift to the hue, almost a bluish light.

He didn't have to push away the sense of lorcith to know that this was alloy. And if they were beneath the palace, then this would be the strange structure outside the palace that they'd broken into in order to reach the palace. Instead of breaking in, now he was simply standing beneath it.

Sarah pressed something into the wall—a slender length of alloy, he noted—and a section of the wall slid away. Valn stepped inside, disappearing.

"You wanted to see your sister, didn't you?" Sarah asked.

"Not like this, Rsiran," Jessa said. "You don't know what's on the other side."

But he did know what was on the other side. They had been in the palace before. He had Slid them away, using the sword as an anchor, even before he knew how he managed to do it. At least now, he knew that the alloy wouldn't be able to prevent him from Sliding. If Sarah and Valn were Forgotten, or even if they were with Venass, regardless of what they might claim, they would know that the alloy didn't obstruct him as it did others with the ability to Slide.

"Come," Sarah urged.

She stepped inside. Jessa pulled on his hand, but Rsiran shook his head. "This is something I have to do. I can get us to safety. You'll have to trust that I can."

"I *do* trust you. I don't trust *them*." Jessa sniffed at the pale white flower tucked into the charm.

Rsiran kissed her on the cheek. "I'll keep you safe," he whispered.

"I'm not sure that you can."

Rsiran swallowed, and then they stepped through the door.

It slid closed behind them. Soft blue light glowed all around. Rsiran's eyes took a moment to adjust but when they did, he nearly fell over. He'd been here before.

The Alchemist Guild house.

When Haern had mentioned that the map he'd found seemed to be directions to the Alchemist Guild, he wasn't sure what to make of it. But it made sense.

Rsiran thought about the contours within the map, the way the heartstone flowed. All of it had been familiar when he first held the brick after it came from the mold. He hadn't understood why it would have been familiar, but now he thought that he did.

It was a map for how to find the Alchemist Guild.

Not only that, but the map—the contours that he detected in the grindl and had been recreated for him in heartstone—was the way to reach the guild through the tunnels beneath his father's smithy. He could practically see it in his mind.

But how would his father have followed it?

Even for that, Rsiran thought he had the answer. Like Jessa, his father was Sighted. Had Jessa known what she was looking for, she might have been able to follow the map without him needing to make the form.

Then what about the other scrap of metal that he'd found in Thyr? That hadn't been a map, at least not one like the one that he'd discovered in the hut.

Rsiran stared at the line of drawers. The last time he'd been here, he'd stolen from the Alchemist Guild and had nearly lost Haern. "I'd thought that they had forgotten," he said.

Where had Sarah and Valn gone?

"The Forgotten?" Jessa asked.

Rsiran could Slide from here. He'd done it before, so he didn't fear that he wouldn't be able, but why would they have brought him here? Did they intend to prove a point to him, to show him that they knew he had been the one to break in that night?

"Not the Forgotten," he said. He had been wrong about Sarah and Valn. They were neither Venass or the Forgotten. But they might be worse. "I thought they had forgotten, but apparently they didn't."

"What are you talking about? Where are we?"

The light began to increase in intensity, and he shielded his eyes. Jessa didn't. Either the light didn't bother her, or… it was heartstone alloy.

A door opened. The light made it difficult for him to see clearly, but he sensed the change in the lorcith. Heartstone came with it. Not alloy, but pure heartstone.

How was he able to sense both at the same time?

"Rsiran Lareth," a voice said. It was deep and carried. "We've spent a long time trying to find you."

He reached for Jessa and found her still holding onto his arm. He wanted to be ready to Slide if needed. "What is this? Why does the Alchemist Guild have my sister?"

A man appeared from the blue light. He had a long face and a thick graying beard. In some ways, he reminded Rsiran of his father when he'd found him in Asador. Beards were uncommon in Elaeavn. Traders, and men from outside the city wore beards, but those within the city, especially those who wanted to impress the Elvraeth, made a point of remaining clean-shaven. The man shifted a long, light blue robe around his shoulders and smiled.

"You don't deny that you're him?"

Rsiran shook his head. "Why would I deny? It seems you already know. You've sent your—" He hesitated, looking for signs of Sarah and Valn. Sarah stood against one of the walls, and the bright blue light made it difficult for him to tell clearly where Valn had gone. He still sensed the lorcith, but it moved. Either Valn paced nearby or, more likely given the way the lorcith flickered, he Slid from place to place. "Your Slider and whatever she is looking for me."

The man smiled. "Whatever she is? I thought that with everything you've been through, you'd have come to appreciate the role of a Thenar."

"Thenar? That's what you call them when they can detect Sliding?"

The man glanced at Sarah. "Oh, she can do much more than detect, though from what I hear, she hasn't had the same success with you, now has she. May I ask why that would be?"

Could that be the reason that they'd brought him here? It seemed strange if true. They wouldn't have needed to bring him to the Alchemist Guild to ask, unless they wanted to prove something to him.

"You can ask," Rsiran said, noting that the bracelets on his wrists went cold. The last time he'd felt them go cold had been while in the smithy. Someone, either here or hidden where he couldn't see them, was trying to Read him.

He watched the man's face, but it remained neutral, only the hint of a smile present. Not him, at least he didn't think so.

"Where are we?" Jessa asked.

Rsiran looked over to her. With the blue light all around, she had an ethereal glow about her, making her look lovelier than he'd ever seen her.

Jessa elbowed him. "Rsiran?"

"This is the Alchemist Guild," he said then nodded toward the man. "And I presume this is the guildlord."

It was a title that gave him even more power than almost anyone in Elaeavn other than one of the council. He'd never even seen the smith guildlord, though he knew that each guild had one.

The bracelets flashed colder again.

The man nodded his head. "Not the Alchemist Guild house, but close. And you may call me Ephram."

"Only Ephram?"

He tipped his head. "Do last names matter?"

"They do if you're Elvraeth." He gambled, not certain whether that was true, but the way that Ephram watched Rsiran left him with the impression that he had Elvraeth features that reminded him of Josun. That, and the fact that he attempted to Read him. Rsiran was certain that it was Ephram.

Ephram's smile tightened. "Now you make dangerous claims."

"How many of the guildlords are Elvraeth?" Jessa asked.

Ephram turned to her, studying her. His eyes darkened as he did, and Jessa's hand squeezed Rsiran's briefly. He suspected that Ephram attempted to Read her as well, but the bracelets would have prevented it.

"Interesting," was all that he said. "You must be Jessa Ntalen?"

"Where is my sister?" Rsiran asked.

Ephram nodded to the end of the room, and Valn disappeared in a flash. Ephram paced a moment. "We have been searching for you for some time."

"Why me?"

Ephram chuckled. "Asks the man able to manipulate lorcith and heartstone." He watched Rsiran, but he made a point of keeping his face as calm as possible, not willing to reveal more than necessary. They might know what he was capable of doing, but he didn't need to share anything that they *didn't* know. "And who can travel through both. Such a man is dangerous. And useful."

"Others have tried to use me. They have failed."

Ephram nodded to Rsiran. "Oh, I understand that they have."

Rsiran cast a look toward Jessa. Were it not for the desire to see what they might have done to his sister, he would Slide away. "Which side are you with?"

"Side? Doesn't the guild side with Elaeavn?"

"I don't know," Rsiran said. "If you sided with Elaeavn, you would bring me before the council."

Ephram pursed his lips. "And how would that serve Elaeavn?"

Rsiran frowned.

Colors shifted and he felt a soft surge of something like movement. Valn appeared, and with him, was Alyse.

She looked different than she had the last time he'd seen her. Then she'd been dressed in clothing suited to Lower Town. She'd been carrying a basket full of fish, and had been working. None of it was what he would have expected from Alyse, not the sister that he had known.

Now she looked... well. Her golden hair was pinned up, and she wore a deep green dress, cut to fit her well.

When she saw Rsiran, her eyes widened, and her hand went to her neck to grab at the necklace that she still wore. It was lorcith—and pulled on Rsiran, now that he recognized it—and made by their father as a gift. It was the type of gift that Rsiran would never have received.

"Rsiran?" Her voice was a near whisper.

"Are you harmed, Alyse?"

She shook her head. "What are you doing here, Rsiran? You shouldn't have come… don't let them—"

With that, Valn Slid her away in a flash of colors and a shifting sense of movement.

When she was gone, Rsiran focused on the sense of lorcith from the necklace that their father had made. It faded and then disappeared. Wherever they had taken her was likely surrounded by either too much lorcith, or enough alloy that he wouldn't be able to reach it. It had been the same when Josun had taken Jessa to Ilphaesn. The lorcith charm she wore should have allowed him to find her, but surrounded by that much lorcith, Rsiran hadn't been able to detect anything.

"Where did you take her?" Rsiran demanded.

"She is unharmed, as you can see," Ephram said.

"What do you want with me?"

"We want your help."

"You think to get me to help by holding my sister hostage? Do you think that's going to get me to help you with whatever you plan?"

Ephram crossed his arms over his chest. "Hostage? We're protecting her. Our plan is to serve the people of the city and to keep them safe. That has always been our plan."

Rsiran looked past Ephram to Sarah. The Thenar stood watching him, her dark eyes unreadable and a deep frown on her face.

"Why me?"

"We've already discussed the particular skillset that you possess, Rsiran Lareth. I'll admit that I wasn't certain, not until you demonstrated your ability so… clearly," he said, his eyes sweeping around the room. The blue light had dimmed somewhat, but remained bright.

"What was it?" Rsiran asked. "What did I take from here?"

Sarah took a step forward. "You didn't know?"

"Know what?"

She turned to Ephram. "Valn is right, Father. This *is* a mistake. If he didn't know what he took, he's not what you—"

Ephram cut her off with a wave of his hand. "I think he's exactly what we thought. Perhaps more raw than I realized. I thought your time on the streets had trained you more than this, but you have either proven lucky—and I doubt that given where I have seen you travel—or you simply do not fully understand the extent of your abilities yet."

"Where have you seen me travel?" Rsiran asked, his confusion—and frustration—rising. He'd done so many things since leaving his parents, almost all of which would lead to the kind of punishment that he once would have feared. Rsiran no longer worried about exile. Banishment—making him one of the Forgotten—would not hold him from Elaeavn. Even were the council to use Elvraeth chains on him, the kind of punishment he knew had been reserved for those with the ability to Slide, such chains no longer held him.

But there were other punishments that he feared. Anything that might be done to Brusus, Haern, or even Della. And anything that would be done to Jessa.

Ephram's smile widened. "So many questions. And answers will come, but after."

"After what?"

"After you help us."

Rsiran stifled a laugh. "It seems you don't want help, you want to tell me what to do. You're no different than *them*."

"Not tell you, and we *do* want help."

"What kind of help? What do you want me to do for you that you can't do yourself?"

Ephram shifted his attention to Sarah and she nodded. "We have seen your ability to travel beyond barriers. The palace did not restrict you and it should. It is this ability we need."

"Why? If you're Elvraeth, and since you haven't denied it, I'm guessing you are," Rsiran said, only vaguely aware of the way he was speaking to one of the Elvraeth. Once he would never have thought to speak so brazenly to them. "Then you know what's inside the palace."

"Do you?" Sarah asked.

Rsiran shook his head, backing up a step. "Yeah. I do. And I'm not taking anything from the palace for you, the Forgotten, or Venass."

Ephram focused on Rsiran, his gaze heavy and intense. "And you should not."

Rsiran hesitated. He'd prepared to Slide away. Jessa clung to him, so he didn't fear losing her, and he could detect the distant sense of lorcith in the smithy, so he had the anchor he needed. Even were he not able to sense it, he thought that he could reach the smithy, anchor or not.

"You don't want one of the Great Crystals?"

Ephram's eyes narrowed. "Why would we want the crystals?"

Rsiran laughed. "The same reason the others do. Power."

"You don't understand, Rsiran Lareth."

"No, I think that *you* don't understand. I'm not willing to be used. You've had your… daughter chasing me throughout Elaeavn, maybe outside of the city as well," he said, thinking of what he'd detected when they went to Thyr. "And you've abducted my sister. I might not know where she is now, but trust me that I will find her. And I will get her back."

He turned to Jessa. "Are you ready?"

She squeezed his arm.

"Please…"

This came from Sarah.

The pleading note in her voice caught him off guard, and he paused.

"We need your help. We didn't take your sister to force you to help, but to keep her safe. That's the only reason that she's here." She turned to Ephram. "Tell him, Father. Tell him that we don't want to steal the crystals. Tell him what you do and why he needs to help."

Ephram watched Rsiran's face. "I don't know that it will matter. He's been changed, hardened. There's nothing that I can say that will make a difference."

"He needs to know that the guilds don't want to steal the crystals."

Ephram motioned to Rsiran. "Look at him. He has held one. I see it in his face. He should know the truth then."

"What truth?" Rsiran asked. "What don't you want to tell me?"

Ephram eyed him with a hard expression. "We don't want your help to steal the crystals because we already possess them."

CHAPTER 33

Rsiran started laughing. "You expect me to believe that you possess the crystals?" he asked. "I've seen them. There's no one who would be able to take them from that place."

Ephram nodded. "It is good you feel that way."

"And I know how hard it was to reach. You can't expect me to believe that you have some way of accessing it to have taken them."

Sarah looked at her father, her eyes practically begging him.

What weren't they telling him?

"Come with me then, Rsiran Lareth."

Ephram started toward one end of the room.

Rsiran looked over at Jessa, and she shook her head. "We shouldn't be here. I'm not sure what this is, Rsiran, but it's dangerous."

"Please," Sarah said to him. Her entire demeanor had changed. When Rsiran had seen her while she shadowed him, chasing him through Elaeavn, he had viewed her as angry, and hard, but that wasn't the woman he saw before him. This woman was uncertain, and practically begging him to help.

Why?

It was nothing like the way that the Forgotten or Venass had demanded his help. And he had no fear that he couldn't Slide from here. The connection to lorcith remained, and he doubted there was anything they would be able to do to prevent him from escaping.

Then what did they want from him?

The only way to know was to follow.

"I have to know," he told Jessa.

She sighed softly, breathing in the fragrance of the flower tucked into the charm.

Rsiran started after Ephram and exited through a wide doorway at the other end of the room, with Jessa by his side and Sarah following. A long hall opened up, with glowing blue lanterns hanging on the walls on either side. Elvraeth lanterns, much like he'd seen in the palace. Jessa pulled on his arm and motioned down the hall.

Farther down the hall, Rsiran saw a small shape moving. At first, he thought it was a young child, but that wasn't what he saw. Then the figure disappeared.

"What was that?" Rsiran asked.

Sarah motioned him to move faster.

The hall changed. The walls were silver and dark gray, and he realized they were formed from lorcith and heartstone, but neither pulled on him, as if his awareness of the metals suddenly faded. He attempted to reach for the metal, but found nothing. As if they weren't there.

He began to feel uncertain.

These were the alchemists he dealt with now. Even more than with Venass, if there was anyone with the knowledge of how to prevent him from reaching the metals, wouldn't it be they?

They turned down another hall. Carvings in the walls seemed to move, and to follow them. Rsiran had the sense of pressure all around him, but didn't know where it came from. The air felt thicker and smelled a bit like lorcith, mixed with the sweetness that he associated with heartstone.

Another door.

Sarah pushed it open. Blue light spilled out from the other side.

The light was similar to what he'd seen in the room at the Alchemist Guild, but less blinding, and with more a sense of purity from it.

He had seen this light before.

Rsiran started forward, but Ephram grabbed his shoulder.

"You have already held one of the Great Crystals, Rsiran Lareth." His voice was a reverential whisper. "You will not be allowed to hold another."

Rsiran stared, unable to believe that Ephram had simply *walked* him to the crystals. And that the tunnel that connected his father's smithy, the one that essentially connected to the Alchemist Guild, connected to the crystals room in the palace as well.

The crystals sat atop platforms much like they had the first time he'd seen them, only this time, none of them pulsed with any regularity, calling him to it. Rsiran didn't even know which of the crystals he had held. From here, they appeared much the same.

"You… you can access them?" he asked.

He watched Jessa try stepping forward, as if drawn to the crystals, but something seemed to push against her. Not Ephram, and not Sarah, but a force. She winced, and tried again, but again she failed.

"The crystals are only able to be held once, and only by those with the blood of the Watcher." He studied Rsiran as he said it, as if waiting for some sort of reaction.

"I don't have the blood of the Watcher."

"And yet you held one of the Great Crystals," Ephram said. He nodded, almost a bow, and then turned away from the crystals. Sarah motioned for them to follow.

Rsiran started to follow, but Jessa held back. "I can see them… One. It's like it's drawing me," she said in a whisper.

Rsiran considered the crystals and wondered which of them drew Jessa. Would it be the same one that he'd held or would she be drawn to a different crystal? What would she see if she held one? Not lorcith and heartstone, as he suspected he had seen. Rsiran didn't know the purpose of that vision, but that must have been what he'd seen. And his had been so different from what Della had described.

"It's like it wants me to go to them, but won't let me," Jessa said.

Rsiran nodded. He could feel the presence now that he knew to pay attention to it, almost like a physical sense, an invisible barrier that blocked access to the crystals. Would he be able to Slide past as he had when he reached them the first time?

He didn't know. And he didn't care to try.

They turned and followed after Sarah. A door that he hadn't seen closed behind them, moving as if on its own.

They found Ephram and Sarah back in the room at the Alchemist Guild house. The blue glow had shifted, turning softer, less intense.

"You can see that we have not stolen the crystals, nor do we need you to steal them for us," Ephram said.

"What then? What do you need me for?"

Ephram motioned for him to follow. A different door opened, and they walked through a narrow hall. This was less ornate than the last, and the walls were stone rather than lorcith and heartstone. Rsiran didn't have the same hesitation to follow as he had before, and Jessa trailed along with him silently.

Rsiran lost track of the number of turns that he took. Enough that he could no longer remember them. The heartstone map, the one that he kept fixed in his head, didn't help. The connection was either too weak, or the map didn't include this place.

Ephram led them to a simple room. Stone benches lined the walls and a massive table sat in the middle, filling the small space. Marks were made on the table, and Rsiran noted that some were done in lorcith. Others were made with heartstone. Still others were either metal or stone.

He motioned them to sit and took a seat at one end of the table. Rsiran couldn't see the mark in front of him. Sarah stood behind him, watching Rsiran with uncertainty.

"When you reached the Heart and held one of the Great Crystals, we were aware of you, Rsiran Lareth," he began. "Though we were aware of you long before that."

Rsiran felt a flush come to his face. "What was on the pages that I took from the drawer at the guild?"

Ephram clasped his hands together on the table and leaned forward slightly. "That room is the Hall of Guilds," Ephram said. "It is a place where all of the guilds can meet privately."

"Why would the guilds need to meet privately?" Jessa asked.

It was the first time that she'd spoken since they had seen the crystals. Rsiran wondered what she was thinking. He'd told her what he'd seen when he'd held the crystal, and she knew how his Sight had changed.

"Because the guilds protect Elaeavn."

She snorted. "Protect? You think that you're more powerful than the council?"

Ephram tipped his head. "Not more powerful, but complementary."

"And you want us to believe that you protect the crystals?" Jessa said.

"You have seen that we do."

Rsiran rested his hand on Jessa's arm. "Why show me? If you have the crystals, and if they're protected, then what do you need me for?"

"To correct a mistake."

"Whose mistake?" Rsiran asked.

"Yours." Ephram leaned back. He let the word linger. "You see, when you penetrated the Hall, you inadvertently reached something that you should not have been able to."

"What was it?" Rsiran asked. The drawer had pulled on him, almost as if he had been meant to reach it. In that way, it was much like the crystal and how it glowed for him, the color pulsing until he lifted it, held it in his hands...

Even now, the memory of the way the crystal called to him remained strong.

He watched Jessa, wondering what it must have been like for her to see the crystal pulsing, to feel it drawing her, but be unable to reach it.

"It was a list," Ephram answered. "Encrypted, so as to keep it safe, but we have reason to believe that safety has been compromised."

"A list of what?"

Ephram frowned. "Many things, but within the pages you took was a master list of the guilds and the guildlords."

Rsiran felt his heart flutter. How would he have managed to get a list of the guilds? And why would that have been what called to him? Unless there was something more that Ephram wasn't telling him.

"I didn't take—"

Ephram waved his hand and cut him off. "Oh, I know that you didn't take it intentionally, or at the very least, that you didn't know what you had taken, but that doesn't change the fact that you *did* take the list. And now, others have begun searching for the guildlords."

Rsiran swallowed. "The smiths?" he asked. "That's why the smithies have gone empty?"

Ephram nodded. "They started with the smiths. The Miner Guild has been impacted, but we managed to keep the guildlord safe. The

Travel Guild remains intact, as does the Forest Guild. And the Thenar Guild"—he motioned to Sarah—"they are too few to ever really be in danger."

"I don't understand." Those weren't the guilds he knew about. The alchemists, miners, and smiths, but the others? The weavers? The Potter Guild? The fishmongers? He could name a dozen others, but… none were as powerful as the first three. And none with the power of the alchemists.

Ephram sniffed. "That much is clear. When you took the list, others managed to claim it. They think to break the code and identify the guildlords. They have started by claiming the great smiths, taking as many as they can, thinking that one of them has to be the guildlord. We have tried summoning the remaining smiths, especially those with smith blood."

Rsiran blinked. "Like my father?"

Ephram nodded. "Like your father."

If they had been summoning the smiths, that meant the map that Rsiran had found had been *for* his father, not *from* him. "And when I claimed the map?"

"You have a quick mind. The map, a guide to the hall for each master guild member. It was for your father when we tried to call him in. You… you reached him first, it would seem. Better than the alternative."

"The alternative? He's in Venass. Is that any better than with the Forgotten?" Jessa snapped.

Rsiran thought of what he'd seen in Asador, the way that his father had been trapped. After speaking to his mother, he had thought it was tied to that, but what if there was a different reason?

And there were other smiths that had been taken there. Rsiran had seen the smithies, had detected lorcith. Had the Forgotten really thought to try to find the guildlords?

"You don't understand," Ephram said. "The smiths are part of something greater. *That* is what the Forgotten seek."

"Just why should Rsiran care?" Jessa asked.

Ephram's dark green eyes flared a moment. "It is because of Rsiran that we have to worry about the guilds."

She laughed. "You think that he cares about the guilds? After what he went through, and the way that his father treated him? Why should Rsiran care about the guilds?"

"You were treated poorly," Ephram said. "That is not something that can be changed. But we can correct other mistakes, ones that put not only our people, but everything in danger."

Jessa laughed again. "You have a high opinion of what the guilds can do."

"And you have a mistaken opinion if you think all that my guild does is create metal," Ephram said. He slapped a hand down on the table. "You have seen the crystals, and he has *held* them, so I know he understands what this is about, even if he needs me to tell him explicitly." Ephram leaned forward. "The guilds, and the guildlords in particular, protect the crystals. Without us… Without the guilds, there would be chaos."

Jessa shook her head. "Why, because someone else would use one of the crystals?" She stood, pushing back her chair. "You're no different from the Elvraeth, thinking that everything you do has such meaning. And like them, you want to use whoever you choose to accomplish your goals. The exiles wanted to use him, you know that, right? And Venass. They wanted to use him. Both thinking that he can reach the crystals. And he can. So what makes you think that you can keep them safe?"

Ephram glanced to Sarah, and sighed. "There is only so much that we *can* do, but without the guildlords in place, we cannot keep the crystals safe. Rsiran reaching them is proof of that."

"How do you know that Rsiran is proof?" Jessa asked. Rsiran touched her arm, but she shook her head. "No, Rsiran. They make assumptions, but what if you can reach the crystals even after they have their guildlords intact?"

"From what we can tell, the exiles are on the move. Knowing that they have abducted members of the guild, and their families, we sought out your sister before they could claim her too. Not to draw you in, as you believe."

"You sent them searching for me."

"Because we need someone who can help us reach them before they can cause more harm to the guilds," Ephram said.

Rsiran thought of the Forgotten Palace, and when he'd gone there alone. They had spoken of taking the smiths. That had to have been what he'd overheard. Had they taken other guild members? "What of the miners?" Rsiran asked.

Ephram sighed. "Most are safe. They began shifting lorcith, pulling what needed to be removed from the mines to protect it." Rsiran arched a brow at this, wondering if that was why all the lorcith he'd discovered in the mines had been mined, and wondered why they had chosen those pieces "But the Forgotten have spies among us, and we fear what they know," Ephram continued. "That is why I only trusted Sarah to watch your sister." He rested his hands on the table and leaned toward them. "*That* is the reason why we need your help, Rsiran Lareth. We must stop them before they bring the fight to Elaeavn. We must stop them before they attack us here."

Had Haern Seen this? Was this why he told him that he would need to pick a side?

Rsiran hadn't thought there was a side he could choose. How could he choose between either the Forgotten or Venass after what they had done? But the guilds…

With a sigh, he looked to Jessa. She stared back at him, the look in her eyes telling him that she already knew what he intended to do.

CHAPTER 34

"I don't like this, Rsiran," Brusus said.

Rsiran crouched on the hillside outside of Asador, the wind whistling around him. The distant city was mostly dark, but occasionally, he noticed lorcith. Never any heartstone. He didn't know whether to be reassured or worried by that.

He glanced at Brusus. He wore a long black cloak and carried the lorcith sword that Rsiran had made along with a pair of lorcith knives. His eyes were drawn tight as he stared through the darkness.

"I can do this, Brusus."

"I'm not questioning your ability, it's whether you *should* do this that I question."

"What did Della say?" Rsiran asked. That had been the reason they had delayed before departing. After leaving the Alchemist Guild through the Hall of Guilds, he sensed Brusus and Haern wandering in the tunnels beneath the city. He shouldn't have been surprised that it had been they who had followed Jessa and him into the tunnels. They hadn't gotten anywhere near the guild. Without the map, Rsiran wondered if they would have been able to reach it.

"She said... She said to listen to you." Brusus shook his head.

Rsiran smiled, knowing how hard the words would be for Brusus to say. "I brought you along, didn't I?" he asked.

"I don't count?" Jessa said.

She crouched next to Haern, armed with a half-dozen knives and carrying her lock-pick set rolled in her pocket. No flower was tucked into the charm tonight. Rsiran wondered when she would grab one to rectify the fact that she hadn't picked one earlier. Haern stared briefly at the bracelets Rsiran had made for him. The lorcith had almost grudgingly acceded to allowing him to make them. No heartstone had been added, not for Haern. Every so often he touched them, prying his fingers underneath. Rsiran hadn't been willing to have Haern come with him without a way to know that he couldn't be Compelled.

"You brought me," Brusus said, ignoring Jessa, "but you also brought *them*."

He pointed to where Sarah and Valn stood. Neither bothered to crouch down, not as Rsiran did. Another man, one they called Usal, stood next to Valn. Rsiran had learned that he could Slide as well.

"We need them if we're going to get the smiths back to Elaeavn."

"What if they don't *want* to come back to Elaeavn?" Brusus asked. "You know what it was like with your father. He was half-mad and angry that you took him from there. What happens if *they* support the Forgotten as well?"

Rsiran hoped that wasn't the case, but if what Ephram said was true, they had been abducted. Much like the Forgotten had abducted him.

"We need to take them back," Rsiran said.

Brusus shook his head and grunted. "I'll go with you, I'm just saying that I don't like it."

Rsiran looked over at Sarah. Since learning that she didn't want to hurt him, a change had come over her. He couldn't explain the change, nor could he explain what it was about her, only that she was different.

"We don't have to like it. But it's my fault, Brusus. If they find the guildlord—"

"It's not your fault," Haern said. Rsiran shot him a look, but Haern ignored it. "You might have taken those pages from the Alchemist Guild, Rsiran, but it's my fault that they reached the Forgotten. Had I not gone around showing them to others to try and understand what was on them, they would never have discovered them."

"They were already after the guildlords before the pages were stolen," Sarah said.

Rsiran hadn't noticed her coming toward them. She moved silently, nearly as silently as Jessa, and stood shadowed against the night.

"Their plan may have changed, but they had already begun." She nodded to Rsiran. "His father was one of the first of the master smiths they took. They might not have known the others then, but they would have found out. That would be why they took Lareth."

Rsiran hadn't considered that. Within Elaeavn, there were master smiths, and there were master smiths. Few knew the difference. Rsiran had never known that his father was of the latter. In order to be a full member of the guild, a smith had to be a master smith.

Sarah considered Rsiran for a moment. "Are you certain this is where we must look?"

Rsiran nodded. "It is where I found my father. There was a place here, one where there must have been others." He thought of the smith where he'd discovered lorcith. Better here than returning to the Forgotten Palace. They didn't have the numbers, or the preparation to go there yet.

"They could have moved to any number of places by now," Brusus said. "Especially if they know you are after them, they would have no reason to remain in place."

The comment made him check his mental barriers. Rsiran didn't think Brusus knew he'd returned to the Forgotten Palace. "The smiths were here."

Brusus climbed to his knees and peered toward the distant city. "So what's your plan, here?"

"There is a place," he said, thinking of where he'd first found his father. "I don't know if there will be others there, but it's a start." He looked up to Sarah. "You can follow?"

"I can follow if you don't obscure your travels," she said.

Rsiran nodded. Getting Brusus, Haern, and Jessa here had taken multiple Slides, only the last of which he stepped into the Slide. It hadn't taken a long time for Sarah and the others to reach him.

"How many can they carry with them?" he asked, motioning to Valn and Usal.

"Valn is strong. He can take himself and possibly two others. Usal will only be able to take one more."

Strong. What did it mean that Rsiran could fairly easily take three, and likely a fourth? He hadn't tried, not wanting to weaken himself for such a long Slide, but this close to Asador, he wouldn't trust the others to Slide with his friends.

"Fine. Then you will follow me."

Valn stepped forward. "I will take Sarah. How many can you take?"

Rsiran nodded to his friends. "All of them."

He grabbed Brusus and Haern, and Jessa held onto his arm. He focused on the street outside the building where he'd found his father, and *pulled* himself there.

The Slide drew him slowly. He had only carried three with him one other time, and that had been with Lianna after she'd died. That had nearly incapacitated him. This Slide, while difficult, was less challenging. Rsiran didn't know if it had to do with the way that he Slid, or whether his practice had truly strengthened him so much, but either way, when he emerged, he didn't struggle as he had.

He stepped briefly into a Slide, enough that Sarah would be able to detect, and then studied the street.

The last time, it had been empty. This time was much the same, though voices drifted down the street, carried on the wind to him. The long, low building appeared much the same as when he'd been here before, and the strange pull of heartstone remained.

A swirl of colors emerged out of the corner of his eye, and he felt a slight pressure against his skin, then Sarah and Valn emerged, with Usal trailing behind.

Usal studied Rsiran curiously and Slid to him. "Just how many *can* you carry?"

Rsiran focused on the building, running his hand along the door as he searched for a way in. He sensed the alloy as he had before. Had he Slid past the alloy or had he forced the lock? He couldn't remember. Now it didn't matter.

"I don't know."

"How many have you carried?"

"Four."

"And you're not exhausted."

Rsiran shook his head. "Not like I was the first time I did it."

Usal glanced over at Sarah. "What did you detect when he Slid?"

"Now is not the time," she said.

"What did you detect?"

She sighed and shook her head. "Nothing. Not until he made a small Slide here."

"How?" Usal asked, looking to Rsiran. "Tell me how you did that without detection."

He grabbed Rsiran's shoulder and pulled on him. The bracelets on his wrists went cold.

"Rsiran!" Jessa cried out, but she didn't need to. Rsiran felt the building effort of Usal trying to Slide with him.

It was the same sense he'd detected before, when his Sliding had been influenced. This time, with the direct contact, he thought that Usal might actually be able to Slide with him.

He did the only thing that he could think that might work: he focused on the inside of the building, and *pulled* himself with Usal inside.

They drew through the alloy around the building. The Slide was more effort than it should have been, likely because of the recent Slide. He'd have to be careful and avoid over extending himself tonight, especially if he wanted to get everyone home.

Once inside the building, the sense of lorcith flared.

He shrugged Usal off him and *pushed* on a pair of knives.

Usal Slid, emerging behind Rsiran.

"What are you doing?" Rsiran asked.

Usal Slid again, not answering.

Rsiran thought he understood. The guilds had been infiltrated. Ephram had known, but not who. "You're with the Forgotten, aren't you?"

Usal shrugged. "Can't help but get recruited when you've got this ability," he said.

Rsiran *pulled* himself to the end of the room where he detected lorcith. He left his knives hovering behind him, the soft white light glowing from them lighting the way for him to see. "And the smiths?"

Usal Slid, colors swirling moments before he did.

Rsiran nearly lost focus. Was that what Jessa saw when he Slid?

"They don't share plans like that with me," he said.

Rsiran flicked the knives toward Usal, but they missed. Usal Slid, emerging nearly in front of Rsiran.

The streaks of color around Usal as he Slid revealed him. Rsiran Slid to the side, sending a pair of knives flying as he did.

Usal unsheathed a sword and, in one smooth motion, sent the knives flying off to the side. "They warned me that you'd be skilled. They tried drawing you to them like they did me, but there's something different about you. That's why they sent me." He lunged with his sword, and Rsiran Slid back a step. Usal grinned. "Thought I might have a chance to grab you earlier, but this will do."

Rsiran focused on lorcith, Sliding back as he did, making a point of staying away from Usal, checking on his friends outside. He detected Brusus and Jessa, but where was Haern?

He would have to figure that out later. For now, he focused on Usal.

With another Slide, this time emerging behind Usal, he sent a knife streaking toward his back. Usal turned, starting to Slide. He wasn't sure how he managed to see the Slide, or what it even meant that he did, but when Usal Slid, the colors around him shifted.

Rsiran anticipated where Usal would be.

With a flash of lorcith knives, he caught the man in the chest.

Usal grunted and started to fall toward him. Rsiran darted back a step, getting away from his sword. Then Usal Slid away.

Rsiran tracked him. The lorcith knife was still in his chest. He could follow him, maybe use him to learn where the other Forgotten had taken the smiths, but not without checking on Jessa and the others first.

Focusing on the street, he emerged to chaos.

Haern battled another scarred man, his knives sweeping quickly. Brusus used his lorcith sword and fought a shorter man. Even Valn and Sarah fought, Valn Sliding from place to place, knives flashing each time he emerged. Sarah used a slender sword—surprising since she came from Elaeavn.

Where was Jessa?

Another half-dozen men closed in from down the street.

Rsiran jumped, sending knives flying, sweeping toward the approaching men.

Three fell quickly.

He *pulled* his knives back and sent another pair of knives at two more men. One ducked, but one wasn't quick enough, and the knife caught him in the face, slicing through his eye. Rsiran forced himself to watch.

Rsiran hesitated.

"Damn, Rsiran! Don't stop!"

This was Brusus.

"Where's Jessa?"

"Some dark-haired woman appeared and grabbed her," Brusus said.

Dark-haired and Sliding meant Inna.

Rage surged through him. He *pulled* on the lorcith he sensed from the knives he'd already used, and Slid, appearing briefly above the street, and *pushed* on the knives. Then he Slid again, focusing on the street behind the remaining approaching men, and sent the knives flying toward them.

The three men fell, knives slicing completely through them.

Rsiran Slid again, appearing behind the man fighting with Haern. With a sweep of his knives, the man fell. He did the same with Brusus, finishing that man.

Valn and Sarah didn't need his help.

The street fell silent.

"What happened?" he demanded. "Did you know that Usal worked with the Forgotten?"

Sarah shook her head. "Do you think we would have fought with you had we known?"

"Rsiran…"

He glanced up the street. More men approached, some carrying lorcith, but the nearest had crossbows. He could avoid swords and knives, but he'd already seen how crossbows could catch him even if he Slid quickly.

Focusing quickly on the charm Jessa wore—and feeling a relief that he could still sense it—he grabbed onto Brusus and Haern and locked eyes with Sarah. "Follow us."

CHAPTER 35

The Slide was a slow, drawing sensation and seemed to move more slowly than it should. Within the Slide, he was aware of colors and the oozing sense of movement, and he caught the odor of lorcith.

Had he not needed for Sarah and Valn to follow him, he would have *pulled* himself in the Slide, but he needed their help. In that moment, he prayed to the Great Watcher that they would help.

Then they emerged.

There was nothing but darkness all around. Rsiran noted the stink of blood, and something else, a sickly odor that he'd smelled before. Haern sucked in a quick breath.

Rsiran *pushed* one of his knives away from him to better see. The light was bright enough for him to make out a figure lying unmoving on the ground.

Jessa.

He started toward her, but Haern raised his hand, holding him back.

"Hold on," he whispered.

The air whistled. Had Haern not warned him, he doubted that he would have realized the danger. Lorcith flared with it.

Rsiran jerked back in a quick Slide, pulling Brusus and Haern with him.

A crossbow bolt streaked through the air, just missing where he'd been standing. Rsiran sent a knife streaking after it. He *pulled* on it as it flew, changing the direction of the knife and sending it sweeping around the room. From the light off the blade, he saw that there was no one else in the room.

The lorcith that he'd sensed disappeared, fading as if it hadn't been there.

Rsiran rushed to Jessa's side. Her skin was cool and blood trickled out from a spot on the back of her head. Glassy eyes looked up at him.

He choked back an anguished sob.

In that moment, he thought her dead.

Then she took a single breath, barely more than the tiniest movement of air, but enough that he knew she still lived. She blinked once, but then her eyes fell closed. Rsiran held his breath, waiting, until she took another breath on her own.

He needed to get her to Della.

He looked up at Haern and Brusus, already preparing to Slide, when Sarah and Valn emerged. They glanced down and saw Jessa lying motionless.

"I'm sorry," Sarah said.

"Don't," Rsiran warned.

Haern crouched next to her and touched her forehead, sweeping her hair back with a more gentle touch than Rsiran would have expected from the man. He checked her neck and leaned to her, listening to her chest, placing a hand over her nose. "She breathes. I can help her—"

"I can get her back to the city," Rsiran said. "We're in the same prison where the Forgotten held me before. I won't have her stay here and die."

Haern nodded. "You can take her back to the city, but you don't need to yet. The head wound bleeds a lot and looks worse than it is. The rest," he said, motioning to her, "is more about herbs and medicines than anything Della can do."

"Haern—"

"This is what I did, boy. Trust me on this."

"I… I want to, but it's Jessa," he whispered.

Haern glared at him. "You think I don't care for her too?"

"No. I know you do—"

"Then finish this, Rsiran. I told you that you can't let your feelings for her disrupt what must be done. Brusus can stand watch while I do what I need to with her."

Rsiran stared at Jessa. He couldn't leave her, could he?

"We need to find the other smiths. If Usal told the Forgotten we were coming…" Sarah started. The urgency in her voice was clear.

"Can you See anything?" he asked Haern.

"Not when it comes to you. You know that. Now go!" Haern urged. "I can keep her alive. Find them."

"I need your help," Rsiran said to Haern. If he was hunting for someone like Inna, he needed more than simply himself and the skills that he'd picked up over the last few weeks. Without Jessa… He couldn't let himself think that way.

Haern crouched on the ground and reached into his pockets, pulling out a few powders and setting them next to Jessa. "Not from what I saw back there. You've been practicing, haven't you?"

Rsiran nodded. "Not much good it did me."

"It did *us* good," Haern said. "Now go."

Rsiran looked over at Sarah and found her watching him. He nodded. "I'll be back. How long can she hold out?"

"As long as I'm left alone," Haern said.

Rsiran turned to Brusus.

"Don't worry. I'll make sure he's got the time he needs," Brusus said. "Besides, we all care about her."

Rsiran touched Jessa again, praying that it wasn't for the last time, and stood to face Sarah. "Come on."

He Slid forward, reaching the door, and then sent a knife floating down the hall. Nothing moved.

"Where is this place?" Sarah whispered.

A flash of lorcith appeared before Rsiran could answer.

Rsiran Slid toward it, *pushing* with his knife as he did, angling toward the sense of lorcith. The last time he'd been here, he'd been weakened, poisoned with slithca syrup. This time would be different.

A soft grunt sounded nearby, and he knew that his knife had struck. Rsiran *pulled* it back to him, not bothering to check on the man that he'd injured.

Sarah and Valn reached him. "This is a place of the Forgotten. This was where they poisoned me and tried to Read what was in my mind," he said.

There was a whisper, nothing more. By the light coming off his knife, he noted a shifting of shadows. Without thinking too much of it, he grabbed Sarah and Valn, and *pulled* himself toward the shadows, sending a knife flying from him as he did.

It sank into a man's back, and he fell to his knees. The crossbow in his hands dropped to the stone with a soft clatter.

"You're more dangerous than we knew," Valn noted.

Sarah shook her head, and Valn fell silent. She took the crossbow from the fallen man. "He won't need this," she said as she stood. "Where next?"

If Inna was here, she would know that he'd follow, but why grab Jessa? What would she have hoped to gain separating him? Based on what happened the last time he'd been here, she would have known how Rsiran would respond to Jessa's capture, and she would know that he would have come for her…

"Damn," he whispered.

"What is it?"

"They wanted to pull me away," he said.

Sarah frowned. "How do you know?"

Rsiran grabbed Sarah and Valn and Slid them back to Jessa. As they emerged, he realized that Brusus was under attack, fending off a man Sliding in his attack, while Haern tried to minister to Jessa. But each time he did, a man appeared, swiping at him with a short sword.

Rsiran split two knives and sent them at the two attackers. They both fell before they would even have known he appeared.

He considered his options. Jessa needed to get back to Elaeavn to keep her safe. Inna was using this time to move the smiths; he was certain that was why she had drawn him here. And he couldn't do what he needed alone.

He looked to Valn. "Can you return her to Elaeavn?"

Brusus shook his head. "No, Rsiran—"

"They want me to stay here, Brusus," he said. "That's the reason they took her. I need to find out what Inna is after, and I can't do it while worrying about Jessa. Haern was right when he told me that."

Haern shook his head. "I think Haern was wrong. Worry for this one made you stronger. I have never seen anything like what you did on that street up there, Rsiran."

"We're not in Asador anymore. This is part of the Forgotten Palace. I need to see her to safety." He fixed his gaze on Sarah. "If I know that she'll be safe, I can do this." Then he turned to Valn. "Will you take her to Elaeavn? There's a place near Lower Town, a Healer by the name of—"

"I know the place," Valn said. There was a hint of surprise in his voice. "If I do this, what will you do?"

"I'm going to go find the smiths," Rsiran answered.

Valn looked over at Sarah, and she nodded. "Return when you can."

"I won't know where to find you."

"Same place we just came from," Rsiran said, kneeling next to Jessa. She breathed, but the color had faded from her cheeks.

Whatever Haern had done had eased some of the injury, and she rolled her head toward him. "Are you sure this is the right thing to do?"

"I can't do this if I'm worrying about you."

"Not that. Trusting them."

Rsiran looked over his shoulder at Sarah. She whispered softly to Valn, something Rsiran couldn't hear. "We have to trust someone, Jessa. It might as well be the people fighting along side us."

She coughed and reached for his hand. "You had better come back to me."

"You had better not leave me."

She smiled. "That will never happen."

He scooped her up and held her out to Valn who stood waiting. "Please," was all he could say.

Valn took Jessa, and nodded to Rsiran. Then he Slid.

Rsiran looked at the faces of the others with him. Sarah held one hand on the hilt of her sheathed sword. Brusus stood back, watching Sarah carefully, and Haern packaged up the powders that he'd withdrawn, placing them back into a pouch before slipping them into his pocket.

"What now?" he asked.

Haern grunted. "It's your show, Rsiran."

"You don't See anything we need to worry about?"

Haern smiled at him. "That wasn't what you asked, now was it?"

Rsiran glanced at the others and held out his arms. When the others grabbed onto him, he *pulled* himself back to Asador.

CHAPTER 36

When they emerged, nothing moved on the street. The bodies of the men Rsiran had slain were gone. The only thing that remained of the attack was blood splatters on the hard-packed earth.

"Do you sense anything?" Brusus asked.

Rsiran listened for lorcith. Without another way to reach the smiths, he needed to search for something, but didn't find the lorcith he expected. What had been here was now gone.

"Not like I should," he said.

"What do you mean?" Sarah asked.

He scanned the street. The absence of *anyone* here was almost as worrisome as when there had been the steady movement toward the attack. "I can sense the presence of lorcith," he started explaining.

Sarah nodded. "Of course. You have the blood of the smiths."

That she should accept the statement without questioning was so very different from what Rsiran was accustomed to with his ability.

"And you've seen how I can… control it," he said, not certain what better word to use.

"Father said your abilities have not been seen in generations," she said.

Rsiran glanced at Haern, and then Brusus. "Strange that Venass would know how to replicate it if it hasn't been seen in generations."

Haern shook his head. "Venass has many experiments, but what you've witnessed is nothing like what I knew them capable of doing when I was there."

Sarah spun. "You were in Venass?"

"Venass once claimed me," Haern answered. "They no longer do."

Sarah studied Haern and then turned to Rsiran. "Not only are you dangerous, but you keep dangerous friends. I have told my father that he made a mistake in thinking that you could help, but he was adamant that you would be able to."

"I've said that I will," Rsiran said. "But I need to be able to detect the lorcith. There was lorcith in the city when I was here last." And he had detected lorcith when they first Slid to the city this time, but now there was none. Either they had been expecting him, or they managed to mask it from him.

He didn't know which answer was right.

"Come," he said. He grabbed the three others and *pulled* himself to the smithy that he'd discovered when he had been in Asador the last time.

They emerged in darkness and Rsiran sent a knife spinning into the room.

Nothing moved.

He *pulled* the knife back to him, and realized that wasn't exactly true. Shadows moved.

Throwing four knives into the air, he pushed them into each direction, filling the smithy with light, at least for him. He held the knives in the air, suspended but not moving.

The shadows faded.

"What is it?" Brusus whispered.

"Do you see anything?" he asked.

Brusus sniffed. "Other than you throwing your damn knives all over the place?" He shook his head. "No. And when we get through this, you're going to have to explain why you keep doing that."

Sarah eyed him strangely before speaking. "You see it, don't you?"

"See what?" Brusus asked.

She didn't take her eyes off Rsiran. "The metal. Each metal has its own properties. Some, like lorcith, can be accessed. The power held inside is potent, almost *too* potent. Others are inert. Iron, for example, can take many shapes, but it has none of the retained power that something like lorcith—"

"Or heartstone," Rsiran said.

"Heartstone does not have that kind of potential," she said.

Rsiran drew the sword from his sheath and held it out. To his eyes, the sword glowed with an almost angry deep blue light. "It does for me."

She ran her fingers along the surface of the blade. "It should not. Heartstone is… unusual. The potential cannot be accessed. That is why it is mixed. Even then, the potential of heartstone cannot be accessed."

"As I said, it does for me." He pulled on the alloy, holding it in the air with his connection to the metal. "That's part of the reason why Venass wants to reach me."

Sarah took a step back, eyes fixed on the sword. "You see the potential with heartstone? And you have a connection to heartstone the same as your connection to lorcith?"

"Not the same, but a connection. That's why I can Slide into the palace."

Sarah shook her head. "There should not be. Which means that Elvraeth chains wouldn't hold you, either, would they?"

Rsiran shook his head, remembering the helpless feeling he had the first time that the chains were placed on him. Until he had learned how to reach the alloy, to press and control it the same way that he did with lorcith, he had felt isolated.

But then, had he not been, he would never have learned that he was capable of controlling the alloy. He never would have learned about heartstone, and the potential that existed within him.

"At first they did," he said.

"You have suffered more than he Saw." She covered her hand over her mouth and her eyes widened.

"Who Saw?" Haern asked, stepping forward.

"It doesn't matter," Sarah said. "Not until we save the guildlord. Then he can have answers."

"That's just it, all the lorcith that was here is..."

He turned slowly, thinking. All the lorcith was gone, and he didn't think the Forgotten had much heartstone, but could he reach for a particular piece? When Usal had attacked, he'd managed to Slide away, but Rsiran's knife had stuck in his shoulder. It was how he Slid to find Jessa.

If Rsiran could detect that knife, he might be able to find Usal, and might be able to find the others.

And then?

Then he would find the missing smiths, and he would find Inna.

He pressed the anger and rage at what had happened to Jessa into his search for lorcith. Lorcith flared all around him. There were a few small pieces in the smithy, some others nearby, but nothing of much quantity.

Rsiran pressed farther, reaching for the lorcith. It had been *his* knife, forged for him to use, drawn from the ore that he'd asked to take shape. There was a connection to that lorcith, and he had only to reach it.

Distantly he felt it.

At first, it was little more than a soft pinprick on his awareness, but that gradually increased, growing in intensity the longer he focused. The pinprick grew stronger, brighter within his awareness, and Rsiran *pulled* on it, drawing the sense toward him.

He held out his arm. "Be ready," he said to the others.

Brusus and Haern grabbed onto his arms. Sarah watched him a moment, as if uncertain, then took his arm as well.

Rsiran *pulled* on the sense of lorcith, anchored to it, as he drew them all forward.

The Slide was agony.

Colors flashed, and the air took on the hot, bitter scent of overheated lorcith. Something was wrong with the Slide.

He couldn't pull away. Doing so risked the others.

Rsiran cursed himself. He'd been foolish to not investigate before bringing everyone with him. There were dangers to Sliding. Less when he Slid this new way, but still dangers.

Someone screamed near him.

Rsiran didn't have a chance to check who.

They emerged.

As they did, Rsiran knew immediately that something was wrong.

The air was hot and bitter, and far too bright. Lorcith burned everywhere, blinding and overwhelming.

Someone—Brusus, he thought—grunted near him.

"Where are we?" Sarah asked.

Rsiran blinked, letting his eyes adjust. Lorcith was all around, filling walls with their bright light. The knife that had drawn him here lay on the ground, blood covering the hilt but no sign of Usal. The place was different from the last time he'd been here.

"The Forgotten Palace," Rsiran said.

"I don't see any palace," Haern said with a grunt. "Can't really *see* anything."

Brusus shuffled around them, staying close, and picked up the knife off the ground. He held it close to his face, as if struggling to see it. Rsiran realized that he might be. To Brusus and Haern, this might be utter darkness. With Brusus's Sight, he would be able to see something, but without the ability to see lorcith, everything would be shadows and shades of gray.

But not Sarah.

"This is lorcith," Sarah said. She stared at the tunnels, as if seeing easily… or as if she saw the lorcith.

The realization of the fact that she saw the light from the lorcith made Rsiran lose his focus. "You see it, too?"

She cupped a hand over her brow and scanned around her. "I am of the alchemists. That is our gift."

Haern and Brusus looked at each other.

"Why can I see it?" Rsiran asked.

Sarah shook her head. "You are smith blood. Smiths can hear lorcith sing, can use that song to give it shape, but should not be able to see the potential within. That is the gift of the alchemist."

"I thought you were of the Thenar Guild," Rsiran said.

Sarah frowned.

"You said alchemist, but Ephram mentioned that you were guildlord for the Thenar Guild."

"My mother. She was Thenar. Through my father, I have alchemist blood, so I am connected to both."

"Like I am?"

"What you describe hasn't been seen in many generations," Sarah said.

"Rsiran," Brusus interrupted, "as much as I'm curious about what the two of you are talking about—and I am—I think we need to finish the assignment. This place is making me uncomfortable."

Rsiran looked around, scanning the rock. "It's different from when I was here last."

"You've been here?" Sarah asked. "This is not Ilphaesn."

"No, but it's somewhere near the Forgotten Palace." He turned to Brusus who stared into the darkness. Haern stood motionless, as if afraid to move. "When we escape the last time, we left the palace through someplace like this. I didn't know what it was, or where it was, but I know this is the same place."

"You said it's different?" Brusus asked. "How?"

"It wasn't this hot, for one. And the air didn't have the bitter scent like…"

Like working at the forge, he realized.

The light was different, too, but he figured that was more due to the change within him rather than anything of the metal in mine itself.

But the change he felt, that of the air and the heat, that was more like a forge. That meant smiths. He needed to find them.

"They're here," he said softly.

"How can you be sure?" Haern asked.

"Whatever the smiths are doing is changing the metal," he answered. Rsiran turned to Sarah. "You said the light that I see is from the potential of lorcith." She nodded. "Is there a way to determine if that potential is disturbed?"

Her brow furrowed in a frown. "Disturbed?"

He nodded. "When lorcith is forged, if there isn't a connection to it, if the smith doesn't listen to the ore, something about it changes." He hadn't been certain how to explain that, but knew that it was true. It was the reason the lorcith forgings *he* made were harder, and less brittle. When it was forced, the lorcith still took on the shape, but something was lost.

"These are master smiths. They can all hear the song—"

"They may hear it, but they don't listen. That's why lorcith has changed so much for them." He was certain of that. He might never be a full master smith, but he understood the call of lorcith, and what the metal asked of him. Unlike his father, Rsiran wasn't afraid to listen. How many of the smiths were like his father? He suspected that most were.

"I do not know if such a thing is possible," Sarah admitted. "I didn't realize that the smiths no longer listen to the song."

Rsiran started away from the others, listening for lorcith. To find the smiths, he needed to know where they worked. He could understand what they did later.

The bright glow of lorcith was all around. There was pressure and a sense of power to tit. Rsiran listened to it as he had long ago learned to hear the call of the metal, to listen to the song, and heard the way that it sang.

The sound was soft at first, as it often was with lorcith. When heating and hammering it, the song became louder, picking up intensity, but he had no heat, no forge to work. But he could listen, and could focus on what the lorcith wanted to tell him.

The sound increased, growing stronger.

Within it, Rsiran became aware of parts that felt off. One in particular was close…

He Slid to it.

There was danger in Sliding as he did, and he knew better than to Slide blindly, but he emerged into something like an open room, a man working coals that were layered on the rock itself. Smoke spiraled up, but not entirely, and the room was thick with it. Light—real light and not that coming off the lorcith—filtered through windows high above.

What was this? Better yet, *where* was this?

A bearded man held a long hammer, one end flatter than the other, and he looked up as Rsiran appeared. The man's haggard appearance was no different from how Rsiran's father had looked when he had brought him back from Asador. Wild eyes widened, and he lifted his hammer and came racing at Rsiran.

He Slid, emerging behind the man, and grabbed him. Then he Slid back to where the others waited.

The man sprawled across the stone.

Brusus sucked in a quick breath. "Where was he?"

"I don't know."

The man reached for his hammer, but Rsiran grabbed it and wrenched it free from his grip. The man was strong, but Rsiran used a single small Slide to jerk it free.

"Take me back," he said. "If they find that I'm gone—"

"Who are you?" Brusus asked.

The man shook his head. "Names don't matter, not here."

"Your name," Brusus said. He pulled a knife out and pressed it toward the man.

He looked around, blinking, but Rsiran suspected the darkness was overwhelming, especially after coming from the lighted, makeshift smithy where this man had been. The wild expression in his eyes faded somewhat. "Eldon Farnam."

Brusus glanced to Rsiran.

"He's one of the master smiths," Rsiran said.

Sarah stepped to Eldon. "We're here to help. Where are the others?"

"Help? You can't help. And now my family… everyone I care about…"

"What are you saying?" Sarah asked.

Eldon shook his head. "You think I don't know that I shouldn't be doing this? You think that I would if there were any other choice? If

I'm gone, they'll… they'll…" He sobbed, unable to finish his thoughts. "They've already shown me what they will do." He turned toward Rsiran, somehow picking him out in the darkness. "Take me back. I haven't been gone long enough for them to notice…"

As he trailed off, his eyes went wide. "Oh, Great Watcher," Eldon said.

"What is it?" Brusus asked.

"They know I'm gone."

"How can you tell?" Haern asked.

Rsiran didn't need Eldon to answer. He could *feel* it, like a change in the way the mine felt around him. The air cooled, and the strange song of the lorcith shifted, as if in warning. For Eldon to know, that meant that he heard it, and more than that, he *listened*.

"How many are there?" Rsiran asked.

Eldon shook his head. "It doesn't matter. They have taken my family, everyone I care about. That's how they get others to work for them. If I don't…"

Rsiran knew without him finishing what would happen. He'd seen that darkness from the Forgotten before, but for them to torment entire families, for them to tear those families apart—families that from what he could see of Eldon, wanted to be together—told him all that he needed of the Forgotten.

"Come on," Rsiran said to the others, holding his arms out.

"Rsiran?" Brusus said. "What are you doing?"

"We're going to end this." One way or another, Rsiran was determined to stop the Forgotten. They would not continue to tear families apart. It had been bad enough when his father had been forced to work with the Forgotten. If what his mother had said was true, his father had done what he did to protect his family.

Now they were using other families? Now they would attempt to destroy all the smiths?

Not if Rsiran could help it.

"Rsiran?" Eldon said, stepping toward him. "You're Lareth's boy?"

"Why?"

Eldon reached for him, but Rsiran shook him off. "You shouldn't be here," he said. "You're the one they *want* to be here."

Rsiran felt anger surging through him. "That's their mistake."

He held his arms out, and Brusus and Haern latched on. Sarah took a moment, and then took his hand.

"Where are we going?" she asked.

"The palace."

CHAPTER 37

Rsiran focused on what he remembered of the Forgotten Palace. He had only been there once, but the memory of it was locked in his mind. He needed only to think of it, and he could find it.

But he had more than that. With the heartstone that he knew was there, he could anchor to the palace, and he *pulled* himself to the room where he'd first met Evaelyn.

When he emerged, the room had a soft blue glow to it that reminded him of the Hall of Guilds.

"Where are we?" Brusus asked.

"I don't know what they call it, but I call it the Forgotten Palace," he answered.

Haern sucked in a breath. "Cold."

As he did, Rsiran felt the bracelets on his wrists go cold as well. "They know we're here," he whispered. "Be ready," he said to Brusus.

He glanced at Sarah. He hadn't thought about providing protection for her and wondered if Evaelyn or someone with her would Compel

Sarah. If they did, Rsiran wouldn't have the same hesitation that he had with Haern or Jessa to do what he needed to keep the rest of them safe.

A door opened at one end of the room. Evaelyn led a group of five others with her. Rsiran noted that Inna was among them. Inna smiled knowingly at him.

"Great Watcher," Brusus whispered, "she looks like Della!"

"Yeah, they're sisters," Rsiran said. "She didn't tell you?"

"There's much that Della doesn't tell me," Brusus said.

"You shouldn't have returned," Evaelyn said. "I allowed you to leave the last time. You will not find me as accommodating this time."

Haern dropped to the ground. He clawed at the bracelets on his wrists, trying to pry them off. "They burn!" he moaned.

"Leave them on," Rsiran urged.

"I *feel* her reaching into my mind!" Haern said.

"Let her reach," Rsiran answered. "So long as she doesn't control."

"Control? You think that I can't learn as well?" Evaelyn asked. "When you made the mistake of coming here again, I decided it was time to act."

She stalked toward them, but Rsiran stood his ground. He sent the knives in his pockets out and let them hover in the air, and held them in place. "Not any closer. We will have a talk, you and I."

Evaelyn's gaze shifted to the knives and she smiled. "That is how you would like to do this? You think violence and your control over lorcith grants you anything?" She smiled, and an anxious feeling settled through him. "I have learned your limitations, Rsiran Lareth."

Rsiran realized that he might have made a mistake. He thought that Inna had pulled Jessa away as a distraction, something that would buy them time to move the smiths, but he'd been wrong. They had used Jessa to draw him here.

He had done what they wanted.

He glanced at Sarah who stared at Evaelyn. Her eyes flared a deep green that matched Brusus's. Any fear Rsiran had that she would be Compelled eased when he saw that. Brusus winced, his face screwing into tight concentration, but he remained standing.

"You think I have maintained my position this long without learning when compromise is needed?" Evaelyn asked.

With dawning horror, Rsiran felt the knives he held in the air begin to spin.

He reached for lorcith and realized that the five people with Evaelyn all had lorcith piercing them. They could control lorcith.

The knives *pushed* against him. Rsiran *pushed* back, but they outnumbered him.

"Venass?" he asked. "You've partnered with Venass?"

Evaelyn smiled then. "Partnership is a strong word," she said. "This is more an exchange of knowledge."

Inna and two others stepped forward. The knives pressed even more.

"Release your knives and you may yet live," Inna said.

"Why the smiths?" Rsiran asked Evaelyn. If he had to run, if he had to Slide from here, he would have answers first.

Evaelyn looked past Rsiran to Sarah. "You haven't told him?" Her smile deepened. "Interesting. And here I thought that the alchemists cared about purity."

Sarah took a step forward. "I am not of the alchemists," she spat, and threw something.

Light exploded at Evaelyn's feet.

"What are you doing?" Rsiran yelled. He managed to maintain control of the knives, but only barely. The sudden explosion had startled him, and he'd regained control, but almost not quickly enough. The knife nearest him *pushed* forward.

If he Slid, he risked losing control of the knives altogether.

Another door opened in a surge, and six more Forgotten spilled into the room.

"Damn," Haern muttered and streaked toward the new arrivals. Brusus raced after Haern.

"They were coming. I detected the travel," Sarah said.

"Help them," Rsiran told her.

Her eyes drifted to the knives. "And what about you?"

"These are mine," he answered through gritted teeth. "And they will not be used against me."

He turned back to face Evaelyn. She stood, watching him with amusement, as the five Forgotten attempted to surround him. Behind him, he heard the sound of metal on metal as his friends engaged the newcomers.

"Soon I will reach into your mind and take what I need," Evaelyn said.

Rsiran focused on lorcith, pushing against the knives. *He* had forged them. The connection was to him, not these Forgotten.

He reached through the lorcith, recognizing the quiet song that had helped him forge them, and felt the knives respond to him.

Rsiran *pushed*.

The knives moved.

Two of the men nearest jerked their heads back, as if startled.

Rsiran used that moment to *push* on the knives and sent them sinking into their necks.

As they fell, another three came racing into the room. Attuned to lorcith as he was, he detected their piercings immediately.

They pulled weapons of their own from their pockets and threw them into the air.

Rsiran shifted his attention and *pushed* against them. He hadn't forged them, and his connection to them was not the same.

Lorcith pressed near him. He could feel the onslaught all around him. Someone cried out behind him. Brusus? Haern?

He needed to gain control of his knives.

Haern had thought that he might have learned enough to keep them safe, but he hadn't expected the Forgotten to have sided with Venass, and he hadn't expected them to learn to control lorcith.

He *pushed* against the attack, but he was not strong enough.

If he Slid, there was no guarantee that he could Slide fast enough to escape the attack. And his friends would be forced to face those who now controlled lorcith.

No, he needed another solution, but what?

Through it all, he felt Evaelyn's eyes on him and saw the dark smile on her face.

Lorcith was his! The connection was his, not borrowed, not stolen, and not faked.

He could hear the song, could feel the ore within Ilphaesn, and knew the weight of it within the mountain. Weight that he'd used before.

Rsiran inhaled, drawing on the distant sense of lorcith, that from Ilphaesn, and *pushed*. Pain shot through his head in a way that reminded him of when he'd first begun to detect heartstone.

As it receded, he *pushed* with the weight of all the lorcith that he could.

The knives and the strange weapons the other Forgotten tossed at him slowly shifted.

One of the Forgotten gasped. Rsiran reached deeper, drawing on the connection with even more strength, and *pushed*.

He did not *push* blindly. Rsiran focused his efforts, using the ties to Ilphaesn, and the sense of the lorcith, to guide his attack.

Weapons streaked from him, racing toward the Forgotten.

All but one struck true.

Inna escaped. He saw her Slide as a flash of color, but also sensed it, a prickly sensation along his skin. She emerged a step away from him.

"You should not have been able—" she started.

He didn't let her finish. Using the connection to Ilphaesn, Rsiran *pulled* on the lorcith knives, *pulled* on the strange weapons the Forgotten had used, and sent them at Inna.

Her eyes widened, and she Slid, again avoiding attack.

Rsiran *pulled* on the lorcith and sent everything he sensed near him, even weapons Inna carried, slamming into the wall until they were buried in the heartstone.

At first, Inna was dragged with them, but then she flicked the lorcith free and Slid. She emerged near Evaelyn.

Rsiran wanted to turn. He wanted to see how his friends in the attack behind him fared, but he didn't dare risk it. Not with Inna still standing, and not with Evaelyn watching him. The darkness in her eyes frightened him, as did the sense he had that she might somehow manage to crawl beyond the barriers created by the bracelets. He could fortify them with his own mental barriers, but he lost something when he did, there was a weakened connection to the metal then.

"How many more do you think you can stop, Rsiran Lareth? How many until you grow tired?" Evaelyn asked, her lips pulling into a tight smile. "I can see it now. You begin to grow fatigued, the effort of the fight wearing on you. You were never trained for this. Fighting does not come naturally for you, not as it does to the exiles."

"The Forgotten," Rsiran said. "Call yourselves exiles all you want, but you, Evaelyn, should be Forgotten."

Rsiran realized that he could sense both lorcith and heartstone at the same time. Never before had he been able to detect both at once.

A flash of color from Inna told him that she began to Slide.

Rsiran *pulled* on the heartstone pin in Evaelyn's hair, grasping onto it tightly as he *pulled* it to him. The sense of the metal was slippery, but he clung to it, drawing it to him.

The bar of heartstone reached him at the same time as Inna emerged from her Slide, holding an unsheathed steel sword.

She smiled and swung it toward Rsiran.

Drawing on the sense of heartstone all around him, he *pushed*. The bar streaked toward Inna. She attempted to Slide, but Rsiran had timed his attack, and she wasn't fast enough.

It struck her in the chest, flying completely through her.

Once Rsiran would have felt remorse or horror or revulsion. He felt nothing for Inna. She had been willing to poison him for the information she wanted, and had attacked Jessa to get to him. A woman like that deserved no sympathy.

He stepped toward Evaelyn.

She eyed him with dark hatred. "You have made a mistake, Rsiran Lareth, if you think your barriers can withstand me. I've forgotten more about my abilities than you will ever learn. The Great Watcher smiled on us when Venass couldn't contain you as they promised they would in Thyr. When I suggested that *we* could draw you here, and that we would share our knowledge if they shared theirs…" She glanced at Inna. "A costly trade, but you are the price for knowledge. With this, we will finally be able to return. The guilds will fall under our rule."

Rsiran looked at the fallen Forgotten all around him. "I'm the price of what you learned? And you think learning how to control lorcith was worth it? How many did you sacrifice for this? How many will suffer for what you want?"

His bracelets began to cool. "As many as it takes for victory," she said.

Cool turned cold, and the bracelets flashed a bright blue and burned painfully. It lasted only a moment, long enough for Rsiran to feel Evaelyn attempting to reach his mind, and then he slammed his barriers into place on top, augmenting the bracelets.

Evaelyn staggered and fell, a piercing scream echoing from her.

He glanced back, and saw Brusus and Haern still standing. Seven Forgotten lay on the ground around them. Sarah held her hand over a gash on her arm, but she managed to stand.

Satisfied that they were safe, Rsiran knelt in front of Evaelyn. "You are mistaken if you think I haven't learned anything in our time since we met."

She looked up at him and managed to smile. "You are weak. All of your kind is weak. And you were never meant to rule."

He noted that she looked past him. Sarah stood behind him, watching Evaelyn with disgust. "What do we do with her?" Rsiran asked.

Sarah's eyes widened suddenly, and she grabbed her head. She brought her sword up, swinging it toward Rsiran.

Without needing to stand, he pulled himself to the side in a Slide. "You should have known you were beaten," Rsiran said to Evaelyn sadly.

"I'll never be beaten. So long as I live—"

He *pulled* on the heartstone pin that had gone through Inna, and slammed it into Evaelyn. He looked away in disgust as it crushed her throat.

Sarah sagged. Brusus reached her and placed his hands on either side of her head. Within a moment, what Evaelyn had done to Compel her faded, and she blinked her eyes open again.

"Thank you," she said to Rsiran.

"Why?"

"You could have simply killed me when she took hold of my mind."

Rsiran glanced over at Brusus and then Haern. "That's not how I do things. I help my friends."

"We're friends now?" she asked.

Rsiran stood. "When I first learned you chased me, I thought you were like them," he said. His gaze swept around him, at all the dead. He sighed. So many had died because of Evaelyn's thirst for power. He feared that many more would have to until the Forgotten were completely stopped, but this was a start. Without Evaelyn and Inna, they wouldn't have their leader.

It was one less threat for him to worry about.

Now, he only needed to focus on Venass.

"You proved you weren't, but you and Ephram have still kept things from me. Friends can't keep secrets that put the others at risk." He glanced over at Brusus, who flushed slightly. "I think it's time that I have answers. Real answers."

Sarah met his gaze and nodded.

EPILOGUE

Rsiran watched Jessa resting soundly. He had been relieved to learn that she was fine, and that Valn had kept his word. There had been a part of him that feared Valn would betray him, but he had proven reliable. And had proven that he knew of Della.

More questions for later.

"Your sister is returned?" Della asked.

Rsiran didn't look up, content to watch Jessa sleep. After what they'd been through over the last few days, sleep was a comfort he wasn't sure they would have. "She has returned to Lower Town. The alchemists… they told her the constables kept her for her safety. I haven't gone back to see her."

He still didn't know what to make of the fact that the guilds ran the constables. Perhaps Ephram was right in telling him that the guilds truly protected Elaeavn. If they protected the crystals, and the city itself, what other explanation was there.

"You should. She is your sister. You have shown how important family is to you," Della said.

Rsiran closed his eyes. "I'm sorry about Evaelyn."

"You have nothing to apologize for," Della said. She stood behind her counter and mixed a mug of tea. "It is my fault for not recognizing the extent of danger she posed before now. She… she has always been dangerous."

"Still."

Della nodded as she stirred. "And the smiths?"

He sighed, appreciating that Della simply changed the topic. "We found most within the Forgotten Palace. Valn and the others search for their families. We think we've found most of them."

"And the guildlord?" Della asked.

He shook his head. "I don't know."

She pursed her lips. "They should not keep that from you, not after what you did to help."

He wasn't sure that they should share with him, not after how he was at least partly responsible for endangering them. "Did you know?" Rsiran asked. "About the guilds?"

Della nodded. "There are things that I cannot fully explain, especially as you didn't want to get too deeply involved."

"Like Evaelyn? Like the crystals?"

She met his eyes. "Yes."

A knock at the door interrupted them. Brusus and Haern stirred from the chairs near the hearth and stood. Della opened the door, and saw Sarah and Ephram on the other side.

She stepped aside to let them in.

Brusus and Haern stayed by the hearth. Della moved behind the counter, again turning to her mug of tea. Sarah and Ephram both remained by the door. In some ways, it seemed everyone tried to gauge who would speak first.

Della cleared her throat and nodded to Ephram. "The boy deserves to know." His eyes narrowed. "All of it," she went on.

Ephram studied Della for a moment and then nodded slowly, shifting his gaze to Rsiran. "What have you told him?"

"It was not for me to share."

"A dangerous plan, Della, even for you."

"As I said, it was not for me to share."

Ephram crossed his arms over his chest. "After how his father was used, you thought you should keep it from him?"

"I could not See how his father was used," Della answered over her tea. "Much as I cannot See when it comes to Rsiran."

"What is this?" Rsiran asked, looking from Della to Ephram.

Ephram sighed and his shoulders slumped. "We have been watching for you, Rsiran."

"Watching?"

Ephram tipped his head in a nod. "The ability to travel is rare these days. Once it was not so, but much has happened."

"Like the Elvraeth forbidding it."

"Forbidden for reasons they claim protect the city. Travel, what you call Sliding, is rare enough, but for one with the blood of a smith to possess such an ability…" He turned to Rsiran, his face intense. "That has never happened."

Rsiran fingered the knives in his pockets through his cloak. "And now here I am."

"Here you are. As was Seen long ago."

Brusus sucked in a breath. Rsiran looked over at him and then Della, but neither met his eyes.

"Seen?" he asked.

"There has long been dissention between the bloodlines. The blood of the Watcher and the blood of the elders. It has long been the source of much conflict, but an end was foreseen."

"What are you talking about?" he asked.

Ephram sighed. "The greatest Seers have long expected one of the ancient bloodlines—in your case, smith blood—and the blood of the Watcher to join. And with that will come great power. That is why we wait, why we serve."

"I might have the blood of the smiths," Rsiran said, "but I don't know anything about the blood of the Watcher."

"You don't know, and you could not. You were never privy to your birthright."

He snorted. "My birthright? You mean the smithy that my father took away from me? You mean the fact that he made me believe what I can do is some sort of dark ability?"

Ephram looked over to Della, as if asking for help, but she only shook her head.

"What do you know of your parents?"

Rsiran looked to Della. She nodded. "I know that my father is a smith. From what you've told me, maybe a master smith."

"As are you. You hear the song of lorcith. You are a smith," Ephram said. "And your mother?"

Rsiran shrugged. "My mother. Other than the fact that she hides in Lower Town now? That she didn't object when my father abandoned me? That she, like Brusus, is a child of exiles?"

Ephram nodded. "Exiled. Yes. And did she share with you who her father was?"

He shook his head. "She said it didn't matter."

Ephram looked to Della. "This should be you," he said.

Della set the mug on the counter. She made her way around, leaning on a cane as she did. "Your grandfather," she said, "was one of the Elvraeth."

An amused smile came to Rsiran. "You're saying that I'm descended from the Elvraeth?"

Ephram nodded. "The blood of the Watcher flows through you. That is how you were able to hold one of the Great Crystals."

Rsiran laughed. "And just how do you know this?"

Della looked down a moment, and then seemed to force herself to meet his eyes. "I didn't know. When you first came, I did not know. With your ability, I cannot See you as I can others. That protects you in some ways, but it prevented me from understanding sooner. With what you shared about your mother, I went to her to understand."

"You went to her?" Rsiran asked.

Della didn't looked away from him. "I Read her. She has some skill, but that can be weakened." She eyed the herbs on her counter but didn't explain. "That is when I learned."

"What did you learn?" His heart fluttered in his chest. So much had happened to him because of how little he knew about his family, and now it turned out that there were even *more* secrets kept from him?

"Your mother is descended from one of the Elvraeth and born outside of the city."

"And what proof is there of that?"

Della sighed and looked to Ephram as if for support, but he said nothing. When she looked back to Rsiran, tears had welled in her eyes. "Because he was my brother."

DK HOLMBERG is a full time writer living in rural Minnesota with his wife, two kids, two dogs, two cats, and thankfully no other animals. Somehow he manages to find time for writing.

To see other books and read more, please go to www.dkholmberg.com

Follow me on facebook: facebook.com/dkholmberg

Word-of-mouth is crucial for any author to succeed and how books are discovered. If you enjoyed the book, please consider leaving a review online at your favorite bookseller or Goodreads, even if it's only a line or two; it would make all the difference and would be very much appreciated.

Manufactured by Amazon.ca
Bolton, ON